Douglas Skeggs read Fine Art at Magdalene College, Cambridge and has an international reputation as a lecturer on European art and history. He has made numerous TV documentaries and is the author of *River of Light*, the best-selling biography of Monet. *The Claimant* is his fifth suspense novel.

Also by Douglas Skeggs

FICTION

The Estuary Pilgrim
The Talinin Madonna
The Triumph of Bacchus
The Phoenix of Prague

NON FICTION

River of Light: Monet's Impressions of the Seine

THE *Claimant*

DOUGLAS SKEGGS

A *Warner* Book

First published in Great Britain in 1998 by Warner Books

A CIP catalogue record for this book is available from the British Library.

ISBN 0 7515 2440 9

Typeset in Perpetua by M Rules
Printed and bound in Great Britain by Clays Ltd, St Ives plc

Warner Books
A Division of
Little, Brown and Company (UK)
Brettenham House
Lancaster Placc
London WC2E 7EN

For Jack & Harry

PROLOGUE

Fetevis Palace, Hungary, January 1945

News of the Russian advance came in the evening.

Captain Gabler brought it up from the village on his motorcycle, the sound of its unsilenced engine shattering the peace of the still winter air, announcing his arrival long before he came in sight.

It had snowed earlier in the day but by three the sky had cleared and across the frozen lake the Palace now lay serene and majestic in the evening sunshine.

Propping the machine against the central fountain, Gabler pulled off his gloves and slapped them in his helmet which he hung from the handlebars. A footman opened the door as he reached the top of the steps. He offered to take the captain's coat but Gabler refused; this wasn't a courtesy call. He was only going to be there a few minutes, he didn't need all the social niceties. In the situation they seemed somehow absurd.

Twenty-six years old, strong and stocky, Gabler was commander of the small unit of soldiers billeted in the village, a member of the Arrow Cross, the Hungarian Nazi Party. He was under no obligation to keep the Count informed of events, his duty at this moment was solely towards his men, but he felt it was only fair to warn him of what was to come.

The footman led him back to the small octagonal reading room where the Count was taking tea. The house was still fully furnished, Gabler noticed: silver laid out on the dining table, oil paintings hanging on the walls, tapestries and Persian carpets in place. It was as though nothing of the past five years had managed to penetrate the tranquillity of the huge house. Here there was no war, no threat of invasion, nothing to shake the ordered routine of aristocratic life. In the past Gabler had found this sense of permanence annoying. Now he couldn't help feeling a twinge of respect for it.

The butler knocked on the door, opened it and stood back to admit the officer.

Count Karoly Kasinczy-Landsberg was standing at the window, his back turned from his visitor. He was dressed for riding in a waisted tweed jacket and jodhpurs, a pair of velvet slippers on his stockinged feet. There was no artificial light in the room. A log fire burned in the grating, its flames glowing on polished woodwork, ormolu fittings and silver tea service. This was not the main library of the house, Gabler knew that. It was a private room where the Count liked to relax in the evenings. There was a wind-up gramophone on the side, a humidor of cigars and a tray of cocktails on the central table.

Gabler drew his heels together and lifted his arm in the ghost of a salute. 'I have to tell you that the Russians have broken through in the eastern sector.'

The Count turned from the window. He was in his mid-thirties: tall, fine-featured with a wing of blond hair that fell over his right eye and that slight aura of aristocratic sadness about him, as though the long lineage of his family had served only to increase the burden of his life.

His face betrayed no sign of emotion at the news. 'How unfortunate.'

'We have orders to draw back at dawn tomorrow.'

The Count put down his cup and saucer. In the evening light the fine porcelain was translucent, the level of the tea quite visible through the sides. 'When do you expect them to be here, Captain?'

'They're thirty miles or so north at present. Unless something unexpected stops them they should be here by tomorrow evening.'

The Count nodded. Nothing would stop them; he knew that. They would advance as fast as their tanks could move, destroying anything that came in their path, gobbling up as much territory as they could before the war could be brought to an end. That was their aim.

Gabler said, 'I thought you should know.'

'And I'm most obliged to you.'

Count Karoly looked across the darkened room at the officer. Gabler seemed to have aged twenty years in the past few weeks. His face was grey and haggard, a couple of days' growth on his chin. Quite different to the arrogant young man who had come here two years earlier, so sure of himself, so sure of the new order that would follow their victory. Then he had treated the Count with disdain: he was an anachronism, a remnant of the past that would shortly be swept away. Gabler had put it in those very words. Now he seemed gentler, more tolerant. Standing there in his worn coat, his eyes sunk with fatigue, crushed by the knowledge that neither of them was to outlast the coming storm, the hostility had gone. In other circumstances the Count might have found some shred of satisfaction in this change. As it was, he felt only sorrow.

'And what of you, Captain? Where will you go?'

'We are ordered back into Budapest.'

'I'm told the Russians are surrounding it.'

'Some of the men are staying on, going up into the hills. They're from these parts, they don't want to leave.'

'And you?'

'I shall follow my orders.' There was no bravado in the words. He spoke quietly and mechanically, as though he knew he were signing his own death warrant.

'I wish you well, Captain.'

'And you, sir.' There was a moment's silence. Then Gabler said, 'Will you be leaving, sir?'

'I don't see there is much alternative.'

Gabler glanced around the room as though he too found it hard to believe that all this, the accumulated wealth and possession of four centuries, could be gone in a matter of hours. 'The bridge is still standing,' he said. 'On the river. It's been left, to let people get out. There's still a route out, south-west from here.'

'When will they blow it?'

'At dusk tomorrow.'

Twenty-four hours. The Count gave a small frozen smile. 'Then that gives us a little time.'

After the soldier had gone, Count Karoly opened the french windows, the glass white with frost, and stepped out on to the terrace. In the still air he could hear the puttering of the motorbike as it returned down into the valley. He walked over to the stone parapet and sat down.

Strangely, now that they knew what to expect, he felt a sense of calm. For weeks they had been surrounded by rumours. Some said that the Allies would liberate them in time, others that the war would end before the Russians had overtaken the country. But gradually faith had faded and by

Christmas only the optimists believed that there was anything left to hope for.

Lighting a cigarette the Count stared down over the lake. Despite appearances, preparations for their departure had been made long ago. Some of the most valuable possessions in the house, the better paintings, the silver and porcelain, had been buried in the caves up in the hills. He had no doubt that it would be found eventually but the gesture had to be made. Much more important in his mind was the salvaging of the family fortune. The steel mills on which the Kasinczy-Landsberg empire had been built, and on which it still rested, would of course be seized by the Russians. They'd be one of their primary targets. But there were assets abroad. At the outbreak of war the Count had had as much as possible moved over to the States. In total it amounted to only a fraction of what the family was worth but it was better than nothing. It would give them a start.

Karoly had been to the States before the war, just on holidays. He found it bright and amusing but he couldn't imagine living there in that loud, brash, classless society. In fact he couldn't imagine living anywhere else but Fetevis. He looked up at the house, glowing now in the last rays of the sun. This was where he'd been born and brought up; he had assumed, vaguely, that some day he would marry and bring up his own family here. He found it almost impossible to come to terms with the idea that now this could never happen.

Time and again he'd reminded himself that it was not the first time the family had been forced to pack up and leave. During the Turkish occupation they'd been gone for over two hundred years before returning and building the present palace. He'd tried telling himself that this could be the same, that this was just a temporary exile and that the family would return, greater and stronger than before. But he knew he was only fooling himself. They would never be back. Whatever became of Fetevis it would never again be the same as it was that evening. This was the end of an era.

'Can I get you a coat, sir?'

He turned to see Ottokar, his valet, standing at his shoulder. He shook his head. 'No, it's all right. I'm coming inside in a moment.'

Ottokar remained where he was. He was in his sixties with a heavy moustache that had once been black and a high, balding head. On his face were a dozen unasked questions. 'Is it true that you are leaving, sir?'

'I'm afraid so.'

Ottokar stared at him in incomprehension. 'Would you like me to pack for you, sir?' The words sounded foolish. He shook his head.

'Don't worry,' Karoly said. 'I'll do it myself. I don't think I'll be needing much.' A suitcase of clothes, another of jewellery and trinkets, anything small and valuable that could be turned into cash quickly. That was all he intended to take with him.

'Will you be driving yourself, sir?'

'I guess so.' He'd already briefed the staff on what was to happen in the event of the Russians reaching the Palace.

'At what time would you like the car to be ready?'

'I'll have the Mercedes outside the front door at two.'

Ottokar hesitated to speak. It was not his place to question an order. But he had heard that the bridges were to be dynamited. 'Would it not be safer to leave in the morning, sir?'

'Safer, yes, but not practical. Y'see, in the morning I'm going hunting.'

'Hunting, sir?'

'Of course.' Karoly straightened up and, flicking his cigarette away into the distance, he smiled. 'Can't just sneak away, can we? We'll have a hunt, like the old days. I'll ring my brother.'

'He's mad. Absolutely stark raving mad.'

The resentment in Mary-Louise Kasinczy-Landsberg's voice was sharp as glass as she sat in the back of the black Rolls-Royce.

Her husband, Sandor, made no reply. This was the fourth time she had offered her opinion of his brother's sanity since they set out, and God knew how many times before that.

The car was packed tight. Perched opposite them was their son, Zoltan, fifteen years old, pale-faced and intent; in the front seat, beside the chauffeur, Eleanor Hargreaves, the English girl who'd been his governess for the past six years. And every other available piece of space between was packed with luggage. More cases were stashed in the boot and strapped along the running boards. Sandor had forbidden them to have any on the roof. He said it made the car top heavy, although he was secretly more concerned that if they appeared too obviously to be refugees they would attract the attention of looters.

Mary-Louise gave a little sniff and opening her pigskin vanity case she inspected her reflection in the mirror. She was wearing a long dark fur coat with a pillbox hat perched on the side of her blonde curls. She had wanted to wear the Tyrolean one but its long feathers were inclined to get broken in a car and, besides, someone might think she was wearing it in honour of the day's sport. And that she was not. In the past she'd rather enjoyed hunting, provided Karoly gave her a sensible horse for the day rather than one of his wild creatures, and provided the head forester rode beside her. But she was having nothing to do with this ridiculous scheme of hunting wild boar on the day they were leaving the country. Only the Hungarians would think of doing something so stupid, so totally irresponsible.

She didn't understand the Hungarians. For twenty years she'd been living here and she still found them as strange and disturbing as on the day she'd arrived. On the surface they seemed so gracious and cultivated; a little flamboyant in their manners, but charming just the same. But there was a dangerous streak in them, a total disregard for the laws of common sense. They rose horses to break their necks, gambled for the drama of losing, committed adultery for the thrill of being discovered. It was as though that civilised exterior was just a mask to disguise the dark, primeval face of their character beneath.

She snapped her compact closed. 'This whole thing's a waste of time. If we weren't having to come out here we could be packing. I didn't have time to pack properly. Do you realise that?'

She hadn't done any packing at all. The servants had done all that. Mary-Louise had fussed about them, ordering cases to be opened once they were closed, changing her mind, taking out clothes, replacing them with others. The only thing she'd packed herself was her jewellery, which she had forbidden to be strapped to the side of the car but carried inside on her knee.

She turned to her husband. 'I don't know why you agreed.'

'It's the way Karoly wants it.'

'You should have been firm. You're never firm with him. You should have told him it was a mad idea.'

'It's not a mad idea.'

'No?' Whenever she was angry her Californian accent became more pronounced. 'The Russians are a few miles up the road and we're heading straight for them. You think that's not a mad idea?'

'It's perfectly safe. The bridges are open until this evening.'

'A few hours left, so your brother decides to hold a party.'

'It's his way of saying goodbye.'

'Saying goodbye?' She slung the words back at him in disgust. 'Holy mackerel. The man wants to say goodbye so he fixes a hunt. He must be out of his mind. If he wants to know how to say goodbye I'll show him how. You get in the car, you give a quick wave and then you hit the gas hard and get the hell out of it. That's how you say goodbye.'

'Karoly wants it this way.'

'And you have to obey him, right?'

'He is the head of the family.'

'So you do what he wants. However stupid, however impractical it may be, you go along with it.' She couldn't understand why her husband let his brother dictate to him. They were twins. Karoly was only forty minutes older than Sandor and yet with that tiny advantage he had gained not only the money, the title and the fifteen estates the family owned, but also the right to rule their lives as head of the family.

They, in their turn, had been allowed a single house. Granted, it was a very nice house, better than most of her friends' houses, but still just a fraction of what they would have owned had her husband been an hour older.

She put her vanity case down on the floor and sat back, trying to console herself with the thought that in a matter of weeks they'd be in the States. If they ever got there. In typical Hungarian style her husband seemed to have no idea of where they were heading once they crossed the Danube or how they might find a ship. It was terrifying. She'd heard talk of roving groups of deserters attacking cars that were leaving the country. When she mentioned this to Sandor he said it was scaremongering. There would be no danger, he'd assured her. But she'd seen that he'd tucked a revolver into the side pocket of the car and that Elek, the chauffeur, had another in the front. If they'd left a week ago it wouldn't have been needed. There would have been no risk. This sudden last-minute dash was insanity and it was all Karoly's fault. She couldn't forgive him.

'He's mad,' she sobbed. 'Quite mad.'

In the front, seated beside the chauffeur, Eleanor Hargreaves was separated from the other passengers by a pane of glass and she was glad of it. She didn't want to hear Mary-Louise's endless list of tearful complaints. Risky and irresponsible it may be, dangerous even, but personally Eleanor thought this hunt was the most perfect way to leave. Only a Hungarian could have thought of something so romantic.

The past six years, since she came to this country from the dreariness of England in the grip of the Depression, had been the happiest of her life. She knew that. It was not something she'd discovered afterwards, once it had gone; it was a happiness she'd lived consciously every day. When war broke out she'd remained. She had her reasons. It was not just the depressing thought of returning to London that held her. There were other considerations that she didn't dare to tell anyone, in fact she hardly dared to admit them to herself. Had she done so she might well have lost her job.

By rights she should have been interned as an alien. But on the Kasinczy-Landsberg estates the law didn't apply as it did elsewhere and she'd been able to stay unnoticed in the country. What would become of her now she didn't know. And she wasn't going to spoil the day by thinking of it at this time.

They had entered the gates of the Palace, the car sweeping round the side of the two-mile-long lake. From his perch in the rear, Zoltan Kasinczy-Landsberg gazed across at the Palace. He hadn't said much on the journey; in fact he'd said very little since he'd heard the news of their hurried departure. He was too angry for that.

He couldn't believe they were going to abandon Fetevis. It was theirs. It belonged to them. It had belonged to them for centuries. Everyone knew that. They didn't have to leave, the Kasinczy-Landsbergs didn't have to do anything they didn't want.

And the war was nearly over. Even the newspapers said so. In a few weeks there would be no more fighting.

'That may be so,' his father had said when Zoltan confronted him the night before. He had been sitting in the study, smoking a cigar as he did every evening after dinner. 'But it ain't going to end our way,' he'd explained. 'The Russians are moving in. And they are not here to liberate the country, they're here to take it over. We've got to go, start over again.'

Zoltan had stormed out of the room in disgust. He didn't want to start over again; he didn't want to go to America and live with all his mother's relations. He wanted to live here in Fetevis. And he would one day, he was sure of that. He was the heir, the eldest son. His uncle had never married and Zoltan was sure he never would. The time would come when he inherited Fetevis. And when he did he would return. He'd sworn that to himself.

One day it would be his.

Preparations for the day's sport had already started as they arrived, the driveway was crowded with men and animals. The huntsmen in their red coats, the foresters in their gaiters and heavy green jackets, stood drinking tankards of mulled wine. Over by the Palace steps the pack of hounds were whining and baying in anticipation of the kill.

As Mary-Louise stepped out of the car, Karoly came over to greet them, walking, as all men who live in the saddle walk, with a flick of the right arm as though he were perpetually urging on a horse with an invisible crop. He was in high spirits, his hair spilling over one eye. As he bent to kiss her on the cheek he took in the fur coat and dainty hat.

'Are y'not coming out with us then?'

'I hardly think this is the day for it.' Mary-Louise spoke with an icy dignity.

'Well, there ain't going to be another one.'

Angrily, she moved away towards the house. How could he be flippant on a day like this? A servant hurried up with a tray of champagne but she brushed him away and went indoors.

Sandor drew his brother aside, out of earshot of the others. 'How far away are they?'

'The Russians?' Karoly wasn't concerned with their achievements. 'They moved forwards about five miles in the night.'

'When will they be here, d'you reckon?'

Karoly glanced across the lake in the direction they would be advancing. 'Nightfall, I should think. Maybe earlier.'

Sandor voiced the thought that had been nagging at him as much as at his wife. 'Do you think we should be doing this?'

'What, hunting?'

'Isn't it a bit of a risk?'

Karoly smiled at his brother, the green-grey eyes confident and slightly mocking. ''Course we should, San,' he murmured. 'Scent's good, ground not too hard. It's going to be a beautiful day. Besides, there's something you and I must do later.' He gave him a tap on the shoulder. 'Now have a drink and enjoy yourself.'

'Later,' Sandor said slowly. 'I think I'd better go and see where Mary-Louise has gone. She's very upset.'

'Seemed a little brisk,' his brother agreed.

Sandor found his wife in the study next to the main drawing room, a tea tray on the table beside her.

'He's left everything,' she hissed as he came in.

'Left?'

'Furniture, silver; he's left everything. I can't believe it.'

Sandor took one of the tiny cucumber sandwiches from the plate. 'There's no point in hiding it,' he said as he chewed it. He'd talked it over with Karoly for hours in the past few weeks. 'They're bound to find it sooner or later.'

'But just leaving it for them!'

'He's put a few things away in the hills. If he leaves the rest he reckons they might not realise there's any more.'

'What's he hidden?' she asked quickly.

Sandor shrugged. It didn't really matter. They'd never be back to claim it anyway.

'The Venus?' she asked. 'What's he done with the Venus?'

It was the most valuable of all the family possessions, a Renaissance silver figure they'd owned for five hundred years.

Sandor didn't know what had happened to that. It wasn't in the niche off the Long Gallery where it usually stood.

'I suppose he's had it put somewhere.'

'I hope so,' she said crossly. She flicked invisible crumbs from her lap. 'You know why he's doing this, don't you.'

Sandor didn't reply. He knew what she was going to say.

'It's because he's not married.'

'You know that's not true.'

'If he had a son of his own he wouldn't be so irresponsible,' she snapped. 'You know he wouldn't.'

'He thinks of Zoltan as his son.'

'Well, I wish he'd show it,' she said and looked away out of the window.

In the driveway Karoly was climbing on to his horse, springing up with the quick, light movement that came from years of experience.

'Do you mind if I take your picture?'

He looked round. It was Eleanor Hargreaves who'd asked, the pretty, pink English girl his brother employed to knock a bit of Latin into Zoltan's head. She was standing at his stirrup holding the black box of a camera in her hands.

'Don't see why not,' he said. 'Always fancied myself as a film star. Might become one when we get over to the States.'

She stood back, squinting down into the lens as she calculated the mysteries of focus and exposure. She often took pictures, he'd noticed. It was her way of overcoming her natural shyness, a sort of defensive system.

'What y'going to do when you leave here, Eleanor?' he asked.

She looked up at him, shielding the bright winter's sun from her eyes with one hand. 'I don't know.'

'Are y'going to stay on with my brother?'

'I couldn't say,' she said primly. 'He hasn't talked to me about anything like that.'

'You should get yourself married,' he said. 'Pretty girl like you shouldn't have much trouble finding a rich husband out there.'

She flushed to her roots but before she could reply there was a commotion in the driveway, a high, boyish voice raised in anger.

Karoly slipped down off the horse and, with Eleanor at his heels, went over to see what the trouble was.

He found Zoltan confronting a hushed group of grooms.

'What's the bother then?' he asked.

The boy turned to him, face flushed with fury. 'They've brought out the wrong horses.'

Karoly looked at the two animals who stood saddled ready, their manes plaited, coats glossy. It was a policy of the house that guests were always offered a pair of horses to choose from.

'Wrong?' he inquired. Both horses were in perfect condition. He'd singled them out for the boy himself. 'What's wrong with them?'

'I want to ride Evergreen.'

'He was out yesterday. I thought one of these two would suit better.'

'I prefer Evergreen,' Zoltan told him.

'You can have him if you like but he's not ready. It would take a little time to get him saddled up. And time ain't on our side today.'

Zoltan's eyes flashed. 'Just because you're running away does it mean I have to ride a horse I don't like?'

'Zoltan, really!' It was Eleanor who spoke but Karoly held up his hand to stop her. It was a fair point. No one at Fetevis had ever gone out hunting on a horse they were anything but satisfied with.

'No, it don't.' He gave a smile, as though apologising for his lapse in manners and, turning to the grooms, he gave them instructions to go and prepare the horse.

'Thank you,' Zoltan said gracelessly.

Karoly waited until the two horses had been led off towards the stables before saying, 'Y'reckon we're running away, do you?'

'Aren't you?'

Karoly took the silver case from his pocket and put a cigarette to his lips. 'You'd have us stay and wait for the Russkies then?'

'Yes,' the boy said, 'I would.'

'It ain't entirely practical, y'know.'

'You've no right to throw everything away,' Zoltan said in a low voice. He was shaking with anger. 'Fetevis is not yours to give away. It belongs to me as much as to you.'

Karoly drew in a feather of smoke. He knew what the boy felt about the estate; he'd seen the gleam of possession in his eyes before.

'One day,' he said lightly. 'Maybe one day it would have come to you.'

'It *will* come to me!'

Karoly didn't want to be hard on the boy. He understood the emotions raging in him that day. He felt them himself, so he said, 'Then I hope the time comes when you can come back and claim it.'

'It will,' the boy snapped and, turning on his heel, he marched away.

Sometime just after midday the hounds picked up the scent of a boar and began to give tongue.

Karoly didn't hold with the modern methods of hunting. He had the beaters comb the woods but, rather than drive the boar out past a row of carefully positioned guns so that they could bring it down at a safe distance, he used dogs, following the hunted animal on horseback as his ancestors had done.

The chase was short and hard, the hounds bringing the furious creature down on a patch of open ground high above the valley. Karoly jumped from his horse, plunged in amongst the snarling, fighting dogs and, taking a pistol from his belt, he put a bullet through the boar's head. It was the one concession to the modern world he allowed. The boar's hind legs kicked convulsively and fell still.

Zoltan also dismounted and watched in cold fascination as the boar was rolled on its back and gutted. The head huntsman, Alajos, first cut off the animal's genitals and threw them to the dogs, a primitive ritual that sent shudders down Zoltan's back. Then he slit his knife up the boar's belly and hauled out the entrails in a warm pile.

When this was done, the carcass was trussed up over the saddle of a horse, limp and glassy-eyed, and taken off down the hill. Only four of them remained up there: Zoltan and his father, his Uncle Karoly and Alajos, the huntsman, whom Karoly had asked to stay.

After the fury and excitement of the hunt, it was suddenly very quiet up there. Across the valley, now grey and misted in the afternoon light, rose a column of black smoke and in the distance they could make out the low, unmistakable crump of the guns.

The huntsman fetched a spade and began to dig a hole in the patch of grass, blackened with blood, where the boar had met its end.

'Now that we're alone,' Karoly said to them, 'there is something that we should do.' From the saddlebag on the back of his horse he hefted out a large box. It was covered in velvet with brass corners but Zoltan knew that underneath the ornamentation it was made of thick steel, a tough watertight casket. 'The Russkies will be here in a few hours,' Karoly continued, putting the heavy box on the ground. 'They're going to get nearly everything that belongs to us. But I don't think they should be allowed to get their hands on this. And so, if it's all the same with you, I thought we should leave it here.'

He glanced up at his brother who nodded. Zoltan felt a

stab of annoyance. They'd clearly talked about this before but they'd never said anything of it to him.

The huntsman had dug down two feet into the hard earth now, the rhythmic crunch of the spade breaking the silence and sanctity of the moment.

'That way just the three of us will know where it is,' Karoly continued. 'If any one of us is able to come back,' for an instant his eyes rested on Zoltan, 'he will know where to find it.'

But it wasn't just the three of them, Zoltan thought angrily. There were four. Alajos was there too, patiently digging in the ground as he'd been told to.

'Of course,' Karoly said, 'if for some reason we're not able to come back,' the quick, mocking smile flickered across his face at the enormity of what he was saying, 'then maybe we can pass on what we know.'

Alajos had finished his work. Setting aside the spade he climbed out of the hole.

Zoltan watched as his father and his Uncle Karoly lowered the box into the ground. 'I'd like to see it,' he said.

Karoly paused and then reached down and opened the velvet lid. The Venus lay there beneath them in her bed of silk, a slim, silver figure, glittering in the darkness of the earth, her arms raised as though she were waking, her shining hair flowing with the rhythm of the sea that washed around her feet.

Since he had been a small child Zoltan had known the story of how the Venus had been given to one of his ancestors by Janos Hunyadi, the greatest of all the Hungarian warlords, after the Battle of Belgrade. And to him it was the most beautiful possession in the world.

Carefully, his uncle lowered the lid again and nodded to Alajos who started to cover it over, the earth crashing loudly on the box, fouling the pristine red velvet.

When it was done and a mound of soft soil stood on the grass like a new grave, Karoly looked across the landscape to where the smoke rose in the valley and said, 'And now I reckon we'd better be going.'

They swung themselves back into the saddle and moved off. Zoltan was the last to mount. He stood for a few minutes, adjusting his stirrup, staring across the patch of grass at the mound of fresh earth.

As the others moved on, he took the knife that they all carried when hunting and, running his hand down the horse's leg, he nicked the skin across one tendon. A line of bright red blood sprang out, seeping into the black coat of hair. The animal tossed its head and gave a quick, high whinny of pain but before it could move away he had climbed up into the saddle and spurred it to a canter.

The four of them rejoined the other huntsmen about a mile further down the hill and together they made their way into the valley. They were riding hard now, not wasting any more time than they needed to.

After a while Zoltan fell back in the group. As he came level with Alajos he called across to him. 'Could you take a look at my horse? I think he's gone lame.'

'Where's Zoltan?' The accusation was sharp in Mary-Louise's voice as she came out on to the steps of the house.

The two cars were standing ready: the Rolls-Royce was loaded with baggage, the chauffeur waiting by the rear door; the white Mercedes next to it was almost empty apart from a pair of cases strapped to the running boards.

Sandor dismounted, looking round in sudden anxiety. 'I don't know,' he said in a rush. 'He was with us until a mile or so back. I saw him.'

'Sandor!'

'I'll go back and find him.'

The huntsmen were pouring into the driveway around them. Sandor climbed back on to his horse.

'What's up?' Karoly asked, coming over.

'Zoltan!' Mary-Louise screamed. 'You've left Zoltan.'

'He can't be far back.'

'I'll go and look for him,' Sandor told his wife but as he spoke Zoltan rode into the yard.

His mother hurried down the steps. She had been waiting for what seemed an eternity; she was scared, tired and white with anger.

'Where have you been?'

Zoltan climbed down off his horse and let a groom take it away. 'Brute got a stone in its hoof,' he said casually. 'I had to stop and get it out.'

'Get in the car,' his mother ordered.

The boy threw himself into the rear seat of the car, legs sprawled out in front. His mother took her place opposite. His father was on the point of following when he hesitated.

'Sandor!' Mary-Louise barked.

'Just a moment—'

'It's half past two, for God's sake!'

Sandor went over to his brother Karoly. He was standing on the steps of the porch, cigarette in hand, gazing out across the lake as though there were no sense of urgency at all.

'Time to go,' Sandor said quietly.

'Looks that way,' Karoly agreed. He turned and looked at Sandor; he, who as the elder brother had always made the decisions, always known what to do, and said, 'You go ahead. I'll be along in a minute or two.'

'There's nothing for us here.'

'No, I guess you're right. But I'll just go round to the stables, check everything's all right before I go.'

Sandor paused. 'You will come?'

His brother smiled and touched the cigarette to his lips. ''Course I'll come, San.'

'Sandor!' His wife's voice was on the point of hysteria.

Karoly gave a wink. 'You run along, San. I won't be a moment.'

Sandor stared hard into his brother's eyes and then ran down the steps and jumped into the Rolls. Before the door was closed his wife was rapping on the glass with her umbrella and the car moved forwards.

'What on earth is he playing at?' she asked, sitting back.

'He wants to see the horses.'

'Horses?' She spat back the word as though it were a fly that had stuck on her tongue. 'Horses. That's all he ever thinks of.'

'It is not all he thinks of!' Sandor turned on her and the look of fury in his green-grey eyes stunned his wife into silence.

With his back to the driver, Zoltan looked out through the oval rear window. He saw his uncle standing on the steps, still smoking, as if there were all the time in the world, and behind him the great palace of Fetevis sinking away into the distance as the car rolled off down the hill, and he thought, 'He's not going to leave. The bastard is going to stay right where he is. In his home.'

There was a small sound behind him. He glanced round and saw it came from Eleanor who was sobbing quietly into her handkerchief.

1

December 1996

The town was an hour's drive north of Budapest. It had a plague column, a population of ten thousand and an unpronounceable name. They arrived at dusk and parked in the square.

Sergeant Norton eased himself out of the driver's seat. 'Do we have an address?' he asked.

'Shouldn't need one,' Max Anderson told him. 'There can't be more than one hotel in a dump like this.'

Max was First Secretary at the British Embassy, thirty-one, slightly built with ruffled hair that might be blond in the sun but since it hadn't seen much sun of late was closer to brown.

Norton nodded and buttoned his coat, taking in the details of the town with the jaundiced eye of a military man examining a pack of new recruits. 'Let's take a look then, shall we?' he said.

They walked up the most promising of the streets. The air was bitter, and tatty patches of snow lined the pavement. Three men were drinking in a café on the corner. The waiter gave Max directions while the Sergeant stood outside the street, patiently slapping his arms to keep out the cold.

'My mistake,' Max said as he came out of the café. 'It's got a couple of hotels.'

The first was little more than a dosshouse. There had been no foreigners staying there and from the look of the place it wasn't surprising. They moved on to the second. It called itself the Station Hotel although there was no sign of a railway track.

The reception desk was unstaffed. Max rang the bell and the manager appeared from a cubby-hole behind the desk. He was balding and plump in all the wrong places; a skinny man who'd let himself run to seed. His name, according to the wooden plaque on the desk, was Oskar Hemszo.

'We're looking for someone called Verity,' Max told him. 'Dr Verity. I think he was staying here.'

The manager tried out the name to himself and shook his head. 'No one here with that name.'

'He was here last week. English.'

'I don't think so. Maybe another hotel.'

'There aren't any others worth the name.'

'We don't have many people staying,' the manager told him. 'It's low season.' He spoke softly but all the while his eyes darted over them, taking in the silk ties, the black city overcoats and the pigskin case that Max was carrying.

Max smiled. 'Let's have a look at the register, shall we?'

Technically speaking, he shouldn't have been doing this job. Missing persons were generally handled by one of the junior members of the staff, a Second Secretary or lower. But they were in the run-up to Christmas and that's a lousy time to be hanging around the Embassy. It's the time of year when every diplomatic mission feels obliged to down tools and put on some festive charade. Even countries which have no idea who's birthday Christmas celebrates join in. In the last week Max had found himself attending a couple of carol services, a Nativity play in Dutch and, had he not cleared out, was due that evening to be at a rendering of seasonal folk songs in the Romanian Embassy.

Faced with that prospect, the thought of a wild goose chase out into the countryside had seemed positively attractive.

The manager opened the book where it was marked with a wooden ruler. His finger ran down the column of names, still shaking his head.

'Turn back a bit,' Max suggested.

'I don't see it, sir.'

Max stopped the man's hand, put his finger on a name at the bottom of the page. 'There, that's him.'

The manager studied the entry and gave a shrug. 'Ah yes, I remember him now.'

'I thought you might.'

'The natives don't seem entirely friendly,' the Sergeant observed. He couldn't speak more than a few words of Hungarian but was picking up the mood of the conversation from expressions and gestures.

Max said, 'He's warming up.'

'It's your accent, sir.' The manager understood he was being talked about. 'I didn't recognise the name when you said it.'

'Sure. Is he still here?'

'No, sir. He left about a week ago.'

'Did he say where he was going?'

'No, sir.' He said the words with a shade more feeling as though no resident at the hotel would ever dream of imparting such confidential information to him.

'Isn't it customary to leave some sort of forwarding address?'

'Not in this hotel.'

Max looked round the tobacco brown hallway. There were a couple of framed prints on the wall and a cigarette machine in the corner. Through an open doorway was a dining room, the chairs turned against the tables to discourage anyone from going in.

'What was he doing here?'

'I couldn't say sir.'

'You didn't speak to him?'

'I hardly saw him.'

'How long did he stay?'

'About a week.' He gave another shrug; it could have been more, could have been less. He didn't remember; didn't care.

The Sergeant diagnosed the problem. 'He seems to be having a bit of trouble with his memory, Mr Anderson. I was wondering if you have anything . . . medicinal in your wallet that might help.'

Max took out a note and passed it over the desk. The manager took it, folded it in two with a deft flick of his fingers and burrowed it away in his upper pocket. A couple of spots of pink appeared on his cheeks. He'd sold out to the opposition.

'He went away for a few days.' He spoke hurriedly. 'And then he came back, just for a night. Then he left again.'

'And you didn't speak to him in all that time?'

'He was out most of the time.'

'Not even a few cosy words when he asked for his key; a chat in the bar before dinner?'

'We don't have a licence.' The effect of the note was rapidly wearing off.

'Did he have a car of his own?'

'I didn't notice.'

'We're not accusing you of anything. It's just that he was supposed to be back in England by now but he hasn't turned up. This is the last place he was seen.' Max tried being a shade more conciliatory but it wasn't going to wash. Oskar was becoming difficult.

'He left a week ago; that's all I know. And now, if you don't mind, gentlemen, I have work to attend to.' He disappeared into the rear room from which he'd emerged.

The Sergeant watched the curtain swing back across the entrance. 'Looks like we're back to square one.'

Max said, 'We never left it.'

'What now?'

'We'll ask a few questions around town; see if anyone has a better memory than this fellow.'

'Are we staying?'

Max thought of those folk songs at the Romanian Embassy and said, 'I guess so.'

'Here?'

'Why, did you prefer the look of the other?'

Constable Zwickl dabbed at his forehead with a handkerchief. When he'd first joined the police he'd been drinking eight litres of lager a day. There was nothing wrong with that. He was a big man; he led an active life. He could drink a lot more than that and not let it affect his work. With the extra pay of promotion he'd begun interspersing the lager with a chaser of slivovitz. It heightened the effect and kept out the cold in winter. Between the two of them they gave him a gut that hung over his belt and stretched the buttons of his khaki shirt. In summer he sweated copiously and even now, with the temperature outside five degrees below, there was a sheen of sweat on his upper lip and temples.

He tucked away his handkerchief and stared sullenly at the two strangers. He didn't like being asked questions. This was his office. If anyone was going to ask questions it would be him. 'It is not my concern,' he said. 'It has already been reported. Your Dr Verity has been registered in the missing persons file.'

'And when can we expect a progress report?' Max asked.

'On what?'

'Your investigation into his disappearance.'

'We're not conducting an investigation.'

'Then might I suggest you begin one.'

'There is no need.' Zwickl wasn't going to be pushed. He decided what he did and when he did it. 'You said yourself that he left this town a week ago.'

'He left the hotel. There's nothing to say he left the town. He might have walked out of the door and been mugged in the street.'

'If he had been mugged I would have heard of it.' Zwickl shook his head, terminating the conversation. 'Your friend has left this town. If you want to find him you must look somewhere else. I don't have the time or the staff to start searching for someone who has already gone.'

'Was he ever in this office?'

'I never saw him; I never heard of him.'

'He was a historian,' Max said. 'A specialist in twentieth-century affairs. I can't help wondering why he should want to be here in particular.'

Zwickl shrugged. There were probably a dozen reasons, none of which interested him in the slightest.

'Is there a museum in the town?'

'No.'

'A library? Any sort of archive from the war?'

'There is nothing like that.'

'Odd, don't you think? There has to be some reason he was here.'

'Maybe he was on holiday.'

'Maybe,' Max agreed. 'But somehow I doubt it. Whatever else this town may be it's hardly an advert for the Hungarian tourist board.'

Sergeant Norton buttoned up his coat as they came out into the night. 'Not the most communicative of types.'

'No—'

'Hands shaking like a leaf.'

'Slivovitz,' Max said. 'Reeked of it.'

The Sergeant dug his chin into his scarf with disapproval. Like most ex-military men he forbade weakness in himself and despised it in others.

From the pay-phone in the passage of the hotel, Max put through a call to the Embassy.

'Nothing,' he told Stratton. 'This guy wasn't big on charisma. No one who saw him can remember anything about him. The police aren't interested and the hotel where he was staying doesn't want to know.'

Stratton gave a grunt. It said that this was to be expected in a country in which, until a few months ago, it wasn't clever to be involved in anything that looked or smelled of officialdom.

Max said, 'It would help if I could get some line on what he was doing here.'

'Research.'

'That's a vague word, Jimmie.'

'It's what the man said. I could find out more if you reckon it'll help.'

'It'll help. There has to be something. This isn't the kind of place you need to hang around for long. Even stopping here for petrol is overdoing it.'

'I'll give them a ring. Where will you be tomorrow morning?'

'Here.'

'You're staying on are you?'

'I'll hang about until you ring.'

There was a pause. 'The Romanian Ambassadress is going to be very disappointed.'

'Happy Christmas,' Max said and hung up.

Later that evening, while they were having dinner in a *csarda* off the square, the Sergeant asked, 'Where do you reckon he's got to then, Mr Anderson?'

'God knows. He might be on the track of a piece of red-hot research and decided to hang the lecture he was giving, or he might be holed up in Budapest with a gypsy dancer. It's anyone's guess. He's sure as hell not here.'

Just after nine a 4 x 4 Toyota Jeep drew up opposite the Station Hotel, its thick tyres scratching on the icy tarmac as it braked to a halt. Jeno Strossmayer killed the engine and sat staring across the road at the hotel. He was in a vile mood. He'd been playing cards with some of the boys from the depot when the call came. They were going on to dinner afterwards; one of them was bringing a couple of girls for company. Strossmayer had had high hopes that with a few bottles of wine, a few laughs and a bit of persuasion the evening would end in a most satisfactory way for him. It usually did. He was a handsome man, if he said it himself, thick-chested and dark-eyed, with a heavy black moustache. More than that, he had a presence, a sense of physical authority that women responded to. But as soon as the call came he knew that this was important. The rest was going to have to wait.

He jumped down out of the Jeep and slammed the door behind him. He didn't own the machine; it belonged to the haulage company he worked for, its logo was painted on the side, but he thought of it as his. With its solid body and powerful engine, it was like an extension of his own persona.

He was in the hotel for half an hour. When he came out he lit a cigarette, cupping the lighter in his hands, and walked off down the street. He wore a black leather jacket belted at the waist and a matching leather cap, and he walked with his hands in his pockets which lent him a slight swagger. The light in the police station was burning. He thought of going in and venting his bad temper on Zwickl but the slob would have drunk himself into a stupor by now. He wouldn't get anything but self-pity from him.

At the end of the street was a phone box. Strossmayer dropped a coin in the slot. Giving his cigarette a couple of puffs he perched it on the metal casing and punched in a number. A woman's voice came on the line.

'Let me speak to Vargas.' He didn't have to be polite; it was evidently some sort of maid.

'Who shall I say's calling?'

'Just get him, lady.'

He took a drag at the cigarette while he was waiting. It was perishing cold out there; he stamped his feet to get the circulation going. Then Vargas came on the line.

'I've checked them out.' Strossmayer didn't bother to introduce himself. Vargas would now who it was; he would have been waiting for the call ever since he sent him off on this job. 'There's two of them; they're from the British Embassy. One's the real thing but just a punk; name's Anderson. The other's a driver. They've been asking questions all over town.'

'Do they know where he is?'

'No idea. They're just acting on a report that he's missing. They'll be gone in the morning.'

'I hope so.'

'It's nothing.'

There was silence on the line as though Vargas was searching for precisely the right words to phrase what he was thinking. Then he said, 'It's essential that you find Verity. It's essential that you find him before they do.'

'I will.'

'I'm holding you personally responsible.'

'I'll find him.' Strossmayer snapped his answer. He didn't need any poncing city lawyers telling him his business.

There was a pause. 'I hope so,' Vargas said. 'Things could go very wrong for you if you let us down.'

Strossmayer nearly laughed out loud. It wasn't he who would be for the high jump if they lost Verity. There was always going to be work for a man with his skills. It was Vargas who had to worry. He was the one who'd fouled up and he knew it.

'Don't wet yourself, Vargas.'

'Just find him.'

Strossmayer hung up. As he drove back through the night, he smiled to himself. He'd track down Dr Verity. The little bastard couldn't have gone far in a couple of days. But he didn't have to get there first. That's what Vargas might want; that's what he might order him to do. But he knew nothing about this kind of work. If someone else were to find Verity first it wouldn't matter.

In fact it could make things all the sweeter.

2

Max sat in the little hotel dining room and sipped at a cup of coffee, his thoughts drifting forwards into the future. In five days' time he was going on leave, the first time he had been back in England in two years, and by Christ he was looking forward to it.

He could have gone before. The opportunities had been there. But since being kicked out of the Embassy in Moscow he'd preferred to stay and keep his nose to the grindstone.

It had been a simple tit-for-tat affair. A group of Russian diplomats in London had been accused of spying and told to leave. The Russians had immediately responded by ejecting an identical number from the British Embassy in Moscow. The list of names ordered to go had been almost arbitrary and Max had found himself on it for the simple reason that he was Second Secretary, approaching thirty years old, and that, in the minds of the KGB, meant he could be a spook.

It wouldn't affect his career. The Foreign Service had made that absolutely clear. He was just an innocent bystander in an international incident. No mud would stick. But when Max was transferred to the Embassy in Budapest he had found himself working remorselessly. He wanted to prove himself, to show he was capable of handling the new job.

In two months he had mastered the language and acquainted himself with the political and economic structure of the country, and in under a year he had been promoted to First Secretary. He could honestly say that his time in Budapest had been successful, but the thought of getting back home for a few weeks, of wearing an old T-shirt and trainers, of drinking beer from the bottle, getting chucked out of pubs at closing time, to live a few days without rules and regulations, was going to be marvellous. There were a couple of girls he was going to look up. The trouble with the Embassy was that they treated any unmarried girl as a potential threat to security. Before they were allowed near the residency they had to be screened, vetted and approved which meant almost invariably that the ones Max had in mind never made it past the polished doors.

A few days back home would change that.

As with most diplomats, a career in the Foreign Service had never been part of Max's grand scheme of life. At university he'd read law. But by the time he came down, with an overdraft, an ability to punt and a respectable enough degree, the chances of getting into chambers in London weren't looking good. It was the late eighties and Britain was in the grip of a recession. It didn't mean that there were any fewer burglaries, any fewer City frauds or fiddles on the tax system but, in the mood of self-flagellation that recessions bring, fewer lawyers were being taken on. And so he'd turned to the diplomatic corps. He had connections there; his father had been an ambassador. Not a bad one in his own way. That's not to say Max had strings to pull but it was a world he understood, rather like going into the family firm.

Max didn't look on the diplomatic service as a life's mission, more like a stepping stone to higher things, a post in one of the City banks, say, or a seat at the board of a big industrial company. But he was in no hurry. He'd already seen some of his friends burn themselves out by the time they were thirty-five, pulling down incomes of a hundred and fifty, two hundred thousand a year, but into the office at seven in the morning, working through to ten at night, never able to get away, never able to spend the money they earned, crushed by the pressure of their responsibility. For the time being he preferred chasing around after missing university lecturers.

The Sergeant came into the dining room, neat and punctual as always, and joined him at the table.

'I've ordered a pot of tea,' he told Max in a confidential tone, as though he was worried that the whole room might hear the news and stampede the kitchens.

'You amaze me. I'd have put shorter odds on getting a bottle of whisky out of them.'

'I gave them the bags. I always carry them with me.' The Sergeant was one of the old school, a man who carried a tiny piece of Britain around with him wherever he travelled, avidly reading the football scores in the papers, listening to the BBC World Service, playing bowls on the Chancery lawn on Sunday mornings.

'Sleep well?' Max asked.

'Well enough.' He sounded distant. 'The room's adequate but they're no respectors of privacy, are they?'

'Why? Did you find yourself sharing your bath with a large Hungarian lady?'

The Sergeant wasn't easy with that kind of talk. 'No sir, nothing like that. But I can swear someone went through my room last night.'

Max took a bread roll and broke off the end. He was used to this line of conversation. Communism was over, dead and buried, but when people came to Central Europe they were still convinced that there were bugging devices in the flower vases, two-way mirrors in the bathroom, a whole army of secret police checking through the laundry bags.

'What makes you think that?'

'A few things moved. Only slightly, but moved just the same. I always lay out my kit in a certain way, neat like and orderly. When I came back last night some of it had been moved.'

'Probably the maid.'

'Probably.'

'They always go through foreigner's luggage. In the old days they took anything they had a fancy to. It was one of the perks.'

'I'd make a complaint but I don't think it would do any good.'

Not forgetting that they wouldn't understand a word he said, Max observed to himself. It was a miracle the Sergeant had managed to convey the principle of brewing tea the way he liked it.

Jimmie Stratton rang on the dot of nine.

'I had a chat with the college bursar in Oxford last night,' he said. 'He doesn't know much about Verity himself but he's given me the number of one of his assistants, name of Lennox. It's probably best if you talk to him yourself.'

Max jotted down the number he read out. As he tucked the notebook back in his upper pocket he asked, 'How were the folk songs last night?'

'Agony.'

'I was thinking of you.'

'Three hours of it without a break, Max. You've no idea. Then they were handing out free CDs at the end for anyone who wanted to hear more. Simon Whittaker took one.'

'Which proves he's either tone deaf or a Romanian mole.'

'It proves he's a prat,' Stratton said as he rang off.

Max went round to the reception desk and asked the scraggy girl for his briefcase. The Sergeant had had it put in the hotel safe overnight with the observation that there were people out there who'd kill their grandmothers for it.

The girl put it on the desk. Max turned the two outer wheels of the combination lock one notch with his thumb and pressed the clasps but they didn't open. He glanced at the numbers. They were nowhere near right.

He beckoned the Sergeant over.

'This thing's been tampered with.' He was surprised as much as anything. On the whole, diplomatic staff were treated with a kind of reverence.

'Are you sure?'

'Dead sure. I only ever turn one wheel of the lock when I close it. These are way off.'

'It's been in the safe all night.'

Max turned to the girl, who was gaping vacantly at them as it dawned on her that something wasn't right, and said, 'We'd like to see the manager.'

'He's busy at present.'

'Get him, please.'

'He never comes to the desk before ten.'

'Tell him that unless he's out here in the next five seconds his feet won't hit the ground.'

She looked from one face to another, realised they were serious and vanished again. Max waited for a moment before lifting the flap of the reception desk and following her.

The office behind was small, dark and smelled of cigarette

smoke. Sitting at a desk crowded with papers was the manager. He was talking urgently with the girl, making small rapid gestures with one hand. As Max came in, the Sergeant behind him, they both turned and stared stupidly for a moment, like a couple of schoolkids caught smoking behind the shed.

'What are you doing here?' the manager asked.

Max jerked his head at the girl and she fled. Putting his briefcase on the desk he said, 'I want a few questions answered.'

'Such as?'

'Such as who went through our rooms last night.' He had no doubt that his own had received the same treatment as the Sergeant's, it was just that he wasn't able to detect it in the same way. 'And who has been fiddling with the lock on this case.'

'I don't know what you mean.'

'No?' Max brushed aside a plate of sandwiches and perched on the side of the desk. 'Now, Oskar, I think it's time you and I stopped playing silly buggers and had a serious talk.'

The manager sat perfectly still.

'Someone has fiddled with the lock on this briefcase. And since it has been shut away in your safe all night I can only assume it was you.'

'That couldn't be. You must be mistaken—'

'No mistake.'

The manager looked round the office, remembering who he was. 'I must ask you to leave. This is a private area.'

'If I go now I'll be back with the police. And I don't mean your fat Constable Zwickl. I mean the real police, men with search warrants and guns and no sense of humour. Tampering with diplomatic property is a serious business, isn't that right, Sergeant?'

Max looked up at the Sergeant who nodded solemnly. He hadn't followed a word so far but he knew when to come in on cue.

'You could find yourself doing three years for this, Oskar.'

The manager shook his head as though he couldn't believe what he was hearing.

'If nothing else they'll close this place down round your ears.'

'I don't understand. This is all most unfortunate.'

'Damned right it is.'

The manager stared up at Max. His resistance was weakening, his eyes pleading. 'He said no one would know,' he whispered.

'He?'

The manager swallowed hard, his Adam's apple sinking into his collar like an unbroken egg slipping down a python's throat. 'The man who came last night.'

Max glanced up at the Sergeant. 'You're saying someone came round here last night and searched through our belongings?'

The manager nodded.

'Who is he?'

'He didn't give a name.'

'Describe him.'

The manager shook his head again, his brain unable to come up with adequate words. 'He's a big man – with a moustache.'

'And you opened up the safe for him and let him break into my case, did you?'

'He told me to do it.'

'Just like that.' Max was sarcastic. 'You didn't think to tell us about this later?'

'I couldn't.'

'He cut your tongue out, did he?'

The manager coloured slightly and gave an impatient shake of the head. 'You don't understand. He's a dangerous man – violent. I can tell. There's no knowing what he would do.'

'Mafia?'

'He could be – something like that.' The words were stuttering out. 'I run a hotel. I can't afford to make enemies of men like that.'

'You've seen him before, have you?'

The manager paused and then nodded quickly. 'He's been here before – several times, waiting for your friend to return.'

'Return?' There'd been no suggestion of Verity returning. He was supposed to have paid his bill and left.

The manager looked up, his eyes flicking between the two of them, realising he'd let slip more than he intended. A bead of perspiration appeared on his balding forehead. He was scared stiff. 'Return,' he explained, 'to pick up his luggage.'

'Are you telling me that Dr Verity never checked out of here?'

The manager shook his head.

There was silence in the little office. The Sergeant could see that the conversation had twisted in a new direction but he was too polite to ask where. He just said, 'Are you getting anywhere with him, sir?'

Max took a little time in answering. 'It seems our friend Oskar here has been a shade economic with the truth. Verity didn't leave; he just didn't come back one day. In the meantime some goon's been looking for him. He worked over our rooms and broke into my briefcase.'

The Sergeant thought this over, nodded to himself as though it were to be expected and said, 'Messy.'

The manager's eyes were darting uneasily between the two of them as they talked. 'It's not my fault,' he whined. 'I didn't want to be involved in this. I just run a hotel.'

Max wasn't interested in Oskar's problems at that moment. He had enough of his own. 'Is Verity's luggage still here?'

The manager nodded.

'Let's have a look at it.'

The manager unlocked a room on the first floor. The place was a shambles, clothes strewn around the floor, drawers hanging out, the wardrobe gaping wide. The bed had been stripped back, the mattress thrown to one side.

The manager made a little gesture of apology. He didn't want them to think this was of his making.

Which it wasn't, Max thought to himself. He'd just stood and watched and said nothing, locking the door afterwards and hoping the whole sordid business would go away.

'I take it your friend with the moustache has been here already.'

'He searched through everything.' Oskar had a gift for converting the obvious into an understatement.

'When was this?'

'A couple of days ago.'

There was a pair of jeans lying on the floor, beside it a sweat shirt with some bright-coloured logo. Because Verity had 'doctor' before his name, because he lectured at a university, Max had assumed that he would be elderly and tweedy like a benign old vicar. He should have known better. The real world didn't deal in stereotypes.

'Look at this, sir.' The Sergeant had found a cheap suitcase.

He held it open. The crimson lining had been slashed to ribbons. He dropped it on the mattress. 'Wanton destruction,' he said. 'That was a good case before he did that.'

Max looked round at the sordid remains of Dr Verity's possessions. He didn't know anything about this man. He had no idea what he was wanting in this drab hotel. But he had the powerful impression that he had got himself tangled up in something very nasty.

He went over to the manager who sidled away towards the bed. Max gave him a prod and he sat down on it.

'Okay, Oskar, let's have some talk out of you. Who was this man who came here?'

'I have told you all I know.' He was watching every move that Max made.

'You've told me he's a big man with a moustache.'

'It's true.'

Max made no reply.

The manager stared at him, realising he wasn't disputing these facts, just wanting more. 'He has black hair,' he added lamely.

'Did he take anything while he was here?'

'I wouldn't know.'

He was still playing the innocent bystander bit but Max wasn't having it. He would have been there; he would have witnessed the whole event.

'What did he take, Oskar?'

'A passport,' he said quickly. 'Some money.'

Both inevitable in their own way. He'd have taken the passport to stop Verity leaving the country, and he'd have taken the money because he couldn't stop himself from doing so.

'How does he get here?'

The manager didn't appear to understand the question.

He mouthed a couple of words to show willing but no sound came. The Sergeant encouraged him with a cuff to the shoulder. 'Come along now, sir. Answer the gentleman.'

'By car.'

'What sort?'

'I don't know.'

'You're standing at the reception desk and a man comes in, wrecks one of your rooms, searches through the safe, puts the fear of God into you and you don't notice what car he leaves in?'

'I don't know the make. It's one of those cars they use in the country, a sort of Jeep – big wheels, a roll-bar.'

'A 4 x 4?'

The manager didn't know the expression. He couldn't really be expected to know all the makes of car. Most of them had only appeared in Hungary in the past few years.

'It's blue,' he said, 'with the name of some company on the side. Yellow letters.'

'You don't know the name?'

He shook his head again.

A man with a moustache who drove a blue 4 x 4. That's all they had. No facts, no names, just an image. But it was probably the best they could hope for.

From the phone box in the passage Max rang Jimmie Stratton.

'This isn't looking too clever,' he said. 'Our friend Verity's luggage is still here. It's been worked over by some heavy who's tearing up the place looking for him.'

Stratton said, 'Hell's teeth.'

'I don't know who this guy is but he's found himself a pretty nasty class of enemy.'

'Looks like you've dropped yourself in it, Max.'

'His passport's been nicked so he can't have left the country. I reckon we'll have to call in the police.'

'I guess so.' Stratton didn't sound too happy about it. There was an unwritten law at the Embassy that the Hungarian police were never involved unless absolutely necessary. Experience had proved that affairs could be tidied up more quickly, cleanly, and with a great deal less fuss without their assistance. 'Can the police your end handle it?'

'No way. The only policeman here is a piece of suet pudding in a uniform. Most of the time he's pissed. You'll have to send someone out here.'

'I'll see what I can do. You'd better stay where you are. Don't let anyone touch his things.'

'They won't; I've got the key to the room.'

'I'll be in touch. It's going to take a bit of time to get the cogs grinding, Max. There won't be anyone out there until later this afternoon. You'd better twiddle your thumbs for a bit.'

Max hung up the phone, listened to the coins rattle into the box. The thought of hanging around the hotel with nothing to do all day didn't fill him with joy. Taking out his pocket book he rang the number in Oxford he had been given earlier.

A woman's voice answered.

'I want to speak to someone called Lennox,' he said. 'It may be Dr Lennox.'

'Just Ruth,' she said evenly.

It hadn't occurred to Max that Verity's assistant might be a woman. For some reason he found that made it easier.

'I need some information about Dr Rupert Verity.'

'Rupert? He's in Hungary as far as I know.'

'So am I.'

'Ah, I see.' She spoke with a touch of amusement. 'I'm sorry. How can I help you?'

She didn't need to have the situation spelled out to her. After the dithering of the hotel manager Max found it a relief.

He explained who he was. 'I'm trying to find out what he was doing.'

'Research, I imagine.'

'Can you be more specific?'

'No.' She drew out the word as though she were thinking. Was she sitting in some venerable college study, Max wondered, with the morning sunshine streaming through mullioned windows? He liked to picture people when he spoke to them. 'Most of his work,' Ruth Lennox went on, 'is concerned with Central Europe in the years between the two wars. Social history, on the whole. But exactly what he is doing at present I couldn't say.'

It didn't sound too hopeful. 'You've no idea why he should be holed up in a one-Skoda town to the north of Budapest?'

'No. Perhaps I should explain that Rupert Verity is a colleague of mine. We share a study at the faculty but I can't say I know him personally.'

Which was another way of saying that she didn't like him very much. 'You must have formed some impression of what he's working on.'

'He's a very private man. He doesn't give much away.' A thought struck her. 'Actually, there was something. He was looking for an address in Hungary a few weeks ago. I took a message for him. It was some extraordinary name. I jotted it down at the time – hang on.' The phone went down.

Max waited in the plywood cubicle.

'Here we are,' she said, returning to the phone. She

sounded pleased with herself. 'I wrote it on the back of a file. He was wanting the address of someone called the Countess Kasinczy-Landsberg. I don't know whether that means anything to you. I've got the address here if it's any use to you.'

Max had never taken an interest in the now-defunct Hungarian aristocracy, who hung around embassy parties hoping for a free drink and the chance to fill a friendly ear with tales of their sorrow. But he knew the name Kasinczy-Landsberg. They'd been in a different league to the rest, one of the super-rich families of Central Europe with estates the size of southern England.

Not that they'd have a bean to their name now. Much of their land would have been confiscated after the Treaty of Trianon, and the commies would have taken care of the rest. The chances were that this Countess had hung on to her title and not much else.

She must also be getting on, Max calculated as he drove over to see her. It was almost fifty years since the use of titles was abolished. If she'd been around long enough before that to have got in the habit of calling herself Countess she must be pushing eighty.

Before leaving he had given Sergeant Norton the key to Verity's room. 'Go through it with a toothcomb. I doubt whether there's anything of interest left but you never know.'

The Sergeant nodded sagely. He wasn't a man of any great imagination but he could carry out an order to the last detail. If Max asked him to search the room he could guarantee there wouldn't be a square inch he'd leave untouched.

'You're going out are you, sir?'

'I'm going to check out this old biddy.'

She was the reason Dr Verity had come here to Hungary;

Max had no doubt of that. The address Ruth Lennox had given him over the phone was for the Palace of Fetevis. And that was just five miles away from the hotel.

Too close for coincidence.

He got directions from a shop in a village he passed through. The woman behind the counter seemed surprised he should be asking and a mile or so further on he realised why. The Palace of Fetevis didn't need directions. It just presented itself.

Max had seen a lot of stately homes in his time but not many to better this one. It was the kind of house that appears on the covers of smart travel guides, the kind that makes you stop the car and say, 'Christ, would you take a look at that.'

It stood on the far side of a half-mile-wide stretch of smooth water, its broad pilastered facade rising above the winter trees. Slim turrets and spiky dormer windows in the roofs gave it the appearance of something from a fairy tale.

Max had heard stories of the Kasinczy-Landsbergs' wealth. How they had smashed the hand-made Herrand porcelain after each party so that they wouldn't bore their friends with it a second time. How, when they travelled by train across Europe, they had their own private carriages fitted out with dining room, library and sleeping quarters and staffed by a small army of butlers and chefs. But it was only now, as Max stared across the lake at this vision, that he realised the full extent of their riches.

Buildings like that weren't knocked up overnight. Valleys had to be flooded, trees grown and vistas engineered. The whole of nature had to be cajoled into co-operating and that took time and the kind of money that would take most people all their lives to count, let alone work out what to do with.

What he couldn't see was how to get into the place. There was a gateway further along the road but it was chained up. He drove on round a bit. If it was anything like the big English piles there'd be a long driveway at the front to impress the guests and a much shorter one round the back to get the tradesmen in and out as quickly as possible.

He did find a second gate but, like the first, it was chained up. There was nothing for it but to ditch the car and walk. He climbed the low wall and headed up the driveway. Sweeping up it in a horse and carriage would, he had no doubt, have been an exhilarating experience. On foot it was a twenty-minute flog and by the time he arrived he was beginning to wish he'd stayed back at the hotel and played Scrabble with the Sergeant.

The driveway brought him in by the side of the house. It towered above him like a fortress. He worked his way through a couple of small, deserted courtyards to the driveway at the front, and it was there that the whole image came crashing down.

At a distance Fetevis had been a magnificent sight, shimmering above its reflection. Up close it was a wreck: the plaster was flaking away, raw brick showing through the scars; weeds were growing up through the paving stones, wooden boards pinned to windows where the glass had broken.

There was no sign of life.

Max walked up the flight of stone steps into the porch and looked to see if there was a bell or knocker to the double doors. But there was nothing like that. He supposed that in the old days there were flunkies to spot you coming and open the door for you. He tried the handle and somewhat to his surprise he found it was open.

He went through into a long hallway. It was completely

unfurnished, the floors and walls bare. The smell of neglect hung in the air. He looked up at the domed ceiling far above. There were large bare patches between the mouldings where he guessed there had once been paintings. As he stared at them a woman's voice behind him said, 'Would you leave please, this is private property.'

3

Max turned around.

There were two figures framed in the open doorway. The shorter of them was an old man. He had a beard and bright black eyes beneath shaggy white eyebrows which gave him the look of a tough little border terrier. He was carrying a shotgun. It wasn't actually aimed at Max but held high enough to keep the option open. He was bent with age so that he only came up to the shoulder of the girl beside him.

She stood with her hands on her hips, long legs clad in blue jeans that were tucked into riding boots. Her hair was tied back in a scarf, peasant style, and the look on her face was far from friendly.

'You have no right to be here.'

'I'm sorry,' Max was conciliatory. 'I didn't mean to barge in but I couldn't find any other way of letting you know I was here. I would have rung earlier but there's no phone here.'

'That doesn't give you permission to come sneaking in through the back way.'

'I wasn't intending to sneak anywhere but the gates are all locked.'

'That's to stop people like you getting in,' she said archly. 'And for your information there is a phone.'

'Not according to the directory.'

She shrugged. 'Then it's out of date. Now I'd like you to leave, please.'

'If you insist. But I came here to talk to Countess Kasinczy-Landsberg and if you don't mind I'll still do so.'

'That's not possible.'

'That is for her to decide.'

'She doesn't speak to anyone. Now go or I'll set the dogs on you.'

She was certainly one of the rudest girls Max had ever come across but he was rapidly coming to the opinion that she was also one of the most beautiful. It was a cool, arrogant beauty that gave her the confidence to stare unwaveringly at him with her green-grey eyes. It was a perishing cold day but she was wearing nothing warmer than a shirt, the sleeves rolled to the elbow. He guessed she must have been in some other part of the house when he turned up and had come running across without bothering to throw on a coat. The raw air had brought a flush of colour to her cheeks.

The old man had shuffled round to one side as they spoke and was keeping him covered with the muzzle of the shotgun. Max watched him out of the side of his eye.

'Look, lady, I don't know what your problem is but I think you've got the wrong person.'

'I know exactly who you are and what you want.'

'Really.' Max allowed himself to be edged over to the doorway. 'You must have remarkable powers of perception. I can see now why you have so many empty guest rooms in this place.'

Her eyes flashed with anger. 'I hardly think you count as a guest.'

'No? Why was Verity any different?'

'Verity?'

'Thc English historian.' Max spoke quietly as though to a dangerous animal. 'The one from Oxford University.'

'What has this to do with him?'

'I don't think he has anything to do with what you're talking about; but he has everything to do with what I am.'

'I don't follow you—'

'I'm trying to trace him. He was here a few days ago.'

A moment's hesitation. 'Who are you?'

'Anderson – I'm from the British Embassy.'

'I see.' She studied him in silence for a moment. This was the moment when Max reckoned she should realise she'd made a mistake, give a grin and show him that she wasn't the hard-nosed madam she appeared to be. But that wasn't how she handled matters. With a frown she said, 'That would explain your terrible accent.'

'Quite. Who did you think I was?'

'That doesn't matter.'

'Well, now that we've tidied up the formalities I'd like to speak to the Countess.'

'About what?'

'I'd rather tell her that, if you don't mind.'

'Oh don't be so pompous,' she said impatiently. 'Tell me.'

'I'm talking only to the Countess.'

'Then get on with it.'

'Are you her?'

'Of course.'

'Why do you stare?'

'I can't see how you can be.'

'No?' She gave him a wintry smile, revealing strong white

teeth. 'Then you don't read your papers, Mr Anderson.'

'I somehow thought you'd be older.'

'Did you?' She held up one finger and revolved it beside her temple. 'Then it seems we are both a little confused.'

It was as near as she was going to get to apologising. Turning on her heel she walked out on to the porch. Max followed. Reverentially, the old man closed the doors behind them. As they went down the steps she asked, 'What is it you want to know about Dr Verity?'

'He was supposed to be back in England by now but he hasn't turned up. I'm trying to find him.'

'He's not here.'

'But he did come here?'

'Yes.' She was looking down over the lake. 'He came here.'

'What did he want?'

She shrugged. 'To see the house.'

'Just that?'

'He seemed interested in all this.' She gave a brief flick of her hand which Max took to mean not only the house but the history it represented, the wealth and power it had once commanded.

'And you let him look around, did you?'

'Yes, I let him,' she said evenly.

'Did he say anything about what he found?'

'I hardly spoke to him.'

'He just trotted around sizing the place up and making notes and then left, did he?'

She turned and looked at him appraisingly, seeing if he was mocking her. 'Yes, that's about it. And now if you don't mind I must ask you to go. I'm very busy. You know the way out.'

With a nod she turned and stalked away round one end of

the house. A spaniel was sniffing along the wall. She snapped her fingers and it fell in behind her, tail wagging. It didn't look a particularly fierce creature, hardly the type to see off intruders.

Which was more than you could say for its mistress.

On the way back, Max stopped in the village for petrol.

'I see you've got your old bosses back in charge,' he said to the boy in oil-stained overalls who shuffled out of the wooden garage to operate the pump.

'How's that?'

Max nodded back towards the house. 'The Countess Kasinczy-Whatshername.'

'Oh, her.' He couldn't have sounded less interested. 'She's only been here a few weeks. Won't last long, if you ask me.'

'Why do you say that?'

'She hasn't got a penny to her name and the place is falling down around her ears, from what I hear. Friend of mine went up there a few months back; he said it was in a fine mess, all rotted away. Take a fortune to restore it.'

'I'm surprised she wanted it back.'

'Don't think she did. Just got it handed to her – because of her name being what it is and all that. She didn't want it and you can't blame her. Mind you, I'm not too sorry for her. She can be a right bitch when she wants. Kicked someone in the village out of his house. Soon as she moved in she calls him up to the place and tells him to get packing – no reason – just ordered him out.'

'Can't have been popular.'

The boy lifted the nozzle and held it in his hand as he stared in the direction of the house. 'No, it wasn't, I'm telling you. I reckon they're all alike, these people with titles and all the rest of it. Bastards under the skin. But you can't turn the clock back. I'll bet you what you like she won't be here come the New Year. Without any money she'll have to sell up and get the hell out of it again. Serve her right, that's what I say.'

'Where did she come from before?'

The boy shrugged. 'God knows. They say in the village that they put her old man in jail.'

'Her husband?'

'Father – the old Count who used to live here. Locked him up for being such a rich pig all those years. Mind you, she'll be all right. With legs like that she'll get herself a rich husband and live in America.'

Living in America, Max knew from experience, was an expression used to describe a life of unimaginable luxury in any country apart from Hungary.

'Do you think so?'

'Sure.' The boy seemed to be an authority on the subject. 'Bound to happen. Sometimes when I see her, I wouldn't mind a bit of it myself. But she shouldn't have got it, should she? It's not right for a woman to get everything. It should be a man who inherits.'

'I didn't realise these things were being handed out at all.'

'Oh, there's been a big court case. Don't you read the papers then?'

He was the second person to have asked that question in the past hour.

Sergeant Norton knew that the secret of control lay in holding the high ground. He had moved a chair into the narrow hallway of the hotel, from where he had a view of both the reception desk and the street outside. No one could come or go without his knowledge. He could also see down the passage to the phone booth and the stairs beyond, should anyone try going up to Verity's room.

To pass the time he was reading the edition of the *Daily Mail* he'd brought with him the day before. It always took a day to reach Budapest and so he was catching up on news that was already two days out of date, but he found it comforting to hear of rugby scores, burglaries and insults in the House that were still taking place without him.

In his twenty-three years in the Diplomatic Police Corps he had performed a large number of tasks, some of which were covered by the Official Secrets Act, others which were more mundane. But he found the disappearance of this university gentleman strange. There was more to it than met the eye. It wasn't his place to say but if he were asked his opinion, he'd recommend the whole business should be passed over to the police as quickly as possible.

It was after three when Max returned. He parked across the street and came in, stamping his cold feet to warm them. The two men went through into the empty dining room.

'Any word from the police?' Max asked.

'Not yet, sir.'

He unwound his scarf and draped it over the back of the chair. 'I saw this Countess that Verity was so interested in. She's not as old as I thought – mid-twenties at a guess – lives in a huge rotting palace with a dog and a bad-tempered old man with a gun.'

'Did you learn anything from her?'

'Not a thing. Damned aggressive, told me to get off her land. Verity wanted to see the place and she didn't even bother to ask him why.' He grinned quickly as though he'd made a fool of himself by going all the way over there. 'How about you?'

'I checked through the gentleman's belongings, as you asked. I can't say there's anything of interest. He was travelling light. Of course, you can't tell what might have been taken already but I doubt whether he was carrying anything of any interest. I did find this.' From his pocket he drew out a magazine and laid it on the table. It was a copy of the *New Statesman*. 'It was on the floor below the bed. I assume it was his; I can't believe there's been anyone else English in that room of late. I found this in it.'

He thumbed through the crumpled pages until he found his place, then handed it over to Max, pointing to the upper corner. A series of numbers had been scribbled down there in Biro, then enclosed in a box.

'You reckon he wrote this?' he asked. Only the Sergeant would have checked through every page of a magazine for information.

'I'd say he was talking on the phone, sir, jotted those numbers down on the first thing that came to hand. The box is a sort of doodle, isn't it? People do that when they're talking on the phone.'

There were eight numbers in a row with two capital letters at the beginning and a dash and another letter at the end.

'Mean anything to you?' Max asked.

'Nothing that springs to mind. It might be worth showing it around the Embassy, see if it rings a bell anywhere.'

'It's not a telephone number. More like a reference number.' He handed it back and got to his feet. 'Hang on to it, Sergeant, I'd better call the Embassy, see what's going on.'

'Panic's over,' Stratton told him as he got through. 'We've just had a call from the university. Our friend's turned up.'

'Oh, brilliant. Where is he?'

'Not far from you. Hopping mad and demanding to be shipped back to Blighty.'

'I bet he is.' Max felt a slight sense of anticlimax now that the business was over. 'He won't get far without a passport.'

'No, he won't. Get him to the airport. I'll fix it for him to be repatriated. And watch out for him, Max, he's pretty jumpy.'

'So he should be.'

'Demanded to have a description of you before he'd agree to have you pick him up.'

'I trust you were flattering.'

'Aren't I always?' Stratton gave a little chuckle. 'Get a pencil, I'll give you directions.'

In the office at the back of the hotel, the manager was perspiring slightly into his woollen cardigan as he stared at the maid. She was perched on the edge of the desk, her ear to the telephone receiver, one hand clamped over the mouthpiece.

As Max rang off she very gently replaced the receiver on its cradle. Her eyes were thoughtful.

'What did they say?' the manager asked.

The thin girl wasn't sure of her English. 'They've gone to pick someone up. Then there were a whole lot of directions.'

'Did you get them?'

'Oh yes, they're not difficult.'

'Write them down,' the manager said. He opened the desk drawer, took out a pen and paper and passed them to her. His heart was pounding as he watched her write. He had never done anything like this before; he had never been guilty of such a breach of etiquette. But this would be the end of it. This was the important part. After this he'd done his bit, kept his side of the bargain.

The girl paused and sucked the end of the pen. Oskar was concerned. 'Have you forgotten something?'

'Oh no.' She was rather enjoying her role. She'd never been so important to the boss before; it was a new experience. 'Just remembering the right order.'

'Get on with it, girl.' Outside in the hallway, he could hear the two Englishmen talking. They went out into the street. The buzzer to indicate the front door opening rang briefly. Then there was silence.

The manager took the directions the girl had jotted down and checked them through. He dialled a number and spoke briefly. After a few moments he read out what she had written, repeated it once and rang off.

As he put down the receiver his hands were sweating.

4

In the days of the Empire, when Hungary was four times larger than it is today, sheep and cattle were kept indoors. It gives their farms, with their high outer walls and single entrance, something of the appearance of the forts the US Cavalry put up in Indian country, except that instead of being rough stockades of wood and stone, they are often elaborately decorated with moulded and painted plaster work.

The one Max reached that afternoon stood a mile up a track. It was set in a valley and surrounded by cherry orchards. Collectivisation had done it no favours: the walls were cracking, the double-headed Hapsburg eagle above the door pock-marked with bullet holes where some wit had expressed his political opinions with the aid of a rifle.

They parked on the edge of the track and went in through the heavy wooden doors that stood partially open. A few pieces of farm machinery stood around, rusting with age, but apart from that there was no sign of human life.

Max looked in through the window of the living quarters but he could see at a glance it hadn't been used for some time.

'Are you sure this is the right place?' the Sergeant asked.

'Fits the description.'

'Strange place to be staying.'

Max looked around the deserted yard. He was getting fed up with playing games. Cupping his hands to his mouth he shouted: 'Dr Verity!'

The words echoed around the courtyard and then died away.

Max tried again.

'Maybe he's moved on,' the Sergeant said.

As he spoke a voice came from one of the barns off to their right. 'Turn around, please!'

There was no sign of anyone. The barn doorway from which the voice had issued was dark, the low windows too dirty to see through. But they did as they were told.

Again the voice spoke. 'Who are you?'

'Anderson – from the Embassy. We've come to take you to the airport.'

There was a moment's silence. Although he could see no one, Max could sense eyes on him, assessing him, sizing him up.

'What's the name of the DHM at the Embassy?' the voice inquired.

'Stratton – James Stratton. He sent me over here. Now could we come in and talk?'

'Very well.'

Max went across to the barn and ducked in through the low entrance. It was dark in there, the air heavy with the fertile smells of soil and animal manure. In the gloom he could see wooden fencing separating the cattle pens. The ground beneath his feet was cobbled.

At first there was no sign of Verity. Max peered around. The man was turning caution into an art-form. Then there was a movement at the end of the barn and a figure emerged from the shadows.

Max screwed up his eyes in the low light. 'Dr Verity?'

The figure came closer, stopping a few yards away from where they stood. He held out one hand. 'Do you have some form of identification, Mr Anderson? I'd like to see something.'

Max took out his wallet, held up the diplomatic pass.

'Just to be sure,' Verity said. 'One has to be sure. Who's the other one with you?'

'Sergeant Norton. He's my driver.'

Verity turned his gaze on to Norton for a moment then back to Max. 'You took your time coming.'

'We came as soon as we heard where you were.'

'Two days I've been here, holed up in this stinking place. And that's not nice, you know. I've hardly eaten a thing.' There was an expression of self-pity in his pale face as he stood there, like a child who has been denied a sweet. His flesh was soft, his lips full and red and hanging slightly open as though he were about to say something but had been forbidden to do so by a severe nanny. His chocolate-brown eyes were on Max. 'Do you have anything to drink on you?'

'No, not on me. You can get something when we get to the other end.'

'You're taking me to the airport?'

'I heard you wanted to get back to England.'

'I want to get out of this country. There's a difference, you know. I need to get my passport first.'

'It's gone.'

'Gone? Gone where?'

'It's been taken. Some friend of yours turned up at the hotel after you'd gone, took your passport and your wallet, wrecked the room while he was about it.'

Verity looked from one to the other, searching their faces to see whether this was some April Fool's trick.

'Didn't you know that?' Max asked.

'No,' he said. He thought about it and for one extraordinary moment it looked as though he might burst into tears. 'They haven't been very nice to Verity, have they?'

Max assumed it was a rhetorical question but Verity appeared to be waiting for him to reply so he said, 'No, they haven't.'

'How am I going to get out of here then?'

'We can fix a temporary visa, just to get you back to England.'

'So that's the way of it, is it? Poor old Verity given the bum's rush. Packed off back home and told not to come back again.'

'What did you expect?'

'I don't know. Manners, I suppose.'

Well he wasn't going to get them. Not from the Customs, and not from him at the rate he was going. Curtly Max said, 'We can pick up your things on the way back.'

'Oh no, I'm not going back there.'

'They've been thrown around but most of the stuff's still serviceable. And you can pay your bill while you're about it.'

'I'm not going back to the hotel.' Verity was definite. 'I want to go to the airport, straight away. And anyway, I don't see why I should give them anything. After the way they treated me they don't deserve to be paid. Send your driver; he can pick up my luggage. We'll wait here.'

Max supposed there was no reason why he had to go to the hotel in person. 'Okay,' he said. 'If that's the way you want it.'

'It is.'

*

Strossmayer sat behind the wheel of his 4 x 4 Jeep. He had pulled it in off the road about a hundred yards from the farm, nosing its bulk into a clump of trees where it wouldn't be seen by anyone passing. From there he could see the high-walled building, even catch a glimpse of the courtyard inside.

He was smoking as he waited, trying not to let the ash break off the tip of his cigarette. Each puff had to be slower, more careful than the one before so as not to disturb the lengthening grey pillar. It was a game he'd played in his days as a policeman. There had been a lot of waiting then also, a great many hours spent in cars and darkened houses with nothing to do to pass the time but smoke and watch and listen.

In many ways the job he had now was better. The hours were good and the pay no worse than it had been. But there was one thing missing and that was respect. As a policeman he had been respected, often feared. He had been someone in the district; he'd had status. You didn't get that working in an office on the banks of the Danube. That's why he'd taken on this work now. It gave him back some of the respect that he needed; some of the respect that he deserved.

Strossmayer shifted slightly in his seat, holding the cigarette up vertically. He touched it to his lips, craning back his head so that the fragile column of ash didn't topple. He didn't know who employed him. He knew it was the lawyer, Vargas, who gave him orders, who paid him his wages. That was the only face he knew. But who gave Vargas his instructions Strossmayer didn't know. He had a fair idea but no proof and that's the way he wanted it to remain. Without a visible employer there was no question of loyalty. Strossmayer hated the idea of loyalty. He was his own man, answerable to no one.

He paused. Someone was coming out of the farm. He flicked the cigarette away, ash scattering in the breeze, and watched as Sergeant Norton climbed into the black BMW. The engine started. Instinctively Strossmayer sank down in his seat as the car came bumping down the track, passing on the other side of the trees not twenty feet away from where he was concealed.

Strossmayer was thinking. He had arrived with no clear plan in mind. He tried never to preconceive his actions. It was better to rely on the moment, to see how events turned out before acting. But now that Sergeant Norton had conveniently removed himself, he knew what he had to do. It was suddenly clear, suddenly simple.

'How long will he be?'

'An hour, maybe more.'

'It's only a few miles back. Why does it have to take so long?' Verity was sitting on a straw bale, holding his jacket tight around his neck with one hand. With the other he was cradling a half bottle of whisky which, despite what he'd said earlier, he'd had tucked away in his pocket. He'd had to pawn his watch for the money, he told Max when he produced it. This was another item on his list of grievances.

'These things always take time.' Max was pacing the cobbled floor of the barn, partly because he was restless and partly because he didn't want to sit beside this morose man with his half bottle of whisky and his endless complaints.

Verity took a pull at the whisky, straight from the bottle. He bared his teeth at the shock of the spirit and looked up at Max. 'We shouldn't be wasting time like this.'

'Why are you in such a hurry to leave?'

'I was supposed to be back a couple of days ago, remember?'

'So what stopped you?'

Verity jerked his head up at the barn they were in, as though it were to blame for his present condition. 'There are people who aren't too happy with Verity.'

'Why? What have you done?'

'You're giving me a lift to the airport, Anderson. That doesn't mean you can put me in the confessional.'

'I think we should know something. You're in hot water – hot enough to cook crabs in. I think we should know why.'

'It's my business, Anderson.' There was a note of warning in his voice but Max was becoming impatient with these evasions.

'If you want to get through Customs and on to a plane back to England, you'd better start being a little more co-operative.'

Verity glared at him. Then he gave a little shrug. 'There's no big deal. I have some information, that's all. Turned it up in the course of my work.'

'What sort of information?'

'Nothing important.'

'You've got nothing important. You're holed up here while someone is turning the country upside down looking for you and you say you've got nothing important.'

'Nothing important to you, Anderson,' he snapped. 'Nothing important to Her Majesty's Government.'

'I'll be the judge of that.'

'I've lost my passport and I need to get out of the country. That's all you need to know.'

'You're not going anywhere until I get something from you.'

Verity took another pull at the bottle, slower this time, more thoughtful. 'You'll find out soon enough. Once I'm out of this hellhole and over the border you can know as much as you like. But not until then. Not until poor old Verity's had first bite at the cherry.'

Strossmayer came in through the gates of the farm. His hands were buried in the pockets of his leather jacket, hat pulled over his eyes. He glanced round the yard but he already knew they had gone into one of the sheds.

He checked through a couple of them. His shoes were rubber soled and he moved lightly for such a large man. Back in the yard he paused and listened. There was a murmur of voices from the barn at the end, faint but just perceptible.

He went over to the doorway. Quietly he eased himself in, just a yard, no more, far enough to let his eyes grow accustomed to the darkness. That was important. Coming in from the light put you at a momentary disadvantage.

The voices were clearer now. He could distinguish between the two: the lower tones of the man from the Embassy, the higher, rather wheedling note of the other. That was Verity. Strossmayer couldn't understand what he was saying but he knew the voice and the recognition brought a smile to his face.

He'd been waiting for this moment.

He rolled around the door frame. The two men were further down the long barn, Anderson with his back turned, Verity sitting on the straw bale, bottle in hand, looking up towards him.

They didn't see him coming.

Strossmayer moved swiftly along the barn, keeping to the shadow of the wall. He took the gun from his belt; held it by the barrel.

It was Verity who saw him first. He was speaking as

Strossmayer came into view and froze mid-sentence, the words drying in his throat. His eyes bulged with fear.

Anderson swung round.

To Strossmayer the Englishman appeared to be moving in slow motion. It was a sensation he'd felt before. At moments such as these, moments of high emotion when he lived life more intensely than was otherwise possible, the whole velocity of time seemed to alter. It was not that he himself was able to act more quickly but rather that the rest of the world became slow and cumbersome.

As Anderson turned round, realising too late what was happening, Strossmayer had time to step up behind him and hit him with the butt of his pistol. He had time to aim the blow neatly at the base of the neck, where the spine links with the skull. The Englishman fell without a sound, his knees collapsing beneath him.

Strossmayer reversed the gun, nestling the butt into the palm of his hand again.

Verity had hardly been able to move. Slowly and laboriously, as though moving under water, he began to get up off the straw bale. He lurched backwards. His mouth had come open to scream but there was no sound in the barn.

Strossmayer raised the gun.

Verity's face had crumpled, his eyes were bursting from his head. A man knows when he is going to die. It's the only moment when he loses all self-consciousness and surrenders himself completely to the primeval forces of terror. The strength had gone from his legs and he fell to his knees. His hands were stretched out, body cringing in anticipation of the impact of the bullet.

Strossmayer squeezed the trigger and the blast of the muzzle engulfed the silence of the barn.

He could have hit Verity in the head; he could have put the

bullet straight between his eyes. But marksmanship like that was a dead giveaway, the hallmark of the professional. So instead he deliberately shot Verity in the chest.

The force threw the man over on to his back. His legs scrabbled on the cobbles. Strossmayer dropped the angle of his arm and put a second shot into him, lower down near the base of his ribs. Verity's body jerked and lay still.

The blood was roaring in Strossmayer's ears. Stepping over the fallen man, his gun held down at arm's length, he studied the effect of the two shots.

Verity was dead. He lay twisted over to one side. His mouth was open, the bright, frothy blood that comes only from a hit to the lung, dripping to the ground. The fingers of one hand fluttered.

Carefully, Strossmayer cleaned the gun with the handkerchief that was tied around his neck, wiping the prints from both the butt and the barrel. It was a 9 mm Colt automatic, a common, urbane weapon, available in any country.

Still holding it in the handkerchief, he went over to Anderson. Putting a foot beneath him he gave a heave, rolling the man over on to his back. He tucked the gun into his opened palm, folding the fingers around it. Then, straightening up, he kicked it away into the darkness.

He felt calm now, almost detached from his actions. Going to the door of the barn he paused and looked back at the two figures. First impressions were important.

Satisfied, he went out into the evening light. By the time he reached the 4 x 4 he was humming to himself.

5

At first there were just sensations.

Max could feel the cobblestones pressing against his face. They were cold and hard, foul smelling in his nostrils. He could feel a relentless pressure on the back of his neck. But there was no thought, no recollection, no understanding of what had happened. Gradually, as he groped his way up towards consciousness, he realised it wasn't pressure on his neck but pain, a dull throbbing pain that filled his whole head.

He gave a groan and pulled himself up into a kneeling position. In the darkness of the barn he could make out the other man lying crumpled on the ground.

In the distance came the wailing of sirens.

Max stood up and went over to the man. There was blood on the ground, black and sticky, more on his shirt. It was Verity. Christ, it came back to him now. This was Dr Verity. He had been talking to him – just moments ago he had been standing in here talking to him. Now the man was dead.

As the first shocks of memory hit him, Max stood there, staring stupidly at the prone figure.

And that's how the police found him.

The car had come to a halt outside in a screech of brakes. There was the sound of running feet and two rookies burst into the barn. They paused, transfixed by the scene before them. One held a gun in his hands, its barrel pointed towards the ground as he gaped. Then the doorway darkened and a third figure came into the barn.

He was large and slow moving. Max recognised the thick body, the short cropped hair, the sheen of sweat on his face.

It was Constable Zwickl.

His small eyes took in the dead man, the blood on the cobbles and Max standing over him. He turned his head to one side, spat on the ground, and said, 'Well, well, and what have we got here then?'

'Ring the Embassy!'

'In time, all in good time.'

'I'm on the staff there.'

'So you keep saying.'

'Ring them; they'll tell you. Anderson – Maxwell Anderson. I'm First Secretary.'

'Sure.'

'I'm telling you.'

Zwickl smiled. 'Oh, I've no doubt that a Maxwell Anderson is First Secretary at the Embassy. The question is, how do we know that you are Maxwell Anderson?'

The hands on the clock of the small, stuffy interview room at the back of the police station stood at eight-thirty. Across the desk, Zwickl sat with his hands folded over his belly. A mug of coffee stood before him. After each sip he stiffened it with a slug of slivovitz. By now, Max reckoned, it must be straight alcohol the man was drinking and it showed in the glazed look in his eye, in the damp sweat on his upper lip, in the slow, robotic movements of his body.

When he'd first arrived, Max had been put down in a cell. It had a bed with a single blanket, a bucket in the corner and a naked light bulb dangling from the ceiling. His coat, his shoes and belt had been removed; he was given nothing to eat or drink. For three hours he'd sat waiting, watching the sky darken through the one grille-covered window high in the wall. Then they'd brought him up here. Another wait. Only fifteen minutes this time, and Zwickl had come in, plumping himself down in the chair behind the desk.

'I was here yesterday.' Max fought down the urge to lose his temper with this dull-witted official. 'I showed you my diplomatic pass which has now been taken.'

'That could have been anything.'

'You saw it. I remember you looking at it.'

'All I saw was a man who burst in here asking a lot of questions. I have no evidence of who you are or what you are wanting. All I know is that you were hell-bent on finding someone who is now dead.'

'That doesn't mean I killed him.'

'You were there. Your fingerprints are on the gun.'

'And my wallet is gone and I've got a bump on the back of my head the size of a plum dumpling. Doesn't that suggest anything to you?'

Zwickl wasn't getting drawn into this. 'First I want to establish who you are.'

'Ring the Embassy,' Max told him in exasperation. 'They have my passport; they can tell you who I am.'

'How would they be able to tell from the phone?' Zwickl was pleased with the way he was handling the interview. His little eyes gleamed, his fingers drummed on the desk.

'Let me talk to them.'

'That's not permitted.'

'I have a right to contact the Embassy.'

'And if you worked there, as you say, you'd know that they are closed at this time of night.'

'I can give you the private number of the residence.'

Zwickl hefted himself out of his chair. 'In the morning, sonny,' he said thickly. 'In the morning.'

The car came to pick him up at 7 a.m.

Max was brought up from the cell, blinking in the morning light. He'd hardly slept a wink on the iron-framed bed, there was a day's stubble on his face and he felt cold and hungry.

Waiting for him out in the street was Simon Whittaker. He was a thin twenty-five-year-old with a cold, his nose red from constantly blowing it on the handkerchief he was clutching in one hand. As Max came out he was looking cross and impatient to have been sent out on this mission at such an ungodly hour.

'Morning, Simon.'

Whittaker nodded and smothered any further conversation by sneezing into the handkerchief.

'How's the CD of Romanian folk songs then?'

Whittaker looked at him stonily but made no reply and Max realised he was on trial.

The police officer handed him his overcoat, along with his small change and keys. He held out a clipboard for Max to sign for them.

'What about my luggage back at the hotel?'

Whittaker said, 'Sergeant Norton's picking all that up. He'll bring it round to you later.'

They drove back to Budapest in silence. When they reached the Embassy Max went up to the first floor, Whittaker on his heels. He pushed through the door of the cloakroom.

'Stratton wants to see you,' Whittaker said.

'In a minute.'

'He said straight away.'

'Simon, when you've been banged up in a cell for a night with nothing more for company than a bed with a bucket under it you'll find there are more pressing matters than talking to Jimmie. Don't look so shifty; I'm not going to run away.'

He hadn't the kit to shave but he was able to wash and brush his hair so that when he emerged ten minutes later he felt closer to belonging to the human race than he had for the past twelve hours.

Stratton was on the phone as they were ushered through into his office. He swung round in his chair, nodded in greeting, and indicated for Max to sit down at the same time. As soon as he had finished speaking he put the phone down and stared across the polished desk at him for a moment. Then up at Whittaker.

'Okay, Simon,' he said, getting to his feet and going across to the door. 'I'll take it from here.'

As soon as Whittaker had gone, Stratton closed the door softly and came back to the desk. 'What the heck's going on, Max?'

In the warmth of the office with its beautifully crafted bookshelves and marble mantelpiece, Max felt suddenly drained. He gave Stratton a smile, his stubbled cheeks pricking his skin with the movement, and said, 'Next time there's a missing persons I think I'll let someone else handle it.'

Stratton was staring at him intently, his sandy lashes giving his blue eyes a dry, dusty appearance. 'I've had the police on the phone, the press causing merry hell outside the gates. What's it all about?'

'It was a set-up.'

'But this Verity character is dead, is he?'

Max nodded. 'Oh, he's dead, Jimmie, there's no getting round that. I was there.'

'So I gather.' The voice was dry. 'Do you know who did it?'

Max shook his head. As he had lain in the cell throughout the night he had regained a few snatches of memory. He could remember his conversation with Verity, the look of surprise that had come over his face. He remembered turning around but after that very little. He had an impression of a figure, just a dark shadow looming up by his ear. And then nothing.

'To be honest, I didn't see him, Jimmie. I went round to that farm you told me about. I found Verity. He was hiding in one of the barns and like you said he was jumpy as a flea. I sent Norton back to the hotel to get his luggage; he didn't want to go there himself. After he'd gone I was talking to Verity, trying to find out what his problem was. He suddenly dried up and wham, the next thing I know there are police swarming around the place.'

'Your prints were on the gun.'

'It doesn't take a genius to fix that.' Of all that had happened to him, the thought of an unknown man manipulating his hand around the butt of the pistol as he lay unconscious was the one that Max found most distasteful.

'No,' Stratton said, 'I suppose not.'

'Like I said, it was a set-up. Not a very subtle one, just knocked up on the spur of the moment, I should think.'

'Damnedest thing I've ever heard.'

'But it doesn't look good, does it?'

Stratton flashed his sharp, inquisitive glance over the desk at him. 'No, Max. It doesn't look good. These things never do in our line of business. I had the police department on the phone just now. They want to talk to you.' He paused, gauging the other's reaction. 'If you like I can tell them to go to hell.'

'No, I'll talk.'

'They've got no authority. If you'd prefer I can lock the door in their faces.'

Under the terms of diplomatic immunity, Max could have simply refused to explain his actions. There was no force on earth that could make him speak if he didn't want to. But they both knew that to take that line would be tantamount to an admission of guilt and so he said, 'I'd better go and talk to them, Jimmie. Set the record straight from the start.'

As children of an ambassador, Max and his two brothers had been sent to a prep school in Norfolk. One of the perks of the diplomatic service is that the Government coughs up for private education fees.

It had been one of the old-style schools where beatings were commonplace and as regular as cricket matches. There'd been a ritual to the process. After lunch the headmaster would summon the victim to his study and inform him of his fate. He would then be told to wait in the next door study while the headmaster finished his business with the other pupils.

For Max the experience of standing in that empty room, waiting to take his punishment, was the most vivid memory of his schooldays. The cane stood behind the curtain, just visible; the large carriage clock ticked on the mantelpiece; there were faded team photographs on the walls, a rack of pipes below, the scent of eau de Cologne in the air. The beating when it finally came was a relief. It was that dreadful period of waiting that was unbearable. Max could remember the sick feeling in his stomach, the twinge of anticipation in his backside.

And he felt it now as he walked up Andrassy Utca to talk to the police.

In many ways it annoyed him. He had done nothing wrong; he had nothing whatsoever to hide. And yet he knew instinctively that his career hung in the balance.

He had been back to the residence before setting off, soaked in a bath, shaved and eaten a good solid breakfast with more calories than molecules per square inch and so it was after ten when he arrived at the granite-grey building.

Ferenc Biszku saw him straight away. He was Colonel of Police, a man with more power at his fingertips than most will wield in their lifetimes, but from his baggy suit, his spectacles hanging around his neck, and his thick black hair which appeared never to have come under the guidance of a comb, he could have been the manager of a local library. Only his eyes, which were sharp and black, betrayed the inner man.

'I'm sure you don't need to be told that this is purely informal, Mr Anderson,' he said after he had busied himself around the untidy office, arranging for coffee to be sent up, positioning chairs, inquiring whether Max wanted to smoke. 'There's nothing you have to say if you don't want to.'

'After last night I'm happy just to find someone who knows who I am.'

'Ah yes, I'm sorry about that. I'm afraid the local police can be overenthusiastic. It's not every day that they get a murder case on their hands.' He touched the pencils, telephone, empty coffee cup on his desk, arranging his thoughts in their pattern. 'Tell me, you claim you were assaulted—'

'It's not just a claim. It's the truth. You can feel the bump on my neck if it helps.'

A quick smile that said that wouldn't be necessary flickered across the policeman's face. 'So you didn't actually see Dr Verity killed?'

'I didn't see the gun fired, no.'

'Were you able to see who did it?'

'No, I wasn't. But my guess is that whoever it was drives a blue 4 x 4 with a company logo on the side.'

'What makes you say that?'

'Because he was raising hell around town trying to find Verity earlier on, ripped his room to pieces.'

'Ah yes, his room. Unfortunately we have no evidence of that. You had sent someone to tidy the place up before the police got there.'

'I didn't have it tidied up,' Max said carefully. 'Verity asked us to go back and pick his things up. He seemed scared of going himself.'

Biszku's black eyes studied him across the desk. 'Because of this man who was searching for him?'

'I imagine so. You can check with the hotel manager.'

'He seems to be vague on the subject.'

Does he, Max thought; how very convenient. Thanks a bunch, Oskar. He said, 'Then you need to talk to Sergeant Norton. He was there with me.'

Biszku made a note and tucked the pen into his upper pocket. 'Do you have any idea why anyone should want to kill Dr Verity?'

'No.' Max had given this some thought in the past few hours. 'He told me that he had information.'

'Did he say what sort of information?'

Max shook his head. 'Just that it was valuable.'

'You think he was blackmailing someone?'

'Possibly.'

Biszku repositioned the objects on his desk again. Then he said, 'How well did you know Dr Verity?'

'Not at all. Until I was sent out there I'd never heard of the man.'

'But you weren't sent out there, Mr Anderson. You volunteered.' Again the black eyes studied him across the desk. 'I spoke to your Embassy earlier. They said you were eager to go.'

Max could feel a chill coming into the conversation. 'I'd been cooped up in a meeting all morning. I wanted a bit of fresh air, that's all. It was still my job. The chances are that it would have been passed on to me even if I hadn't volunteered.'

Opening the drawer of his desk, the policeman took out a key. He held it up for Max's benefit. 'Have you ever seen this before, Mr Anderson?'

'Not as far as I know.'

'It was found in the pocket of your overcoat.'

'Can't say I've ever seen it before.'

Biszku laid the key down on the desk. 'We were able to trace its code. It comes from a luggage locker on Nyugati station. In it we found this.' Reaching down below his chair he hefted a green canvas holdall on to the desk and slid open the zipper.

With a sickening sense of impending disaster, Max watched as he took out a couple of icons, some pieces of silver tableware and another object rolled up in a cloth. Carefully, Biszku unfolded it to reveal a gold cross. He smoothed out the material and arranged all the pieces in a neat row on his desk. Then his black eyes came up to meet Max's.

'Have you seen any of these before, Mr Anderson?'

'No I haven't.'

'Dr Verity was a lecturer at one of your most prestigious universities. He was also involved with the smuggling of art treasures across the border. How he got them out of the country we don't know as yet, but we have been aware of the leakage for over two years now.'

'You think this is why he was killed?'

'How long have you been in the country, Mr Anderson?'

Max could feel the questions closing in on him, each one in turn condemning him. 'Two years.'

'That's what we thought.'

'Are you suggesting that I am responsible for this man's death?'

'I'm not suggesting anything as yet. I am simply explaining why it is I'm forced to start an investigation into your conduct.'

Max could feel the panic rising within him. He was concerned that it might show in his voice so he spoke slowly. 'This is absurd. I'd never even heard of this man until I was sent—'

'Volunteered, Mr Anderson.'

'Until I volunteered to go out and see him. It was just a routine piece of work. I'd never seen him before, I'd never seen that key and I know nothing about these trinkets you've got here. I wasn't reckoning on staying out there for more than the time that it took to pick him up and deliver him to the airport.'

'But when you couldn't find him you stayed on. You went to great lengths to track him down, from what I hear.'

It was no good trying to explain to him that twenty-four hours tracing a missing lecturer was a lot more fun than staying back in Budapest listening to folk singers caterwauling, so he said, 'I stayed out there because that's my job and if you are going to accuse me of anything else I must ask to have a lawyer present.'

Biszku held up his hands; he didn't want to be misunderstood. 'I'm not accusing you of anything, Mr Anderson.

Please believe me. This is just an informal discussion, a chance to talk the problem over. But I must unfortunately ask you to remain in Budapest until our investigations are over.'

'I'm going on leave at the end of the week.'

The policeman made a small gesture of apology and said, 'Ah no, I'm afraid that is out of the question.'

'Take a few days off work.'

'I'd rather not, Jimmie.'

'Relax a bit. It'll do you good.'

Max looked across the café table at Stratton. The expression on his face was gentle, almost concerned, as he stirred his coffee.

'Are you saying I'm suspended?'

'Just for a few days,' he said quietly. 'Just until they get things straightened out, Max. It won't take long. Go back home, read a good book, chat up those girls you're always sneaking into the place.'

'Jesus, Jimmie.'

'You're a lucky dog. I wish I could take a few days off myself.'

'You don't believe I've got anything to do with this, do you?'

'No, of course not.' Stratton looked at him steadily, his blue eyes very bright beneath their sandy lashes. 'And we'll back you to the hilt on this, Max, you know that. But just while the police are sniffing around it's probably best to keep out of the limelight.'

To be suspected by the police was one thing; it was their job to be suspicious. But to find that some of their suspicion had rubbed off on Jimmie Stratton came as a shock to Max. They'd worked together for two years; they were colleagues, friends. Only last week he'd attended Jimmie's daughter's

confirmation party. Max looked out through the g
window at the empty expanse of Varosomarty Square, whe
pigeons were hopping about in search of scraps, and felt
betrayed.

'I'd never even heard of the bastard until his name came up on your computer.'

'You don't have to tell me, Max. You're preaching to the converted.'

There was nothing Max liked better than to have time on his hands. To lie in bed in the morning, to spend two hours over lunch, to go to the cinema in the afternoon, were pleasures that normally he'd kill for. But to have them forced on him was a different matter. Within hours his mind rebelled at the enforced idleness. He found himself chafing to be back in the office, to have all the usual, dull, familiar life going on around him.

To make matters worse, the papers picked up on the story. At breakfast the following morning, he was horrified to find the whole thing spread across the front page. His name wasn't actually mentioned but to anyone in diplomatic circlcs it was quite evident who was involved. He found himself watched in the Embassy, eyes following him and sliding off again when they caught his. He rang Biszku to complain.

'Not me,' the policeman said. 'We haven't said a word to the press. They probably picked it up in the town.'

Max could believe it. It wouldn't have taken much spadework to have turned up the dirt. Oskar at the hotel would have been quick enough to pass on the information and it would only have taken the price of a drink to have got Constable Zwickl to spill the beans.

To get out, he went for a run up to Margit Island.

Afterwards he was taking a shower when the phone rang. It was the reception desk of the Embassy.

'There's someone here to see you, sir.'

'If it's the press you can tell them to get knotted.'

'It's not the press, sir; it's the Countess Kasinczy-Landsberg.'

6

She looked different this time. The jeans and peasant scarf were gone. In their place she wore a long grey overcoat, buttoned up to her throat, with a fur hat above, her mane of tawny hair spread out across her shoulders. In her high heels she was almost as tall as himself.

She was waiting in the hallway of the Embassy when Max arrived, studying the pictures on the wall, her back turned from the two Embassy guards who were watching her with open curiosity.

'I thought I should come to see you,' she said, offering him a gloved hand in greeting. 'But if you're busy?'

'I've never been less busy in my life.'

'Ah, that's good.' She was civil but still cool. 'I would have rung you but I couldn't remember your name.'

Couldn't you, Max thought. Good to know he'd made an impression.

'Max Anderson,' he said.

'Yes, I found it just now. There's a list at the desk.' She spoke lightly, quickly, skimming over these preliminaries. 'I read about Dr Verity, in the newspaper this morning. It sounded terrible. I take it that you were the other person they said was there?'

'Unfortunately.'

'And the police think you are involved?'

'They're born with suspicious minds.'

She studied him gravely with her green-grey eyes. 'And is it true that he was smuggling things over the border? Art treasures?'

'According to the police.'

'Is that why he came to Fetevis?' she asked. 'To try to steal things?'

'Yes, I think it probably was.'

'God, if I'd known I'd have rung the police and had him thrown out of the house.'

She spoke calmly, almost dispassionately, but the edge in her voice convinced Max she meant exactly what she said.

'He sounded so respectable,' she went on. 'Coming from that great British university with all those letters after his name.'

'What did he say he was doing?'

She gave a shrug as if it was irrelevant what story he'd sold her. 'He told me he was making a documentary about the Hungarian aristocracy and wanted to look through some of the family archives. It sounded reasonable. I let him see what he wanted.' She tossed back her head, annoyed at her own naiveté. 'And all the time he was just trying to pinch a few things.'

'Have you checked to see that he hasn't?'

'I had a look through this morning. I don't think there's anything missing. But I can't tell. There's so much of it.'

'What sort of things are we talking about?'

'Oh, pictures, old books, bits of china. There's crates of it. After the war it was all taken away and stored. It's just come back. I've hardly had time to look through it all myself. But I don't know what he thought he was going to find.

There's nothing valuable. All the good stuff's in the museums now. He must have known that.'

'I'd like to have a look at it,' Max said. 'When I was with Verity he said he'd found some information, something he reckoned was really valuable. That's why he was in such a heck of a hurry to get out of the country.'

Her eyes narrowed. 'You think he found it in my house?'

'That's where he'd just been.'

'But it's just a load of old books. Nothing good. Most of it's going mouldy round the edges. I had half a mind to chuck it all out.'

'There must be something there that interested him. I'd like to see it, if I could.'

'If you like.' She wasn't bursting with enthusiasm. 'It could take ages. He was up there for three days.'

Was he just. She hadn't told him that before. From the way she'd put it the first time round, it sounded as if he'd been in and out in half an hour. 'I'll come round tomorrow, if you don't mind.'

'Okay, if you think it'll help—'

'It'll help.'

Glancing at her watch she told him that she must be going. From the reception desk she collected a small leather suitcase. 'I'll see you tomorrow then,' she said, holding out her hand in parting.

As Max shook it he said, 'And one other thing.'

'What's that?'

'Could you leave the gate open this time? It's one hell of a long walk up your drive.'

As soon as she was out of sight of the Embassy, Terezia dumped her suitcase down on a litter bin, clicked it open and pulled out a pair of wellington boots. Ignoring the glances of a couple of passing tourists she tugged them on in place of her high heels. They were the only smart pair of shoes that she owned and she didn't want them ruined in the slush of the Budapest streets. Then she walked the two blocks to where her car was parked. It was a ten-year-old Lada van, a battered vehicle that had had so many parts repaired and replaced that very little of the original remained. Hardly the kind of car that the British would want to see sitting outside their Embassy.

Tossing her case across the seat she drove out through the suburbs of Budapest. There'd been a time when the family estates had reached right up to the edge of the city. Her great-grandfather had been able to boast that he could walk from Budapest to Transylvania without leaving his own land. Now she owned the houses in the village and five hundred acres of land around it, of which only a hundred could be used for farming, the rest was forest. It was all hopelessly impractical. The total annual rent was a fraction of what she needed.

Earlier that day her accountant had given her the bare facts. 'The estate needs to earn four times its present rate just to break even, Countess. And that's without any further expenses incurred in restoration work.'

'But how can it earn more?' she'd asked.

'Are there no other assets on the land you can draw on?'

'No, none.'

'How about the stud fees from your stables? Won't they be enough to cover the difference?'

The task she'd set herself when she came to Fetevis was to revitalise the decaying stable block in the Palace and run it as a commercial stud farm. She was sure she could do it. She'd worked with horses all her life; she had the experience and the knowledge for the job. But a stud farm needed time and money to get itself established, neither of which she had at this moment.

'Then you must borrow,' the accountant had said. 'And go on borrowing until you can find a way of providing some sort of income for the place.'

She didn't like to tell him that in the past few weeks she'd already borrowed from two banks. It hadn't been easy getting money out of them. She had no real collateral to offer. Under the terms of restitution, the Palace belonged to her but she wasn't allowed to sell it. If she wanted to be shot of the damned thing she had to return it to the Government. But the bank managers had been impressed by her name and softened by her evident distress as she explained her predicament and had advanced her fifty thousand forints. But that had been swallowed whole by the rebuilding work she was doing on the stables.

What was of more immediate concern to her was that she owed her cousin three million forints (about £100,000). He was threatening to sue her unless she paid. He knew she couldn't and the weight of the responsibility hung round her neck like a millstone.

The New York café was built at a time when no self-respecting Hungarian would dream of taking a glass of wine without being surrounded by mirrors, marble pillars, gilded swags and painted cherubs who perched their butts on improbable pink clouds.

Max sat at a table by the window and read a newspaper. Gallagher was late. He was always late. Max had never known an occasion when he'd shown up on time. It wasn't that he tried to fit too much into his crowded schedule but simply that he had no concept of the time of day. How he ever reached a news conference before it was over was a mystery.

When he'd arrived, Max had ordered coffee but after half an hour he moved on to white wine. He was ordering a second glass when Michael Gallagher finally slumped into the chair opposite.

'Good to see you, Max.' He didn't bother to apologise for being forty-five minutes late; it wouldn't have occurred to him that he was. He just looked at Max through his hooded, sleepy eyes and said, 'I thought you were on house arrest.'

'Town arrest actually.'

Gallagher nodded vaguely. He was dressed in a baggy green jersey and pale chinos that looked as though he'd slept in them; no socks but a pair of espadrilles so unsuited to the weather that they were beginning to fall apart on his feet.

'So,' he said. 'Now that you've had me haring across town, what are you going to give me?'

'Tortoising would be more accurate.' Max summoned a waiter. 'Actually I wasn't reckoning on giving you anything more than a drink.'

'I've had worse offers.'

'In the hope that it'll loosen your vocal cords.'

'Oh, Christ.' Gallagher craned his head back at the waiter. 'I'll have a double whiskey just to be getting on with. Bushmills – and don't go chucking ice cubes into it.' As the man withdrew he flopped one leg over the arm of the chair and said, 'So what are you after?'

'I want you to tell me what you know about the Countess Kasinczy-Landsberg.'

'Ah, the lovely Terezia.' He smiled dreamily as though there were a joke somewhere here which he couldn't remember. 'Have you met her then?'

'A couple of times—'

'Twice.' He was impressed. 'That must be close to a record.'

'I want to know who she is, where she's come from, and why she lives in a great pile of rotting masonry.'

'Is there a shred of reason behind this?'

'I'll explain later.'

'You're not going soft on her or anything?'

'Nothing like that.'

'If you were you wouldn't be the first in the past few weeks. She's set one or two hearts bumping around town.'

'I just want to know who she is, Mike.'

Gallagher leaned back in his chair and spread his hands as if to explain that this was something that was going to take some time and several rounds of drinks. Max had no qualms that he was the man for the task. Michael Gallagher had been *The Times* correspondent in Budapest for four years in the late eighties. In that time he'd taken such a liking to the city that he'd abandoned his post on the newspaper and stayed on, writing a guide book to keep the wolf from the door. Now he worked freelance for any newspaper that would carry his material. No difficulty there; he was good. There was nothing that he didn't know about the city and what he wrote was read. His marriage might lurch from one drama to another as he forgot birthdays, anniversaries and rendezvous but there wasn't a name, a contact, a piece of scandal that slipped his mind.

'Terezia Kasinczy-Landsberg,' he tried out the name for size. 'Do you want the short version or the de luxe?'

'Can I afford the de luxe?'

Gallagher sipped at his drink, put down the glass and turned it in his fingers as he collected his thoughts. 'You have to go back a few years to understand this one, Max.'

'How far?'

'Nineteen forty-five.' He glanced up at Max, unwilling to go on until the ground rules had been cleared. 'Is there an angle in this for me?'

'Could be. Tell me what you've got.'

'I reckon there's still a lot of mileage in this story. I'd hate for someone else to get there before me.'

'You're the only person I've talked to so far.'

Gallagher nodded, took another pull at his glass and said, 'The war didn't have a happy ending here, Max, as you know. The Russians moved in and knocked the crap out of the place. Buda Hill was flattened, the whole city looted, men interned, women raped; you know the form. The Hungarian aristocracy didn't wait to see what was going to happen to them. They got the message and legged it out of the country. The Kasinczy-Landsbergs went along with them. They left it until the last moment but they went in the end. That is, except the Count himself. For some reason he stayed behind.'

'Why do you think he did that?' Max put the question lightly. He didn't want to stop the flow.

'Goodness knows. If it was anything sentimental he was nuts. The Reds locked him up.'

'And the others?'

'They made it over to America and got rich again. I guess they'd stashed away quite a pile of cash there anyway, so they weren't exactly beggars when they came off the boat. They got themselves back into the steel business, branched out into armaments in the sixties, landed themselves a few hefty contracts with the American Navy, and made themselves a packet. It was all ivy-league colleges, country clubs and trips round the European watering holes for them. Back to the good old days.

'When the old man died his son, Zoltan, took over the

firm. He'd been about thirteen when the family left Hungary and fancied himself as the heir to the title. He cut quite a dash around Beverly Hills; he'd hung on to his accent and called himself the Count Kasinczy-Landsberg. The girls thought he was the bee's knees.'

'Mothers, too, with that much cash behind him.'

'Yeah, well he got himself married into one of those old families that can date back ancestors on both sides to the *Mayflower*.'

'An overcrowded ship.'

'But Zoltan wasn't interested in America. The only thing he wanted was to get back to Hungary and claim his rightful place as heir to Fetevis. You've no idea how he's been working on it, Max. The guy's nuts about it. He put a fortune into propping up the Hungarian steel industry and bunging bribes into Party funds. In the end the commies let him move back here. They didn't want him but they could recognise a good thing when they saw it. They allowed him to become an 'Adviser to the State on Industry,' or some such damned-fool name. But then the Wall came down and he got his real chance. He moved the headquarters of his entire Empire back here – including the armaments bit which up to now the Americans had insisted stayed on their side of the pond.

'Now Zoltan moved his sights. Instead of pouring money into the steel business he started giving huge donations to the Government – just gifts, you understand, no strings attached. But he made it pretty clear that what he was expecting in return was the family estate back: house, title, the works. A few months ago they gave in and let him have it. The lawyers drew up the contracts; it was all signed and sealed. Zoltan was the pig in clover. Then came the bad news.'

'He wasn't the heir.'

'You got it. One of the lawyers got out the old Count's will. He'd made it in jail and since he didn't own anything no one had paid it much attention at the time of his death. But now, when they looked it over, they found he had left anything he might have owned to a daughter.'

'Terezia.'

'She got the lot.'

'He must have hit the roof.'

'Took her to court on the spot. But it didn't do him any good. The contract said that the estate went to her and that was that.'

Max drank some wine. What he heard made sense; it fitted what he had already seen.

Gallagher was drying up. 'All of which is a lovely story that gives a man a powerful thirst.'

Max called the waiter, ordered more whiskey. Bushmills, Gallagher put in, still with no ice chucked into it.

'So you've met her?' he said when it had arrived and been tested.

'I've talked to her.'

'A right little firecracker she's turned out to be, from what I've heard. Locked herself in that house with some of her cronies and won't let anyone near.'

'You're right there.'

'Refuses to be interviewed. I'm told *Hello!* magazine tried to do a glossy on her the other day; turned up at the door, full of hope and charity, only to be sent away with a flea in their ear.'

'She let Verity in.'

'How's that?'

'Dr Verity was round there last week, going through all the books and pictures.'

'Is that so?' Gallagher's voice took on a quietness that

came only when he smelled a story. 'Is that the angle then, Max? Is that the pay-off you have for an old mate?'

'Verity was searching through the house; three days later he's dead.'

'You think he got himself caught up in the Kasinczy-Landsberg business?'

'It could be.'

'It could,' Gallagher agreed. 'Or it could be that he was a grubby little man who met someone who objected to him smuggling knick-knacks out of the country.'

'You don't get murdered for handling dodgy icons.'

'Maybe not. But from what I heard, your friend Verity made enemies more easily than most and that's not an advantage in the smuggling business.'

'I'm just telling you what I know, Mike.'

Gallagher drank whiskey and smiled. 'And I'm glad to hear it, Max. Really I am.'

He didn't believe him any more than the police had, Max realised.

Across the crowded floor a violinist had started to play. It was high, soaring gypsy music that swooped between the cherubs on the ceiling.

Max checked the bill and thumbed coins on to the marble table. 'What's going to become of her, do you think?' he asked.

'Terezia? She'll get thrown out of the place.'

'Do you think so?'

Gallagher was sure of it. 'If she's got any sense she'll make a deal with Zoltan and run for it.'

'She is the heir.'

'And it's a lovely fairy tale. But Zoltan will get his way. He's been building up to this all his life; he's not going to let a slip of a girl get in his way now. She should get out while the going's good.'

'She is his daughter, presumably? There's no doubt about it?'

'None at all.'

Max didn't see how she could be. 'But how can her father have produced a child when he was in jail?'

'He was let out in '56,' Gallagher said, rolling his feet on to the ground and getting up. 'They opened up all the prisons during the revolution, let the whole lot out. The Count was in Vac jail. They didn't bother to wait, just seized a gun, shot the locks off the prison and ran for it.'

'And he met some girl and married her?'

'Yeah,' Gallagher said. 'Well, I don't think it was quite as easy as that actually.'

7

1956

The cart moved at a snail's pace along the road towards Budapest. On the front seat Erzsebet Sarvar sat huddled beside her brother, numb with cold, the shawl that she clutched to her face against the biting north wind making her appear older than her fifteen years.

Behind her, strapped under a bulky canvas cover, were the few treasures that they had managed to rescue from their home, and beyond that, lounging on the tailboard, his feet dangling over the road, was Antal, one of the farm hands. A cigarette dangled from his lips. It wasn't lit. He smoked only in the evenings when they stopped to make camp but he found it comforting to keep it there in the daytime.

Three days they had been travelling, coming up across the Hungarian plains, heading into a horizon that was lost beneath the snow clouds. They weren't alone. A steady stream of traffic was making the trek with them up towards the Austrian border: carts and wagons, some with solitary drivers, others packed. They didn't speak to each other when they passed, Erzsebet noticed. At times they scarcely managed a nod of greeting. It was as though they were all on this long, endless road alone.

Occasionally a car would putter by, its exhaust corkscrewing out from its rear end. Erzsebet's family had owned a car themselves, a black Citroën with headlights the size of soup bowls and a door that hinged at the rear. That was so that ladies could climb out elegantly, her father had said. Although, in practice, her mother had very rarely driven in the front. The limp leather seats behind had made Erzsebet feel sick so her father would let her ride up there beside him. He had let her do most things she wanted.

They would have brought the car now but there wasn't the petrol to go such a distance and besides her brother, Peter, had said it couldn't carry enough baggage. So they'd sold it, for a fraction of its value, and loaded their possessions into the cart instead. Peter said it was more practical that way. They could sell the horse when they reached Austria. It would give them something to start with.

Erzsebet didn't want to sell this patient animal who plodded along in front of her, its eyes fixed on the road a few feet before its head; she was part of the family – almost all there was left of it. But she would do as her brother said. He was head of the family now and that gave him the right to decide.

In the afternoon, as they were approaching a small town on the outskirts of Budapest, two Russian jets swept across the sky, swooping low then banking off to the north as one, like a pair of puppets controlled by the same strings. Later another appeared. It was smaller and slower and came up the line of the road. The eyes of the travellers watched it in silence as it roared overhead.

'Spotter plane,' Peter said and Antal, standing up in the back of the cart, prodded the cold stub of his cigarette at it, mouthing something to them that was lost in the din.

Erzsebet asked her brother what they could be spotting for and he shrugged and said, 'Rebels.'

She hated that word. She knew nothing about war or fighting but she sensed that rebel was the word for the underdog, the victims of the revolution. Rebels were men who must be hunted down and killed. They weren't rebels, she told herself angrily. They were simple, everyday people, the farmers and workmen from the factories she'd known all her life, who wanted to see their country free of the Russians.

Erzsebet had never known a Hungary that was free. When she had been born the country had been under German occupation. She wasn't sure whether she remembered the Nazis, in their peaked caps and long, low cars, or whether the memory was prompted by the films and pictures she'd seen later. But she knew the Russians who came after them, with their flat faces and piggy eyes. She knew them all right. They'd been there in all their lives, a heavy, sullen presence.

At first the thought of getting rid of them had been almost shocking to her. It went against everything she had been brought up to believe. She disliked the Russian soldiers, the pale conscript boys who watched her listlessly in the street. They were lazy and rude and hostile. But in some way she understood that they were guests in the country and should be tolerated, even welcomed. It was the common law of hospitality. But as the realisation that they could be thrown out of the country dawned on her she found herself filled with a hot, guilty excitement.

In the evenings the farm hands had gathered in their parlour and listened to the radio broadcasts out of Budapest. They had smoked their cigarettes and stared down at their hands, shaking their heads as they listened to the reports of fighting in the streets of the city. The Red Star had been pulled down, they heard, and the Hungarian flag was flying over the parliament building again. When the news had come that Imre Nagy had been elected President and was demanding the withdrawal of Russian troops, her father had opened a bottle of Tokai that he had been keeping for a special occasion and the men had stood, solemn and awed, and drunk a toast to their new future. She'd been allowed a sip from her father's glass. It had tasted sweet and strong as the pride that filled the room.

Two days later he'd driven down into the town. There was a protest march taking place and he wanted to be there. There wasn't much work to be done around the farm at that time of the year and it was going to be a great sight.

He didn't return. The Russians had posted machine guns along the roof tops and opened fire on the crowd. Just a single burst to clear the square but her father had been amongst those hit. And all because he didn't have any work to do that day, she thought to herself. Had it been summer he'd have been in the fields harvesting and he'd still be with them now.

Her brother had said they must leave the country. There was talk of Russian reprisals and the border with Austria had been opened in the summer. It was their only chance to get out. And so, as soon as the funeral had taken place, they'd begun the long journey north.

Already the dusk was drawing in as they came into the town. A statue of Lenin stood in the square, one arm raised. Calling for a taxi, her father had called it. 'There's Papa Lenin calling for a taxi,' he'd say to Erzsebet. 'Let's hope he finds one and clears out of here quick.' And he'd chuckle at the idea. He'd hated the Russians as the others did but unlike them there was no real fury in his hate, any more than there was towards the weather that ruined his crops. He'd treated them all as part of life.

Lying in the gutter beyond the statue was a bundle of grey

rags and with a chill of recognition Erzsebet realised it was the corpse of a man. He was lying on his back, his arms over his head and shirt front open, a look of patient expectation on his face as though waiting for a doctor to plant a stethoscope on his bare chest.

At the sight of the body, Peter gave a curse under his breath and flicked the reins, urging the horse forwards. There was a stillness to the town, Erzsebet noticed. A silence. The doors were all closed, the windows empty.

A group of men ran up the street in their direction. They were carrying a telegraph pole between them. The spotter plane was flying overhead again, flitting over the roof tops like a mosquito over stagnant water.

The men had pressed themselves against the wall, crouched low, looking away down the street, and above the drone of the plane Erzsebet could hear another noise now. It was a deep, distant roar. She'd never heard anything like it before but it filled her with a primeval terror.

Slowly, as though in answer to her question, a Soviet T32 tank lumbered in from a side street and stopped, sluggishly rocking back on its suspension. For a moment it paused as though looking about itself and then black smoke squirted from its rear exhausts and it turned around, its tracks tearing up the tarmac as though it were made of unset cake icing.

Peter was yanking on the reins, pulling the horse's head around. The animal took fright and began bucking and stamping in the traces, bright sparks spitting out from its hooves.

As the tank came lurching up the street, Erzsebet saw the rebel soldiers dart out from their hiding place and run in on it, carrying the pole between them like a battering ram. What good would that do, she wondered, as she watched frantically over her shoulder. What hope had a piece of wood against this metal monster?

But they didn't ram the tank. Dropping to the ground, they lifted the pole and thrust it into the rear end of the tracks as it passed. For a moment it looked as though they'd disabled the machine. The pole locked in the drive wheel and leapt up out of their grasp and with a squeal of metal on metal the tank slewed round like a gored bull.

The men had scattered and were running up the street towards them. Only one had remained. He'd climbed up on the turret of the tank and was tearing at the hatch cover with his bare hands. There was a rattle of gunfire and Erzsebet saw him stand up and turn around, his arms spread wide, as though greeting an old friend. Then slowly he toppled off into the road.

With a roar of anger the tank had begun to move forwards again, the wooden pole lifting and splintering like a toothpick before dropping away behind.

Their cart was half round in the road now but the horse had panicked and was thrusting back in its harness, reversing them into the wall, Peter cursing and sobbing with fear as he tried to right it. Orange light winked from the tank and with a sudden cracking sound, the windows behind them shattered, bullets whipping along the walls.

Peter dived off to one side, yelling at them to run.

A second burst of machine-gun fire ripped along the wall above their heads and the air was full of hot, stinging shrapnel that tore into the side of the cart.

Erzsebet threw herself down into the road and began to run, her legs hampered by the long coat she was wearing. The wagon behind them had spilled its load as the travellers tumbled off and the street was suddenly full of terrified, fleeing figures, stumbling into each other in their haste.

As she ran, Erzsebet heard a crash behind her and above it the high, screaming neigh of a horse.

She glanced round over her shoulder.

Their cart had toppled over on its side and the horse, trapped in the traces, was rolling over with it, her legs flailing in the air.

Erzsebet stopped, breathing hard. She looked round for help but Peter and Antal were gone.

The horse lay in the road, pinned down by the harness. Her neck was stretched out, nostrils dilated, her flanks, flecked with sweat, heaving as the tank bore down on her.

Without thinking or reasoning Erzsebet began running back to her. She didn't know why or what she could do to help the poor animal. All she knew was that she couldn't leave her there to be crushed by this vile machine.

The buckles of the harness were stiff with age. She tore at them with her fingers but they wouldn't loosen. She could hear the thunder of the tank's engines, the angry rattle of the tracks as it came towards them.

Then she saw that there was blood on the ground and that one of the horse's forelegs lay at a strange angle and she realised she didn't need to unbuckle the harness.

The creature couldn't get up anyway.

The tank was close now, a dark mass rearing up above her. Every instinct told her to get out of the way but her arms were around the horse's neck, its head on her lap, and she held on tight. Above the din of the tank's engine she could hear her own voice screaming in defiance.

A burst of sniper-fire from the rooftops. She saw the bullets slapping across the armoured body of the machine. The turret turned, the gun rising like a crude eye searching for its prey, and the tank swung round in the road, missing them by a few feet away. She saw the mud-stained bogey-wheels chattering over the tracks as it passed, the tarmac buckling under its weight, the debris spitting out from the rear drive-wheel, and her head was full of the concussion of its engines and the stench of oil and diesel fumes.

There were soldiers behind, following under the cover of the tank. She stared up at them and then something hit her from behind.

For a moment she thought she'd been shot, but with surprise she realised it was one of the rebel soldiers landing on her.

'Keep your head down, little one,' he breathed.

The tank had swung over to the other side of the road. Its barrel raised high and it fired, rocking back under the impact of the recoil. The upper two storeys of the building across the square dissolved into brown rubble and the shock of the blast hit them where they crouched behind the horse, the air suddenly filled with the sweet, acrid smell of cordite.

The tank moved forwards, its turret creaking round, the soldiers huddling behind the safety of it bulk.

The rebel pushed her out from under the shelter of his body. 'Run for it,' he shouted in her car.

'I can't.'

'Quick, go now,' he said, pushing her towards the pavement.

Erzsebet held the horse's neck. 'I can't leave her.'

The rebel looked across to the animal's broken leg. Up the street a second tank was coming.

'There's nothing you can do,' he said. 'You must go now. Save yourself.'

'I won't leave her!'

'Run, little one.' Above the din of the fighting he spoke gently, almost softly to her. 'Don't worry, I'll do what has to be done. Now get out of here.'

'No!'

'It'll be quick. I promise. She'll feel no pain.'

Erzsebet clutched thc horse's coat tightly to her. Every instinct of decency in her rebelled at the thought of abandoning this wretched creature who had brought them all this way. 'She mustn't die!' she shouted above the fighting.

'It's the only way.'

'No!' she screamed at him. 'Not here; not like this.'

The rebel looked at her. He had extraordinary green-grey eyes. 'Her leg's broken,' he said. 'She can't work again.'

'I don't care! I don't want her to die.'

The tanks were firing, slowly and systematically, the crackle of rifle fire between. The rebel glanced round over his shoulder. Then he looked back at her and the green-grey eyes smiled. 'Then let's make sure she doesn't,' he said.

Taking a knife from his back pocket he cut the harness and tugged it free of the horse's neck. The shaft beneath had broken and he pulled it round in the road.

'We must get her out of the way,' he said.

Bent double he scuttled down to where there was a shop, its door and windows barred. Throwing aside some empty vegetable boxes he pulled out a plank of wood and came back with it.

'Can you lift her head?' he shouted.

Erzsebet took the horse's head and raised it in her arms. The animal gave a snort of fright, its eyes stretched wide.

'Pull it down towards her legs,' he told her.

Panting with the exertion she drew the head round, the animals' hot breath on her hands. As the neck turned the horse rolled obediently on to its belly. Quickly, the rebel thrust the wooden plank and the broken shaft of the cart beneath its ribs, resting the other ends on his shoulders.

'Now back the other way.'

She hefted the horse's head across and almost magically it rolled back the other way, turning on to its back, its weight taken by the two wooden supports. As its broken foreleg moved the animal gave a snort of pain but the rebel was already dragging her back across the road.

Reaching the pavement, he dropped to his knees, running his hands across the animal's sweating neck and flanks, soothing her with small sounds and words, and Erzsebet, crouched beside him, realised for the first time that he was not a soldier as she'd supposed. He wore a patched corduroy jacket and trilby hat with a feather tucked in the side. Both had once been stylish but were now so faded and battered that they gave him the look of a tramp, although unlike any of the tramps she'd seen, his face wasn't tanned and ruddy but pale as a lily, a wing of fair hair falling over one eye.

He turned to her, breathing hard. 'Bandages,' he said. 'Have you anything that I can use for bandages?'

Desperately she looked around for inspiration. Their overturned cart had spilled its load across the road. Scrambling over to one of the cases she unstrapped the lid and pulled out the clothes she'd packed so carefully four days before.

A nightshirt was the first thing to come to hand. She wrenched at its hem but it wouldn't give. Tearing at the thick linen with her teeth she managed to make a rent and then it gave easily, shredding into long strips.

With a crack of splintering wood, the man had broken a chair on the road. It was one of the polished ones that used to stand in the dining room. Gathering the remains of it like a bundle of firewood he knelt beside the horse.

Erzsebet held its head in her arms. One wide, frightened eye stared up at her and in its dark orb she saw herself, pale and intent as she watched the man at work.

His hands were on the horse's upper leg, massaging the muscles, working his way down, slowly and rhythmically. His fingers were strong and slender and very pale, she noticed, like the fingers of a concert pianist. And again he spoke those soft, crooning words to the creature.

As he came to the break in the bone she felt the horse twitch and snort, its rear legs giving a spasmodic kick, and then he had it straight and the animal lay still.

'Where are you heading?' he asked as he tied a length of the bandage to one stave of the chair and laid it against the horse's leg.

'Austria—'

He glanced round. 'And what's your name?'

'Erzsebet.'

She watched in fascination as he ran the bandage round the leg, slipped another piece of wood into the loop and twisted it twice so that it lay snugly against the broken bone.

'Well, Erzsebet,' he said, 'you picked your moment to come through here.'

She glanced up across the square. It was quieter now, the fighting had moved further on across the town. She stroked the long nose of the horse and felt its soft mouth working against her palm.

The man strapped the splint tight. 'Where's the rest of your family?'

He had a curious accent, slow and almost drawling, not like anyone's she'd heard before.

'I don't know,' she said. 'My brother was here but I don't know where he is.'

'How about your parents?'

'I don't have any,' she whispered.

He looked round at her with his green-grey eyes. His face

was grave and lined but the deep crow's feet gave her the strange impression that he was always smiling.

'I'm sorry,' he said.

She gave a shake of her head.

He tightened a knot on the splint and rolled back on his heels, inspecting his work. 'It ain't the most artistic achievement but I guess it'll do.'

'Will she be all right?'

He stroked the curve of the horse's flank. 'If you keep her steady until the bone's set she'll be fine. She won't work again but she'll be fine. The foal too.'

'Foal?'

He seemed surprised she should ask. 'She's in foal. Did you not know that?'

She shook her head. They'd taken her as she was the youngest and the strongest of her father's horses.

He took her right hand and laid it on the horse's belly, finding the right spot. 'Here,' he said, 'feel there.' But she couldn't feel anything apart from the warmth of the animal's body.

The street was quiet now, one or two figures straggling back down the pavement.

'Two, maybe three months into it,' the man said. 'What's her name?'

'Twilight.'

He nodded as though that were natural.

'My father always named his horses after the time of the day they were born.' Erzsebet felt she should explain.

'Then you must make sure you're there when the foal's born.'

She smiled. 'I will.'

'Erzsebet!'

It was Peter, coming scuttling down the pavement, Antal in his wake. His hair was ragged, eyes wide with shock.

'Erzsebet. Where have you been?'

She straightened up. 'Here,' she said simply.

Peter looked at the horse with its splinted leg. 'What happened?'

'The tank.' She didn't want to talk about it. 'It broke her leg.'

'You stayed?'

'Yes,' she said. 'I didn't want to leave.'

And Peter dropped his head and looked down at his feet because he knew he'd thought only of his own safety as he ran.

Erzsebet glanced round. The man in the battered jacket was walking away down the street, a canvas sack over his shoulder.

She ran after him, calling for him to stop.

'Where are you going?' she asked as he turned around.

'I'm heading on south,' he said. 'See if I can find some work.'

Erzsebet was suddenly shy, aware that she couldn't hold him and unsure how to say goodbye. 'I don't know your name.'

The crow's feet held their smile. 'Karoly.'

'Karoly? Karoly who?'

'Just Karoly.'

'You must have another name.'

'No,' he said. 'I don't think I do.'

On impulse she held out her hand. She didn't usually shake men by the hand but instinctively she wanted to touch him. 'Thank you, Karoly.'

He bent and took her fingers, lifting them to his lips. 'Good luck, Erzsebet,' he said.

For a moment the smile was gone and he looked at her, sharply and keenly, as though something was worrying him. And then he touched his hat and walked on down the street.

As she came back, Peter and Antal were standing glumly around the fallen horse.

'What do we do now?' Peter asked her.

'We go back,' she told him. 'Where we come from.'

8

At dawn the following morning Joszef rapped on Terezia's door. Lazily she rolled over in bed and stretched out her legs, letting the creak of the springs tell him she was awake.

She glanced at the clock. The luminous hands stood at 6.50 a.m. In winter her working day started an hour later than in summer but summoning up the enthusiasm to get up on freezing cold mornings was much harder.

Venturing one arm out from the warmth of the bedclothes she twitched aside the curtains and looked up at the sky. Heavy clouds were lumbering overhead, their grey undersides brushing over the chimneys of the house. Not too friendly. But at least she could see them. That meant it wasn't raining. She hated having to exercise the horses when it was raining.

Kicking her feet out of bed she padded over to the basin and washed her face. The little wing of the house they lived in was the only part of the building that had water and electricity. Not the original systems, they had all packed in years ago. The primitive network of pipes and wires that now wormed across the walls dated back to the time when this part of the house had been home to a caretaker.

It was idiotic. He'd had nothing to take care of. All he'd done for fifteen years was sit and preside over the disintegration of the house, a pointless occupation with no other purpose than to make the unemployment figures look good.

Occasionally Terezia came across mementoes of his days there: an old shoe, a couple of tins with labels blackened with damp. When she first arrived she'd found a stack of faded pornographic magazines behind the boiler which Rozsa had promptly burnt, washing her hands afterwards as though they were contaminated.

Terezia tugged on jeans, pulled a double layer of sweat shirts over her head and a thick white jersey on top of them. In the past she'd been inclined to be untidy with her clothes but now that it wasn't easy to replace them she found herself treating them with rather more respect, examining them each evening for tears, folding and laying them out on a chair for the morning. She even kept her laddered tights, divided into various categories of dilapidation.

Dragging a brush through the thick golden mane of her hair she tied it back in a handkerchief and went through to the kitchen where Joszef was making tea. He handed her a cup and took another through to his wife Rosza. She liked to stay in bed for another half hour while they did the rounds of the stables. It was one of the few luxuries she allowed herself.

Joszef and Rosza had been her foster parents since she was twelve years old. It was an unofficial role, never quite defined or explained, but all the stronger for that. When Terezia's father had been arrested they had taken her into their house. Her mother had died when she was a baby and so there were no immediate relatives to turn to. As the weeks passed and the awful realisation began to dawn on them that her father wasn't returning, the arrangement had been extended until it became permanent. Middle-aged and childless, this couple had gradually adopted her as the daughter they'd never had.

Dawn was just an idea on the horizon as Terezia and Joszef walked down to the stables. Waiting in the archway were the stable lads: Elek, eighteen, shy and tongue-tied; Gyorgy, two years older, with a good feel for horses. He'd been smoking as they approached, she'd seen the gleam of a cigarette tip in the dawn light, but he stamped it out as they arrived. He knew that smoking and drinking were banned during working hours. She didn't mind him playing the radio in the stalls but that was only because the horses seemed to like it.

She could never escape a little thrill of pleasure as she came into the stable yard. The stables had been derelict when she first arrived; a sad, neglected memory of another age. The local collective had used them as storage barns for their unwanted farm kit and it had taken her weeks to clear out the forty years' worth of accumulated rubbish. Joszef had tried to help but he was touching seventy and most of the heavy work had been left to her, a back-breaking task that had left her so tired in the evenings that she'd often fallen asleep at the dinner table.

But now she had them going again, roofs patched, woodwork repaired and painted, and for an hour she went around the stalls with Joszef, checking the condition of the horses, feeling their warm, powerful presence in the darkness.

She had fourteen of them under her care at present and hoped for another five by the end of the winter. Finding owners who wanted to use the stables of Fetevis had proved easier than she expected. Joszef had spent most of his life in the Bukk mountains, working on the Lippizaner horses, and his reputation went before him. She was also shrewd enough to know that her own name and title carried some weight. But really it was the stables themselves that sold the business. They had style and class and a flash of romance to them that the owners wanted to be part of.

To avoid confusion, she always mentally linked the owner with the horse. It reminded her which animal belonged to whom and at the same time produced strange and almost magical names for the animals: 'Tempest Banker', 'Bald Man Lucky', or, her favourite, 'Snowflake Dancer', a grey mare that belonged to an elderly lady who'd once been a member of the Kirov Ballet.

At nine they knocked off for breakfast. Terezia took a bath, with a cup of coffee for company, while Rosza cooked eggs in the kitchen for the men. As she was towelling her hair she heard a knock on the outside door. Joszef called out to her.

'It's that bloke from the Embassy.'

Max Anderson. She'd clean forgotten he was turning up this morning. Launching herself out of the bath she threw on her clothes and went outside.

She found Max in the driveway, standing with the slight awkwardness of a man who has been told to wait but not invited inside. Beneath the black overcoat, he wore a grey herringbone jacket and guernsey jersey. It made him appear slightly younger, more boyish, than before. He gave a little salute as he saw her.

'I'm sorry. I didn't mean to get you out of bed.'

'You haven't,' she said quickly. 'I've been up for hours.' She found the suggestion that she'd been lying in bed at 9.30 faintly annoying. She went back and fetched the keys from the peg behind the door. The eyes of the three men at the breakfast table followed her.

'I'm going over to the main house,' she told them. 'I'll join you at the stables later.'

As they came around to the front of the house she glanced around the driveway. 'How did you get here?'

'I drove.'

There was no sign of a car. There wouldn't be, she realised. The gates were still locked.

'Oh, hell. I was going to send Joszef down to undo the chain, wasn't I? I'm sorry. Did you walk up?'

'Seemed the quickest way.'

The reply was easy, rather mocking. Terezia flashed a brief smile in his direction. 'I'm sure the exercise did you good.'

She was surprised by her own sharpness. She wasn't usually rude to people, particularly people she didn't know. But there was something about the smooth, confident way this man spoke that goaded her into it.

The smell of decay greeted them as she opened the high front door and led the way up the broad double staircase. It had been designed, she was told, so that two ladies in crinolines could sweep down it side by side without crushing their ridiculous skirts together. Now the boards were bare and riddled with woodworm.

'You'd better keep to one side,' she warned. 'It's not very safe.'

Max was looking around with curiosity at the crumbling splendour of the Palace as he followed her upstairs.

'You don't live in this part at all then?'

'It's hardly habitable, is it?'

'Has it been used at all since your lot were moved on?'

'My lot?' She paused, not understanding the expression.

'Your family—'

'Oh, I see.' She didn't entirely like the idea that her family had been 'moved on', as though they were a pack of gypsies.

'Yes, it's been used. There were conferences and so on after the war. Then it started to get run-down and they turned it into a barracks. When they couldn't use it for that any more they just let it go. It was deserted for about fifteen years.'

'Lucky the roof didn't cave in.'

'It did,' she said as they reached the library door. 'But my cousin had it repaired.'

'Decent of him.'

'Yes.' She smiled briefly. There was no point in explaining to this man that the only reason that her cousin Zoltan had repaired it was because he thought the house would belong to him. Now that it didn't he was suing her for every forint he'd put into the place.

She sorted through the enormous bunch of keys, trying to remember which one fitted the lock. None of them was marked. She tried a couple but they didn't work. As she stooped over the lock to put in another, she was suddenly acutely conscious of Max standing behind her.

She felt the faint, familiar clutch of panic. Straightening up, she spun around. But Max wasn't where she'd imagined. He was over by the window, looking down into the courtyard.

He glanced round. 'Having a problem?'

She shook her head, feeling the adrenaline die in her veins as quickly as it had come, and turned the key. 'No,' she said as she opened the high door. 'I was just wondering where you'd got to.'

The library was large and spooky, the empty shelves grey with dust, the twin fireplaces gaping holes in the walls. What had once been cosy was now cold as ashes. In the centre of the floor were a dozen or more tea chests, most of them already disembowelled into piles of books.

Max picked one up and flicked open the cover. As he read

the title page, Terezia studied him from the doorway. He wasn't particularly good looking, with his unruly hair and sticking out ears. In fact she'd put him down as rather ugly if it were not for his eyes which were dark and bright and seemed always to be moving.

He put the book down again.

'Is this it?'

Terezia shrugged. 'Yes.'

'This is what Verity was looking through?'

'Yes—' It wasn't her fault if he'd come all this way to look at a heap of mouldy books.

'And he seemed interested in them?'

'He must have been. He spent hours up here going through them.'

'He didn't give you any idea of what he was looking for?'

'I hardly spoke to him,' Terezia said. She'd made certain of that. There'd been something about the whiteness of his skin, the slight bulge of his eyes that had repelled her. On the one occasion she had spoken to him for any length of time, he'd quizzed her on her family. There wasn't much she could tell him; he'd known more about them than she ever would but that hadn't bothered him. The subject fascinated him and for over an hour he'd sat in the office going through her entire family tree, analysing the marriages, the friendships and alliances, pronouncing the names and titles of her ancestors with the loving care of an antiques collector examining a hoard of priceless porcelain.

Max was walking round the piles of books as though trying to assess the task he'd set himself.

'There has to be something here he was looking for,' he said. 'Something he *knew* he would find.'

'He might just have been trying his luck.'

Max shook his head. 'He came the whole way out from England to get his hands on these. He wouldn't have done that unless he was pretty certain of what was here.'

'When I talked to the police, they said he was smuggling things out of the country and got himself killed for it.'

'Did they say who by?'

'The Mafia.'

She dropped her voice at the mention of the name. The Mafia didn't operate in Hungary but the word was used for every black-market outfit and protection racket that had spawned since the Wall came down. It was the flipside of democracy.

Whatever name they used, Max didn't rate them.

'That's what we're supposed to think,' he said. 'If the Mafia had got rid of Verity they'd have done it quickly and quietly and disposed of his body afterwards. They wouldn't have played games putting that key in my pocket. They'd have taken back their little trinkets and no one would have been the wiser.'

The offhand way he dismissed her opinion stung her to say, 'That's not what the police think.'

'This is nothing to do with the Mafia.' He gave her a quick, penetrating glance with his dark eyes. 'The reason that Verity was killed is that he found something up here that he wasn't meant to know about. He practically told me so himself.'

'You spoke to him?'

'Only briefly.'

'What did he say?' She couldn't help being intrigued.

'Not much. He was scared out of his wits. He knew someone was after him and he wanted to get out of the country as fast as he could. He wanted me to fix it for him.'

'But why should anyone be after him?'

'Because he was blackmailing them and he wanted to get somewhere where he could do it from a safe distance.'

'He told you this?'

'Not in so many words but he managed to get the idea over loud and clear.'

'Damn him,' Terezia said flatly. 'He swore he was doing some research for a TV programme.'

'He didn't try to touch you for money, I suppose?'

'Me?' She almost laughed at the absurdity of it. 'There'd be no point in blackmailing me. I couldn't even afford the stamp to send him money.'

'That bad, eh?'

'This place burns up anything we earn before we've had a chance to get our hands on it.'

'How long have you been living here?'

'About three months now.'

Max put the book he was holding back on one of the piles very carefully as though it's position there had been arranged by an extremely expensive interior designer. 'Isn't there some argument about this place? I heard there'd been a court case recently.'

'Oh, that,' she said. 'That's over now.'

'What was the problem?'

Terezia shrugged. There was no secret. The story had been all over the papers at the time. 'It was my cousin Zoltan,' she said, 'He didn't think this place should be inherited by a woman.'

'He thought it should be inherited by a man – like him, for instance.'

She couldn't resist a little smile. 'That's about it.'

'But the court came down on your side?'

'Yes,' she said carefully. 'They came down on my side.' She'd never been involved in a lawsuit before and she hoped she never would again. It had been sordid and humiliating. All the more for her as she wasn't actually part of the case, just a name that was thrown back and forth by the lawyers as they played their long-drawn-out and highly lucrative games with each other.

'That can't have pleased him,' Max said.

'No, it didn't. But I don't think you'll find anything in these books that would have made any difference, if that's what you're thinking.'

'Probably not. But there's something in here; I'm sure of it.'

'Well, good luck.' She glanced at her watch. It was 10.30. The others would be waiting for her. 'I must go. I've work to do. You'll have to be through by about four, I'm afraid.'

'Why? Do you need the place for a party?'

'No,' she said. 'It gets dark then. There's no electricity in this part of the house.'

As she hurried back down the stairs, Terezia didn't look at the disintegrating house around her. She didn't want to know about it. The stables she could handle, even love. They had a purpose and future. The rest she hated. It was just a burden that drained her meagre finances. As far as she was concerned, the sooner it was pulled down the better.

The trouble was she'd been given no warning of its coming. Until the day before she was summoned to the solicitor's office in Budapest she'd been plain Terezia Kovacs, working on a stud farm up in the Matra mountains, paying weekly instalments from her wages to earn herself a place in the co-operative. And that had been the extent of her ambitions. She'd known who her father had been but she'd heard nothing of the restitution of the estates or that she could be involved in it.

It had been a man's voice on the phone, quiet and formal. He'd asked her for her name. When she'd given it he'd said, 'Can I inquire, is that the name you were born with?'

'It's the name I use.'

'As I understand it, that is the name of your foster parents. What I am trying to establish is the name you were born with.'

'Kasinczy,' she'd said cautiously.

'And would I be right in thinking it is in fact short for Kasinczy-Landsberg?'

She'd felt the first ache of apprehension. That second part was never used. It was banned, never mentioned. Twice in her life they'd had to move to escape it.

'Why are you asking me these questions?'

The man hadn't given a reply to this. Instead, in his polite voice, he'd said, 'Could you give me your father's first names?'

'I want to know why you are asking me this.'

'We are trying to trace Count Kasinczy-Landsberg's daughter.'

'Karoly,' she'd said quickly. 'Karoly Istvan.'

'And where was he born?'

It was no longer a crime to be descended from the aristocracy, she'd told herself. The regime was gone, the files of the AVO, the Hungarian secret police, had been scattered. But still she'd felt her hands shaking as she held the receiver. In a small voice she'd said, 'The Palace of Fetevis.'

This appeared to satisfy him. 'If it's not too much trouble, Kisasszony Kasinczy-Landsberg, we'd like you to come to our offices tomorrow afternoon.'

'But why?'

'We have been going through your father's will. There are some aspects of it we'd like to discuss with you.'

Terezia didn't understand. It was ten years since her father had died. She hadn't been at the funeral. The ministry had informed her of the date and place afterwards, a brief typewritten note in a brown envelope. There had been no mention of a will at the time and she hadn't expected there to be one. He'd had nothing to leave. What few possessions he'd had on him at the time of his arrest had already been returned. He hadn't owned anything else.

'Can I count on your attendance, Kisasszony Kasinczy-Landsberg?' the solicitor had asked. She'd noticed, even then, that he seemed to hesitate as he used her name, as though not sure of the correct way to address her. But she'd thought nothing of it.

'Yes,' she said. 'If you think it's necessary I'll come.'

She'd arrived at the address he'd given her in Andrassy utca on a still, autumn day with the leaves dripping off the trees. A young man had led her up marble stairs to an office on the first floor. In a soft, deferential voice he'd introduced her to Victor Szelkely, the senior partner of the law firm.

'We spoke on the telephone yesterday,' he'd said, raising her hand to his lips in the manner still preferred by those of the older generation. He had silver hair and the lazy, hooded-eyed charm of the Hungarian intelligentsia.

She hadn't been the first to arrive. Across the room had been a group of smartly dressed people. They had glasses in their hands as though this were a party. When she'd come in they'd been talking loudly, cheerfully, but at the sight of her they'd been struck silent and now stood watching her.

Victor Szelkely had offered to take her coat but she'd refused. The dress she'd been wearing beneath was white and flimsy. She'd bought it for a wedding that summer and it was quite unsuitable for this occasion. She'd only put it on because she'd had nothing better. He'd offered her a drink but again she'd refused. There'd been a tension in the room. She hadn't known why she had been summoned to this beautiful, book-lined office, but she'd sensed she was unwanted here, an intruder on something intimate and personal.

'First allow me to make some introductions,' the solicitor had said.

She didn't want to meet these wealthy, confident-looking people but his hand had been on her elbow, drawing her across the floor towards them.

They'd waited to meet her in silence, the hostility naked in their eyes. Seated in the midst of them, dressed in an immaculate grey suit and silk tie, one leg tossed negligently over the other, had been a man in his sixties. He was strikingly handsome, his face tanned, the skin devoid of all sags and wrinkles in the manner that only the very rich can achieve.

'May I present Zoltan Kasinczy-Landsberg.'

She'd known the name; she'd heard it spoken over and over again by her father and by Rosza. Her American cousin; the one who had left the country, the last member of the family to have known Fetevis in its heyday.

She couldn't have put it in words but suddenly she'd had an intimation of what was happening that afternoon and she'd felt her knees beginning to shake beneath her long coat.

Gravely the solicitor had introduced the rest of the family: the wife with pale blue eyes, arrogant and remote, who'd nodded briefly and looked away, and the son and daughter who stood behind. The lawyer, Laszlo Vargas, had been there also although she hadn't caught his name; she hadn't caught any of their names after Zoltan's.

He'd sat studying her, neither speaking nor moving, as the solicitor had made his introductions. As soon as they'd come to an end he'd held up his hand, cutting off any further social niceties and said, 'I think we know who we are. The question is, who is this girl you've brought along?'

'This is Terezia Kasinczy-Landsberg.'

Zoltan had gazed at her for a moment longer, then his eyes had drifted up to Szelkely, 'And who the heck is she?'

'Your first cousin. Count Karoly's only daughter.'

'The hell she is,' Zoltan murmured.

There'd been a moment of complete silence in the room. Then, lifting her head, her neck lengthening, and with an accent that would have cut stale cheese, the wife had said, 'Mr Szelkely, do I have to remind you that Count Karoly wasn't married?'

'That is what we were told and what we believed,' the solicitor had said. 'But it was not so.'

'It's the first I've heard of it,' Zoltan had said.

'It wasn't widely advertised.'

'Too damned right it wasn't.' He'd banged the glass he was holding down on the table. Festivities were over; he was talking business now. 'I've never heard of any marriage, or any daughter. Where the hell's she been all this time?'

'In the country.'

'Why did no one know about this?'

'For practical reasons she has not been using her real name. We had the greatest difficulty in tracing her.'

'I'll bet you did.'

'It was only when we read the Count's will that we learned of her existence.'

Zoltan had sat quite still. 'What will?' he'd asked softly. 'There is no will.'

'It has only recently been recovered from the archives; we received it earlier this week.'

'I've never heard anything about a will.'

The solictor had remained calm. 'Before we go any further it might be helpful if I were to read it to you.'

Offering Terezia a chair, his hand touching the back as she'd sat down, he'd taken his place behind the desk. From a folder he'd taken out a scrap of paper.

From where she'd been sitting, Terezia hadn't been able to read the words but she'd recognised the close, neat handwriting and the sight of it had sent a little shiver down her spine.

'It states that this document was written in the prison governor's office in July 1987. It is witnessed by the governor and the doctor who attended him in the last months of his life. The Count himself has signed it simply Karoly Istvan Kasinczy of Fetevis.'

At this tiny insight into her father's final days Terezia had felt herself beginning to tremble uncontrollably. They'd had no news of what became of him after the trial. Information on where he'd been taken and his state of health had been banned. The report of his funeral had been the only indication they'd had that he'd lived until then.

'He states that he is of sound mind,' the solicitor had continued, 'and goes on – and here I quote – "In the regrettable circumstances of my life I find myself without resources or possessions. I therefore bequeath on my only daughter, Terezia Erzsebet, all that is left for me to give – my name and my blessing. I do this in the understanding that she is my sole heir and, in different and happier circumstances, would inherit my title, my estates and all that I own under the sun."'

The simplicity of this statement had silenced everyone in the room except their lawyer, Laszlo Vargas, who'd shaken his head gravely, as though deeply moved, and said, 'A charming sentiment and, if I may say so, most touching. But it alters nothing. In Hungarian law the estate passes to the eldest male heir.'

The solicitor had accepted the point with a bow of the head. 'Unfortunately,' he said carefully, 'it is not that simple.'

'There has never been a case of the daughter inheriting while a male line exists.'

'That is true.'

'Inherits?' Terezia had put in. Her mind was reeling with the shock of what she was hearing. 'Inherits what?'

The solicitor had turned to her with a smile of apology. 'I fear we have not put you in the picture. The purpose of this and other meetings has been to settle the restitution of Fetevis Palace.'

'Restitution?' She'd repeated the word stupidly.

'To give it back. Your cousin Zoltan has suggested it might be appropriate, given the present political climate, for the Government to return the estate to the family. And they have accepted. We had been working on the assumption that Zoltan was the heir until we received your father's will—'

'The will changes nothing,' Vargas had cut in. 'It was not in the late Count's gift to leave the estate to his daughter.'

'No,' Szelkely had agreed. 'But the will established the existence of a daughter and that is all that matters.'

Vargas had begun to argue but the solicitor had held up his hand. 'This is not a question of inheritance. The line of inheritance was severed fifty years ago. What we are concerned with here today are the terms of restitution and in the contract – which you have studied – it states quite clearly that the estate will be passed to the next of kin.'

Zoltan had suddenly leaned forwards, as though the full impact of what was being said had only just reached him, and pointed across the room. 'You mean you're going to hand it over to this peasant girl?'

'That is the conclusion we have reached.'

'Are you out of your bloody mind?'

'It is my duty to tell you that in our opinion she is the legal heir to Fetevis which, I should add, was also her father's wish.'

After that all hell had broken loose. Vargas had begun clamouring, the wife had spat out words of disgust. Everybody had been speaking at once and in the midst of it the daughter had suddenly burst into tears.

Only Zoltan had remained still and silent, staring across the room at her with a look of raw hatred in his eyes.

That weekend she'd gone over to look at Fetevis. It was a cold, rainy afternoon and she'd loathed the place on sight. It was dark and depressing, a ruined shell with no resemblance to the house her father had loved and talked of so often.

'You don't have to take it,' Victor Szelkely told her.

'What will happen to it if I don't?'

He shrugged. 'Your cousin Zoltan will have it, of course. He's next in line.'

'Then I must go and live there.'

He'd given her a long, hard look. 'You know he'll take you to court?'

'Will he win?'

'Not if you keep your head. You're your father's daughter. He can't take that away from you.'

In a small voice she'd asked, 'Do you think I'm mad?'

'No,' he'd said. 'I think you're very brave.'

Pulling her thoughts back to the present, Terezia ran down the steps of the porch and went round to the cottage where the men were finishing breakfast.

'Did you ask him over for lunch?' Rosza asked, wiping her hands on a dishcloth. She was in her late sixties, short and sturdy, with a jaw like a boxer and a face that was lost in wrinkles. Iron-grey hair was tied back in a scarf, her black dress hidden behind a faded print apron.

'Who, Anderson? No, I didn't.'

'You should, Tereyki.'

'Why?'

'He's from the Embassy.' Rosza spoke in awe. She was easily impressed by official status.

'Oh, pooh,' Terezia said, going out into the drive with the three men. 'If he wants something to eat he can go down to the village.'

Bela Bessenyei, the Minister of the Interior for the Republic of Hungary, stretched out on the bed in satisfaction.

At weekends he put the affairs of state behind him and dedicated himself heart and soul to his family. In a woolly cardigan and trainers he played football with his son and sat in the stalls of the local ice rink to watch his daughter practise her skating. To the paparazzi lurking around his weekend home in the Buda hills, he was to be seen on a Sunday morning reading the papers in a deckchair, chatting with neighbours and walking the dog in the company of his wife whose guidance and support he cherished above all other political advisers. Which was why his visits to this discreet and very expensive spa-club in Obuda had to be confined to week days.

At the heart of the club was a Turkish bath which drew its sulphurous water from one of the one hundred and twenty hot springs that lie beneath Budapest. But it couldn't have been more different from the municipal baths with their cracked tiles and sullen echoes, that look and smell like a public convenience. Here it was all stripped pine and polished aluminium. Leafy pot plants dripped condensation in the brightly lit pool, piping hot water was propelled through

Jacuzzis and saunas. Membership was restricted to a select few and then only with the unanimous agreement of the other members of the club.

In private rooms off the central pool, girls in short white uniforms massaged away the aches and strains of executive life. They had clever fingers and soft mouths and when they had finished work on the outer man they unzipped the fronts of their tunics and satisfied whatever inner cravings he may have been complaining of.

That morning Bessenyei had chosen an oriental girl with raven-black hair and legs that bowed slightly like sugar tongs. As she disappeared to collect the scented massage oils, he was savouring the moment of anticipation. And so he was not best pleased when Laszlo Vargas appeared in the doorway.

''Morning, Bela.'

Bessenyei swung his feet over the bed and sat up. Damn the man, didn't he know that it was a house rule that no one was ever disturbed in the rooms?

'Sorry to barge in while you are resting,' Vargas said with a little smile of apology. 'I have been meaning to have a chat with you for some time but just haven't got round to it. Then seeing you here I thought I'd take my chance.'

Bessenyci glowered at him. He'd have to talk to the committee about this. It was quite outrageous. He'd had no idea Vargas was a member here; certainly the man's name had never come up during his time at the club. Must have been here before he joined. Lucky for him. If Bessenyei had been there at the vote he'd have had the man blackballed. He couldn't stick lawyers, particularly this new suave, overpaid breed who'd come in since the revolution.

'You don't mind?' Vargas inquired.

'No,' he heard himself saying. 'No, I suppose not.' He

glanced towards the door. But it was going to have to be quick. The girl would be back in a minute and he didn't really want anyone seeing him talking with Vargas. Even high-class tarts.

Vargas caught his meaning. 'I've asked her to give us a moment to ourselves,' he said smoothly, drawing his white robe around himself and sitting down in a wicker chair. His smile was momentarily roguish. 'Nice choice, if I might say.'

'What can I do for you?'

Vargas steepled his fingers beneath his chin. 'As you know, my client is most disappointed by the court's ruling last week.'

'There's nothing I can do about it,' Bessenyei said roughly. He wanted that point made clear from the start.

'No, of course not. That goes without saying, Bela. Naturally my client will appeal. But appeals can be slow and their outcome . . . unpredictable, shall we say.'

Bessenyei didn't know why he bothered to talk of his 'client', as though this was some mysterious person who had to be kept anonymous. Everyone knew he acted for Zoltan Kasinczy-Landsberg. Vargas was on the corporation pay-roll, a puppet lawyer who said and did what his master ordered.

'The courts have ruled that the girl inherits,' Bessenyei said, 'And as far as I'm concerned that is final.'

'My client cannot accept this.'

Well, bad luck. Zoltan could rage until he was blue in the face, he was never going to get his case past the judges. 'The title goes to the nearest blood relative and she's his daughter.'

'That's his point.'

'What is?'

'How do we know she *is* his daughter?'

'Because she's called Kasinczy-Landsberg and she was

brought up by the man. How much more do you need?' Bessenyei couldn't see what he was driving at.

'She could be adopted. For all we know she could just have assumed that name after the Count went to jail.'

'You're not serious?'

'She says she's the daughter and the courts have taken her word for it. There's no evidence. Nothing concrete. No one has actually seen a birth certificate.'

'Well, you could find it quick enough.'

'That's what I intend to do.'

'So what's your problem?'

Vargas paused, phrasing his thoughts carefully. 'My client would prefer it if there weren't a birth certificate.'

'I'm sure he would; I'm sure it would suit him just dandy. But it's not missing, is it?'

'No, no, it's not. Not at present, that is . . .'

There was a moment's silence in the little room as Bessenyei grasped what the other was saying. 'Holy Mother,' he said, lowering his voice. 'Are you telling me you're going to destroy the thing?'

'Of course not.' Vargas was shocked. The very thought of such an act was abhorrent to a lawyer. 'What I am telling you is that when I arrive at the town hall the day after tomorrow, my client would prefer it if the thing were found to be missing.'

'You mean you want me to do it?' Bessenyei stared: he couldn't mean that, could he? It was unbelievable.

'Well, I can't do it myself.'

By God, he did; the bastard was asking him to do his dirty work. 'Now hang on a moment.'

'Municipal Halls have an annoying habit of keeping records of the documents they show to the public. And that would rather defeat the purpose of my visit. But the police can examine documents as much as they like. There's no record of what they look at . . . or of what happens to them.'

'The answer's no.'

'I must ask you to reconsider.'

'Hell, you're asking me to commit a crime.'

'I'm asking you to infringe a bye-law.'

'The answer's no, dammit.'

Vargas took on the pained expression of a man who has tried to be reasonable, tried doing things the civilised way, and got nowhere with it. 'I need hardly remind you of the contributions my client has made to your Party funds.'

'I don't give a damn about his contributions. What he pays helps the Party; it doesn't buy it.'

'Or of the payments made directly into your account.'

'I can't order the police to destroy a birth certificate.' Bessenyei was getting angry but Vargas wasn't listening.

'If my client fails to acquire the estate,' he spoke distantly, as though voicing thoughts to himself, 'he will undoubtedly move back to the US, taking his entire corporation with him.'

At that moment there was nothing that Bessenyei would have liked more than to see Zoltan Kasinczy-Landsberg heading off into the sunset taking his family, his business and his Godforsaken bribes with him.

'I imagine the massive loss of revenue would be something that both the public and parliament would want to have explained to them.'

'You're asking too much.'

'The work of a few minutes. You must have men you can trust for such tasks?'

'What am I going to tell them?'

'You don't have to tell them anything, do you?'

Bessenyei weighed it up in his mind. He was going to have to do it, he knew that. They'd got him on a spit. 'Oh, God, get out of here.'

Vargas stood up, retying the belt of his robe. 'Naturally, my client will be wanting to offer you a small token of appreciation when the job is done.'

'Stuff his tokens.'

'As you like.'

As he was leaving, Bessenyei said, 'You're taking one hell of a risk coming here like this. How do you know I won't go straight back to the office and report this conversation?'

Vargas paused in the doorway and considered the question as though it had never occurred to him. 'Because if I were put in the embarrassing position of admitting to it, I'd be almost bound to let slip where it took place, wouldn't I?'

'How did you get on?' Terezia asked without looking up. She was working at a paper-strewn desk in a back office of the stable block as Max came in. It was four-forty. Dusk was gathering in the yard outside, the light over the doorway making it appear almost night.

'Hardly started,' he said. 'It's taken me all day just to list all the books you've got up there.'

'He was at it for ages – Verity, that is.'

'And he knew what he was looking for.'

Terezia sat back, thrusting her long legs out under the desk. One golden lock of hair had escaped the control of the handkerchief. She tucked it in and studied him thoughtfully. It was as though she'd only just focused on his arrival. 'So that's it, is it?'

'No, I'll come back tomorrow, if that's okay.'

There was a moment's hesitation. Then she said: 'Yes, if you want.'

From the tone of her voice she might as well have said: 'If you must.'

Flipping shut the file on the desk she got to her feet. Max followed her out into the stable yard.

It was a separate world within the Palace. He would never have known it existed at all if the old woman hadn't pointed out the way in to him. And the mood was different here too. There was a sense of purpose and organisation.

'Quite an empire you've got here,' he said.

'It's a start,' Terezia said, glancing round the yard critically. 'There's still a lot to be done.'

'Until what?'

'Until I can get the place going properly and start breeding horses of our own.'

'How many of these do you own then?'

'These? None of them. I just look after them. But soon we'll be able to afford a mare and then things will get going.'

She spoke with a quiet pride and he realised the project was precious to her. One of the stable doors was open. She went over and swung it shut.

'How about the rest of the stuff?' Max asked.

She glanced round the yard. 'What stuff?'

'The pictures, the furniture, all the rest of it. Where's that all got to? There must have been truck loads of it originally.'

'Oh that,' she said, clanking the bolt into place. 'That all went after the war.'

'How come those books have survived?'

'They didn't survive. Nobody wanted them, that's all. When the Russians took over the house they had the whole place forked over by art experts. They took away everything they wanted and put it in the museums. The rest was sold.' She paused and turned to him, thumbs hooked into the belt of her jeans. 'I saw a picture of it from the newspapers. They got everything out into the driveway and auctioned it off. "Liberated goods" they called it. Anything that hadn't gone at the end of the day they packed up and stuck in a cellar somewhere.'

'And that's what you got back.'

She nodded thoughtfully. 'That's what I got back.'

'What about the pictures?'

'They're still in the museum, I guess.'

'The Hermitage?'

'No, the Fine Art Museum in Budapest. At least, I suppose that's where they are – I've never been to see.'

'Aren't you going to get them back?'

She was amazed by the suggestion. 'Heavens, no. They'd never let them go.'

'They let the house go.'

'The pictures were all nationalised; they belong to the State.'

'So did the house. You should have asked to have them back, and anything else they've got stuck away in their museums.'

In the light above the entrance her eyes were the colour of honey as she studied him. 'They'd never do that, would they?'

'Tell them you'll take them to court if they don't. They'd hate that.'

'So would I.'

'You don't have to do it, just threaten it.'

'Are you a lawyer?' She sounded interested.

'I studied law, but I didn't stay the course.'

'Were you going to be a solicitor or one of those ones in hats – I don't know what you call them.'

'Barristers. And they're wigs.'

'What are?'

'They wear wigs, not hats.'

'Wigs? How very strange. Are you sure?'

'Quite sure.'

'Well, I'll think about it.' She looked at him in silence for a moment. Then she said, 'Shouldn't you be getting back to Budapest?'

9

For the first time in two months, Laszlo Vargas felt at ease as he settled back in the rear seat of the long-wheelbase Mercedes and studied his notes. He wasn't reading them, just using them to avoid making conversation with the junior lawyer who sat opposite. Vargas didn't want to talk. He was mentally preparing himself for the coming confrontation with Terezia, rehearsing the words he would use, the exact timing he would employ as he hit her with his bombshell.

And, Christ, he was looking forward to it. Ever since she'd shown up at that solicitor's office his life had been hell. It hadn't been his fault. No one had known about her. There had been no mention of a daughter living in Hungary – no one had even known the old man had married. But try telling that to the boss. Zoltan had been like a man possessed, ringing him at all hours of the day and night, demanding to know what was being done to remove her. God, it had been a rough time. For the past eight weeks his job had been on the line. He'd lost five pounds in weight and more hours of sleep than he cared to count.

But he could put all that behind him now. His trip out into

the countryside the day before had been successful, more successful than he'd ever dared to hope. It had been almost amusing to watch the officials at the Town Hall scrabbling through their disorganised filing system, fussed and bewildered as they realised they couldn't find the document that was requested, eventually announcing that it didn't exist.

The car slowed and swung in through the gates. Vargas put his papers into the briefcase and snapped it shut.

'I don't want you to speak during the meeting,' he told his junior. 'Just take notes, that's all that is required. I want an exact record of what she says.'

The junior nodded. He knew that he wasn't needed for any practical reason that day. He was there to add weight to Vargas's presence, to increase his sense of importance. Given half a chance he'd have a whole retinue of junior lawyers fluttering around him.

They were rounding the curve of the lake, the great house coming into view across the water. Vargas sat back and wondered how Terezia was going to react when he told her that the entire basis of her claim to the estate was non-existent. Would she flare up in indignation or dissolve into tears? He rather hoped it would be anger. He'd enjoy seeing her lose her temper, all that coolness of hers melting into helpless fury as she realised she'd lost the battle.

It was long overdue. Since she'd walked into their lives, unknown and unannounced, she'd been having it all her own way. But that was over. It was time to turn the tables on her, explain to her that her brief reign in the Palace had come to an end.

His arrival at the house was not exactly as he'd planned. As he got out of the car, the driver holding open the door for him, his junior carrying his briefcase, there was no sign of anyone waiting to meet him. He walked across to the side wing where he knew Terezia was living. But it was an old woman who opened the door. She stood with a broom in hand, solid and hostile, blocking the door like a sentry.

Vargas said, 'I'm here to see Terezia Kasinczy-Landsberg.'

'She won't be wanting to see you.'

'Could you tell me where she is?'

The old woman shrugged. 'Could be anywhere. She doesn't tell me what she's doing.'

'I rang yesterday to say I was coming.'

'She'll be gone then.'

Vargas could feel the eyes of his junior on him. He let a note of weary impatience come into his voice, as though this kind of opposition was to be expected.

'Then I shall just have to come in and wait.'

'You can't come in here. I'm washing the floor.'

He was saved from what could have been an embarrassing scene by Terezia, who appeared round the side of the house at that moment. Her eyes narrowed as she caught sight of him.

Christ, she was a good-looking girl, he thought as she approached. Even in jeans and baggy sweater, her hair tied back like some bloody washerwoman. He wouldn't mind seeing her in something more revealing – a little black cocktail dress maybe. Very short, with high heels. She'd been wearing a long overcoat when he'd last seen her in the solicitor's office but he'd glimpsed enough to know that it was hiding some spectacular legs.

'*Jó reggelt*,' he said.

'What do you want?'

'Perhaps we could go inside to talk?' He found it undignified to be standing here in the doorway with the old woman blocking the way.

'If it's about the money you're wasting your time,' Terezia told him. 'I've already told Zoltan how I'm going to pay him.'

'It's not about the money.'

'Then I can't see what else there is to discuss.'

Vargas was becoming impatient. This was not the way it was meant to be. 'If we could go inside.'

She considered for a moment and then said, 'Okay.'

The kitchen was sparsely furnished and spotlessly clean. Terezia told them to sit down at the table but Vargas objected. He didn't want the old woman there. Terezia spoke to her and she left, not before throwing him a look that was intended to stick two inches into his gut.

Taking the chair opposite the two men, Terezia rested her elbows on the table, hands clasped beneath her chin.

'So what brings you here?'

'There are a few points I'd like to go over with you.'

'You'll have to be quick. I'm going out in a few minutes' time.'

Vargas gave a smile, just sour enough to convey that what he had to say was of far greater importance than any engagement she might have. Opening his briefcase he took out the sheaf of papers. They were the transcript of the lawsuit Zoltan had filed against the Government.

'You were not often in court during the recent hearing but I assume you gathered the gist of its outcome.'

'I wasn't aware that I had to be there.'

Vargas assumed a slightly pained expression at such naiveté. 'My client was searching for clarification on the wording of the contract issued by the Ministry of the Interior concerning the restitution of the family estates.'

'Your client was trying to get the contract torn up so that he could have the place for himself,' Terezia said bluntly.

'The wording was open to interpretation,' Vargas replied vaguely. 'It was necessary to have a ruling on its exact meaning.'

'Which now you have.'

'Indeed. And my client is happy to abide by it.'

'He is?'

'Naturally. Now that the meaning of the contract has been made clear he has no argument with it. As far as he is concerned the subject is closed. I suppose I should take a look at the documentation.'

'Documentation?'

'Birth certificate or the equivalent. To prove that you are the Count's daughter. Under the terms of restitution the estate passes to the nearest blood relative. That's you, of course. We all know that. But I'd be failing in my duties if I didn't ask to see some evidence of it.'

'You'll have to go to wherever it is they keep birth certificates.'

'I am assuming you have it. We made a request at the Municipal Hall where you were born but they don't hold anything in your name.'

'They must do.'

'I checked the files myself.'

'But I don't have it.'

'No?' Vargas's expression was one of puzzled incomprehension. He wasn't expecting a problem here. 'But surely you have already been asked to show it. Didn't Victor Szelkely ask to see it when he first contacted you?'

'No.'

'Then how did he establish your credentials?'

'He asked me my name, and who my father was.' A flush of pink had appeared on Terezia's cheeks.

'Just that?'

'Yes.'

'With nothing to corroborate it?'

Terezia looked at him steadily. 'Are you suggesting that I am not the daughter?'

Vargas hadn't the slightest doubt that she was exactly who she said she was. It was her eyes. As he faced her across the table he couldn't fail to notice that her eyes were identical to Zoltan's – the same green-grey tone, the same steady, penetrating gaze. He found the resemblance unnerving. Zoltan was the one man he respected in this world, the one man he could admit to himself he feared.

'I'm saying that there is no legal evidence that you are,' he put in smoothly. 'Frankly, I'm astonished that matters have been allowed to get this far as it is. It's incredible. And it casts a slightly different light on matters. This whole business – the fact that you're living here now – is based on the assumption that you are the daughter. It never occurred to me that there was any doubt.'

'There is no doubt.'

'I'm afraid there is.' Vargas hated to be the one to disillusion her. 'Unless you can provide some sort of documentation I'm afraid we'll have to go back to the beginning and start again.'

This was the moment when he was expecting Terezia to begin to crumble. But she just stared at him pensively. Then, with a quick drumming of her fingernails on the table top she got to her feet and said, 'Will you wait here please?'

'Are you going somewhere?' Vargas was expecting tears, abuse, even violence but not an unscheduled departure.

'I'm just going to get someone.'

'Are you busy at present?'

Max looked up from his book. 'Hardly the word I'd use.'

'Could you come downstairs please? There's something I want you to hear.'

He threw aside the book and got up. There was something about her presence there in the doorway, a sort of static electricity, that didn't invite argument. 'Sure,' he said.

He'd hardly spoken to her in the past two days. She was never around in the mornings when the old woman let him into the house, and usually out when he left in the evenings. He'd seen her ride by in the distance from time to time, loose-limbed and nonchalant as a young Cossack, and that's as far as it went. She was either avoiding him or had forgotten his existence completely which was hardly flattering to his ego.

'So what's this we're listening to?' he asked as he clattered down the stairs after her.

'Vargas is here.'

'Smooth-looking guy in a black car?'

'That's him. He's trying to tell me I'm not who I say I am. It's unbelievable. He says that I don't have a birth certificate so I can't prove my father really was my father.'

Max hadn't the slightest idea what she was talking about. 'Why do you want me to listen to him?'

'You were a lawyer, weren't you?'

'No.'

Terezia paused on the staircase so abruptly that he nearly ran into her. 'You said you were.'

'I said I studied law at university. I never became a lawyer.'

'Same thing. You know the way they go about things and all that talk of theirs. And you sound like a lawyer.'

'Do I?'

'You did the other day when you were talking about those pictures.'

'I may sound like one; I sure as hell don't know anything about Hungarian law.'

'You don't have to know anything about it.' Terezia was talking over her shoulder, her mane of golden hair flying as she hurried down the stone steps of the porch. 'He'll do all the talking. Just listen to him and remember what he says. I need a witness. I think he's trying to hustle me into saying something I shouldn't. There's a little minion with him writing down everything as he goes along. He thinks that by turning up here and springing this on me he can get away with it. You mustn't let it happen. If I say something I shouldn't, anything, stop me. You understand?'

To say he understood was an exaggeration but Max nodded his head. 'Who is this guy?'

'A bastard.'

Vargas was pacing the floor as they came in.

'This is Úr Anderson,' Terezia said shortly. 'I'd like him to hear what is going on.'

'As you like,' Vargas had elected to treat the arrival of Max as nothing more than a waste of time.

They sat down around the table, Terezia opposite Vargas and the other junior lawyer, Max at the end, slightly away from the others.

'And now, if we could get on,' Vargas said.

Terezia wasn't going to be hurried. 'First, I'd like you to repeat what you said to me to Úr Anderson.'

Vargas turned. He was about to say something when the name struck him. 'Anderson – you say your name is Anderson?'

'That's right.' His black eyes frisked over Vargas quickly and keenly. He must be in his early forties, Max estimated, a touch of grey at the temples, fine lines around the eyes. His face was lean and sharp and agile. A predator, a man who lived by his wits and his instincts.

'You're not Hungarian then?' Vargas said.

'Does that bother you?'

'Of course not.' A smile flicked on to his face and away again. 'I was just wondering whether you will be able to follow what's being said. Since you have been brought here to listen it would be a shame if you had trouble with the language.'

'I can manage.'

Vargas nodded briefly, as if to say he'd given him warning, before going on. 'We've come across an unexpected problem, Mr Anderson. I came here today as a formality. More of a courtesy visit than anything. But in doing so I found that Kisasszony Terezia doesn't have a birth certificate. Before she decided to walk out I was explaining to her that this rather complicates matters.'

'I do have a birth certificate,' Terezia cut in.

'Not that I could find.'

'Then it must be somewhere else.'

'Unless you have it yourself,' Vargas said, 'it would be in the Municipal Hall where you were born.'

'Then it must be there. I was born so there must be a certificate.'

Vargas smiled at the simplicity of this statement. 'There is no doubt that there is a register of your birth. The only question is what your name was at the time.'

'Terezia Kasinczy.'

'And I'm telling you there is no one registered under that name. It must have been something else.'

'What do you mean?'

'There is no Terezia Kasinczy.'

'Of course there is.' She was becoming angry now. 'There's me. I'm Terezia Kasinczy.'

'I'm afraid not.'

'How can you say that?'

'It is quite clear that your father thought of you as his daughter and legal heir. It is also quite clear that you were not born with his name.'

There was a moment's silence. Terezia stared at him, wide-eyed with astonishment as she realised what he was saying. 'Are you suggesting I'm adopted?'

'It's the rational explanation.'

'That's ridiculous!' Terezia cried. She was leaning forward now, her eyes blazing with anger. 'How dare you say such a thing. Of course I'm not adopted.'

Vargas made a small, defensive gesture of his hands that said, 'Hey, what happened in the past is not my fault; I'm just breaking the news.'

Terezia wasn't interested. 'I would know if I was adopted. He would have told me.'

'On the contrary. Foster parents very rarely let on to children. They're worried it might jeopardise the relationship.'

Terezia shook her head. 'I would know.'

'How old was your father when you were born?'

'In his mid-fifties.' A note of caution came into her voice. 'Fifty-eight to be exact.'

'That's not too old to have children. Men have had children when they're much older than that.'

'But it becomes increasingly unlikely after fifty. There's not a doctor in the country who won't testify to that.'

'He *was* my father!'

'Yes.' Vargas nodded; he was prepared to be reasonable here. 'In legal terms he was your father. He made you his legal heir and as such you are entitled to everything he owned at the time of his death. But he was not a blood relative and that's what matters.'

Terezia sat back, arms spread wide on the table. 'You've planned this, haven't you?' she said coldly. 'This wasn't a courtesy call. You knew I didn't have a birth certificate all along. You've just been playing me along.'

'There is no evidence that you are who you claim to be.'

'I am his daughter.' Her voice was low and dangerous. 'Nothing you say can change it.'

'That's not the way the courts will see it.'

Max said, 'Then we'll have to wait for the result of the tests.'

The two heads snapped round. In the heat of the argument they'd both forgotten of his existence in the room.

'Tests?' It was Vargas who asked.

'The tests,' Max said. 'In a situation like this you're bound to have DNA tests done. They'll prove whether she's a blood relative or not.'

For one brief moment Vargas was caught off guard. He hesitated, searching for words. Then he said, 'Yes, well. I don't think we could subject my client to such an indignity.'

'I would have thought these courts you keep talking about are going to be very surprised if you don't.'

'And besides,' Vargas said, recovering rapidly, 'you may not be aware of it in the diplomatic service, Mr Anderson, but DNA tests would be quite inconclusive in this situation. There are too many outside influences to take into account. Cousins have nothing more in common than one set of grandparents. Genetically that makes the link between them tenuous.'

'I'm not suggesting you check her against her cousin,' Max said. 'I'm suggesting that you check her against her father.'

'And how do you intend to go about that?' A slight smile curled on to his lips. 'I can't believe Kisasszony Terezia would want to have her father's body exhumed for the purpose – even if it were known where he is buried.'

'No, but she has a locket upstairs which belonged to her grandmother. There's a piece of her father's hair in it. It was put there when he was a child. That should be enough to run a test on.'

Terezia opened her mouth to say something but thought better of it.

Vargas was studying Max appraisingly. 'I didn't know you were an expert on these things.'

'You don't have to be a botanist to know what an apple is.'

'An interesting analogy,' Vargas murmured. He was playing for time, giving himself enough time to come up with an objection. 'And what evidence have you that this piece of hair came from the Count?'

'It's got his name on it.'

Vargas smiled, back in control again. 'Hardly cast-iron proof. You'll have to come up with something more substantial than that, I'm afraid.'

'This is his daughter,' Max said. 'You only have to look at her. There's a photo album in the library with pictures of the Count as a young man. I was looking at it just now. They're the spitting image of each other.'

'That's purely circumstantial.'

'Are you going to try telling a judge that the girl who has been known as the Count's daughter all her life, who looks extraordinarily like him and who can be genetically matched to a lock of hair that has his name on it, is adopted? You'd be laughed out of court.'

'Then why is there no birth certificate?' Vargas inquired.

'Probably because it's been misfiled, or it's been lost, or it's just been turned into a paper aeroplane and thrown out of the window by the lady who makes the tea. I don't know, there are a hundred reasons why it might not be there, all of them grouped under the heading "clerical error", something that the communists turned into an art form. But just because you can't find one scrap of paper there's no point in going around announcing that she's adopted and making a complete fool of yourself.'

'I wasn't intending to make a fool of myself,' Vargas said. He pronounced the words shortly and quietly as though he couldn't trust himself to speak without betraying the anger that glittered in his eyes.

'You're barking up the wrong tree,' Max said. 'Terezia's his daughter; it's clear as day.'

'Without a birth certificate she can't prove that.'

'And without one you can't prove she's not.'

Vargas knew when to beat a retreat. He straightened the papers on the table and put them in his briefcase.

'Yes, well, let's hope the Government see it in that light,' he said distantly. He was the weary *aparatik* again, engaged in the endless task of overseeing the mechanisms of Government legislation. He snapped the briefcase shut and got to his feet. The junior took this as his cue to break off his chronicles and get up also.

10

After Vargas had gone, she said, 'I don't have any locket.'

'No?'

'No.'

'That's a shame.'

Her cool green eyes studied him across the table. 'You were just gambling, weren't you?'

'Yes, I was in a way. But I reckoned you'd reached the point when there wasn't much left to lose.'

'What would you have done if he'd asked to see it?'

'That was the last thing he was going to do.'

Terezia smiled. It was a slow, gentle smile that touched her eyes first and only then curled the corners of her mouth, giving a glimpse of her strong white teeth.

'Perhaps you should have been a lawyer,' she said. 'In a little hat.'

'Wig.'

'Whatever.'

'He'll be back – you know that. This is only a temporary let-off. As soon as he finds something new he'll be back.'

'I know.' Terezia pushed back in the chair and looked

away. 'I thought it was over. Now that horrible court case is over and I've paid him what he wants, I thought that would be an end of it. But I suppose that was just naive.'

'Why's he so hellfired up about owning the place?'

'He knew it,' she said, 'in the old days. He must be the last person who did. He can remember how it used to be.'

'You reckon that got to him?'

'Oh, yes. He's obsessed by the idea of owning Fetevis. It's eaten into him so that he can't think of anything else. He was the heir, you see. When he was here as a child, he was the heir. My father wasn't married so Zoltan was next in line. And he thought he still was. All these years he's convinced himself he was going to inherit the place.'

'So meeting you must have come as something of a surprise.'

'Yes,' she said. 'It was.'

'How come you owe him money?'

Terezia looked up from her thoughts. 'What's that?'

'You said you had to pay him something.'

She gave a slow shake of her head as though this were the least of her problems. 'He had a lot of work done on the place when he first came to live in Hungary. Roofing, foundations. Structural stuff. It cost a fortune. As soon as the trial was over and he realised he wasn't going to get his hands on the estate he said I had to pay it all back to him. I suppose he thought that if he could bankrupt me I'd have to pack up and go.'

'But you found the money, did you?'

'I made a deal with a bank. They're going to pay him in monthly instalments. I wrote to tell him last week. But now he's come up with this new scheme.'

'Which some dog's widdled on already.'

'He's never going to give in, is he? He's going to go on

digging and digging until he finds something that will get me out of here.'

'It's not that,' Max said. 'He's just a bad loser.'

She studied him for a moment and then, throwing her head back, she laughed.

'Is that what they call the English understatement?'

'He's a rich man; he's used to getting what he wants and gets dead pigged off when he doesn't.'

'Well, he's going to have to get used to the idea,' she said. The laugh was still bright in her eyes. Getting to her feet she stretched, hands on hips, head back, exposing the curve of her throat. Then glancing at her watch she said, 'I've got to get something for supper. Would you like to come with me?'

'Down to the shops?'

'No, the woods.'

She picked up the shotgun that stood propped behind the door, broke it open and glanced up the barrels to check they were clear.

He said, 'You're reckoning on knocking down a couple of pigeons, are you?'

She made a face. 'I hope not, they're stringy old things. But there should be some pheasants. They used to breed them for the commie top brass to come and shoot at weekends. The woods are still crawling with them.'

Shrugging on a jacket she filled one pocket with cartridges from a bag hanging on the wall and went outside. From the shed next door she let out the spaniel which bounded ahead of them, tail wagging, as they made their way round to the front of the house.

Darkness was drawing in, the lake beneath them glinting like oiled metal. On the far shore they could see the lights of Vargas's car bumping its way along the driveway. Terezia paused, the gun over her shoulder, to look at it.

Beside her Max said, 'Their information's good.'

'About me?'

'About what's going on up here. I've never met him before but he knew my name.'

'Do you think so?'

'Nearly jumped out of his skin when you mentioned it.'

'That was because he was expecting you to be Hungarian.'

'No, he knew the name,' Max said. 'I could see it in his eyes. And later, when I started to argue with him, he started on some patronising crap about how diplomats can't be expected to know anything about the law. Which is true. But had anyone told him that I was a diplomat?'

Terezia thought it through. 'No,' she said. 'God, you're right.'

'So how did he know unless he's had his spies out?'

Terezia studied the car crawling away into the distance. 'Little creep,' she said.

'Don't start feeling too sorry for him. He's got some explaining to do when he gets back.'

'Serve him right.'

'From what I hear,' Max said, 'I wouldn't want to be in his shoes this evening.'

'I hope Zoltan fries him alive.'

Shooting with Terezia was an experience.

From the lower terrace with its two ruined fountains, she led the way down into the woods, moving forwards quickly and silently in the overgrown parts where it wasn't possible to get a shot, beckoning him to do the same, then advancing more carefully in the clearings, pausing between each step to watch the dog working its way through the undergrowth. Her eyes never left it, except to flash a look above her head to check the arc of fire allowed by the trees.

As they were approaching the edge of the lake, the water showing blackly through the branches, a bird burst out in front of them. Wings clattering, it towered up, turning back over their heads. Even to his inexperienced eye, Max could see it was a difficult shot but she hit it fair and square. He heard the pellets slam into the bird's body a split second after the blast. It's head went back, it rolled over backwards in the air and hit the ground with a heavy thump.

Ejecting the spent cartridge, Terezia bounded down to where it lay. The dog had got there first and hoovered it up in its soft muzzle, bringing it towards her, one wing dragging along the ground. Terezia tugged on the glove she'd removed to keep her trigger-finger free and took the bird. Holding it up by the legs she began brushing down the feathers, which erupted in a red-gold cloud around her.

'If you do it quick they come off easily,' she told Max as he reached her. 'It's something to do with rigor-mortis.'

'Christ, that was quite a shot.'

'It was, wasn't it?' She laughed, the adrenaline of the kill still on her. 'I'd never shot anything until I came here.'

'You seem to have picked up the rudiments quick enough.'

'There's nothing like being hungry for improving your aim. Here, you can finish off the rest of this.'

She dropped another cartridge into the breech of the gun while Max plucked the last feathers from the pheasant. After a while he asked, 'Was your father really fifty-eight when you were born?'

'If that's what Vargas said it must be true.' She gave a little grin.

'Actually I thought he was older.'

'How come no one knew he'd got married?'

A feather had caught in her hair and she brushed it away with the back of her hand.

'They thought he was in jail. He'd been arrested by the Russians at the end of the war. They'd fixed up one of their trials and made him confess to being an enemy of the people and all the rest of that rubbish. But then he was let out in '56. There was an amnesty and they let him go. It didn't last long but by the time it had been turned over he'd disappeared into the country.'

'And they never tracked him down.'

'He worked all over the place until eventually he got a job on a stud farm in the Bukk mountains,' she said. 'They fixed up some papers for him. People did that then. It's odd; I don't think they'd liked the old regime much—'

'It's just that they liked the new one even less.'

'Yes, I suppose so. That's when he met Joszef; they worked together. Papa was good with horses.'

He'd never heard her call her father by that name before. It was strangely intimate.

'And he got himself married.'

She nodded.

'What do you want with this?' He held up the pheasant.

'Can you put it in your pocket?'

'There isn't room.'

She took it and tucked it away inside her jacket.

'What's become of your mother?' he asked as they walked along the edge of the lake.

'She died.'

'Oh, I see, I'm sorry—'

'It's all right,' she said lightly. 'It was a long time ago. I never really knew her.'

Max glanced at her as she walked beside him in the twilight, the gun over her shoulder, her attention on the dog bounding ahead.

'You don't mind me asking you these questions?'

She considered for a moment. 'No. I don't mind. Sometimes it's good to talk about these things. Otherwise you don't know what you think about them yourself, do you?'

'I suppose not.'

'I know Rosza thinks it's lucky she died. If she hadn't she'd have been arrested along with my father – me too, I suppose. She doesn't say anything up front but I know that's what she believes. I've heard her talking to Joszef.' She shivered as though the image had suddenly chilled her. 'I can't think of anything worse than being locked up in jail for the rest of your life, can you?'

'Probably not.'

'Never seeing the sun, never having anyone to talk to. It's horrible.'

'But your father was arrested again, was he?'

'Yes,' she said. 'He was turned over to the police.'

'By someone he worked with?'

'Oh, no.' She turned and faced him. 'It happened here.'

'In the house, you mean?'

'He came back here one night. Didn't you know that? Someone in the village spotted him and called the police.'

'But why did he come back?'

'I don't know.' She was standing very still, her face pale in the darkness. 'I never saw him again. He just left one day and didn't come back. He didn't say where he was going or why. I think maybe he just wanted to see the house again, to see if it was still here. He thought about it a lot; I know that.'

Max glanced up through the branches to where the house stood. From this distance you couldn't tell it was just a ruined shell of a building. Set against the sky it looked serene and magnificent, a symbol of everything a man could want.

'It is very beautiful.'

'Do you think so?' She tapped a pebble with her toe, watched it skitter away across the ground. 'I hate it.'

'You must feel something for it.'

'I don't,' she said quickly. 'I wish it had been knocked down years ago.'

'If you hate it why do you live in it?'

'I have to.'

'You could always sell it.'

'I can't,' she said with sudden force. 'That's the trouble. I'm not allowed to sell it. If I want to get rid of the place I have to give it back to the State and I can't afford to do that. I've borrowed so much money to pay bills and debts that the only way I can get it back is to keep the place on and try to make a profit out of it.'

'I see—'

'So I'm stuck.'

'Between a rock and a hard place,' Max agreed.

'Probably.' Her eyes flashed up to him for an instant and away again. She gave a shiver.

'Are you cold?' he asked.

'Perishing, let's get going.'

They started back up the hill. Away from the mirror of the lake what light there was faded away and darkness closed in around them. As she followed along behind Max she said, 'What's it mean then – a rock and a hard place?'

'Not much.'

'You have the weirdest expressions sometimes.'

From the bar in the village, Max bought a couple of bottles of red wine. When he returned the kitchen was warm with the smell of cooking, Rosza supervising operations on the oven, Joszef sitting at the table reading a newspaper. There was no sign of Terezia but Joszef said she was having a bath.

'She tells me you gave that lawyer a hard time this afternoon,' he said, folding the newspaper and setting it aside.

'I gave him a few things to think about.'

Joszef pictured the scene for himself. 'I think I'd like to have been there to see that,' he said thoughtfully.

He must be over seventy, Max reckoned. His face, with its stubbly white beard, was scored with wrinkles and tanned from a life spent outdoors in all weathers, the small, bright eyes belonging to someone half his age.

Max stripped the covers off the two bottles and, cranking out the corks, he filled three glasses.

Joszef tasted his. 'Is it true he's trying to make out she's not Karoly's daughter?'

'That seemed to be the line.'

He shook his head at the absurdity of it. 'You've only got to look at her,' he said.

'Of course she's his daughter,' Rosza said gruffly from her place at the oven. 'It's a wicked lie to suggest she's not.'

'Did you not know her parents at the time of her birth?' Max asked. He put the question carefully. In the past few hours he'd been thrust unexpectedly into what was a private, family matter and he didn't feel it was his place to pry.

But Joszef didn't mind speaking of it. 'No,' he said. 'She must have been two or three years old when Karoly arrived. She'd been born in the place he was working before.'

'I heard you and her father were close friends.'

'We worked together for ten years,' Joszef said. 'And in that time we became friends. At least I like to think we did.' He spoke with the strange, open honesty of a country man, laying claim to nothing that wasn't his.

'Did no one guess who he was?' Max asked.

'Oh yes, we knew. I think everyone knew. Not exactly who he was, or what his name had been, but that he had been someone before. It was in his manners, the way he spoke.'

'But no one thought of reporting him?'

'No,' Joszef said. 'There was no need. He did no one any harm and he was good at his job. Extraordinarily good at it. I don't think I'll ever know a horseman as good as Karoly. It was a gift. Terezia has it too. When she concentrates and works at it.' There was a touch of parental pride as he spoke. He glanced around the room to indicate the whole inheritance of hers. 'If it wasn't for all this, she could be an international rider, certainly in dressage.'

The thought of Terezia in top hat and tail coat was one that Max was happy to give a little living space in his mind.

'She has something of him when she rides,' Joszef said. He looked away into the distance. 'Sometimes when I see her, particularly when she's some way off, she's the image of him.'

'Did you ever know her mother?'

'No, poor girl. It was just the two of them when they arrived. Erzsebet had died. I think that's why he moved on from his last job. They were very close.'

'She must have been quite a bit younger than him.'

He nodded. 'She was. I'd like to have met her. From what I hear she was quite a remarkable person.'

'How did they come to meet?'

Joszef shrugged as though there were no telling the ways of fate. 'Chance,' he said.

11

1967

It was after seven in the evening when the stranger arrived. Erzsebet was in the kitchen serving up dinner with Margit. Next door the men were sitting around the long pine table, a bottle of Barak between them, talking in the slow, drawn-out way of those anticipating a meal.

She heard one of them get up to go and see who it was that had come calling at this hour of the night. Certainly not anyone from the village. They'd have come round to the kitchen door and walked in as they knocked. The ground floor of the farm was a public place, shared by everyone who worked there. It was only upstairs that Erzsebet could lay claim to anything that might be called privacy.

Carrying the tureen through she began ladling soup into bowls, the men passing them down the table. Her husband, Gyula, planted at the far end, was the first to get his and began to eat straight away.

There was a gust of cold air from outside. She heard a few words exchanged and then the yard-hand returned.

'It's for you,' he told Gyula, taking his place at the table.

Her husband looked up from his steaming bowl.

The stranger stood in the doorway, his cap held loosely in

both hands. His face was in shadow so Erzsebet saw only that he wore a long coat over worn overalls and an army belt round his waist. Seeing them at the table he gave a nod of apology. 'I'm sorry t'disturb you when you're eating.'

It was the voice, the soft, almost drawling pronunciation of the words, that made her pause and turn around as she carried the soup back into the kitchen to warm on the range.

'What can I do for you?' Gyula asked. He had put down his spoon and sat back in his chair, looking the stranger over with the mild annoyance of a man whose routine has been disturbed.

'I was wondering if you had any odd jobs you needed doing around the farm?'

He'd moved forwards into the light now and she could see that he had changed slightly in his outward appearance. His face, which had been pale when she last saw him, now had the mahogany tan of a man whose life is spent in the open air. The lines were scored deeper, the flesh more gaunt and there was a week's beard on his cheeks. But the eyes were as she remembered.

Gyula gave a grunt. 'At this time of the year?'

'I heard you keep a fair number of cattle here.'

'What of it?'

'Cows need tending to as much in the winter as the summer.'

Gyula didn't need to be told his job. He took a mouthful of soup, wiping the back of his broad fist over his lips.

'We milked them this morning without your help,' he said gruffly. 'And I dare say we'll manage to do it again tomorrow.'

'It wouldn't cost you anything. A place to make a bed and an evening meal is all I need.'

He spoke politely, neither begging for the work nor disdaining it; almost, Erzsebet felt, as though he were asking on behalf of someone else.

But Gyula was wary now. 'That's all you need, is it?' he asked softly. He stretched out one hand. 'Let me see your work papers.'

The crow's feet around the stranger's eyes deepened as if he found some amusement in the question. 'Now that's the irony of it,' he said lightly. 'I seem to have mislaid them.'

Gyula nodded grimly. 'There's no work here,' he said.

The stranger was used to this reaction. 'Then I'm sorry to have taken your time.'

Gyula put his head down and began to eat again, leaving him in no doubt that he was dismissed. But the stranger hesitated a moment. 'Could I ask one thing of you?'

'What's that?'

'Would y'mind if I used one of your barns for the night?'

'This isn't a hotel.'

'No,' he said carefully. 'I can see that. But I couldn't help noticing as I came in that the chestnut mare of yours has cast a shoe. I'd fix it for you in exchange for a night under a dry roof.'

Before Gyula could answer, Erzsebet said, 'Yes, of course you can stay. There's a bunk house in one of the barns you can use.'

The stranger looked at her across the room, noticing her there in the shadows of the room for the first time. He gave a little bow.

'Thank you. That's very kind.'

Gyula was glaring at her in fury. It was not her place to interrupt; it was not her place to contradict what he said.

Ignoring him, Erzsebet put the tureen back on the table.

'Take a seat,' she said quietly to the stranger. 'You must be hungry.'

Rolling his cap he tucked it into his pocket and sat at the end of the table. She passed the bread down to him and watched how he ate, slowly but intently, and she realised that this was probably the first hot food he'd tasted in days. She looked hard at Gyula.

Grudgingly he poured a glass of Barak and pushed it across the table to the stranger. 'What's your name?' he asked.

'Karoly.'

'Where were you working before?'

'On a farm on the other side of Szentes.'

'Why did you leave?'

'The harvest wasn't good.' He gave a shrug as though the rest spoke for itself.

When they had finished eating, Erzsebet collected the bowls and carried them through into the kitchen. Gyula followed her, glancing quickly round the room to check they were alone.

'Did you have to do that?' he asked roughly.

'Do what?' Her back was turned to him as she ran water into the sink.

'Humiliate me like that.'

'I didn't humiliate you,' she said evenly, turning to face him as she dried her hands on a cloth. 'All I said was that he could stay here for the night.'

'Why, for God's sake?'

'I couldn't push him out into the dark on a night like this.'

'He'll be used to it.'

'Have you been out there?' she said crossly. 'It's freezing.'

'It wouldn't be the first time he's slept under the stars.'

'On a night like this?'

'Where do you think he was last night?' There was a sneer in his voice. 'And the night before that?'

Angrily she tucked the cloth back over the rail of the oven. 'You wouldn't push a dog out on a night like this. Why do you have to do it to a man?'

'Because we've no idea who he is.'

'Just someone looking for work.'

'With no papers?' Gyula dropped his voice. 'He's jail-bait. An undesirable. He's probably on the run from the police.'

'You don't know that!'

'No? He didn't seem keen to give his name. Did you notice that? He didn't seem keen to let us know who he is.'

'Oh, don't be so ridiculous,' she snapped and pushed past him to go upstairs.

She returned with a stack of blankets tucked under her arm. Gyula watched her darkly from the doorway of the kitchen. The other men had melted away and the dining room was empty. Slipping off her shoes she stepped into a pair of clumsy rubber boots and went outside, slamming the door behind her.

She found Karoly in the stables working on the horse's shoe. His back was turned to the rump of the animal, its hind leg held clamped firmly between his knees. One of the stable hands was holding up a spirit lamp as he reset the nails that had come loose.

When he was done, the tools put back in the workshop, she showed him the bunk house, a row of home-made beds in a shed beyond the tack room. It was only ever used in the summer when they brought in extra hands to shear the sheep and it smelled of damp and neglect.

Taking a box of matches from her apron, she lit the spirit lamp hanging from the ceiling. In its soft glow the stranger stood in the doorway. She laid the blankets down on the cleanest-looking of the bunks, suddenly self-conscious now that they were alone together.

'How did you know that horse had a loose shoe in the dark?' she asked him as she busied herself with the bed.

He gave a shrug. 'They move differently.'

'I wouldn't have noticed.'

'It's the same as a man with a stone in his shoe,' he said vaguely. 'Nothing clever.'

He hefted his canvas bag on to the end of the bed and undid the string at its neck.

She paused, not sure what to say, and then reached in her apron pocket. 'I've brought you some soap.'

He took the white block she offered him and touched it to his nose, drawing in the soft aroma of cleanliness, not in the least self-conscious that she should see the pleasure he found in it.

In a small voice she asked, 'Do you remember me, Karoly?'

He put the soap down on the mattress and began laying out his possessions in a neat order beside it. A comb, a razor and a small round mirror that a woman would use to adjust her make-up.

'Of course,' he said.

'I wasn't sure—'

He smiled, the wing of fair hair falling over one eye. 'How could I forget a girl who wouldn't let her horse die in the street?'

'I didn't know. It was a long time ago.'

She'd changed since then. Her hair, which had fallen below her shoulders, was cut short. And she was taller than she'd been then. Stronger too, not only in her body but in her mind also.

'Did the mare have her foal?' he asked.

She nodded, pleased he should remember.

'What did you call it?'

'Grey-Dawn.'

'Ah.' He smiled. 'That's often the time they are born. Just to keep us poor mortals out of our beds.' He took a watch from his pocket. It was one of the old-fashioned type that hung from a chain. Opening the lid he set it on the window sill. 'Do y'still name your horses that way?'

She shook her head, slightly embarrassed. 'No, I don't think my husband would like that.'

'No, I can see that,' he said. 'How long have y'been married then, Erzsebet?'

'About six years.' She ran her fingers back through the short tufts of her brown hair and he saw she found the question discomforting.

'I had the impression that he didn't want me hanging around the place longer than I had to.'

'He's worried that you don't have any papers.'

'Well, you can see his point. If he were to employ me he'd be breaking the law.'

'Is it true that you were in jail?'

He smiled. 'What makes y'think that?'

It was just small things that had come together in her mind. 'You were very pale when I last saw you' – she mentioned the foremost – 'as though you hadn't been outside for a long time.'

'No, I hadn't been outside,' he agreed. 'Not for almost ten years. And that don't do anything for your complexion.'

She stood at the end of the bed, aware of her shabby print dress and the working apron over it.

'What did you do to be sent to prison, Karoly?'

He didn't answer immediately, as if there were no simple

answer he could give to this. 'I used to be someone else, y'see,' he said slowly. 'And they didn't like that.'

'Is that why you had to move on from your last job?'

'It has a habit of catching up,' he said. She had the impression this was not something he'd spoken of before and had difficulty in putting words to. 'They let us all out in '56. There was an armistice and we were all allowed to go. But it don't mean anything any more. They revoked the order so now I can't get any proper work.'

She felt ashamed. 'I'm sorry,' she said.

'It's just something y'have to live with. I'll move over eastwards, see what I can find.'

She thought of Gyula back in the house. 'It would be best if you went early in the morning.'

He nodded in understanding. She groped in her apron pocket and took out some folded notes. 'I brought these for you.'

Gravely, he took them.

'There's not very much,' she whispered. 'It's the most I could take without him noticing.'

For a moment she thought he was going to be too proud to accept the money. He flicked through the notes, undecided, before tucking them away in his overall pocket.

'You're a princess, Erzsebet,' he said. Taking her hand he touched it to his lips. Then leaning down he kissed her lightly on the mouth. 'Now go quickly,' he said. 'Before he begins to wonder where you are.'

The dining room was in darkness when she came in. She sensed Gyula's presence more than saw it.

She switched on a light. He was sitting at the end of the table. There was a glass in one hand and a bottle of slivovitz in front of him. From the sullen glaze of his eyes she could tell he'd already put away quite a bit of it.

'Where have you been?' he asked. There was a sheen to his face and the dark curls of his hair were glued to his forehead.

'Just making up a bed.'

'Does it take that long?'

'I was talking with him,' she said shortly. She didn't have to explain herself to him.

'What about?'

'Nothing in particular.'

He pushed the glass aside and got to his feet. He was a large man, powerfully built. There had been a time when she'd found his strength attractive. Now that he had aged and the drink had slackened the muscles of his belly she found it brutish, almost grotesque.

'You know him, don't you?'

'Yes,' she said. 'If you must know, I do.' She tried to push past him towards the stairs but he grasped her by the wrist, spinning her round to face him as though she were a rag doll.

'Who is he then?'

'Just someone I met a long time ago. He helped me.'

Gyula's fingers bit into her flesh. 'Why's he here now?'

'He was just looking for work.'

'He just happened to come by, did he?'

'Yes,' she hissed. 'That's exactly what happened.' She struggled against his grip but he held her firm.

'Did you tell him to get the hell out of here tomorrow?'

'Yes. I did. Now if you'd let go of me I'd like to go to bed.'

For a moment longer he held her and then, as she pulled, he let her go. She staggered backwards, momentarily off balance. With a quick swing of his arm he hit her across the face with the back of his hand so that she sprawled back against the wall and fell to the ground.

Without another word he turned and went upstairs.

Erzsebet held quite still, listening to his footsteps on the stairs. When he had gone she touched her lip, saw the blood on her hand.

Going through into the kitchen she damped a cloth and held it to the cut. Her cheek was beginning to throb. Upstairs she could hear Gyula moving around as he undressed. She waited until there was silence before creeping up stealthily herself.

In the bathroom mirror she examined the cut on her cheek. It was already beginning to swell and darken, a chain of ruby-red beads of blood running across the line of torn skin.

It was not the first time he'd hit her. It was something that happened frequently now, something that he gave no more thought than he would to hitting a dog that disobeyed him. He never did it in front of anyone, only when they were alone, and she had come to dread the moments they were left to themselves.

As she was putting on her nightdress she caught sight of her reflection in the mirror. She paused and examined her nakedness critically. She'd never thought of herself as beautiful in any conventional sense of the word but she was tall and strong and sleek as a thoroughbred and she knew that men's eyes followed her in the street.

As she switched off the light she saw the glow from the lamp in the window of the bunk house across the yard. He must be reading. There'd been a book amongst his belongings and she'd been tempted to ask him what it was. She was curious to know what he read, what he thought about. She knew nothing about him. He'd said he was once someone else but had given her no idea of who that someone might have been. All she knew was that he was Karoly and unlike anyone else she'd met before. A man who carried an air of sadness with him and yet seemed more at ease with himself than any man she'd known.

When she went next door, Gyula was asleep, his back turned to her. He was breathing heavily as he did when he'd been drinking.

She slipped into the bed and lay on the side of the mattress as far from him as she could. There had been a time when they'd slept as one in the middle, her arms around his chest, knees tucked in behind his, their bodies slotted together as neatly as two silver spoons in the dresser downstairs.

As with most lovers, there had been shared confidences, tunes on the radio they'd thought of as theirs, places they'd liked to be alone in together. They'd made plans, some practical, some just wishful thinking. All of them had included children.

But there had been no children.

They'd made love, at first freely and impulsively and then, as time went by, more carefully, calculating the time of the month and the intervals between each try. But still there had been no baby.

Gyula blamed her for the failure although she knew, from the tests she had undergone in secret at the hospital, that it was not her problem. 'Oh, so you think it's something to do with me, do you?' Gyula had said when she had plucked up the courage to speak to him of it.

He took the suggestion hard, as though it implied some lack of manhood on his part. It couldn't be anything to do with him. She must be inventing it, coming up with excuses to cover her own inadequacy, and that he found contemptible. From then on, in his eyes, she was only half a woman, unable to fulfil the duties of a wife.

She'd responded by letting her looks go, cutting her hair

short, wearing clothes that obscured the graceful movement of her body.

The first time he'd hit her was as they were coming home from a party. She'd let the top button of her shirt fall open. Unlocking the front door of the house he caught sight of it and sharply told her to do herself up. She'd had too much to drink that evening and was in the mood for love. Rather than fix the button, she opened the next one down provocatively so that her breasts showed through the parting.

Gyula had glanced down at them for a moment. His eyes had darkened and with a flick of his wrist he'd clipped her across the cheek.

It had not been hard, just a slap of the hand. But it was as though he was testing the effect, opening a new possibility in their relationship. The first real punch came a week later. He'd been out in the fields working late and she was asleep when he climbed into bed. Drowsily she'd put her arms around his stomach, her fingers just brushing the line of hair that ran down to his groin. Almost out of habit she followed it down. He touched her hand and she thought he was guiding it. She often guided his hand when they made love. But then suddenly he'd erupted in fury, swinging round and hitting her full in the face. Not a slap this time, nothing playful. A hard, aimed punch, the fist closed, that sent lights exploding before her eyes and set her head spinning. She'd cried out, not so much in pain as surprise and shock, blood from her nose staining the pillow. Even then she'd expected him to make up, to blame it on a sudden flash of anger and beg her forgiveness. But with a curt word he'd dragged the eiderdown off the bed and taken it next door.

Not long after that he started going with other women. Nothing lasting, just brief affairs with the girls in the village. She didn't confront him with it or even bother to let him know that she was aware of it. The truth was she found it all rather sordid.

Instead she withdrew into herself. She started to distance herself from their friends. She no longer took an interest in the farm or formed attachments with any of the animals as she had in the past. Gyula decided that she was doing it to be disagreeable. He told her she was cold and haughty but she knew it was not that. She was simply going through the slow and painful process of breaking free.

She didn't sleep that night but lay staring up at the ceiling until the dawn crept in to discover the familiar shapes of wardrobe, wash basin and bed head.

Outside she heard the cow-men talking as the day's routine began. Gyula was still asleep. She slipped out of bed, dressed and went down to the kitchen. The hands of the clock stood at six-fifteen. She put bread and some pieces of cheese and meat into a canvas bag. From the teapot on the top shelf she took the rest of the money and stuffed it into her coat pocket, not feeling guilty any longer, and went outside into the cold morning light.

Skirting the cow sheds she hurried down the road. At first she thought she must have been wrong. She could have sworn she'd heard Karoly speak to the men as he left but there was no sign of him. Then a mile further on, as she was coming to the edge of the village, she saw him ahead of her and called out for him to stop.

He turned and waited for her to catch up, his hands buried in the pockets of his long overcoat.

'Don't go yet,' she said breathlessly as she reached him.

He was looking at her steadily, a look of curiosity on his face, his breath curling out in the cold air. 'You're up early,' he said.

'I heard you leaving and got up.'

'Is there a problem?' he asked.

She shook her head. 'I want to come with you.'

'Come with me?'

She nodded.

He glanced back in the direction of the farm and then at her. 'But I'm not going anywhere.'

'That's where I want to go too.' She'd thought it all through as she lay awake in the night. She knew what must be done. But now that the moment had come, she didn't know how to explain it to him. 'I need to come with you.'

'Come with me?' His voice was puzzled. 'What are you talking about, Erzsebet? You can't come with me. You've got a husband back there. A home.'

'No.' She shook her head violently. 'You don't understand. I've got nothing back there.'

'But you can't just leave them.'

'I must!'

'It's not so easy—'

'I must come with you, Karoly.'

As she said it, he noticed the bruise on her cheek. Reaching out his hand he turned her face to one side to get a better view of it.

'He did that?' he asked.

She nodded.

He glanced back towards the farm and when he looked at her the green-grey eyes had softened and he said, 'Then let's get the hell out of here.'

It was after seven by the time the four of them sat down to dinner.

Terezia was the last to come to the table, now wearing a baggy T-shirt above her jeans, her hair, free for once of its handkerchief, falling in thick gold waves to her shoulders.

'I spoke to Victor Szelkely just now,' she said as they ate. Rosza had cobbled the pheasant together with onions and potatoes flavoured with paprika. Not based on any recipe, Max suspected, just a collision of ingredients that happened to be around. But it was good. There was bread on the table and the two bottles of wine Max had bought down in the village.

'Do I know him?' he asked.

'He's the solicitor who handled the handing over of the house. He says they did check the birth certificate.'

'Has he got it?'

She shook her head. 'He never actually saw it. He said they rang the Municipal Hall to check it was there and they were told it was. They didn't take it any further.'

'Pity.'

'He's very embarrassed about the whole thing,' she said. 'But it proves one does exist.'

'Of course it does,' Rosza said hotly from the end of the table.

'Do you think it would be worth me going down there myself?' Terezia asked Max.

'Might be.'

'No,' Joszef said. 'It's gone.' He broke off a piece of bread and chewed it slowly. Nothing was ever hurried, Max noticed. Everything was done at a certain pace. There was no stress, no agitation in the man. 'The reason Vargas turned up there,' he went on, 'was because he knew it didn't exist. If he'd really wanted to find it he would just have sat on his backside in his office and rung around the place. He went down there himself – the big-shot lawyer from Budapest – because he knew it wasn't there and he wanted everyone else to know it before he came here. I bet he made a heck of a scene; I bet he had them all running about the place like frightened rabbits.'

Terezia studied him thoughtfully. 'But how could he have known it wasn't there?'

'I imagine because he'd already had it removed,' Joszef told her.

'It couldn't have been,' Terezia said. 'I asked Victor that. He said if anyone had been in and touched it there would be a record of it.'

'Zoltan could get round that,' Joszef said. 'He's a powerful man. He's got friends in high places. He's not going to let a few *aparatiks* get in his way.'

'The man's a devil,' Rosza said as she got up to clear away the plates.

'Not that you can ever prove it,' Joszef added.

Terezia turned to Max. 'Do you think he did it?'

'It could be.' What the old man said fitted.

'But that's against the law.'

'Why do you think he keeps a private army of lawyers?'

When the table had been cleared Joszef produced a bottle of Borovitszka and filled four small glasses. They touched them together and drank their health. Terezia put hers down on the table and cradled it in her fingers.

'You said you'd found a photo album,' she said. 'Was that real, or another of your inventions?'

'Oh, that was real,' Max said.

'Could I see it?'

Leaving them, he groped his way up to the library in the dark and brought the album down. It had a brown crocodile-skin cover and black pages as thick as card. Terezia took it gingerly.

'I found it in one of the boxes,' Max said.

Moving her glass aside, she spread it out on the table. The small, browning pictures were held in place with ungainly triangular mounts. Most of them were of the house and the grounds immediately around it and, judging from the women's clothes, were taken in the thirties.

Slowly Terezia turned the pages until she came to a picture that was larger than the rest, filling a whole page of the album. It showed the entire family on some sort of picnic. They were posed by the edge of the lake, dressed in overcoats and fur hats, some of the more dashing ladies sporting dramatic sprigs of feathers in theirs. In front were two rowing boats and behind servants were arranging tables and chairs for lunch. It was a glimpse of another age, a moment that had passed unnoticed at the time and now was all that remained.

Terezia studied the photo in silence and Max realised that this was probably the first time she'd seen pictures of her family.

The Count himself was unmistakable. He was sitting in the centre of the group, his legs crossed, a cigarette in his hand, gazing into the camera lens with that serene confidence of the infinitely wealthy. He wore a high starched collar and black tie. Unlike the others, he was bareheaded, his blond hair parted high on the crown of his head in the fashion of the time. The resemblance to Terezia was inescapable.

Her finger rested on him a moment and then moved to the figure beside him. He was similar but not identical, his face fleshier, body a shade more solid.

'Sandor,' she said. 'And that's his wife. She was American. That's why they went there after the war.'

The woman she was pointing to was thin and somehow brittle, looking off to one side as though she'd lost interest in the proceedings.

'Oh God,' Terezia said, moving her finger down lower. 'And that's Zoltan.'

It was the first image Max had of the man who aspired to be the Count of Fetevis Palace. He was sitting cross-legged on the ground beneath his mother, aged no more than nine but dressed like an adult in a knickerbocker suit and Irish cap. His hands were on his knees, his back was straight as a ramrod and, like his uncle, he stared straight into the camera lens: the heir apparent, a boy with all the hopes and dreams of youth but with the certainty that in his case they would come true.

Max said, 'Looks awfully chilly to be having a picnic.'

'It's the winter pavilion; it's on the lake. My great-grandfather built it over a hot spring he found, like the ones you get in Budapest. They used to go and swim there in the winter. It's still there, you can see it across the other side of the lake.' Terezia turned the page. 'Who took these pictures?'

'There's a name at the beginning.'

She flicked back to the inscription at the front which read: *Eleanor Hargreaves, Christmas 1939*.

'Mean anything to you?' Max asked.

Terezia repeated the name a couple of times, recollection dawning. 'Yes . . . yes, of course. How extraordinary. Eleanor Hargreaves was Zoltan's governess.'

'Sounds English.'

'She was. Everyone had English nannies and governesses then; it was fashionable. She was very devoted to them. When the war started she was meant to go back to England but she refused. She stayed here until the family left. My father always thought she was secretly in love with Sandor.'

Max could picture her: an educated girl from a good family that had hit hard times, suddenly translated from dreary England in the Depression years to the fairy-tale world of Hungary. Quite a change; quite enough to fill her head with romantic dreams.

Terezia closed the album and stood up. It was getting late, Rosza was yawning. Max made his thanks and went outside. Terezia followed.

'You'll die of cold out here,' Max said.

'It's all right—'

'That was a good supper.'

She nodded, hugging herself for warmth, and stared down at the lake. It was a clear night, the sky crusted with stars.

'You know those paintings?' she said after a moment. 'The ones you were talking about the other day? I spoke to the Fine Art Museum about them. They say they're prepared to talk about what happens to them.'

'That sounds useful.'

'They said they're not promising anything but they will talk about it. I'm going round there tomorrow to look at them.' She paused, suddenly shy. 'I wondered if you'd come with me?'

'If you like.'

'You're better at putting these things than me.'

'I'll put my lawyer's hat on. When are you going there?'

'Three.'

After he had gone, Terezia made a tour of the stables, as she did every night, before returning indoors. The others had gone to bed and the room was still. The photo album lay on the table. She knew she should leave it there. The faded brown memories it held were best left to themselves. But the temptation was irresistible and, sitting down at the table, she opened the cover and began going through the pictures one by one.

They were images of another world: shooting parties in winter, the men in their tweed suits and capes, the huntsmen with their heavy black moustaches; summer walks in the hills, flowing white dresses and parasols and siestas under the trees; lazy weeks at Karlsbad and Trouville and St Moritz, the gentlemen sitting in wicker chairs with cigars and spats and panama hats; ladies reading novels, children with impractically dressed nannies, steam-yachts with high funnels lying out at sea.

And there was the house as she had never seen it before, the floors covered with Persian carpets and tiger-skin rugs, huge chandeliers hanging overhead, ornate mirrors gleaming in the magnesium flash of the camera.

Unexpectedly, she felt a tear trickle down her cheek. Angrily she brushed it aside. She hated tears. Taking the glass of Borovitszka she downed it in one. It burned in her throat. She refilled it and pored over the photos.

She could never get the house back to the way it was here; she knew that. Those days were gone, finished. She could live in it, she might even manage to inhabit a few more rooms, but she could never look after it properly. Slowly it would collapse and there was nothing she could do about it.

A tear splashed down on the black page. She wiped it away with her sleeve and drank some more. As she refilled the glass the bottle rattled against the rim.

There were times when she thought she should give in and let Zoltan take the place. At least then it would be preserved. It might even return to something approaching the way it was in these pictures, full of life and elegance, the fountains gushing, the Hungarian flag fluttering from the flagpole and that now lay mouldering in one of the back courtyards.

But she knew that this was forbidden. Whatever happened, Zoltan must never be allowed to own Fetevis.

In the early hours of the morning, seeing the light still

burning, Rosza came into the room. She found Terezia slumped over the table, the glass still in one hand, her mane of hair spread out over the surface, dead to the world.

Rosza pulled the photo album out from beneath her. She glanced at the open page and put it aside.

'Stupid girl,' she scolded under her breath. 'Why do you want to go upsetting yourself with all that?'

She shook Terezia by the shoulder but she didn't stir. Locking her hands under the girl's arms Rosza lifted her from the chair and half carried, half dragged her over to the sofa. Terezia landed in amongst the cushions in a heap. Rosza picked up her legs and stretched her out, then fetched some blankets, covered her over and left, switching off the lights. It was criminal to leave them burning all night.

12

Colonel Ferenc Biszku always held meetings in his own office. There were several reasons for this. For a start he was a busy man and it saved him time. Added to that he found he could get more out of people in police headquarters. The presence of uniformed policemen, the sense of bureaucratic authority and the sombre building itself added the kind of extra weight that one man alone can't achieve. But the most important part of it was that he was naturally rather shy and liked to have the familiar books and furniture around him when he conducted interviews.

But on this occasion he went out. It was necessary. He drove himself; the idea of chauffeurs, assistants and all the rest of the power images didn't appeal to him. So when he arrived at the British Embassy he had some difficulty in getting past the chancery guard who wasn't impressed by the baggy suit, the dishevelled hair. Colonel? This didn't look like any colonel he'd seen. He wanted to see some identification.

Biszku flicked open his wallet. The guard read it, moved

from hostile security official to helpful underling in one fluid action and had the Colonel escorted upstairs. 'No trouble at all, sir. Glad to be of service; have a good day.'

For an hour he was in conference with James Stratton. At eleven-thirty Max was summoned into the office.

It wasn't good news. He sensed it the moment he came in. Biszku was polite but distant, giving him a formal bow as they shook hands, Jimmie Stratton unnaturally helpful, fussing about the office, drawing up a chair. 'Sit yourself down, Max. There we go, that's it.'

Biszku was in no mood to beat about the bush. As soon as they were seated he said, 'I was explaining to your colleague that we've made very little advance in the case of Dr Verity.'

'We've been having a little chat, Max.' Stratton wanted to put it his way. 'Whether his murder is linked to his smuggling activity or to something else, as you have suggested, we cannot discover.'

'An extremely untidy affair.' Stratton's disappointment was in his voice. 'The fact remains that you were found at the scene of the murder and you were holding a key to the locker where the stolen items were found.'

'I think I've explained all this,' Max said.

'You have. And your Sergeant Norton corroborates much of what you said. Unfortunately, your name remains linked with the murder and as such I have asked the DHM that you leave the country.'

Max felt the words sink to the pit of his stomach like lead. 'You can't do that.'

'Unfortunately we have no alternative.'

'I had nothing to do with his death.'

'I take your word for it.' He gave a small shrug. 'Unfortunately we have no proof of what you say.'

'It's just a formality, Max,' Stratton said.

Max took his eyes off Biszku and looked round at him. Stratton's expression was understanding and kindly, like a schoolmaster who knows what's best for his boys.

Max said, 'Like heck it is, Jimmie.'

'Nobody thinks for a moment you were involved.'

'No? Then why are they kicking me out?'

'A doubt exists,' Biszku said. 'And that makes your position as a member of the diplomatic service untenable.'

Max turned to face the policeman. 'Do you personally think I had anything to do with his murder?'

He started to say that it wasn't his place to comment on such things but Max cut him short.

'No, tell me straight. Do you think it was me?'

Biszku drummed his fingers on the arm of his chair. He didn't want the conversation to turn personal. He looked up. 'No. To be perfectly frank I don't think you did any more than you say. But I'm afraid that while we are unable to eliminate your name from the enquiry we must ask for you to be withdrawn from the Embassy.'

'When do I have to go?'

'Shall we say the end of the week?'

'Friday?'

Biszku nodded.

'But that only gives me four days.'

'Do you have a reason to delay?'

'So that's it,' Max said after the policeman had left. 'End of career. Finito.'

'Of course it's not.'

'No trial, no chance of appeal, just told to get out.'

'It's just a way of avoiding any unpleasantness. It won't affect your career in any way.'

'No? It'll be there in the records. Kicked out of Hungary as a suspected murderer.'

'It's not like that, Max. Believe me. I'll see to it that it's not like that.'

'I can hear them now: "Max Anderson? Wasn't he tied up with some sort of fuss in Moscow before that? Nothing proved of course but you know what they say, no smoke without fire." Hell, Jimmie, I'll never work again.'

Stratton shook his head. 'Don't get in a stew, Max. It's really not that bad. It's just that in our line of business we can't allow the mud to stick.'

'It hasn't stuck!'

'I understand how you feel—'

'I don't think you've got the slightest idea how I feel.'

'Don't get cross. I know it's not easy but look at it this way, you'll be getting a new posting in a few weeks, with a bit of free holiday in the meantime and nothing will show up in the files, I can promise you that. Hell, you might even get a promotion out of it. The Service is always generous with those who get mistreated.'

Max didn't want a new posting; he didn't want a compulsory holiday and he didn't want charity from a Service that hadn't the strength to look after its own. What he wanted was to get out of that office. And he did, slamming the door after him.

He took the millennium metro up to Heroes Square. It was snowing again, soft flakes falling casually from a leaden sky. In the distance the Vajdahunyad Castle was just a blur, the lake in front swarming with skaters. With his scarf wrapped round his face, he crossed the huge expanse of the square, past the statues of the Magyar chieftains, craggy and menacing and fierce as hawks.

There was no sign of Terezia until he reached the steps of the Fine Art Museum. Then she appeared from behind a coffee stall, crunching across the snow towards him.

'Where have you been?' she called out. 'I've been waiting for ages.'

He said he'd been held up in a meeting. He didn't want her to know he was being kicked out of the country in a couple of days. He could hardly believe it himself.

'Have you got any money on you?' she asked. 'I had some coffee while I was waiting. It was so cold. But I hadn't got enough money on me.'

Max went over and paid the man. She thanked him meekly and said that it hadn't occurred to her that she'd need any money while she was here. They went up the steps of the museum.

'How are you?' he asked.

'Good.' She ran one hand through her hair. 'Actually, not so good,' she admitted. 'I was feeling terrible this morning when I woke up. I think I drank too much.'

She didn't look terrible. Beneath her fur hat her face was glowing from the cold. They gave their names at the reception and waited. Terezia seemed nervous.

'We're very late.'

'People expect aristocrats to be late.'

She was looking round the hallway of the museum, distracted. 'I'm not an aristocrat.'

'Don't tell him that.'

The curator had appeared down the long flight of marble steps. He was in his forties with spectacles and a small, pointed chin and spoke with a slight bewilderment as though he wasn't used to confronting other members of the human race in his museum. His name, he explained as he shook Terezia's hand, was Janos Ottlik.

He took them down into the basement where a vast number of canvases were stored in several chambers below ground level. Ottlik consulted his file.

'The museum is presently holding forty-seven paintings from the Palace of Fetevis. Eleven of them are upstairs on public display, the others are down here in the reserve collection.'

With the aid of a couple of porters, he had them brought out and lined up along the wall. The sizes varied from tiny Dutch still lives, glittering in translucent shadow, to the vast scenes of ancient mythology that had once been set into the ceilings.

Terezia examined them in silence, walking beside the curator like a visiting dignitary inspecting the troops. It wasn't until she came to some portraits that she said, 'But these should be in the house.'

The curator made no comment.

'No one else wants them. They're only of interest to the family.'

'Well, that may be true.'

Squatting down, she examined her ancestors. To Max they looked a mixed bag, the earlier ones grim-faced and tough, with suits of armour and codpieces and ferocious beards; those from the last century more elegant, the dress uniforms crusted with medals and stars, wispy moustaches on the upper lips, the eyes dreamy.

She wanted them. Max could see it in the intent, almost hungry look in her eyes. She wanted these pictures back in her possession. She may hate her house, hate the burden of its debts and demands, but the sense of dynasty burned in her hard and true.

Ottlik was keen to make his position clear. 'I should remind you, Countess, that all these belong to the State.

While we might not condone the regime under which they were acquired, the fact remains that they were legally passed into our possession.'

'But it's terrible to keep them locked up down here.'

'I agree.'

'Those ones from the ceiling should be put back there. They'd look wonderful.'

'I'm sure they would but sadly it is not so simple. Your family formally renounced all claim to the collection fifty years ago.'

Max said, 'But now that the estate has been returned to the Countess shouldn't the pictures be handed back to her as well?'

'Some of them,' he agreed. 'Not all.'

'You mean not the valuable ones.'

Ottlik didn't entirely like the sharpness of this observation but he accepted the point.

'In a way, yes.'

'So you're not going to give them back.'

'We're not obliged to.' He paused, assembling the information together in his mind. He was an orderly man. 'When the contents of the Palace were removed it was all assessed for value. The more important pieces were put in here, and in the Museum of Applied Arts. I believe they have quite a few items from the house. The rest was stored locally. That has already been returned to the Countess.'

'But why not this stuff?'

'Because the late Count gave them to the State.'

'You mean he was told to hand them over or get a bullet in the head.'

Ottlik made a small gesture of his hand to say there was no telling how the deal was made. 'He gave them to the nation. We have the receipt here in the museum.'

'It's not worth a bean. Any contract made under pressure isn't legally binding.'

'There is nothing to say it was made under pressure. The Count was paid for everything that was put in here.'

Terezia turned. 'I never heard that.'

'Oh, yes. A substantial sum was paid to your father at the time. You are perfectly entitled to buy them back. I'm sure the museum would be prepared to negotiate on the lesser works down here. But there is no question of giving them back. We have not held them under false pretences. I was explaining this to your cousin when he bought one of them last year.'

Terezia was amazed. 'Zoltan bought a picture from you?'

'The Sargent portrait. It was of, er . . . I'm not good at calculating these things . . . your great-grandparents, I imagine it is.'

'But they're mine!'

'I'm afraid not.'

Max was thinking it through. 'How can you have paid the Count for his paintings when he was in jail?'

Ottlik wasn't sure of that. 'There must have been an account,' he said.

'He didn't have an account. He didn't have anything.'

'The transaction was made.'

'The man had just had everything he owned taken away from him. He wouldn't have got an account to pay into.'

'You would have to talk to his solicitors about that.'

'They'll be long gone.'

'Not necessarily. Solicitors have a way of surviving, particularly your English firms.'

'They were English?' Max was amazed.

'The payment was made through a solicitors' firm in London. Did you not know that? They hold the copy of the receipt for the pictures. I can find the name of it if you like.'

'We must ring them, pronto,' Max said as they came out of the museum.

'But why would they have a solicitor in London rather than here?' Terezia asked breathlessly.

'Your family probably reckoned London was safer than Budapest.'

'But why?'

'Because it's got twenty-three miles of water between it and anyone who's thinking of sticking their flag on it, and it's less inclined to have revolutions than you guys. And that makes it a good place to keep valuable things.'

Terezia was running to keep up with him as they crossed the bleak square. 'What sort of valuable things?'

'Money for a start.'

'You think there's some left there?'

'There may be. There's just a chance that your father had accounts outside the country. They may still exist.'

'But I never heard of any accounts.'

'You'd never heard of his solicitors until just now.'

They took the millennium train back to the Embassy and went up to Max's office. As he came in his secretary, Janet, looked up hurriedly from her desk. She spoke in a rush. 'Oh, Max, I've just heard. I can't believe it . . .' Her voice trailed off as she saw Terezia behind him.

Max pulled up a chair for her. She sat down and pulled off her hat, her hair falling in a cascade of gold around her shoulders. Janet stared at her from the other side of the room.

Throwing himself into his chair, Max picked up the phone and dialled the international directory.

'It would be better if you spoke to them,' he said.

'I can't speak English.'

And they sure as hell won't speak Hungarian. 'Okay,' he said. 'I'll give it a go.' The line connected and he spoke into the receiver. 'I want a number in London, England. It's a firm of solicitors, name of Roper & Wilkes.'

The call was routed through to William Pemberton, a specialist in Trust and Probate and a partner in the old, respected and prosperous firm of solicitors whose offices were situated in a four-storey stuccoed building in Lincoln's Inn Fields.

Pemberton didn't usually accept this kind of phone call personally. Inquiries into the archives of previous clients were a waste of his and the firm's time. There was no account that could be charged for the task and consequently they were known as 'nuisance calls'.

But when he heard the name Kasinczy-Landsberg he had the line connected immediately. His secretary went to bring up the file. It was curious, he thought as she plumped it down on his desk, for fifty years it had lain in the vaults untouched. Now, in the space of two weeks, it had been brought out three times. And each time for a different caller.

He sorted through the thick wad of papers.

'Yes,' he said cautiously, 'we hold a receipt for the sale of paintings made between Count Karoly Istvan Kasinczy-Landsberg and the Hungarian Ministry of Culture on 23rd March 1947.

'Was there a payment made for this?' Max asked.

'May I inquire under what authority you are asking these questions?'

'I'm acting as agent for the present Countess.'

'Can you confirm that?'

'How's your Hungarian?' Max asked sweetly. 'She's here with me now, you can speak to her if you like.'

'That won't be necessary. You say you're ringing from the Embassy?'

'That's right.'

Pemberton glanced across at his secretary. She nodded in confirmation. It took only seconds to trace a call these days. 'I think we can take it your credentials are good. Yes, a payment of three thousand American dollars was made at the time of sale.'

'Do you know where it was made?'

Pemberton consulted the document. Surprisingly, a detailed memo on this subject had been added by his predecessor. 'The money was credited to an account in the Count's name in the National Bank in Budapest.'

There was silence on the other end of the line. A hand had gone over the receiver. He was talking to the Countess. Was she like Zsa Zsa Gabor, he wondered, with dripping pearls, a suntanned cleavage and an accent gravelly enough to strip paint? It was a nice idea.

Max came back on the line. 'Can I just get this straight. You say the money went into an account in the Count's name?'

'That's correct.'

'In Hungary?'

'I have an address in Budapest.'

'We don't see how he could have had an account in Hungary. You may not know this but he'd just been put in jail as an undesirable. Everything he owned had been seized by the State. He wasn't allowed bank accounts.'

'It was not opened by him,' Pemberton said. 'It was opened by the Ministry in his name so that the money could be passed into it.'

'So it may still be there?'

'No, the account was closed shortly afterwards.'

'By whom?'

'By the Ministry.'

There was silence again. 'Let me get this straight – are you telling me that the Ministry opened an account, put this money they owed him into it, and then closed it again?'

'That's correct.'

'So where the heck did the money get to?'

'It was returned to the State, Mr Anderson.'

'Jesus Christ—'

'As you said, under the terms of his imprisonment the Count was not allowed to own money or possessions. Anything in a bank account in his name belonged to the State.'

'So they paid him for his paintings, knowing perfectly well the money would be returned to them straight away.'

'That's what the law required.'

'Bastards.'

'That's not for me to comment.'

As he put down the phone, Pemberton took the three closely typewritten sheets of instructions from the folder. It had arrived only days before. Picking up the receiver again he dialled the number at the head of the page.

The voice at the other end spoke in Hungarian. Pemberton gave his name and the other reverted to English.

'What can I do for you, Mr Pemberton?'

'I had an inquiry into the file we hold in the name of Count Karoly—'

'Who from?' The other cut him off before he could finish the name.

'A Mr Maxwell Anderson. He was from the British Embassy in Budapest.'

'Yeah, okay, I know of him.'

'He said he was phoning on behalf of the Countess—'

'There is no Countess, Mr Pemberton.' He spoke with a slight American accent, drawing out the words. 'What did he want?'

'He was inquiring into the sale of the family paintings in 1947.'

There was silence. 'Nothing else?'

'No.'

'What did you tell him?'

'That we hold the receipt for the sale and that the money was passed into a bank account that is now closed.'

'He didn't ask about the rest?'

'No.'

'Is he aware that there is more in the file?'

'I don't think so, sir.'

'Okay. Keep me informed. You hear anything more from him you tell me, you got that.'

'Of course, sir.'

The line went dead. Pemberton put down the receiver. It was idiotic – a man he'd never met in a country he'd never been to, and yet speaking to him made his hand shake. He consoled himself with charging two hundred and fifty pounds for the pleasure.

13

The call came at eight-thirty a.m. Max was eating toast in the tiny kitchen of his apartment. He reached across the table and grabbed the receiver off the wall.

'Yes?'

'This is Laszlo Vargas. We met at Fetevis Palace the other day.'

'What can I do for you, Mr Vargas?' He put down his toast. He was suddenly very wide awake.

'My client feels that some confusion has arisen since our last meeting.'

'Client, Mr Vargas? Just who is your client?'

'Count Zoltan Kasinczy-Landsberg.'

The big cheese himself. For some reason Vargas didn't like saying the name. Maybe he was Jewish and thought it was another name for God. Which, in any case, it probably was.

'And what's confusing him then?'

'He would like to talk to you, Mr Anderson.'

'Fine, put him on the line.'

'No.' Vargas wasn't going to be hustled by any flippancy. 'In person; the Count feels it would be useful if you were to meet in person. Twelve tomorrow would suit him.'

There was no point in arguing. Vargas was just a messenger boy that morning, passing on an order from his boss.

'Okay,' he said. 'Where's he want to meet?'

'He'll send a car.' There was a pause and he added, 'The Count would prefer it if you were not to mention this meeting to Kisasszony Terezia beforehand.'

'Why's that?'

'What he has to say to you is . . . private.'

At eleven o'clock that night the Presidential car drew up outside the large, overheated and over lit house in Szabadsag Ter and the driver went inside to announce his arrival. Within minutes the President appeared, brushing past the journalists who hovered around the doorway, his lower lip thrust out in the familiar bulldog expression that had earned him a reputation for blunt speaking and hard bargaining.

The President left every reception in this abrupt way. It created an impression of a man with pressing matters of State to attend to and disguised the fact that he had precious little small talk. He could make a good speech in the House, under attack from the other parties he could come up with the occasional sharp reply, but when it came to social occasions he hadn't got two words he could string together.

As he was getting into the car he spotted Bela Bessenyei further down the street, who was hoping to use the President's familiar early escape to make his own getaway.

'You want a lift?' he barked.

'It's very kind of you, President. I've got my own car.'

'I'm going your way, I can drop you off.'

Bessenyei didn't want a lift. He had a rather promising offer of a nightcap from an actress he'd met a couple of evenings before. But the opened door didn't offer much in the way of escape and he climbed in. As the car drew out into the stream of the traffic, the President sat back in the deep leather seats, opened his coat and spread his legs wide.

'What the heck's going on, Bela?'

There were innumerable replies to the question. Bessenyei contented himself with one. 'How do you mean?'

'This Kasinczy-Landsberg affair. I thought it was all fixed up. The court case went on long enough. I thought it was agreed that the daughter cops the lot.'

'It was.'

'So what's changed?'

'It seems there's a possibility she's not his daughter. I've opened an inquiry.'

The President shifted in his seat uncomfortably. 'Do we have to get involved with it?'

'It'd look very odd if we didn't.'

It was the image that concerned the President. 'Couldn't we just be looking the other way? We've been the good guys in this business so far, standing up for the underdog. It wasn't meant to be like that but it hasn't done us any harm.'

'And it's not going to do us any good if she turns out to be an impostor.'

'But what evidence have they got?'

'There's no birth certificate.'

The President sat staring out of the window as he waited for Bessenyei to go on. When he didn't he turned, his eyebrows raised in the expression he fondly imagined shrivelled the opposition during parliamentary debates.

'That's it?'

'How much more do you need?'

'A goddamned slip of paper? Is that it? It's probably fallen down behind the filing cabinet.'

Bessenyei shook his head. 'It's not there.'

'Have you been down to check?'

'It's not there.'

'There's bound to be one; it's just a matter of searching.'

'It's not there, President.'

Bessenyei repeated the words slowly and softly, as though speaking to an imbecile. Slowly the President took their meaning. He gaped across the dark confines of the car.

'Jesus,' he whispered. 'You're not saying . . .'

'There is no birth certificate.'

'You mean you . . .'

'I mean we didn't get much alternative.'

'Are you out of your mind?' The President could see the headlines screaming out the story on every breakfast table in the country. 'The elections are coming up. We can't afford a scandal, Bela.'

'And we can't afford to let him go. If Zoltan doesn't get that palace of his he'll leave the country.'

'Is that the end of the world?'

'Apart from the fact that the Landsberg Corporation employs a workforce of thirty thousand and pulls in enough revenue to fund the civil service single-handed, you mustn't forget he also contributes almost a third of Party funds.'

The President swore to himself, not so much because they were caught by the short and curlies but because he was President of this goddamned country and would never pull down a fraction of that kind of money.

'How did the bastard get so rich?'

'Good old American know-how,' the minister said. 'Coupled with good old Hungarian cheap labour.'

'So what do we do?'

'We chuck the girl to the wolves.'

The President totted up the odds. 'The press aren't going to like it.'

'The press will hardly know about it. I was talking to

Zoltan's lawyer this morning. He says it won't go to court this time.'

'Why not?'

'I don't know, but he promised me there'll be no court case. She's going to go quickly – no fuss, no bother.'

'I hope you're right, Bela,' the President said. 'I want this finished.'

He rapped on the glass panel that separated them from the driver. The car slid into the kerb and the door was opened. As Bessenyei stepped out, the President leaned forward.

'You were discreet about this, I trust?'

'What do you take me for?'

'A bloody moron at times.' He thought for a moment. 'Sweeten the pill, Bela.'

'In what way?'

'I don't know. Think of something.'

The young man who opened the door at twelve the following day had short hair, a thick neck and the lazy magnificence of a bouncer. He stared at Max in silence as he passed. A mobile phone bulged from his back pocket but apart from that there was no indication that he had a tongue in his head.

A suited figure materialised from within the house. He was older, deferential, in charge.

'If you'd care to follow me,' he said with a bow. 'The Count will see you directly.'

Max hadn't formed much impression of the building as he approached, except to note that it was large, low and modern – more Beverly Hills than Budapest – but he realised now as he followed the manservant that it wasn't designed to be seen from outside.

It was the inside that mattered.

The hallway was completely black, the floor, walls and

ceiling all cut from the same gleaming black marble. The beam of a powerful spotlight crossed the room and fell on a single painting twice his own height. It was full of convoluted figures, the upper part of the canvas rounded, a sure sign that it had started life over the altar of some Italian church. What it had looked like back in Italy Max had no idea but it was an awe-inspiring sight here on this black marble wall. He found himself almost tiptoeing as he passed the thing.

After taking him through to the living room beyond, the manservant removed himself, murmuring assurances that the Count would join him shortly.

The room was a large open-plan affair, sunk down below ground level. A log fire burned in the grate and there were thick carpets on the ground. More paintings filled the walls, each one nestling in a gold frame and the beam of a spotlight. What Max knew about art could be written on the back of a postage stamp but he could sense that these were the kind of heavyweight masterpieces that you usually queued up to see in museums. Whatever it was that the Landsberg Corporation did with themselves, it was keeping its boss in the manner to which his ancestors would have been accustomed.

There was a portrait of two of them over the mantelpiece: an impossibly elegant couple. The man, wearing an opened waistcoat and a felt hat on the back of his head, a cheroot in his hand, looked as though he'd just strolled in from an afternoon's partridge shooting. Beside him stood a young woman who was at that very moment heading out to a ball in a dress of flashing white satin. On the table between them was what Max assumed at first to be a clock. But when he checked it a little closer he noticed that it didn't have a face. It was just an ornament, like an oversized piece of jewellery.

As he was studying it, a voice behind him said, 'I see you like paintings, Mr Anderson.'

He turned to see a man in his sixties coming down the steps towards him. He was dressed in a cravat and blue blazer, with comfortable suede brogues beneath flannel trousers. He gave Max a handshake that would have cracked walnuts. 'Count Zoltan.'

'Pleased to meet you.' Max recognised him from the photo immediately. Fifty years on, the smooth, boyish looks eroded and lined with the years, but unmistakable just the same.

'Are you interested in paintings, Mr Anderson?' The accent was Ivy League American, soft, patrician, with just a dash of something foreign to give it class.

'I know what I don't like.'

'Very wise.'

Zoltan gave a smile and there was warmth and friendship in the green-grey eyes, in the laugh lines that sprang up in the tanned skin around them and Max thought: Hell, this man should have stayed in America. With looks like this he'd have made President.

Zoltan was looking up at the portrait.

'My great-grandparents,' he said. 'Istvan Kasinczy and Sophie Landsberg. They're the ones who brought the name together. Sophie was Austrian, rather beautiful and very wealthy. Her family didn't mind her marrying into the Hungarian aristocracy, even those who had soiled their hands in industry, provided the name didn't go with it.' He smiled faintly at the thought that there could ever have been a time when it was demeaning to marry one of his ancestors. 'It's by Sargent. He painted them while they were over in England. Sophie was a great friend of the Empress Sisi. They shared a passion for hunting your foxes.'

'It looks as though her husband wasn't averse to a bit of hunting himself.'

'You got it,' Zoltan said with a touch of weariness. 'All my family have been great sportsmen. Horses and shooting, that's all they ever thought of. The one aspect of their character which fortunately they haven't passed on to me.'

Max was tempted to tell him that they had passed on quite a dose of it to his cousin when Vargas appeared in the wake of a tall woman who was immaculately dressed and fitted out with enough jewellery to attend a State banquet.

'My wife, Elaine,' Zoltan said.

She must have been a handsome woman in her prime, and still remarkably well preserved with that smooth, unmoving expression that's the hallmark of the face-lifter's art. She nodded to Max as she was introduced and took a seat, Vargas moving in to touch the back of her chair as she did do.

'And Laszlo I believe you've already met,' Zoltan added.

With the formality of a duellist, Vargas gave him a stiff bow from the waist and clicked his heels, a little performance Max guessed he'd picked up from a film.

As if on cue, the manservant appeared with a tray of champagne and glasses. He removed the cork with a deft twist of the wrist and a soft plop and then withdrew.

'Mr Anderson was just admiring our paintings,' Zoltan informed his wife as he poured the champagne.

'It's quite a collection you've got,' Max said. Embassy life had taught him that the odd compliment never went amiss.

Elaine Kasinczy-Landsberg frowned distantly as though she were being troubled by an irritating fly and said, 'It's a hobby of my husband's. I've tried but I can't cure it.'

The accent was Southern, a slow drawl, redolent of

swamplands, white-columned verandas and the hint of a Negro Spiritual drifting across the plantation.

'Paintings are the one temptation I can't resist.' Zoltan didn't even try to deny the accusation. 'Can I offer you a glass of champagne, Mr Anderson? I can get you something stronger if you prefer but I find myself that champagne is the only appropriate drink at this time of the day.'

There was the merest suggestion that he was being taught how to behave himself in society but in his line of business Max was used to this and he took the glass without comment.

'The one advantage of being a refugee from your own country,' Zoltan continued, 'is that you are able to build up a collection of pictures from scratch. You're not dictated to by your ancestors' taste which is at best eccentric but usually execrable.'

Having never inherited anything more dramatic than a watercolour of Colwyn Bay from his great-aunt, Max had never been faced with this dilemma.

'You're lucky to find a house to fit them all in so well,' he said.

Zoltan was surprised he should think so. 'I never tried. I built the house around the paintings.'

'I guess that gets around some of the problems.'

'My parents lived here before me, of course. But the house they owned didn't suit me. I had it knocked down and started again. It was the only practical thing to do.'

And devoid of any sense of sentiment or nostalgia, Max thought to himself. But then Zoltan didn't want to live in the house he was brought up in; he wanted to live in the Palace he hadn't been.

'I showed the architect my collection and told him to tailor something around it. The one exception was this portrait of my grandparents. That's a recent addition.'

'Is it the painting you bought from the Museum of Fine Art?' Max asked.

'It is.' Zoltan was impressed by the accuracy of his information. 'How very interesting, now how do you come to know that?'

'I was round there a couple of days ago, with your cousin Terezia.'

He nodded as though he was glad the name had been raised and they could do away with the social hors d'oeuvres.

'I hear you have been taking a keen interest in her affairs, Mr Anderson.'

'It's not an interest. I just happened to be around.'

'Laszlo seems to have formed the impression that it's more than that; that you've been lending her expert legal advice.'

Nice of him to rate it as expert, Max thought. 'She asked me to sit in on the meeting the other day. I think she was feeling rather outnumbered.'

'I'm sure she was most grateful to you,' Zoltan said warmly and for an instant his gaze held Max's, hard and unwavering, as though he were trying to extract whatever else Max might be holding back. 'Laszlo tells me she is living in just one wing – part of the servants' quarters?'

'I think it's the only part of the place that's habitable at present.'

Zoltan shook his head, unable to comprehend such a meagre existence.

'You must have seen the place yourself,' Max said.

'Oh, you bet I have, Mr Anderson.'

'It's falling to bits around her ears.'

'A bloody disgrace,' he said, looking away quickly, as if the image of his rotting inheritance had suddenly flashed across his eyes. 'It should never have been allowed to get to this.

Fetevis is one of the best hunks of real estate in the country – both historically and architecturally. To let it fall into decay like that is criminal, quite criminal. But I doubt there is much she's going to do about it, is there?'

'I doubt there is.'

'It'll take more than keeping a few nags in the stables to get the place back in working order. Just reversing the structural damage of the past fifty years will cost a fortune.'

'As I think you made clear to her.'

'I have?' Zoltan seemed surprised to hear it.

'Haven't you been chasing her for some money you put into restoring the roof?'

'Oh, that.' Zoltan brushed aside this small infringement of good manners. 'Yeah, I asked her to cough up a bit but that's because I thought it might inject a little reality into the situation. Please don't get me wrong, Mr Anderson. It's not the money. I'm not bothered with what it cost me to stop the house from collapsing. It's a job that needed doing and I'm glad to have done it. The reason I asked her to pay it back is to try to draw her attention to the kind of figures we're talking about. I don't think she has any idea what it will cost to look after that house.'

'You've practically bankrupted her.'

'Of course I have.' Zoltan could see Max was getting his point. 'Just a simple piece of damage restriction has cleaned out her piggy bank. And it's hardly surprising. This is a peasant girl from the country we're talking about. She hasn't got a dime to spend in a candy store. She can't be expected to preserve a stately home, let alone restore it. Surely she can realise that?'

'It's a difficult position,' Max agreed.

'You see what I'm getting at? I don't want to bankrupt the girl but she's putting me in an impossible position. When I put it to the Government that they should allow me to take on the Palace I knew what I was doing. The house needs work to stop it collapsing into a pile of rubbish, and it needs it like yesterday. And that costs money – money with zeros on the end of it. The Government hasn't got it – what government does – but fortunately I do.'

He filled Max's glass and then waved his arm vaguely around the room, bottle in hand, to indicate the scale of financial clout he had at his command.

'It was just a piece of good old-fashioned horse trading. They had a problem, I had the money to solve it so we struck a deal. Everyone was happy – until this girl shows up.'

'Tactless of her.' Max could see it from his side.

'Tactless? Tactless diddly; it's downright irresponsible. If she stays there any longer the whole darned thing's going to come down round her pretty arse, and that's vandalism, Mr Anderson. Cultural-bloody-vandalism.'

'I think she knows that—'

'If you pardon my French.' The fine aristocratic features he'd inherited from his Hungarian ancestors and the overripe language he'd picked up in the land-of-the-free made a strange combination. He glanced up at the portrait, as if the same thought had struck him, and then down again.

'What the hell's she want to do it for?'

'I don't think she's much option, has she?

'I mean why the tarnation is she up there?'

'She's the heir.'

At the mention of this word, Zoltan's whole manner seemed to drop twenty degrees. Carefully he put the bottle back on the tray and turned to face Max.

'She's not the heir, Mr Anderson. Let's get that straight from the start. She's a claimant.'

'A successful one.'

'At present. The lawyers have got themselves in a tangle. It's going to take a little time to straighten it all out. But I'm the heir to Fetevis. I always was and I always will be. Terezia Kovacs is just a claimant who's had a lucky break.

He believed it, Max realised. He hadn't persuaded himself he was the heir. He knew it like he knew his own name.

'She's the daughter,' he pointed out.

'We have no proof of that.'

'She's just a peasant girl,' Elaine said from her straight-backed chair. She'd been silent while her husband was talking but now that it was a matter of character assessment she wanted her say. 'From what I hear she's practically illiterate. God knows how she got round the lawyers but the sooner she's thrown out of the house the better.'

'What beats me is why she wants to live there in the first place,' Zoltan said.

Max said. 'She doesn't.'

'No? Then why's she hanging on to it tooth and claw?'

'Because she's put a lot of money into repairing the stables and she can't afford to let it go.'

Zoltan hesitated, looking for the catch. 'That's it?'

'As far as I know.'

'Then why did she take it on?'

'I don't think she was given much alternative. But she's not possessive about the place, if that's what you're wondering. In fact, if there were some way she could wash her hands of it I think she'd go for it.'

'No kidding?'

'That's the impression I get.'

Zoltan's eyes flicked across to Vargas for an instant, then back. 'She told you this straight?'

'Not in so many words, but yes, she told me.'

'If the terms were right, you reckon she'd do a deal?'

'I think she might.'

Zoltan took a sip of his champagne, his eyes cool and speculative as he studied Max over the rim of the glass.

'Interesting,' he said. 'It's kind of how we figured it ourselves, Mr Anderson. It's why we called you along this morning.' His voice was warming up again, taking on a richness. 'I'll make her a proposition, Mr Anderson, and you can pass it on to her. She has no right to the estate but I'm sick as a dog of wrangling over it so I'm prepared to make a deal. The day she drops her claim to my family I'll pay ten million dollars into any bank she likes outside Hungary.'

Had he not developed the diplomat's ability to detach his facial expressions from his feelings, Max's jaw would have hit the ground. It was a fortune, even for someone as loaded as Zoltan Kasinczy-Landsberg. He must be desperate.

'How's that strike you, Mr Anderson?'

'American dollars?' He wanted to be sure they were talking the same language.

'Why? Isn't it enough?'

'I've no idea.'

'Ten million American dollars in nice, new, crinkly notes the day she drops all claim to the title and the estate and clears out of the country. And that's my final offer.'

Max shrugged. 'I'll put it to her.'

'Do that,' Zoltan said bluntly. 'Tell her she won't find a better deal anywhere else in town. With money like that she can buy a whole string of stud farms.'

'I'm sure she'll take the offer seriously,' Max said. He also knew she was going to leap at it. From impoverished aristocracy to millionairess in one bound. That's not something that happened to everyone.

'All claim to the family name, mind you, Mr Anderson.

That's the deal. She drops all claim to the family name and gets out or she doesn't get a dime.'

Max told him he'd got it and put down his glass. The meeting was evidently over.

As he was leaving he said, 'Tell me, what's that weird thing up there?'

'What weird thing?' Zoltan inquired.

Max pointed up to the portrait. 'That piece of silver standing there on the table.'

'That's the Hunyadi Venus, Mr Anderson.' He saw the name didn't register. 'You never heard of it?'

'I can't say I have.'

The glittering object was hard to make out clearly in the painting. Much of it was dissolved in shadow, the lit parts a tangle of flashing brush strokes. But from what Max could see it was the figure of a naked girl reaching up out of the sea, or maybe it was from other naked figures who lay at her feet, their hair swirling around them to look like the sea. Whichever way, there was something raw and sensuous about the thing standing there on the table between the handsome, smiling couple.

'Five hundred years that belonged to our family,' Zoltan said.

'Belonged?'

'The Russians took it at the end of the war. It hasn't been seen since then.'

'It looks quite something.'

'It was.'

'You knew it?'

'Oh yes,' he said softly. 'I knew it. And now, if you'll forgive me, Mr Anderson, I must go. I've business to attend to.'

The car that had brought him there was waiting at the

entrance, long and low and black. When it had taken him a mile from Zoltan's house, Max put through a call to Terezia on his mobile. He got Rosza on the line.

'She's not here,' the old woman said, shouting to get her voice down the wire. 'She's gone into Budapest.'

'Do you know where?'

'To see that solicitor of hers. He said something important had come up.'

'An inquiry? It can't be true!'

'It's just a formality, Countess.'

'If I lose the house now I won't have anything at all,' Terezia cried. 'In fact worse. I'll have less than I had before.'

'I know that.'

'They can't just take it away from me.'

'It hasn't come to that yet,' Szelkely said. 'If the inquiry finds there are sufficient grounds for doubt your cousin will be allowed to appeal and the case will have to be reopened. But that's still a long way off.'

'If Zoltan wants to go to court again he will,' Terezia said bitterly.

From the other side of the desk, with its silver-topped inkstands and Galle lamp, Victor Szelkely studied her in silence. It was awe-inspiring to think that but for a twist in the course of history this girl who sat opposite him, an expression of grave indignation on her face, would have been one of the richest women in Europe. As it was she was only just keeping her head above water financially, and just about to drown completely.

He didn't like to say so but he didn't think she stood a chance against her cousin Zoltan. The law had been devised to protect the weak against the strong but, as every lawyer knew, anyone with the time, the money and the determination to slug it out in the courtroom eventually won. And Zoltan had all three of those in bags.

'There's nothing sacred about the birth certificate itself, Countess,' he said. 'It's simply a way of establishing who you are. There are other ways.'

Terezia looked up. 'Such as what?'

'Do you have anything in your real name – a passport, identity papers? Something which will show who you were before you changed your name. Even a bank account would be useful.'

'I don't think there's anything like that. I was only twelve.'

'Is there anyone who was around at the time of your birth who could give evidence?'

Again she shook her head.

'It would only take one solid statement to blow this whole inquiry out of the water.'

'I'm not sure I know anyone from when I was very young,' she said, getting to her feet to leave. 'In fact I'm not sure I know where my parents were living when I was born.'

'The Kovacs – could they help?'

'Maybe. I can ask them.' He could see from her expression that she didn't hold much hope.

After they had parted, Terezia walked back towards the car. She'd parked it on the outskirts of town where you didn't have to pay and taken the metro in but she wanted to walk now. It gave her time to think.

An afternoon concert was ending as she passed the Opera, figures spilling out of the doors and over the steps. None of them gave more than a glance at the tall girl who strode past, her hands buried in her overcoat pockets, eyes fixed on the pavement in front of her.

Some of the confused feelings that coursed through her mind as she walked she could identify. There was anger and frustration, an unbearable sense of unfairness at what was happening to her. But there was something else too, an emptiness, a sort of aching void at the thought of losing Fetevis that she didn't recognise.

What Szelkely didn't understand – probably couldn't understand – was that there was no way she could prove her identity. All references to her true name had been destroyed at the time of her father's arrest. If they hadn't she wouldn't be here now. She could remember Joszef going through their home searching out letters and photos and school reports and burning them.

From that moment Terezia Kasinczy had ceased to exist.

She was close to the British Embassy now. Not that she was heading that way intentionally; it just happened to be on the way. But since she was near she thought she might talk to Max. Actually that wasn't true, she told herself with a flash of annoyance. She badly wanted to talk to him. He was the one person who would understand what was happening, the one person who might even be able to help. Beneath that casual, rather flippant British character of his there was a comforting certainty about Max which was exactly what she needed right now.

The security guard on the desk was understanding. He wasn't supposed to reveal where the diplomats lived. But he recognised her from the time she was last there and the poor girl looked so pale and lost that he couldn't see it would do any harm.

The address he gave her was for an apartment building only a few blocks round the corner from the Embassy. It was a tall, lead-roofed affair put up at the time when Budapest was trying to be bigger, smarter and naughtier than Paris.

As she came to it, searching above the doorways for the

number, a long black car slid up the street from the other direction and drew into the kerb. The rear door opened and a figure climbed out.

It was Max.

Terezia stood stock still and watched as he made some comment to the driver and let himself into the flat. As the door closed, the car pulled out into the street again and came cruising towards her, passing just a few feet away from where she was. It was a long-wheelbase Cadillac, with darkened windows and a silver ornament on the bonnet, the aerial on the rear boot shaped like a boomerang.

She knew this car. She'd seen it parked day after day outside the law courts. There couldn't be another like it in the city.

It was Zoltan's.

14

The phone was ringing as Max let himself into his flat. Without bothering to close the door behind him he picked it up. He was half expecting it to be Terezia returning his call but it was Jimmie Stratton. He sounded genial and relaxed, in the mood for a party.

'How's it going then, Max?'

Max told him that he wasn't too bad, which in the circumstances was optimistic.

'What are you up to at the moment?'

'Not much.'

'How about supper with Sally and me tonight? Nothing formal, just a get-together round the kitchen table.'

'Can't do tonight; I've got to go out in a few minutes.'

'Tomorrow maybe?'

It was just a game. Neither of them wanted to have dinner together but Jimmie had to suggest it to ease his conscience and Max had to think of a reason he couldn't without being openly rude.

'I'm a bit tied up at present, Jimmie,' he said. 'There are a few people I must see before I leave.' Hardly original but it was the best he could come up with on the spur of the moment.

It suited Stratton's mood to read his own meaning into the empty spaces. 'Taking leave of all those names in the famous Anderson black book, eh Max?'

'Something like that.'

There was a pause and he said, 'You're okay, are you?'

'I'm fine, Jimmie.'

'When are you off?'

'Friday – day after tomorrow.' Jesus, Max thought, was it that soon?

'You'll drop in and see us at the office before you go? We don't want you just creeping off.'

'I'll come round.'

'Good.' Stratton sounded relieved as he rang off. Mission completed. He'd made the gesture, he couldn't do more.

Max put down the receiver and looked around the flat. He hadn't even thought about packing up yet. Not that there was much to do. The furniture came with the place, the pictures were on loan from some nebulous department of the Embassy and whatever was in the cupboards that was both edible and durable he'd leave for the next inmate. The rest of his belongings he could pack into a couple of suitcases. It wouldn't take him more than an evening. When he'd left Moscow he'd done it in under an hour with a pair of Russian gorillas standing out in the street to make sure he didn't try to do a runner. Since then he hadn't bothered to accumulate much in the way of possessions around him.

The hour-long drive out to Fetevis seemed shorter now he knew the way. The gates were locked when he arrived, as they had been the first time he turned up, and he had to clamber up the steep driveway. This was another journey that he was getting to know, although for some reason it felt longer every time.

It was Rosza, short and inscrutable, who opened the door when he knocked, her mole's face peering out into the dark at him. Without a word she beckoned him inside and removed herself into the back of the house.

Terezia was leaning against the kitchen range, nursing a mug of steaming tea in her hands. He had the impression she'd only just come in herself; she was wearing a heavy blue jersey and jeans that had been washed so often they appeared pale as moonlight in the darkened room. Her hair was loose and fell around her shoulders, glittering like pirate's gold.

She didn't say anything as he came in. She just put down her mug and placed her hands behind her on the rail of the range. Her stance made her look ominously like a prize-fighter waiting to come out of his corner.

'I rang earlier,' Mas said conversationally, 'but I heard you were in Budapest.'

'I had to see Victor Szelkely.'

'Pity – I could have saved myself another walk up here if I'd known you were there.'

'Yes,' she said. 'You could.'

'Any reason for seeing him?' Max kept his voice chirpy although he could sense a chill in the room that would have scared the hell out of any brass monkeys in the vicinity.

'Zoltan has lodged an appeal against me.'

'On what grounds?'

'That I'm an impostor.' She spoke lightly, as though it were of no importance to her whatsoever but there was a stealth to her, a wariness, like a wild animal that finds itself in unknown territory. 'But I imagine you knew that already, didn't you?'

'How could I know?'

'I assumed he would have told you himself.'

'I see.' The bush telegraph had been working overtime. 'You heard about that.'

'Yes,' she said. 'I heard.'

'He asked to see me.'

'When was this?'

'Yesterday – Vargas rang and said he wanted to talk to me.'

'And you didn't think to tell me?'

'He asked me not to.'

'And you agreed, did you?' she asked. Her voice was still controlled but he could sense the anger beneath the surface. 'Zoltan wants something and you obey – just like everyone else. Whatever he wants he has to have. No one can ever argue with him; no one can ever say no.' Picking up the forgotten mug of tea she threw the dregs down the sink and rinsed it under the tap.

'Sometimes it helps to have a go-between.'

'I'm sure you'd know all about that,' she said without looking round.

He studied her back, still turned to him. He didn't want a fight but sure as hell he could feel one coming on.

'I know you won't get anywhere without talking,' he said.

'So that gives you permission to take the law into your own hands and start plotting with Zoltan, does it?'

'Yes it does, if you must know.' She was being ridiculous. 'And we weren't plotting; he had something to say and I listened. And it's as well for you that I did.'

'Really? And what was it he had to say that was so important?'

Max wondered how long it was going to be before her inquisitive female mind got round to that.

'He wants to do a deal.'

There was a moment's silence.

'What sort of deal?'

'If you let him have the house he'll give you ten million dollars.'

She put down the mug and faced him, wet hands held out on either side of her, the expression on her face as grave and intent as a death mask.

'And what did you say?' she asked softly.

'I said I'd pass it on.'

'Why was that?'

'Because he's not offering it to me.' He was becoming exasperated. 'He's offering it to you.'

'You don't for a moment think I'd accept it, do you?'

'I can't for the life of me think why not.'

'Can't you?'

'No, I can't.'

'Then maybe you're not such a good go-between as you think, Mr Anderson from the British Embassy, if you think I can be bought off like some gypsy.'

'This is one hell of an offer.'

'If you say so—'

'Ten million dollars, for God's sake.'

'I don't care how much it is.' Her eyes were glittering dangerously.

'You could found a whole empire of stud farms on that.'

'I don't care if he gives me everything he owns, I am not selling this house to him!' She was suddenly shouting, the anger bottled up in her exploding into words.

Max was amazed by the ferocity of it. Her face was pale, eyes blazing like emeralds. He hadn't been sure how she was going to react to Zoltan's money but whatever it was he hadn't expected this. He was sure that if she could have laid hands on some useful weapon at that moment she'd have pitched into him.

'How can you just sell the place without even asking me!' she shouted.

'Hang on a second. Are we on the same bloody planet? Just the other day you told me you hated the place; that you'd do anything to get it off your hands.'

Her head flashed round. 'Did you tell him that?'

'Probably – possibly, I can't remember.'

'How dare you,' she hissed.

'It's what you said.'

'It doesn't matter what I said! How dare you pass it on to him. It's got nothing to do with you.'

'No, it hasn't,' Max said. He was angry himself now. 'It's got nothing to do with me at all. I didn't want to get tangled up in your family and all its blasted problems. I was just trying to get someone to the airport and the next thing I know I'm on the ten most wanted people in Europe posters.'

'That has nothing to do with me.'

'It has everything to do with you.' When was she going to wake up and realise what was going on around her?

'That doesn't give you the right to start interfering.'

Max was angry and bewildered. He told her he didn't want to be interfering. It was the last thing in the world he wanted to be doing. If she wanted to keep her house that was fine but he wished she'd just say so and stop whining about how much she hated the place.

At the mention of whining she'd had enough. She told him that if he thought she was whining he'd better go. Max thought so too. The sooner he was out of there the better, and he slammed out into the night.

Terezia listened to his footsteps die away. She was trembling all over but she wasn't cold. The blood was thrumming in her veins, her cheeks flushed. Mechanically she turned from the door and picked up the mug she'd been washing. Eyes burning with resentment she raked back over the argument.

How could he go behind her back like that? Without even telling her that Zoltan had rung. What right had he to start negotiating about her inheritance? What right had he to start talking with him at all? He should be sorting out his own problems, not interfering with hers.

The worst of it was that she'd trusted Max. He was the one person she'd been sure was on her side. A lock of hair fell over her eyes; she swept it aside and banged her nose with the stupid mug. She looked at it in surprise and in her mind she heard Max's steady, reasonable voice: always so considered, always so sensible – always so bloody right about everything – and she slammed it down on the draining board so hard that the handle snapped off.

'No need to take it out on the crockery as well,' Rosza said coming into the room. She swept the broken pieces off into her broad spade-like hand and dropped them into the rubbish bin under the sink.

Terezia watched her sullenly.

'Quite a little set to, wasn't it,' Rosza said comfortably, opening the lid of the range and checking its heat.

'You heard?'

'Of course I heard, Tereyki. I should think everyone in a ten-mile radius heard.'

'I can't believe he did such a thing.'

The old woman paused, hands on hips, and asked what exactly it was she thought he'd done.

'Conspired behind my back.'

The shock of the fight was easing off now and she was suddenly restless. Rosza's gaze followed her round the room.

'You have a reason, I suppose?'

'For what?'

'Turning down the offer.'

'It's just a trick,' Terezia said quickly. 'You can see that. One moment they turn nasty and threaten to take me to court again, then they turn all nice and offer me millions of dollars. They think I'll take it and run.'

'Seems reasonable to me.'

'You didn't expect me to accept, did you?'

Rosza wasn't going to be cornered into an argument. 'Most would have.'

'But I can't – you know that.'

'Why? Because of your father?'

'He'd turn in his grave if Zoltan got the house.'

'Yes, he might,' Rosza agreed. 'But then I don't think he'd want to see his daughter pushed out on the streets either.'

'He hated Zoltan.'

'And that's the reason, is it?' Rosza didn't sound convinced.

'Yes—'

'It's nothing to do with the fact that you are besotted by the place yourself?'

'I am not!'

The wrinkled face was placid. 'There's not a moment of the day when you're not thinking about it, you should see yourself.'

'I have to think about it.'

'You're possessed by the place, Tereyki.'

Terezia couldn't believe what she was hearing. 'I never wanted to come here, you know that.'

'Oh, you rage at it all right. It's not what you expected; it doesn't live up to your dreams but you wouldn't let it go if they locked you up and starved you.'

She felt suddenly very frightened.

'That's nonsense,' she said putting on her coat.

'Then why didn't you take the money?'

She didn't have an answer but went out into the night saying she had work to do.

Max drained his third glass of red wine. It was soft and warm and slipped down very easily. Catching the barman's eye he ordered another. He knew you can't find consolation in a bottle but it wasn't consolation he wanted at that moment. He wanted to blot out the memory of Terezia's furious eyes and he found it was doing the trick pretty well.

God knows where she'd heard about his meeting with Zoltan but she'd got the wrong end of the stick completely. If she'd just listened for a second instead of blasting off like a rocket he might have been able to explain. But she hadn't given him the chance. She'd been so busy shouting he hadn't got a word in edgeways. Bloody women. He'd half a mind to go back up there and shake her until she had to listen but he knew he'd just make more of a fool of himself than he had already.

It was ironic that she'd slung him out of the house, he thought as the barman slipped a full glass in front of him. She'd done it the first time he'd met her and she'd done it the last time. It *was* the last time. He wouldn't see her again. He knew that. Twenty-four hours from now he'd be back in London, cap in hand, the naughty boy who's been expelled from another school.

And Terezia would be just a memory.

'Cold night,' the barman remarked.

Max nodded. 'More than you think.'

'Did I see you coming out of the Palace just now?'

'Climbing out,' he corrected. 'The gates are locked.'

'You know her then, do you – the Kasinczy-Landsberg girl?'

Max took a pull at the red wine and shook his head solemnly. 'No,' he said. 'I don't know her at all.'

'She's a looker though, isn't she? She came in here the other day to get a bottle of wine. It was the first time I'd seen her, you know, up close and she's quite a looker.'

'Yes,' Max said, getting up to go. 'She is.'

As he came out into the cold the alcohol hit him. He could feel the ground rolling as he walked up the street, as though it were the deck of a ship. Probably not a great idea to drive for a bit, he told himself. A woman crossed the road and went into the building next to him. Seeing him standing there she held open the door for him.

'You coming in?'

It looked warm and bright inside; somewhere in the distance he could hear singing. Max nodded. Why not? He had nowhere else to go at that moment.

It was some sort of community hall, functional and unattractive, gaunt iron-framed chairs lined up on a lino floor. Max took a seat at the back. On the raised dais at the end a group of children were rehearsing carols, their teacher thumping out the tune on a piano.

Carols. It was only a few days until Christmas, he realised. He'd liked carols as a child. Not because of the music but because they were a prelude to the great day itself, along with the tree and cards and the chestnuts in the fire.

Strange to hear them here though. Church services had been banned for the past fifty years, the clergy hounded and persecuted. He was surprised anyone even knew the words of carols any more, let alone bothered to teach them to children.

With a clap of her hands, the teacher dismissed the class and the children escaped out into the night, chattering excitedly, collecting their parents as they went.

Max stayed where he was.

The teacher was rounding up the sheet music left scattered around the stage. She was a pleasant-looking girl, plump and pink-cheeked, in a long woollen jersey. As she was switching off the lights she caught sight of Max.

'Hallo,' she said. 'Are you waiting for someone?'

'No, I came in to listen to the carols.'

'That's nice,' she said with a slight blush. 'Did you like them?'

'Yes,' Max said. There was something simple and unaffected about the children singing. He got up to leave with her.

'That carol,' he said as they went outside. 'It was English, wasn't it?'

'Probably. All the carols we sing are English. We were taught them by our gran, you see, and she was English.'

'How did she come to be here?'

'She'd been a governess at one of the big houses before the war and she came back afterwards and became a teacher.'

It was a shot in the dark but the parts fitted in his mind, the shape was right, and somehow Max knew the answer before he'd even asked the question.

'Her name wasn't Eleanor Hargreaves, was it?'

The girl clutched the satchel of sheet music to herself and her eyes smiled over it in surprise.

'Yes – goodness, how did you know that?'

'She used to take photos.'

'That's right, she always took pictures.'

'I saw some she took up there.' He nodded back towards where the house towered above them.

'Oh, at Fetevis, you mean?'

'I found an album of photos in the library. Her name was in the front.'

'She worked for the family, when she was first here. She loved Fetevis, you should hear the stories she used to tell about it – in the old days, I mean.'

'Is she . . .' Max wasn't quite sure how to put the question but she took his meaning.

'Still alive? Oh, yes, very much. She lives over near Eger with my ma.'

She locked the door of the hall and put the key over the lintel. High-security outfit this. Her car was parked further up the road.

As they reached it Max said, 'Do you think I could talk to her?'

'I'm sure.' She cocked her head to one side.' You're English yourself, aren't you?'

He nodded.

'I'll give you my number; you give me a ring and I'll take you over there sometime. Gran likes talking to English people. Weekends are best for me.'

'No, it would have to be sooner than that. Tomorrow in fact.'

She looked dubious about this.

'I'm leaving, you see. But I'd really like to see her. It's very important.'

'I don't know,' she said. 'It's a bit sudden.'

'There's something she may be able to help me with.'

'Oh, my, you are in a rush aren't you?' She laughed, eyes twinkling. 'Leave it with me; I'll see what I can do.'

15

It was the daughter who opened the door. She was pushing fifty, stout and dependable-looking in apron and carpet slippers, with the tired and rather distant expression of a woman who'd had too much to cope with in life to bother about her hair or her figure or showing a flicker of interest in a stranger who'd appeared at her home.

'I've come to see Eleanor Jankovics,' Max said. He'd learned that this was her married name.

The daughter nodded and held back the door to let him in.

'She's in the back,' she told him as she led the way through to a kitchen at the rear of the long, low house.

Max hadn't formed an image of what Eleanor would be like. To him English governesses were trim, starched girls with trim, starched morals who never smiled, never had sex or grew older than their late twenties.

Eleanor was closer to eighty. She was sitting by the range, her knees wrapped in a tartan rug, a newspaper clasped in hands that were bunched with arthritis. Her hair was tied back close to her head, her face severe, the flesh lined but not sagging. His first impression was of one of those tough pioneering women of the Wild West who fought their way through blizzards and swarms of marauding Indians with nothing more for company than the Good Book and a Winchester repeater.

She was dozing when they came in but she woke quickly, glancing up at Max and then round at her daughter.

'Have you got them, then?'

The daughter handed her a packet of Silk Cut, and with slow movements, the packet held up to her face, Eleanor began peeling away the cellophane.

'That's one thing they can't make in this country any longer,' she said to Max. 'Cigarettes.'

'They're not good for you,' the daughter reproved.

'So they keeping telling me. The Government puts this warning on the packet telling me they're bad for my health. But I've outlasted dozens of governments so why should I care?'

She gave a little cackle of laughter and looked up at Max. Her eyes were hazel brown, clear and unwavering, the only intimation of the girl who had come to Hungary all those years ago.

'So you found the way here then?'

'No trouble.'

The council took away the road signs because they said they weren't the approved type. But they hadn't got the money to replace them so now no one can find us.'

'Your granddaughter gave me directions.'

'Ah yes, a nice girl, Trudi. Still thinks she can teach children by being nice to them but she'll learn.' Again she gave a cackle of laughter. The daughter tried to straighten the cushion behind her head but she brushed her away crossly.

'She told me you found some photos of mine,' she said.

'I was looking through the books in the library at Fetevis. I came across an album with your name in the front.'

'I'm surprised there are any books left there.'

'They were given back.'

The old woman nodded and glanced over to the window. 'The commies took all the books away. They thought that if they owned them they'd become more clever themselves but when they discovered they were still as pig-ignorant as they'd always been they gave them back again.' She held out the cigarette. 'Would you mind lighting this, please? My hands are a little unsteady and my daughter is convinced I'll set fire to the house if I do it myself.'

Max flicked a flame from a match and set it to the tip of the cigarette. The old woman took a couple of drags to get it going and then pointed with it towards a chair.

'Sit down, for goodness' sake. You'll give me a crick in the neck standing there.'

Max sat down. The old woman smoked for a moment, taking the cigarette to her lips very slowly as if uncertain she could hit the target accurately.

'They tell me Fetevis is a ruin now. Is that true?'

'More or less.'

She nodded slowly, as if it were only to be expected. 'And she lives in it, does she – Karoly's girl?'

'She lives in part of it.'

Eleanor brooded on this for a moment, the cigarette rising and falling to her lips.

'They never told me he got married,' she said. 'You'd think someone would have told me.'

'I think it was kept secret.'

'He won't let her stay,' she said unexpectedly. 'Zoltan: he won't let her stay there. I hope she knows that.'

'She knows it.'

'He was sure he was going to inherit that house, even when I knew him. He was grooming himself for the part. I could see it.'

'I hear you were his governess.'

She nodded. 'Eight years I was with the Kasinczy-Landsbergs. When this was still a country to live in, before the Russian scum moved in.'

'It must have been something.'

'It was,' she said, touching the cigarette to her lips gently as though she were blowing a kiss. She was back there, Max could see it.

'They say the Hungarians were the Englishmen of Europe,' she went on. 'Because they had good manners and good horses but that's just a load of manure. There was never any comparison. The English have manners but no style. When they become civilised they become dull like a flock of constipated ducks. There's no charm, no romance like the Hungarians.' She blew out smoke. 'Although I don't know where it's all gone now. Everything is grey these days. As soon as colour came into the cinema it started going out of the world, do you know that?'

She gave a cackle of laughter at the over-simplicity of the idea and Max realised she didn't live in the past to the exclusion of the real world. There was still life and humour in this strange old woman.

She waved the cigarette before her eyes. 'But you didn't come here to listen to an old witch telling stories. What is it you want from me that couldn't wait a day longer?'

'It was the past I was hoping you could tell me about.'

'Oh, yes? And what piece of the past is that?'

'What is the Hunyadi Venus?'

There was silence in the kitchen, the hazel eyes rested on him for a moment.

'Ah, so that's it.'

'I saw it in a portrait.'

'It's gone,' she said. 'You know that, I suppose?'

Max nodded. 'I was told. But what was it?'

Eleanor stared away into the distance, as though this were a difficult question to answer. 'It was a piece of sculpture.'

'It wasn't bronze was it?'

Eleanor shook her head. 'No, not bronze: silver, with some parts enamelled in colour. It was very beautiful – more like a piece of jewellery than sculpture.'

'It must have been worth a bit.'

She smiled as though this were more of an understatement than he could know. 'Oh yes, I'm sure it was worth a fortune. It was by Donatello, you see. The only thing he ever made in silver.'

From weekly lessons in the dusty Victorian art room of his school, Max had a vague notion that Donatello was a Renaissance artist, the kind of Renaissance artist who has to be pronounced piously and reverentially in the correct Italian accent.

'You saw it, did you?'

'Oh yes, often. It stood in a little room all by itself. Just off the Long Gallery in the Palace. It was an extraordinary thing . . . quite extraordinary.'

The kind of extraordinary thing that Verity would like to get his hands on, Max was thinking. The kind of extraordinary thing he might come hundreds of miles to find.

'Fabergé saw it there,' Eleanor went on. 'The Czar had stayed at the Palace on a shooting party. They all used to stay there in those days: czars and archdukes and all the rest of the buffoons in their braid and medals. When he was shown the Venus he wanted it so badly he tried to buy it. But the family wasn't selling. So he sent Fabergé down to try to work out how it was made.' She gave a little chuckle at the idea of it, spilling cigarette ash over her lap.

'Why was it so important to them?' Max asked.

'It was a sort of family emblem; it's hard to explain.' The old woman wrinkled her nose, trying to put words to her thoughts. 'It had been in the family for years, you see. It was part of their history, like a family crest.'

'Where is it now?'

'I don't know. It was taken away.'

'By whom?'

She shrugged as though this weren't important. 'By whoever dug it up.'

'It was buried?'

'That's my guess.'

'During the war, you mean?'

She shook her head at his naiveté. 'You don't know, do you?' she said with a touch of amusement. 'You don't know anything about it?'

'I'd never heard of it until yesterday.'

She was studying him thoughtfully, coming to a decision in her mind. Then stubbing out her cigarette she called her daughter back into the room, telling her to fetch one of the photo albums.

It was leather-bound with matchbox-sized pictures on black paper, much like the one Max had found amongst all the mouldy books at Fetevis.

Eleanor turned the pages with gnarled hands, peering at the photos until she reached the one she wanted.

'Here,' she said, pushing the album towards him. 'Take a look at that.'

The photo she found was of Terezia's father on horseback. He wore a soft felt hat on the side of his head and that gentle, rather mocking smile on his face. As well he might, Max thought, while he was posing for his nephew's governess.

'That was taken on the last day at Fetevis,' Eleanor said. 'Karoly fixed a boar hunt and we all went over there for the day. I took the picture just before they set off. Look there. Do you see the saddlebag on the back of the horse?'

'Yes—'

'And can you see what's in it?'

The picture was so small it was hard to be sure. 'It looks like a box.'

'It's the Venus,' Eleanor said. 'That was the box it was kept in when the family wasn't at home. He took it with him when he went off and it wasn't there when he came back. I noticed it at the time.'

'You think he buried it up there in the woods.'

'I suppose he thought it might escape the commies that way.'

'How do you know it didn't? It might still be there.'

Eleanor smiled distantly at his mistake. 'It's not,' she said, 'or Zoltan would have found it by now. He was there that day; he knew where it was buried. If it was still in the ground when he came back here he would have got it. It would be part of that art gallery I hear he's set up for himself. No, it's long gone.'

'But you don't know where?'

'I've no idea.'

Her eyes met his for an instant, clear and innocent as a girl at communion, and Max thought: hell, she's lying. But there was nothing he could do about it. It was already after ten. He had an appointment with Zoltan in half an hour. He hadn't the time to worm any more answers out of her – even if he knew what questions to ask. He got up to go.

As he was putting on his coat he said: 'How well known is all this?'

'Well enough.'

'Has it ever been put in print?'

'Oh yes.' She sounded disappointed. 'I'm afraid it has. A few years ago I wrote an article about it for the local paper. I probably shouldn't have but it's hard to keep a secret all these years, isn't it?

'Could it have been read outside Hungary do you think?'

'If you mean: do I think it could have been read by Dr Verity of Oxford University, then the answer is yes, Mr Anderson.' She smiled up at him, quietly and complacently, the bright young governess one jump ahead of her pupils. 'That is what you're wondering, isn't it?'

Max smiled. 'I guess it is.'

'I'm sure your Dr Verity knew all about the Venus.'

There wasn't much that passed her. Her body might be bent and withered but the mind inside was sharp as a razor. Max thanked her for her help and she smiled sweetly and nodded to him, her hands folded on her lap, just as they had been when he came in.

'I would like to see her,' she said as he left.

Max paused in the doorway.

'Karoly's girl,' she said. 'I'd like to meet her.'

'I'm not sure I can arrange that; I'm leaving in the morning.'

'That's a shame,' she said. 'No one ever told me he had a daughter. I'd like to see her.'

Strossmayer thumbed his pass from the breast pocket of his denim shirt and thrust it out of the car window. The pasty-faced guard in the security post peered at it through the glass and nodded. The barrier cranked up.

'I'm looking for the head office,' Strossmayer told him. He had to shout to make himself heard.

'Straight in, first left; big brick building. You can't miss it.'

He shifted the gear lever into first and gunned the engine, holding it on the clutch. 'Who hangs out there, then?'

The security guard looked nonplussed. 'How d'you mean?'

'Who's the head man here?'

'The Count.'

'Kasinczy-Landsberg?'

'It's the head office of the Landsberg Corporation.' The guard couldn't think who else might hang out there and with an inch of reinforced glass between him and this saturnine-looking man he could afford to sound as though it was a stupid question.

Strossmayer grunted his thanks. That's what he thought; he just wanted to make sure. He'd never come face to face with Count Zoltan before. He'd done his dirty work, taken his money in return, but never actually met the man. In fact he couldn't even have sworn that was who he had been working for all these years. Letting in the clutch, he drove the 4 x 4 forwards.

A steel mill is an awesome sight: ten square miles of industrial jungle, smoking, steaming and screeching, an unholy alliance between man and nature. God's hell on earth.

Strossmayer was impressed. There was wealth here, he told himself; not the flabby wealth of bankers and stockbrokers who make their profits from a safe distance, manipulating money on a computer screen, but the real wealth that comes from sweat and dirt and hard labour. He could see why the old man had his offices here.

Not that there was anything mean about them, he noticed

as he parked the car further up the road. There were uniformed commissionaires on the high glass doors and a brightly lit foyer beyond, more like the entrance to a hotel than an office block. He glanced up at the windows on the first floor. There'd be thick-pile carpets and air-conditioning in there, he guessed, and PAs with painted nails and short skirts that hardly covered your imagination who could do a lot more for you than take dictation. That was the flipside of the coin. You don't make a fortune to live like a monk.

He leaned against the bonnet of the car and watched the current of activity around the entrance to the building, punctuated by the distant hisses and rumblings of the plant behind him. He wasn't due to arrive for another hour but he'd made good time on the thirty-mile journey and he'd wanted to be early. It gave him time to check the place out, to acclimatise himself to his surroundings.

A car came through the entrance, bumping its way over the sleeping policemen in the road. A stupid name that. He'd seen policemen sleeping in their car seats and huddled up in corners on surveillance exercises but never lying down in the road.

One of the commissionaires stepped forward as the car came to a halt in front of the building, and opened the door. A man in a long black overcoat got out. It was the Englishman, Anderson. He'd only seen him for a few moments in the twilight of that barn but he recognised him immediately. It had been a uniquely satisfying moment, one he had savoured afterwards. But what the hell was he doing here?

He watched the Englishman go inside. He was evidently expected. A young man in a suit met him at the front desk, ever so gracious and polite. He watched them shake hands, get into the lift together. As it went up, Strossmayer looked up at the windows of the first-floor offices.

He'd give a bit to know what was going on in there that morning.

'She says no.'

'Just like that?'

'Just like that.'

'You've got to be joking.'

'She won't sell.'

'You told her what I was offering?'

'I told her exactly what you said. She's not interested.'

Max couldn't help feeling a small malicious gleam of humour as he passed on the information. No doubt they'd expected to haggle a bit, even compromise if necessary, but he doubted they'd expected to be turned down flat.

There were four of them in the office that morning: Zoltan in the centre of the stage, sitting behind the desk with its art-nouveau lampshade, gold cufflinks gleaming beneath the sleeves of his charcoal-grey suit, silvery grey tie matching the silvery grey hair; near him his wife, acid blue and pearls, looking remote and yet proprietorial like the vicar's wife in church; Vargas stood behind, sharp-faced and alert, and over by the window was Zoltan's son. He'd been introduced as Sandor although he'd been quick to amend the name to Alexander. He was much the same age as himself, Max reckoned, with the blond, aquiline features of his family, so like Terezia in his expressions that Max had felt a quick, keen stab of pain as they met.

How they took the news was irrelevant. What mattered to all of them was how Zoltan was going to take it.

He shifted his weight in his chair, his eyes locked on Max. 'Are you telling me she wants to go on camping up there like some goddamned Girl Guide?'

'I guess so.'

'But I thought you said she didn't want to be there?'

'That's what she told me.'

Zoltan looked round at the others as though they might hold the secret to the riddle. 'Is this whole world going crazy or is it just me? This stupid broad wants to get rid of the house but she won't sell it for ten times the market rate.' He looked back at Max, his eyes cold as ice. 'Why not, for God's sake?'

'I don't know.'

'She just said no, did she? No reason, no explanation?'

'That's about it.' It was uncomfortably close to the truth.

'She must have said something.'

'Not to me.'

'Then what do you think?' Zoltan didn't shout, didn't even raise his voice, but his fury was in every word and gesture. It was as though some other person had possessed him as he sat there. 'You've got a brain in your head, haven't you? What do you think?'

It was a question Max had asked himself over and over again since he'd walked out on her.

'I think she can't escape the fact that she owns the place.'

The green-grey eyes bored into him. 'She does not own Fetevis, Mr Anderson. I thought I'd made that clear to you the last time. I own it and she is keeping me from it.'

'Which leaves you with something of a problem,' Max said amiably.

'What does?'

'Your only hope of getting the place back now is to go to the law courts and ask them to change their mind.'

'That suits me fine. If she won't give it up the easy way she'll just have to give it up the hard way.'

Max could see his point. 'And there's always a chance,' he said, 'that you might find a judge who believes that your uncle adopted a daughter who grew up to look just like him. But somehow I doubt it.'

'I want you to go now, Anderson.'

Zoltan must have pushed a hidden bell below the desk because the door opened on cue and the young man who'd escorted him up came in. He stood poised in the doorway with that air of cool efficiency that comes from a mixture of ambition, arrogance and good grades in business school.

'Mr Anderson is just leaving,' Zoltan informed him.

The little toady stood back to let Max pass but he was in no hurry to go. He turned back to Zoltan.

'Tell me something.'

'I just have.'

'Did you ever meet someone called Dr Verity?'

'No—'

'He didn't come to see you a few weeks ago?'

'No, Mr Anderson, he didn't. Does that answer your question?'

'He was looking for the Hunyadi Venus.'

Zoltan faced him across the office, the full force of his personality in his voice. 'The Hunyadi Venus is gone; I told you. It was taken by the Russians at the end of the war.'

'Verity didn't come to you claiming he knew where it was?'

'I didn't speak to this Dr Verity; I didn't meet this Dr Verity. Now if you don't leave my office I'll have you thrown out of here.'

Half an hour later, Strossmayer was leaning against the wall of the next door office rolling a cigarette. He was giving it a lot of concentration, keeping in all the little scraggy bits at the end, sweeping aside with his foot any strands that did fall. He didn't need to be rolling it, he usually smoked them ready-made, but it was irritating the hell out of the little creep at the desk and it gave him something to do to pass the time.

It was some time now since Anderson had left. He'd seen him drive away. Then some haughty old cow had been removed in a chauffeur-driven car. So what the hell was keeping them?

'There's no smoking in here,' the creep at the desk said.

Strossmayer paused, as though he had forgotten there was anyone else in the room, and looked him straight in the face. Sticking out the tip of his tongue he ran it along the rim of the cigarette paper and rolled it into shape.

The secretary frowned. There was no point in even trying to argue with someone from the animal kingdom. Why he was here, stinking out his office with his vile leather jacket and do-it-yourself cigarettes he had no idea.

Strossmayer couldn't give a stuff what the creep thought. How he'd even got the job in the first place he couldn't imagine. If he was the boss he'd have something very different in here, something that kept crossing her legs and manicuring her nails as she waited to be taken out to lunch.

The door opened. It was Vargas, the lawyer.

'Would you come in please?'

Strossmayer latched the cigarette behind his ear and pushed himself away from the wall. As he went he gave the creep a long, hard stare. He liked to do that to these overpaid suits. It left them with the impression they'd had a curse put on them.

Count Zoltan was working at his desk as he came in. It must have been really important work because it was almost five minutes before he put down his pen. It was one of the old-fashioned ones with a screw cap and it rested on a little rack on the desk.

Sitting back, hands easy on the arms of the chair, the

Count looked him straight in the eye. Where the hell did he get a suntan like that in the winter, Strossmayer wondered.

'You've done some work for me in the past,' the Count said.

Strossmayer didn't like to be rushed in a conversation. He looked around the room. It had oak panels and large paintings hanging on them, the real thing, not your reproduction scenes of horses cantering through waves, but shiny, hand-painted items in gold frames. Probably cost a bomb. He couldn't see it himself. What was wrong with a nice big drinks cabinet and an executive bathroom next door with gold taps and a king-sized Jacuzzi?

'I don't work for people,' he said. 'I work for money.'

Count Zoltan didn't make any smart reply to this. He didn't even smile knowingly. He just sat there staring at him with those unearthly green eyes and Strossmayer couldn't look back because he knew, in the primitive layer of his mind, that this man was stronger than him.

'I have another job for you now,' the Count said.

'Oh yes?' He wanted it to sound as though he'd decide whether he took it or not. He was beginning to hate this man with all his money and his power.

'You know the Palace of Fetevis?'

Strossmayer nodded.

'There's a girl living there called Terezia Kovacs.'

He knew the one he meant – tall, blonde bit with legs like a model's. He'd seen her picture in the papers. But she was some relation of the Count's, wasn't she?

Zoltan was watching him, gauging the response. 'She calls herself Kasinczy-Landsberg.'

That was it. She'd got the house, right under his nose; he'd read about it. Must have got right up the Count's aristocratic nose that.

'You know her?'

'Yeah, I know her.'

'She has something that belongs to me. I want it back.'

'What sort of thing?'

Zoltan didn't answer that immediately. 'It has to be discreet, Strossmayer. It has to be very discreet. Can you do that?'

'Tell me what I have to do.'

The phone started ringing while Max was packing. He slapped the suitcase shut and with his foot on the bulging lid picked up the receiver.

'Yes?'

'Anderson?' The voice on the other end was American and imperious.

'Speaking—'

'Alexander Kasinczy-Landsberg.' It was the son whose Ivy League education had bred the name Sandor out of him. 'We met earlier—'

'What can I do for you?'

'I want to know what the heck's going on.'

'I'm packing.'

'I need to speak to you.'

'You're doing pretty well so far.'

'Don't get smart with me, Anderson. We need to talk. I'll be at the baths of the Thermal Hotel tomorrow.'

'That's a place for queens, isn't it?'

'Shall we say eleven?'

Max hung up the receiver and bending down he tugged out the socket from the wall. He'd had enough of phone calls. He finished his packing, zipped up the two suitcases and put them in the small entrance hall of his flat. He went out into the passage, locked the door and pushed the keys through the letterbox. Then, carrying only a small airport bag over his shoulder, he took the metro up to Varosomarty Square.

''Evening, Mr Anderson.'

Sergeant Norton was sitting in an alcove at the rear of the bar reading a newspaper. He got to his feet, the surprise clear on his face as he held out his hand. 'Can I get you a drink, sir?' he asked.

Max said he'd get them in but the Sergeant wasn't hearing of it. 'My shout sir. Your money's not good in here.'

He called the waitress over and ordered a couple of beers. The bar was long and low with a painted wooden ceiling and tiled floor, authentically Hungarian as the sign in the window said in four different languages.

'I heard you were being transferred,' the Sergeant said as the drinks arrived.

'Kicked out is the correct terminology.'

'Over that business with the, er . . . missing person?'

'The police don't know who did it so they're shooting all the suspects.'

The Sergeant siphoned off an inch of beer and wiped his upper lip. He gave a slow shake of his head. 'Doesn't seem right to me,' he said. 'I spoke to the police about it. They came round asking questions so I told them how it happened, straight up, not keeping anything back because we had nothing to hide. But they didn't seem that interested in what I said. They just heard the bits they wanted to hear, if you know what I mean. When are you leaving then, sir?'

'The flight's at midday tomorrow.'

'Not too frantic then.'

'In the meantime there's something you could do for me.'

'How's that then, sir?' the Sergeant asked quietly.

'You've got some good contacts in the police, haven't you?'

'I have a drink with one or two of them from time to time.' He was gazing across the table, waiting to hear what was coming.

'Could you get someone to check out a car registration number?'

'Shouldn't be too difficult.'

Max took out a notebook and scribbled down a number. He tore off the page and passed it over the table.

'It's for a blue 4 x 4.'

'Oh yes.'

'You remember that business back at the hotel? The manager said the room had been worked over by a man in a blue 4 x 4?'

'Certainly do.'

'I saw it today at the Landsberg Corporation. I couldn't read the logo on it but I got the number.'

'You're sure it's the same one?'

'The driver had a moustache.'

Norton studied him in silence for a moment, then picked up the piece of paper, folded it and tucked it into his wallet. 'Then we'd better find out who he is, sir,' he said calmly. 'I can't promise to get anything by midday tomorrow though.'

'That doesn't matter.'

'Can you give me a contact number?'

'I can't at the moment,' Max said, draining his glass and getting to his feet. 'I'll give you a ring tomorrow.'

'No offence meant but probably best not to ring the Embassy, sir.'

Max took the point. 'Here then,' he said. 'I'll leave a message at the bar. You can ring me back.'

'That sounds right.'

16

'There's a call for you.' Rosza was standing in the doorway as Terezia rode by on the following morning. She beckoned her inside. 'Come quick,' she ordered. 'They're holding the line.'

Terezia kicked her feet from the stirrups and climbed down from the saddle. She'd been exercising the horses since dawn and felt cold and stiff. The snow of the past few days had thinned to sleet, a cold relentless downpour that had crept into her collar so that her shirt was damp and an icy bead of water was trickling its way down the line of her spine.

She followed Rosza inside, stamping her feet in the doorway and shaking the wet off her long riding coat. The old woman would have a fit if she left footprints on her clean floor.

Rosza was holding out the phone. For a moment Terezia thought it might be Max, but she brushed the thought from her mind. Max wouldn't come back into her life by phone. He might turn up out of the blue but he'd never ring her.

Taking her hard hat off, she dropped it on the table. She only wore it to keep off the rain. She preferred a fur hat when she was riding but they were no good in the wet.

It was a woman's voice on the line, calling from the Fine Art Museum in Budapest.

'Could you spare a few minutes to come round here, Countess?'

'What, now?'

'The curator would like a word with you.'

'Can't he speak on the phone?'

'He's in a meeting at present.' She explained the situation in her chatty voice. 'But he's free later this morning.'

Terezia looked out at the sleet dribbling down the window pane. She had work to do that morning but with this weather the thought of driving into town wasn't unattractive.

'What's it about?'

'I couldn't say.' She was just passing on a message.

'It'll take me an hour or more to get in.'

She took that as a yes. 'Shall we say eleven?'

'Make it half past.' Terezia wanted time for a bath and a cup of coffee.

Twenty minutes later, as she was getting ready to leave, Rosza asked, 'Are you taking the car then?'

'No, I thought I'd walk.'

'I'll come with you to the village, I need a few things.'

'I'll take you into Budapest if you like.' Terezia was putting on lipstick in the mirror. 'You can get them there.'

'I don't think I'd like that.'

'Why not?' She stood back to gauge the effect. 'It'd do you good.'

'There's nothing there I can't get in the village.'

'You'd be surprised.' Terezia gave her reflection a last hard stare and then turned away with the sudden briskness of a woman who's satisfied with her appearance. 'Okay then,' she said picking up her handbag. 'Let's get going.'

From the woods below the house, Strossmayer watched the two women get into the van – the old woman marching over and dumping herself in the passenger seat, basket over one arm, Terezia skittering round the other side on high heels, her handbag over her hairdo.

Strossmayer tucked the binoculars away in their case and moved forward. Four hours he'd been crouched there in the dripping trees watching, waiting for his chance. The time didn't bother him. He would have waited much longer if necessary. Often in the past he'd studied a target for a couple of days before making a move. There were patterns of behaviour to observe, the little trivial comings and goings which must be taken into account if a mission were to be a success.

But in this case he didn't need to see more. The routine was straightforward. All life centred around the stables at the far end of the house. Except for half an hour at breakfast time, the old man and the two stable lads who'd shown up at dawn were down there permanently. The girl appeared periodically through the arched gateway with one of the horses, riding it down through the woods along the lakeside. He'd followed her with his binoculars, watching her thread the animal through the trees, her head bowed, coat glistening in the wet.

The problem he'd seen from the start was the old woman. She was never far away from the part of the house they lived in. When she did come out it was only to shake out a tablecloth, or stump round the back to feed the chickens.

But now, with both the women gone, there was no reason to wait longer. He had his chance.

Keeping to the cover of the trees he moved up closer to the house. Quite how long he had before they came back in that clapped-out car of theirs he couldn't be sure. The girl was dressed to go out; the old woman wasn't. But even if she was going off to post a letter it would take a while to get down the drive. And there were the chains on the gate; he'd seen those. He must have twenty minutes at the least, probably more.

That was enough.

Working his way round to one side he climbed up to the level of the house. It was a spooky-looking place up close, all crumbling and hollow, the windows barred. Why the Count should want it when he already had a brand new place not ten miles away beat the hell out of him.

He would have liked to go in through one of the back windows but there were those chickens round there. Nothing screwed up a job like this quicker than bloody chickens – apart from geese that is; they were one worse. So he walked round to the front door. Not trying to be too unobtrusive at this stage. If anyone did appear he would just say that he was looking for a stray dog. That always worked.

He turned in the doorway and glanced casually around the weed-filled driveway, hands behind his back. He turned the knob, felt the door open a fraction. So much for security at Fetevis Palace. Still watching the drive he stepped inside and closed the door.

Easy as stealing coins from a blind beggar.

The girl's room was at the back. A single bed, neatly made with a plain white nightie folded on the pillow. Hanging at the end was a pair of jeans. He ran his hands over them. They were slightly damp: probably the ones she'd been wearing out riding just now. She must have thrown them over the bed when she came in to change. Beneath them was a white bra. It too was damp. He felt the lacy cups, pictured the breasts they had been cradling until a few minutes ago, the nipples tight and hard in the cold.

He felt a movement of arousal. From his vantage point in the woods he'd watched her exercising the horses. With the sleet drifting down between them he couldn't make out her face clearly but he could sense she was a handsome piece, very sure of herself and confident in the saddle. He could tell that. She probably got a kick out of controlling a horse; she was that kind of girl. He'd watched her around the stables with the two grooms and there was no mistaking who was in charge.

She'd be a damned sight less cool if she could see him now.

He went over to the dressing table with its feminine clutter of bottles and brushes. There was a teddy bear perched against the mirror. She didn't strike him as someone who needed that kind of childlike comfort but you learned things about people on a job like this.

Quickly he searched through the drawers below but there was nothing. Going over to the chest of drawers he went through her clothes, lingering a moment longer over the flimsy underwear. He was no more perverted than the next man but he found this invasion of privacy intensely exciting. He could smell her scent, sense her body in his hands. It was a form of rape – he knew that – distant and remote but no less real than if she'd been there beneath him.

There was nothing in the drawers. He looked around the room and then he saw it. On the bedside table was a jewellery box, half hidden beneath an opened paperback. There had to be one – every woman has a jewellery box. He memorised the position of the book before putting it aside and flipping open the lid. There were the usual trinkets in there:

earrings and rings, a brooch in the shape of a salamander, a watch with no strap. But not what he was looking for.

There was a second layer. Carefully he eased up the tray and a movement behind him made him spin around.

'What are you doing in here?'

It was the old woman. She was standing in the doorway, basket in hand, her face stupid with surprise.

Strossmayer shut the lid of the box, slowly, carefully, feeling the sudden flood of adrenaline burst into anger. What the hell was she doing here? He'd seen her leave. How could she be back so soon?

The old woman's gaze was moving. From his face to the box and back to his face again. Dull and somehow dazed. He could see her thinking, making the connections.

His hand went out, snatched up the bedside lamp. He took two quick steps forward. She shouldn't have come back like this. She'd seen him; she knew him.

The stupid cow was staring at him. She opened her mouth to speak. The lamp swung round in his hand.

And she never said a word.

'It's good of you to come, Countess.'

'Your secretary said it was urgent.'

'It's about your pictures.'

'Are you going to give them back to me?'

Ottlik wished he could say yes. There was a beguiling naiveté to the way she asked the question, like an attractive child who has learned how to twist grown-ups round its finger.

'I'm afraid that is out of the question.'

From the smile that flicked across her lips he could tell that she never believed he might.

'That's a shame,' she said.

They walked down the gallery together. When she'd arrived, Ottlik had been supervising the rehanging of the Bellini portrait of Catherine Cornaro, the plain, middle-aged queen who had spent her last years ruling over a toy court after the Venetians had taken her real one from her. He'd outlined the story to the Countess.

'She looks very sad about it,' she'd commented.

'She had every reason to be.'

'It looks to me as though she took to the bottle,' she'd said. 'That's what most women do when they lose something important.'

Ottlik had run his eyes over the plump, passive face in the portrait and thought: God knows, she's probably right. It had never occurred to him before.

'We can't turn back the pages of history,' he said now as they came downstairs. 'If we gave back every painting because we thought we didn't own it the whole art world would be in chaos, Countess.'

'I wish you wouldn't call me that.'

'What would you prefer?'

'My name's Terezia.'

Ottlik didn't think he could get used to that. She might be Terezia to her friends but to an historian like himself she was heir to one of the oldest titles in the country and he felt more comfortable with the title in place.

'I'll see what I can do.'

She smiled at his discomfort. He couldn't get away from the idea that she was mocking him. He never found it easy to talk to women and she seemed to sense it.

'I've been talking to the minister,' he said, returning to more solid territory. 'About the compensation paid to your family after the war.'

'And what did he say?'

'I read the statement your English friend made after his conversation with your father's solicitors and I don't mind saying I'm appalled. We had no idea the payment was withdrawn.'

'And what are you going to do about it?'

'The minister thought it might be suitable if we were to replace it now.'

'Pay me the money, you mean?'

'After it has been reassessed for inflation.'

She paused in the passageway to consider, hands in her overcoat pocket, weight resting on one leg. The cold winter light from the roof light carved her face with shadows. She really was bewitchingly beautiful, he thought, like a Greek statue.

'If I take the money I'm accepting that you own the pictures,' she said after a moment.

'We do anyway.'

'How's that?'

'We may not condone the past but we can't alter it.'

The girl pondered. 'How much are you offering?'

'We estimated the original sum would be worth four and a half million forints today.'

'Thirty pieces of silver – isn't that what the Bible says?'

He was surprised she knew. 'We have nothing to gain by giving it to you,' he said.

'Then why do it?'

'Think of it more as an apology.'

The green-grey eyes studied him gravely. Then with a sudden smile she said, 'If that is really what it is then I accept.'

She shook hands with him and walked down the steps of the museum. As soon as she was round the corner out of sight she threw her arms in the air and gave a yelp of triumph so that a woman passing by with a child in a pushchair stepped off the kerb into a puddle. But Terezia didn't even notice. For and a half million forints! It may not seem much to the Hungarian Government but it was a fortune to her.

Driving down Andrassy Utca she made a list of priorities. First, and most important, was to complete the payments on the brood mare. That was the beginning they'd been working towards all this time. What was left over must be divided carefully, some of it to make the improvements she needed for the stables, maybe take on another hand. The rest could be put towards paying off some of the debts; lightening the burden of responsibility. Whatever happened, it had to be put to good use.

Having piously decided this in her mind, she walked up the Vaci and bought herself a fur coat. It was long and dark and rippled like light on water, horribly extravagant, almost a fifth of the money that Ottlik had just offered her, but so soft and warm and elegant that she couldn't resist it. Guiltily she put it in the back of the car and drove home.

The door of the house stood open. She hurried in, full of her news, and stopped dead in her tracks.

There were two policemen in the kitchen.

'What are you doing here?' she asked in surprise.

Neither of them wanted to answer. There was newspaper laid out in the passage beyond.

She felt a sudden clutch of panic. 'What's happening?'

One of the policemen asked if she was related to Rosza Kovacs.

'Rosza? Yes . . .' The strength was draining from her legs. 'Oh God, what is it?'

Another policeman appeared from her room.

'Oh God,' she repeated in a whisper.

There was a crunch of gravel behind. She turned around. It was one of the stable lads.

'Gyorgy—'

The whiteness of his face said it all.

'It was an accident, Terezia . . . a terrible accident . . .'

Alexander Kasinczy-Landsberg lowered the polished steel pushbar of the weightlifting apparatus back on to its rest and sat up. He was wearing sports shorts over a tight one-piece bicycling outfit and a sweat band round his forehead, all of them in colours that didn't like each other.

He held his wrist between two fingers, checking his pulse rate, but Max couldn't see he had much to worry about. He looked in pretty good condition. The only damage that his twenty-minute workout in this ultra modern, over-equipped gym had done to him was to knock up a couple of damp patches under his armpits and deepen the pace of his breathing, a combination which conveniently gave his blond good looks a more rugged edge.

Max thought it was time to draw the meeting to order. 'You wanted to see me.'

Without looking up from his counting Alexander said, 'I thought you should be given a chance to explain your behaviour.'

'Behaviour?'

'Yesterday, in my father's office.'

'I was passing on a message.'

'You know what I mean, Anderson.'

'He asked me to be there.'

'And I'm asking you not to give me any of that horse-shit.' A member of the hotel staff passed him a towel. Alexander levered himself to his feet and gave his arms and hair a brisk rub down. 'You were riding him from the moment you came in, asking a lot of damned fool questions about things that don't concern you.'

'I wanted some answers.'

'What is it with you?' he asked, slinging the towel round his neck. 'Do you get a buzz out of needling people, is that it?'

'Not particularly.'

'Because it sure as hell looks like it.'

'I need to know who murdered Dr Verity.'

'Then go talk to the police, better still go talk to Sherlock Holmes back in London, but leave my family out of it because it's got nothing to do with them.'

'Verity was interested in your family.'

'Yeah, all the old ones who died like a hundred years ago. You may think me funny, Anderson, but I'm not too bothered about what happened back in the Middle Ages.'

'Neither was he.'

'What is it with this Verity anyway?'

'He came over here a few weeks—' Max would have given him a brief biography but Alexander didn't need it.

'Yeah, I know who he is. He was the English dude who got blown away for messing with things that he didn't own. Right?'

'That's the one.'

'So what has that got to do with my family?'

'He was looking for the Hunyadi Venus.'

'How do you figure that?'

'It was taken up into the hills and buried at the end of the war.'

'Yeah, I heard that.' He paused and reflected on this piece of history a moment. 'It was on a hunting party; my Pa was there. They shot a pig and buried the Venus in the ground where it came down.'

'That's why Verity came over here.'

'Because they shot a pig?'

'Because some of the books have just been given back. Mountains of them. Not worth much on the whole. I've been looking through them. But a lot of the account books from the house are there. Also the game books.'

'No kidding—' A flicker of interest now.

'That's what Verity was looking for when he went to the Palace. It had me foxed for a while.'

'Does it say where the thing was killed?'

'An exact description – in the hills above the river, in some place they call the Castle Rock.'

Alexander gave a shrug. 'So he was one jump ahead of the rest.'

One of the staff appeared to tell him that his bath was ready. Alexander glanced at his watch, told them to give him ten minutes and the man withdrew.

'So this guy had a line on the Venus,' he said, turning back to Max. 'But he didn't find it.'

'I think he might have.'

'It's gone, Anderson. Didn't you hear my father tell you? Whatever it was they did with it, it's not there now. It's gone, finished, end of story. Sometimes I wonder if the darned thing really existed in the first place or whether it's just another of those goddamned fairy tales they come up with around here.'

'I think Verity found it. Her certainly found something. He told me so himself.'

'You met the bastard?'

'Not socially.'

'Christ.' He didn't like the sound of that. 'You hang out with some wacky people.'

'When I spoke to Verity he said he had something valuable and he was scared out of his wits.'

'Are you suggesting my father has something to do with this?'

Max hesitated. This was a field of tulips that needed to be tiptoed through with some care. 'I think your father would like to have the Venus.'

Alexander Kasinczy-Landsberg stared at him in silence. 'Jesus Christ,' he said quietly. 'I should have you chucked out of here.'

'I had enough trouble getting in.'

'You've got a nerve.' He had those same green-grey eyes that seemed to burn into your flesh when he was angry. 'You've got a goddamned nerve. And what's worse, you haven't a horse's arse idea of what you're talking about. You don't know what kind of man you're dealing with here. Sure my father wants the Venus back. But if some prick had found it he'd have bought it off him. He wouldn't have started throwing threats around, he'd just have bought the darned thing. It would be up there on the mantelpiece and he'd be telling stories about what it cost him.'

'You don't know what Verity was asking.'

'It doesn't matter what he was asking. You may not have noticed it, Mr Anderson, but money's not the problem in my family. Sure, my father has got a bit screwy about all this Hungarian stuff. He wants his house and his title and all the family knick-knacks back. He really believes in all that old-world aristocratic crap. But if you want to suggest he'd bend the law to get it you can talk to my solicitors.'

'If that's what you want—'

'No, that's not what I want, Mr Anderson. What I want is for you to get the hell out of here. What I want is for you to go away, to stop nosing in my family's affairs, and to not come back again. Because if you don't I'm sure as hell going to make your life not worth the living. Now, if it's all the same with you, I'm going to take a bath.'

'The doctors say it's bad.'

'How bad?'

'They've taken X-rays. There's a fracture to the skull.'

'Has she said anything?'

Joszef shook his head. 'She's been unconscious ever since she came here. They say she will be for quite a while.'

'But she'll come round, won't she?' She spoke in a rush. 'They said she'd come round?'

'I don't know, Tereyki.'

He sat in the gaunt plastic chair, elbows resting on his knees, staring ahead of himself as though he was transfixed by an invisible television screen. Terezia stood beside him. Through the porthole in the door she could see into the ward where Rosza lay surrounded by the stark impersonal medical equipment, her life held in the little green bead that scribbled its way across the screen.

'How did it happen?' she whispered.

'I don't know. I think it was a burglar.'

'Burglar?' It seemed inconceivable.

'He was in your room. Rosza must have come in, found him there and he . . . he did it.'

'Did what?'

'Hit her . . . with the lamp by your bed.'

Terezia gazed into the ward. She could see it in her imagination, picture every detail. She felt shock and guilt.

'Oh God,' she said. 'It's all my fault.'

'It's no one's fault.'

'I should have gone back with her. I gave her a lift down to the village. She left her purse behind and got out. She said she'd go down later. I should have gone back. But I had to get into Budapest . . . I was in a hurry.'

'It's not your fault, Tereyki.'

'I shouldn't have left her. If I'd gone back this wouldn't have happened.'

'If you'd been there it would only have been worse.'

She glanced round. It hadn't occurred to her that anyone else could have been the victim; that it could have been her lying there. For some reason she'd assumed that he'd picked on Rosza because she was old and alone, as the street gangs of children in Budapest pick their victims for being old and alone.

She sat down beside Joszef and put her arm around his shoulders, trying to make him feel her there with him.

'What was he doing there?' she asked after a moment. 'What did he want?'

'Who knows?'

'There's nothing valuable in my room. There's not even any money.'

'He must have thought there was something.' He was still staring ahead. 'It doesn't really matter.'

There were a couple of policemen further down the passage, talking together, keeping their distance. One of them took Terezia aside.

'When the lady comes round we'll need a word with her.'

'I understand—'

'Nothing disrespectful or anything, but police work has to come first.'

'I know what you have to do,' Terezia said quickly. 'I'll just be glad when she comes round. God, I'll be glad *if* she does—'

'Don't think like that.' He had a round, kindly face. 'These things are never as bad as they look. My old ma was taken into hospital last year. Pneumonia. We thought her time had come. Three days later she was out and giving us what-for for not hoovering the carpets when she was gone.'

Terezia smiled distantly. He meant well but he couldn't know what she was thinking or feeling at that moment. No one could. Neither love nor tragedy can be shared.

It was after three. From the call box in the passage she rang the stables.

'Gyorgy says he'll stay until I get back,' she said, sitting down beside Joszef again.

'He's a good boy, Gyorgy. I wish I could stay here myself.'

'You can.'

'I wouldn't want her waking up in a strange place. She doesn't like hospitals. I wish I could be there when it happens, just to let her know it's all right.'

'You can stay, can't you?'

He shook his head. 'They haven't got the beds.'

'Who says?'

'Some guy I spoke to earlier – administrator.'

'You told him who you were?'

'He said the place was full.'

'I'll see about that.'

Terezia took the lift up a floor and marched down the passage, glad to have a purpose, something on which to vent her pent-up energy.

The girl in the reception of the administration department didn't rate her chances.

'Úr Dobos is busy at present,' she said.

'I need to see him.'

The secretary shook her head. She'd like to help but her hands were tied. 'I'm afraid without an appointment—'

'Is someone in there?'

'Not as such—' She clambered to her feet as Terezia

swept through into the office without knocking.

Dobos was taking his afternoon cup of tea. There was a biscuit perched on the saucer, like they show in the adverts. It toppled off on to his lap as the door burst open.

'What do you want?' He wasn't used to this kind of invasion.

'I need a bed put into one of the wards.'

'I'm sorry, Úr Dobos.' It was the secretary from behind Terezia. 'I couldn't stop her.'

Dobos nodded and shooed her away with one hand. He could handle this.

'What bed?' he said. 'Where?'

'I need a bed for my stepfather so that he can stay the night with his wife. She's in the emergency ward.'

Dobos was catching on. The GBH on the first floor. He'd already given a ruling on that.

'There are not enough beds in the ward.'

'Then get one,' Terezia ordered.

This was one angry woman but Dobos wasn't going to be pushed around in his own office.

'You run the place, do you, lady?'

'I'm telling you what's going to happen.'

'And who are you?'

'The Countess Kasinczy-Landsberg.'

Terezia had never before used her title to get what she wanted but she gave him the full broadside of it now and saw it hit the mark. Dobos gaped; his Adam's apple dropped into his collar and came up again like a yo-yo on a string.

He was wondering what the hell was going on. He'd seen the old man. Scruffy old fellow with a beard. He'd taken him for a peasant farmer; nothing important. No one had told him he was something to do with a title as long as your arm. But he wasn't giving in yet.

'We can't start changing the layout of the wards just to suit you.'

'No? You'll allow the police to interrogate an old woman but not allow her husband to be there at the same time. Is that it?'

'The police have to be there.'

'And he doesn't?

'I'm only following the rules.'

'What's the problem, Dobos? Filled your quota of decency for this month?'

Dobos was rapidly coming to the conclusion that something had to be done. 'She'd have to be in one of the private wards if he's going to stay.'

'So put her in a private ward.'

'They cost money.'

'So charge it to me. But get it done now.'

'Yes, sure, Countess.' He was reaching for the phone. 'I didn't know that's what you wanted. They didn't tell me.'

'Well, now we understand each other there shouldn't be a problem.'

She shot him a dazzling smile and as she swept out of the office again Dobos found himself feeling pretty good about being able to help.

17

In the office on the first floor of the British Embassy the lights burned late that night. Colonel Biszku stood at the window, staring down at the street. It was not a social visit. His overcoat was unbuttoned, hands thrust into the pockets of his baggy grey suit.

'He's here,' he said. 'Somewhere in the country.'

'Are you sure of that?'

'He wasn't on any scheduled flight out and he hasn't crossed through any of the border passes. I've checked with Customs. And his luggage is still in his apartment. Packed but still there.'

'Then you're probably right,' Stratton agreed politely.

Biszku glanced round at him. 'You had no idea he was intending to do this?'

'No.'

'He said nothing to you about staying?'

'To be honest,' Stratton told him, 'we've seen very little of him in the past few days. He's kept himself busy.'

'Doing what, for Christ's sake?'

'I really couldn't say.' Nor would he if he had known. It was not a requirement of his job to help the police; only to appear to help them. 'I was aware though,' he added, 'that he was not at all happy at the way he's been treated over this.'

Biszku ignored the criticism. He was impervious to the ways of diplomats. 'You realise I have no alternative but to have him arrested.'

'At which point you will, of course, pass him over to the Embassy.'

'I have no reason to do that.'

'I need hardly remind you that he is a member of the diplomatic staff here.'

Biszku wasn't getting tangled up in protocol. 'His diplomatic status in this country ended when the flight left without him. He is a wanted man now like any other petty criminal. I've issued a warrant for his arrest. I've no doubt we'll pick him up pretty soon; he can't get far. The police have his picture.'

To Stratton the whole subject was sordid, distasteful.

'Is this really necessary?'

'Yes,' Biszku said flatly. 'It is necessary.'

'Is there not maybe some compromise we can come to? If we were to agree to—'

'No.' Biszku cut him off short. 'The time for talking with Úr Anderson is over. He has taken the law into his own hands and must face the consequences.'

He turned back to the window.

'If you want my own opinion,' he added over his shoulder, 'I think the man is out of his mind. He must have known his career as a diplomat was finished the moment he decided to stay.'

'And I think he would tell you,' Stratton said with a sudden flash of impatience, 'that he knew it would have been finished if he'd left.'

*

'You've got a room to let.'

'How's that?'

'The sign in the window,' Max said. 'It says you've got a room to let.'

The landlord was chewing on something. He had fair hair cut down to bristle. It was much the same length as the week's stubble on his plump cheeks. His cardigan was parted to reveal a belly partly covered by a dirty T-shirt that his trousers failed to meet as the braces were hanging down. It gave him the look of a middle-aged schoolboy with a large catapult dangling from his back pocket.

'You want to rent?' He was cottoning on fast.

'Not before I've seen the place.'

'I need a week's rent in advance.'

'Let's look at it first.'

The landlord led the way to the second floor, wheezing heavily and muttering what sounded like words of encouragement to himself. A lavatory flushed and a thin young man flitted down the passage ahead of them like a bat. He glanced at them as he vanished into his room but didn't speak. It was that friendly a place.

The room was predictably small with a bed, striped mattress, a chest of drawers and a pair of curtains that didn't try to match the wallpaper.

'How long you staying then?' the landlord, who called himself Gombos, asked when Max said he'd take it.

'Couple of months, maybe longer.'

'I'll need to see some ID.'

'I don't have any with me,' Max said, hefting his shoulder bag on to the bed.

'I'll need to see something,' Gombos told him. 'You could be anyone.'

'I'll give you a month's rent up front.'

That was good enough in Gombos's book. Money spoke louder than references.

'What you do then?' he asked.

'I'm a journalist.'

He gave a grunt. 'That accounts for it then.'

'For what?'

'The way you speak – you American, then?'

'How did you guess?'

'It's your accent,' Gombos told him. 'I can always tell an American by the way they speak.'

Max counted out notes and handed them over to Gombos who counted through them again out loud before folding them away in his back pocket.

'There's no cooking,' he said. 'No smoking and no women in here after six. Got that?'

'No chance of a romantic dinner party then—'

'Toilet's down the passage. Bathroom opposite. You can get the key from me first. It's twenty forints a time.'

It felt like home already.

Max locked the door and went outside into the drab street. From a café round the corner he bought a couple of ham rolls and an evening paper. Later, lying on the mattress, he leafed through the pages but there was no mention of him. There was no reason why there might be. Diplomats who did a bunk were hardly the material that sold newspapers. But he had no doubt that the police would know all about it.

On the third page a small item caught his eye. It was only a short piece. If he hadn't been scanning the text more closely than usual he would have missed it.

It reported that a sixty-eight-year-old woman had been mugged earlier that day by a burglar trying to break into the Palace of Fetevis.

*

Rosza's name was taken off the critical list just after nine that evening. A doctor appeared to say that her condition was satisfactory. She'd have to stay in for a few days but the worst was past. In the meantime she had come round and they could go in and see her.

The visit didn't last more than five minutes. Rosza was disorientated, confused by the strange room, by the presence of the doctors and the two policemen who pressed their questions on her. But she managed to give them a few answers before the doctor announced that she must be left to rest.

'It's good,' Terezia whispered as they came out.

Joszef nodded.

'She remembers more than I expected. I thought she'd be concussed.'

'No,' he said. 'She's all right.'

He stopped in the passageway, head lowered. Terezia put her arm around him.

'Silly old woman,' he muttered into her shoulder. 'I knew it would take more than a hit from a lamp. She's got a head like a rock.'

His face was buried in her neck and she held him as he wept. Then he took out his handkerchief and blew hard.

'You must be getting back home, Tereyki,' he said.

'In a minute.'

She felt physically and emotionally drained. For the past four hours they'd been waiting here, pacing the little room, their nerves stretched to breaking point. She hated hospitals, particularly this one with its drab paint, its air of gloom and its ridiculous little Christmas tree perched in the nurses' dispensary.

'Is there somewhere you can get a drink here?' she wondered. 'I could murder for a cup of coffee.'

They found a cafeteria on the ground floor and sat at a table in the corner together.

'Will you be all right alone?' Joszef asked.

She nodded.

'You'll keep the door locked? I'll be over in the morning.'

'You can stay all day if you like.'

'What, here? I'd go out of my mind. I'll take the bus back in the morning.'

Terezia stirred her coffee, studying the little whirlpool made by the plastic spoon, her mind on the few words that Rosza had mumbled to the police. 'She said it was a man with a moustache.'

'It could be anyone.'

She was watching the spoon. 'Max said the man who was after Verity had a moustache.'

'Lots of people have moustaches,' Joszef said gently. 'It doesn't mean a thing.'

'What did he want, do you think?'

'Money probably.'

'We don't keep any money there.'

'He wouldn't know that.'

She took the spoon out and tapped the last drop of coffee off before laying it on the table top. The cafeteria was almost empty. A woman was cleaning the floor with a damp cloth on the end of a broom. Terezia steepled her fingers against her lips and stared across the foyer.

'Max told them I had a locket in my room. He said it had some hair in it which would prove Papa was my father. That's what he was looking for, wasn't it?'

'I think he imagined we kept the wages in there.'

'It doesn't exist,' she said. 'Max just made it up to give them something to think about. But they didn't know that.'

'Maybe you should tell him.'

She gave a shrug. 'He's not around any more.'

'Maybe it would be better if you stayed here tonight.'

'I'll be fine.'

She kissed him goodbye and drove back home. Gyorgy was dozing by the range when she came in. He awoke with a start and they exchanged their news, quickly and shortly, speaking in whispers as though there were someone else in the house who mustn't be disturbed, before she packed him off to his home.

She went through to her room. Then she remembered the newspaper on the floor, the lamp still white with fingerprint dust, and went next door. She could face all that in the morning. But not tonight. Unzipping her dress she threw it over the end of the bed and crept between the sheets without switching on the light.

Ten miles away, in the book-lined study of his house, Zoltan was cradling a balloon-glass of cognac in one hand. The lamp on his desk cast a pool of light over the polished silver ink-stand, the framed photos and the ornamental dagger that he used as a letter opener. It had been given to his father by Hermann Goering after a day's hunting back in the thirties. Zoltan could remember the Reich Marshal standing vast and gaudy in his mock-medieval hunt gear, announcing, as he made the presentation, the forests of Fetevis to be of a unique mystical significance in the great quest of their nations. Zoltan had been eight at the time and it wasn't until he was three times that age that he realised what a buffoon the man had been.

He listened now as Vargas made his report. When the man had finished he swirled the spirit in the glass and took a sip.

'The man's an arsehole,' he said. He spoke quietly and

calmly as though he weren't voicing an opinion, just trying to locate the species that Strossmayer belonged to. 'I give him a simple job and he louses up.'

'From what I hear, the old woman came back unexpectedly,' Vargas ventured.

'Did she get a look at him?'

'He says not.'

'He'd better be right. I've seen the bastard, spoken to him. He knows me.'

'There's no connection that can be made,' Vargas assured him hurriedly.

'You'd better hope to hell you're right about that. The man's a goddamned amateur blundering around like a bull in a china shop. I can't think why you give him the work.'

Vargas didn't want to go into that right now.

'He's not indispensable,' he observed.

'Damned right he's not.'

'There has been some good from it.' He changed the subject. 'He tells me the locket wasn't there.'

'Did he have time to search the place?'

'Long enough to be sure it wasn't there.'

'You mean it's some place else?'

'I think more likely it never existed in the first place. Anderson just threw it in as an obstruction.' Vargas allowed himself to sound disparaging. 'I can't see why. He must have known we'd see through it.'

'He had you going.'

'It had to be looked into before it could be dismissed,' Vargas said primly.

Zoltan stared down at the glass in his hand and for a moment Vargas thought the meeting was over. Then he spoke.

'I want to know what her price is.'

'She may not have one—'

'Everyone has a price,' Zoltan said harshly. 'Especially women. You've just got to find what it is. Does she want money? Does she want fast cars, smart friends, a part in some goddamned Hollywood film? What is it?'

'Anderson reckoned she wouldn't sell the place.'

Zoltan leaned forward in his chair, the viscous brown spirit rocking in the glass with the sudden movement.

'I don't give a toss about the house. Houses you can build; houses you can buy. What I want is her to drop her claim on the family name.'

'But I understand—'

'I don't care what you understood, Laszlo. She drops her claim to the family name – every aspect of it. I want her to put in writing that she's nobody's daughter at all. The rest she can keep. Got it?'

'You mean she could keep the house?'

Zoltan's face was gaunt in the light of the desk lamp.

'If that's what it takes.

'I see—'

'No, you don't see, Laszlo,' he said coldly. 'You don't see anything and you don't need to see anything. Just find what her price is and leave the rest to me.'

18

At nine the following morning Max was coming down the steps of the Arpad Bridge on to Margit Island. He was wary of being seen out in the streets right now. Budapest has a population of over a million but there's a sod's law that states you'll always bump into someone you know when you don't want to.

Fortunately, the piercingly cold air allowed him to turn up the collar on his coat and wrap a scarf over half his face so that he was hardly recognisable to people passing on their way to work. He'd abandoned his fur-lined hat for a grey herringbone cap he'd picked up in a market stall earlier that morning. If he were being critical, he'd have said that between them the scarf and cap made him look like a gangster from a B-movie but he'd rather that than look like a rogue diplomat who'd just spent the worst night of his life on a mattress riddled with fleas.

In summer the island is crowded with picnickers and sunbathers but at this time of year there was hardly a soul in the place so it wasn't hard to find the Sergeant. He was sitting on a bench overlooking the water, a brown paper parcel on his lap in which he was clasping a polystyrene cup of coffee.

He greeted Max with a slight shyness, his eyes drifting round the trees as he said good morning.

'Did you find out that registration number?' Max asked as they sat down again.

'I did, sir.'

'Who's it belong to?'

The Sergeant put the lid back on his coffee cup and set it down beside him. He was embarrassed. 'No offence, sir,' he said slowly. 'But I'm . . .'

'But you're not meant to be speaking to me.' Max finished the sentence for him.

'Something like that, sir.'

'You don't have to; you know that.' He didn't want to get the man into trouble.

'We've been told to report to the police if we know where you're staying.'

'You don't, do you?'

The Sergeant smiled. 'No, I don't. That's just what I said to myself. A phone number is not the same as an address, is it?'

'Not the same at all.'

'And I reasoned that you're only doing what the police should have done from the start.'

'Tracking down that car, for example.'

'That kind of thing.'

'Who does it belong to?'

The Sergeant took the lid off his coffee again and took a sip at it. Now that he'd squared his conscience he felt better. 'It's a company called Triton. They're a haulage firm about thirty miles up the river.'

'There wasn't a name registered?'

'Just the company.'

The Sergeant stared at the ice flows drifting downstream

like giant lily pads and took another sip of his coffee. 'I thought I might go up there this afternoon,' he said thoughtfully. 'Take a look at the place.'

'It's a nice idea, Sergeant, but you don't have to do that.'

He gave a shrug. 'I've nothing on; I'd rather like a trip out into the country.'

'If you're looking for a bit of fresh air.'

There was a ghost of amusement in the Sergeant's eyes. 'I might even take a camera with me.'

A man with a dog was approaching down the path. Max got up to go.

'You know where to contact me?'

'I've got your phone number.'

'Not the address?'

'Unfortunately, you wouldn't give that to me.'

Vargas swung the Porsche out into the other lane and trod on the accelerator, overtaking the lorry that had been holding him back for the past three miles. He'd passed on the chauffeur that day and was driving himself. What he had to say to Terezia was between them and them alone.

The car coming the other way flashed its lights at him. He hit the horn as he swung back inside. Stupid cow. He hadn't even noticed her there. His thoughts had been miles away.

The conversation with Zoltan the night before had puzzled him. And puzzled wasn't a frame of mind Vargas liked to entertain too often. The one gift he had as a lawyer was that he knew what the boss wanted; often before he did so himself. The house was easy to understand. The old man had let himself go a little crazy over it, pumping huge sums of money into the system to get his hands on it. But still, Vargas could see where he was coming from. It was his inheritance, right? A man has to have his roots, especially a man as rich as Zoltan Kasinczy-Landsberg. His obsession with the rotting pile was no different from that of all those Texas oil millionaires who sink a fortune into finding the miserable little hovel in Ireland or Scotland that some enterprising marketing shark had convinced them was once home to their ancestors.

In some ways Zoltan's passion had been endearing. It was the one soft spot in the old man's character, the one facet of his mind that showed he was at least human.

So why the hell was he letting it go? That was the question that had been bothering Vargas. Zoltan had bribed ministers, blackmailed *aparatiks*, bought up failing and defunct industries where it might be popular, all to get his hands on his family home. So why should he suddenly decide to let the girl have it?

Vargas had been in the office at six that morning, glued to the computer screen, searching through the labyrinthine framework of the Landsberg Corporation. But there was nothing that he could put his finger on: no weakness, no insecurity. The only conclusion he could come up with was that the old man was holding out on him. There was something that he wasn't telling; something that Vargas wasn't allowed to know.

He didn't like that; he didn't like that one little bit. Vargas didn't operate on a need-to-know basis. He needed to know everything. How else could he make himself indispensable?

Vargas wasn't going to let it get to him though. He may not like the situation but it did open other possibilities, one of which was so tantalising that as he approached the Palace he felt a worm of excitement turn in his stomach.

The gates were chained up, goddamn it. He'd have to ditch the car and walk. That wasn't the way he'd planned it.

He'd wanted the Porsche up there, parked amongst the faded ruins of the Palace like a UFO sitting on some primitive planet. A car might be just a substitute for the male organ but the chances were that even Terezia would be impressed by a 200-horsepower male organ that can do nought to sixty in nine seconds.

She was standing in the stable yard holding the reins of a horse and talking to the old man, Joszef Kovacs, when he finally made it up the hill.

'You should have worn something more sensible,' she told him when he showed her the pitiful state of his shoes.

They were Italian, hand-made and ruined by the mud of her blasted driveway. Not that she cared; she just stood there with the suggestion of a smirk in those extraordinary eyes of hers.

'What do you want?' she asked.

He told her he wanted to speak to her in private. She said there was nothing he could have to say that couldn't be said in front of the old man. She might have made a fight of it if Joszef hadn't decided he had work to do elsewhere.

Terezia led the horse across the yard, its hooves loud on the cobbles.

'So?' she said. 'What is it you've got that's so private?'

'You decided to pass on the offer Count Zoltan made.'

She gave a little shrug. 'Of course.'

'Why of course?'

'I'm not going to be bought off like that.'

'It was a generous offer—'

'If I were selling. But as I'm not selling it's irrelevant what he was offering.'

She unbuckled the girth and, with a deft movement, ducked under the horse's belly and slipped the saddle off on to her arm. Vargas kept well back. He didn't share his fellow countrymen's fascination for these large and dangerous animals.

'What is it you want?' he asked.

Terezia turned and faced him. She probably had no idea what a provocative sight she was standing there, her hips swung out to one side to take the weight of the saddle, sleeves pulled back to the elbow, the shapeless jumper emphasising the long, sleek thighs below.

'To be left alone,' she said.

He chose to treat this as a witticism. 'What I meant is, what do you hope to gain from this war with Count Zoltan?'

'I didn't start any war.'

'No, I appreciate that.'

'I intend to keep what is mine,' she told him and, turning on her heel, she carried the saddle off into the tack room.

'The house, you mean?' Vargas inquired as he followed her.

'It belongs to me.'

'You may have some trouble proving that.'

The tack room was dark with polished leather, brass buckles and bits glinting in the light from the open door. Terezia slid the saddle on to a rack and rested her arms on it.

'I didn't ask to take this place on,' she told him. 'But now that I've got it I don't intend to let it go.'

'There's no knowing how the courts will settle in the end.'

'I know that.'

'The case could run for years.'

'Possibly.'

'Unless, that is . . .' He let the words drift away as though they had prompted a new thought. 'Unless I were to make other arrangements.'

Terezia paused. The green eyes studied him for a moment in the darkness of the tack room.

'Other arrangements?'

Gentle, Vargas told himself. Keep it gentle. Don't over-play your hand. This has to sound like just another deal, just another piece of legal manoeuvring.

'It's possible,' he said, 'that I could persuade Zoltan to drop the case completely.'

'On this place?' Irritatingly, she didn't rate his chances. 'You must be joking.'

'I've never been more serious in my life.'

'He'd never do that. He's spent his whole life trying to get it.'

'That's because he's always been advised that it was possible to get it,' Vargas told her. 'I could convince him that it's no longer possible.'

'He wouldn't believe you.'

'Oh, I think he would.' He wanted her to be sure she understood his relationship with her cousin. He wasn't just another hired lawyer. He was an adviser, a spin-doctor. 'Count Zoltan listens to me. On legal matters he listens very carefully.'

'And you'd tell him that there is no chance of his ever getting the house?'

'It may be true.'

'Is it?' she asked bluntly.

'It could be the law is always open to . . . interpretation. Of course,' he added quickly, 'that would have to be the end of it. If I managed to get you the house, you'd have to agree not to try to push your claim further.'

Terezia straightened up and ran her hands slowly down over her hips, hooking the thumbs into her pockets. Christ, what was she like in bed, he wondered. What was she like when all that golden hair came spilling out of that bloody handkerchief over the pillow?

She was looking at him, her head cocked to one side. 'Why should you want to do this for me?'

'Think of it as a gesture of goodwill.'

'Oh yes?'

Vargas leaned back against the door frame. The air was heavy with the scent of oil and leather. He gave a quick smile. 'We haven't got off to a very good start, have we?'

'I hadn't realised we'd made a start at all.'

'I was thinking. What you need here is a bit of financial backing. If you're going to make a go of these stables you need promotion. It's no good just doing up the place. You need to get the name known, get it talked about in the right places.'

'And you'd do that for me, would you?'

'I have a lot of contacts in Budapest.'

'Who'd like to put money into a stud farm?'

'It's worth thinking about. Maybe we could have dinner one evening, talk it over.'

'I'd rather not,' she said quickly.

'It seems a shame to see someone like you working herself to death up here when it could all be made much easier.'

'The answer's no.'

'Don't be too hasty,' he said. 'Think it over.'

'The answer's no, Úr Vargas. I don't know what you're playing at but I don't want to be part of it.'

'It's just a business proposal.'

'I don't know you and I don't trust you. And that's not a good basis for any business.'

'It could be good for both of us—'

'No.'

She went back to the horse in the yard. The darned thing was just standing there, waiting. How could she do that, Vargas wondered. How could she get such authority over a creature that can't speak, can't understand, can't even take a fax for Christ's sake?

He stayed in the doorway and watched as she led the animal into one of the stables and returned with the bridle in her hand. Without speaking she hung it up above the saddle. It was all very ordered in here, the horse's kit arranged on pegs, their names written above. It was rather like a school locker room but, with the darkness and the smell of the leather, somehow sexier.

Terezia still said nothing as she fiddled with the buckle on the bridle. It didn't bother Vargas. He knew these silences; he knew women. Silence meant they were thinking, silence meant they were waiting to be coaxed a little further.

He pushed himself away from the door and sauntered up behind her.

'You can't want to spend your life mucking out stables. There are things to do, places to see.'

Terezia was still reaching up above her head. Her jumper was drawn up, exposing the smooth curve of her bottom.

'You should be seen around the place,' he murmured. 'You're wasted up here.' And almost casually he ran his hand across the tight stretched denim of her jeans.

The effect was instantaneous.

Her head came round, slowly and deliberately, as though she'd forgotten something she wanted to say. But the look in her eyes froze the blood in his veins.

'Don't you dare touch me!' she hissed.

Vargas stepped backwards but before he could get out of range Terezia had hauled the bridle from the peg and swung it round in his face.

It caught him in the side of the head, throwing him backwards. He felt the weight of it, the sudden flash of pain where a metal part cut him. Before he could reach up to assess the damage she had swung at him again but this time he jumped back out of the way and the bridle crashed into the wall. Some tins clattered down from the shelf.

'Get out of here!'

Vargas made it over to the door. But he wasn't going to suffer the indignity of bolting. He brushed his hand across his cheek, saw the blood and gave a little smile.

'Maybe when you're in a more reasonable mood,' he said sourly.

'I am being reasonable. More reasonable than you deserve.'

And it was true. The madness had gone from her eyes as quickly as it had come. This encouraged Vargas to loiter a moment.

'It's a good deal.'

'I'm not interested in any sneaky deal of yours. I'll run this place by myself. I don't need your help or anyone else's.'

'If that's the way you want it—'

'That's how I want it.' She gave a little jerk of her head. 'Now get out of here.'

'What happened?'

It was Joszef who came running. Terezia gave a shake of her head as she hung the bridle back in place.

'It's nothing—'

Joszef looked at the cans on the ground. 'Did you have a fight?'

'No, not a fight. He was just making a pass in a clumsy sort of way.' She felt suddenly light-headed and sat down on one of the feed bins. It was lower than she expected and she came down with a bump.

'Are you all right, Tereyki?' He sat down beside her, one arm around her shoulders.

She nodded.

'Just sit still for a moment.'

'It's not important; I'm all right.'

'He gave you a fright.'

She shook her head ruefully. 'It's silly, isn't it. It shouldn't matter any more.'

'Did he . . . touch you?'

'Sometimes I think it's gone. I don't feel anything for weeks. And then something like this happens.'

'What did he want then?'

'He said he could persuade Zoltan to let me keep the house if I was nice to him.'

'Little toe-rag.'

'He said he could help promote the stables,' she said. 'He must be out of his mind. Did you see him with the horses? I thought he was going to wet himself every time one moved.' She was laughing now, a little shakily, the adrenaline wearing off.

'I bet you gave him one,' Joszef said.

'I did.' She got to her feet, smacking the dust from the back of her jeans with her hands. 'Knocked him right across the room.'

'I always said we could put you in the ring.'

She stared in the direction in which Vargas had gone. 'Why do I always attract the pillocks?'

'You don't, Tereyki. You attract lots of men. It's just that the pillocks try it on with you.'

Sergeant Norton eased down the window. Across the road, in the Triton Haulage works that stretched out untidily along the banks of the Danube, a man was approaching the car. It was parked round the side of the wooden building that served as the main offices of the company: a blue 4 x 4 with the company logo on the door, just as that scruffy little hotel manager had described.

He'd had no trouble finding the machine. Just luck that. It might have been in a garage, tucked away out of sight, or out on business for the day. But he'd spotted it the moment he turned up. There was only a mesh fence around the words, see-through as a string vest. And there it was, sitting in the open, waiting for him.

Bringing the camera up, the snout of the telescopic lens poking from the opened window, Norton examined the man. Looked hopeful, he told himself. He was dark, heavily built, in his thirties. He had a leather jacket and a black cap on his head. But Norton couldn't make out his face as he walked towards the car. He just needed him to turn around, give him a flash of his mug.

'Just a quick glimpse, sir,' he murmured to himself.

Two hours he'd been waiting in the car, watching the cranes unloading wood from a barge, the diesel engines surging and roaring as they swung it ashore. Norton didn't mind waiting. If the 4 x 4 was there someone would use it, if only to go home when they knocked off work. Everyone used the company cars to go home. That was part of the deal. It was just a question of waiting.

The man was unlocking the rear door of the vehicle. His head turned slightly. Not a clear view, but enough to see he had a moustache. No doubt of that. Norton pressed the button. Click. Not enough to identify him but better than nothing. Car and moustache together.

'Come on then, sir. Let's be seeing you.'

From the back of the car the man hefted out a canvas holdall. Norton twisted on the focus. Press, click. Not bad. A glimpse of his face this time. But he could do better; he was sure he could do better.

'Give us a nice one then for the camera.'

The man was carrying the bag back again now. Press, click. That's more like it. Head down too low but it showed the whole face. There was something satisfying about this job. Nothing to do with artistry, more with hunting. The instinct of the predator and his prey. It didn't matter that this was a camera; it could be the crossed wires of a telescopic sight he was looking through. The sensation was much the same.

A car rolled past the wooden office block. The man paused, glanced round. Norton gave a grunt of appreciation.

'Look at the birdie then, sir.'

Press, click. Beautiful, could have been posing for his picture. And another. Press, click. Perfect that one. Caught him just as he was saying something to the driver. Norton cranked on the zoom, pulled the man's face in close. 'Oh yes,' he murmured. He knew the type: thickening neck, jowls sagging below the moustache. Too much drink, my boy. Too much sitting around being cock of the roost. The face of a bully. Oh yes, he knew the type.

The camera clicked as the man went back inside. When he was out of sight, Norton rolled the film through to the end and took it out. He knew someone in Budapest who could develop it for him. It was black and white, the detail was better without colour. It would take only an hour or so to get them done.

'And then I've got you, my boy.'

Ten miles away, in the head offices of the Landsberg Corporation, Vargas stepped out of the lift and stormed down the passage to the double doors at the end. A secretary said good evening but he ignored her and went on through. A man who can walk into Count Zoltan's office without an appointment doesn't need to stand around chatting to secretaries.

The PA in reception picked up the phone to announce his arrival and ushered him straight on through.

Count Zoltan was working at his desk. Was he really working all the time, Vargas wondered, or did he just pretend to be when someone came in?

He sat back in his chair, the light of the desk lamp splashing deep shadows across his face.

'What did you find out?' he asked.

'I put your proposal to her.'

'Was she interested?'

'Emotional would be the word I'd use.'

Zoltan's eyes searched his face. 'Will she sign?'

'She may,' he said. 'When she has had time to think about it.'

'Think about it?' His voice was harsh. 'What's she got to think about? It's a good deal. She's got nothing to lose.'

That's just it, Vargas told himself. She had nothing to lose. That's what was bugging him. Why was Count Zoltan offering her a deal where she had nothing to lose?

'I think the offer came as a bit of a surprise,' he said. 'She needs a little time to get used to it.'

'But you think she'll go for it?'

'She may, if she were given some encouragement.'

'Then we must give her some encouragement.' Zoltan's eyes were on him still. 'What's that on your face?'

'Where's that?'

'Your cheek; there's a cut.'

'Oh that's nothing, just a nick.'

He wasn't letting on how he got that. But Zoltan seemed to know already, as if he could read his mind, see what had happened.

'Did you mess with her?' He put the question softly.

'Mess?'

'Did you try your luck with her, Laszlo?'

'I might have brushed against her while we were talking.' Vargas found himself admitting it.

'And she slapped your face for you?'

He gave a little laugh; there was nothing to be ashamed of. This was man's talk. 'I hardly touched her and she went round the bloody bend. I don't know what her problem is.'

'You would if you'd read the report I gave you on her.'

'I looked through it—'

'The reason I had it made was so that we could learn about this girl, understand how she thinks, not just to keep some firm of private dicks in work.'

'I didn't see anything in it about her being a screwball.' He didn't like the idea that he wasn't up to speed on this.

'No? You didn't see the part that says she doesn't like people coming up behind her. It's a sort of phobia of hers.'

'Why, some guy give her a fright or something?'

'No,' Zoltan said. 'She was raped. When she was twelve years old she was raped by some older boys.'

'I didn't read that.'

'So it would seem.'

19

The following morning, Elaine Kasinczy-Landsberg picked up the phone and dialled the number she had scrawled on her notepad.

She had long suspected her husband of having a mistress. There are small inconsistencies a wife can detect – gaps between the time of leaving work and getting home, nights spent over at the office when it didn't seem necessary – none of them much in themselves but put together they added up to evidence that Zoltan was keeping a woman.

It hadn't really bothered her. They'd lived increasingly separate lives since they'd moved to Hungary. She had her own circle of friends, mainly the wives of American businessmen, who were of not the slightest interest to Zoltan, and he had his business to occupy him. Happily, they no longer shared a bedroom. It was not something they'd openly discussed. It had just been allowed to happen and she found it a quiet relief. Elaine didn't consider herself a particularly cold or inhibited woman – she was the mother of two healthy children, after all – but some of the behaviour that was expected of a wife in the marital bed made her shudder. So if Zoltan had turned elsewhere for what she liked to think of as his 'masculine needs' it had its advantages.

But suspecting and knowing are two very different emotions, and the proof that he was keeping a woman still came as a shock.

It had just been chance. Two weeks ago, a bill for something she had never ordered arrived from a shop in the Vaci. When she looked into it, she discovered that delivery had been made to an address up on Buda Hill. She put a private detective on the job and learned that it was for a flat in Úri Utca belonging to an Anna Eckhart: single, mid-thirties, working as a lecturer in social sciences at the university. Zoltan paid her regular visits and, on occasion, stayed overnight. She had the times and dates in front of her now.

Elaine hadn't taken a knife to his clothing, scratched the paintwork of his cars, or thrown a fit of hysterics as, she learned from her friends, was the fashion these days. She'd accepted the news with the stiff upper lip that had been bred into her back in Virginia.

Rather than angry, she felt isolated. She'd never wanted to come to this country, which after a thousand years of civilisation didn't seem ever to have become properly civilised. She didn't want the title her husband lusted for; she didn't want to be the lady of the great monster of a house that she had never even seen. Her only desire was to be back home in the States, the safe, comfortable US-of-A where people and money both spoke a language she could understand.

She dialled the number of Fetevis Palace. This was not out of spite or revenge, she told herself, but simply because she'd had enough of deceptions.

A man's voice answered. He told her he was one of the stable hands. Elaine asked to speak to Terezia. She didn't hold with the use of Christian names for people she'd hardly met but she had no idea what other name the girl would use.

The boy went off to find her and Elaine waited, phone in hand, in her graceful and very expensively furnished morning room. It was ten-thirty. The thin winter sun touched the Dresden figures on her escritoire and the Renoir pastel that hung above. It was delicate and pretty, a girl carrying a basket of flowers. Now that was civilisation for you, something charming and innocent, not the catalogue of murder, mayhem and torture that the Hungarians offered in its place.

'Can I help you?' The girl's voice came on the line.

'Elaine Kasinczy-Landsberg—'

Terezia hesitated at the name. 'What can I do for you?'

'I think it's time that you and I had a talk.'

'Do we have anything to talk about?'

'Yes.' Elaine knew she sounded aloof and imperious at moments like this. It came from overcoming a natural shyness. 'I have some information that you might find helpful.'

'What sort of information?' Terezia asked.

'I don't want to speak about it on the phone. I shall be at a concert at the Vigado Hall later today. I could meet you in the foyer beforehand.'

'I'd like to know what this is about.'

'Shall we say four?'

'I need to know—'

'I'll explain when I see you,' she said and hung up.

In his office in police headquarters, Ferenc Biszku sorted through the black and white photos on his desk. His jacket hung on the back of his chair, his sleeves were rolled back from thick forearms and his hair was ruffled from his habit of running his fingers through it as he talked.

'When did they come in?'

'About twenty minutes ago.'

'Did you get a description of the man?'

'Middle-aged, short, smartly dressed like a businessman.' The Captain gave the few facts he'd managed to drag out of the duty sergeant at the front desk.

'Doesn't sound like Anderson.'

'He might have hired someone.'

Biszku prodded the prints into order on the desk with the tips of his fingers. They were a professional job. Long range but sharp as a razor. All of them showed the same heavy saturnine face, black jacket and cap, drooping moustache. In the background a 4 x 4. No prizes for guessing who that was meant to be.

'But you reckon Anderson's behind this?'

'It's the man he described.'

Biszku gave a grunt. It was like a kick in the pants having these pictures shoved on to his desk. He was being told how to do his job. He had a cheek, this Anderson.

'Have you got a lead on him, yet?'

'This guy?'

'Anderson—'

'He took twenty thousand forints out of his bank account on the morning he was meant to be going. My guess is he's holed up in some cheap hotel.'

'They'd want to see his passport.'

'He speaks Hungarian well enough to claim he works in the country.'

'Accent's still foreign.'

'Or some friend. He's been here two years; he'll have contacts he can use.'

'He can't last long on twenty thousand.'

'He used a credit card yesterday.'

Biszku looked up from the photos. A credit card was the quickest way of getting a fix on the man.

'Where?'

'Vac Hospital.'

It didn't make sense. 'What do you buy in a hospital?'

'He ordered a bunch of flowers. Over the phone. He wasn't there himself.'

'And they accepted?'

'Seems so.' The Captain gave a shrug. Three years ago credit card payments over the phone were science fiction.

'Who did he want flowers for?' Biszku asked.

'The Kovacs woman.'

'Kovacs?' He didn't know any Kovacs.

'Terezia Kasinczy's foster mother. She was mugged a couple of days ago.'

'Who by?'

'They reckon she surprised a burglar.'

'When was this?' Why was he always the last to hear about these things in this place?

'A couple of days ago.'

A couple of days ago and they'd only just decided to tell him. He aimed the stub of a finger at the man.

'Get me the file,' he snarled.

The Captain knew when to act first and ask questions later. As he removed himself smartly through the door, Biszku called him back.

'And Captain—'

'Sir?'

He threw the stack of photos in his direction.

'Find out who this bastard is.'

Terezia saw the flowers later that afternoon when she dropped by the hospital.

Rosza was on the mend, sitting up in bed, demanding to be out of this place and complaining about the way the staff fussed around her like chickens. Terezia had brought in a stack of magazines to keep her occupied. Rosza didn't hold with women's magazines; they were for empty-headed people with time on their hands. But Terezia knew the old woman liked to work her way through them in private, clucking and tutting at the extravagance of the recipes, the indecency of the dresses worn by the scrawny models, all of whom needed some flesh on their bones. A good square meal, that's what was missing. But Rosza's mind wasn't on anorexic girls at present; it was on the bouquet of flowers at the end of the bed.

'Came in this morning,' she announced.

Terezia fiddled with the note tucked between the stems. It read, '*With the compliments of M. Anderson*'.

'Not the vase though,' Rosza said. 'That came from the hospital. They've got hundreds of them. I must write and thank him.'

'Yes,' Terezia agreed, putting the note back in place. Damn you, M. Anderson, she thought. Why do you have to send flowers by phone? Why couldn't you have just breezed in with them, you stupid stubborn mule?

Rosza was sitting propped up in bed, her stout brown hands folded on the sheet. She looked Terezia over critically.

'Where did you get that coat from?'

'Do you like it?'

'You never had a fur coat before.'

'I bought it the other day.'

Rosza was struck dumb by the news.

'With some of the money I got from the museum,' Terezia prompted.

'You never told me you got any money.'

'Oh,' she said lightly. 'I must have forgotten to tell you.'

They'd talked about it the evening before, discussed what it should be used for in some detail. Now the old woman remembered nothing. It wasn't the first time Terezia had noticed these lapses in memory.

'It's shock,' the doctor told her when she spoke to him in the passage later. 'Her mind's not ready to accept new information yet. It's still coping with the trauma of her attack.'

'Will it get better?'

'With time and patience. But you mustn't expect miracles, Countess. She's not young any longer.'

An hour later, Terezia walked in through the swing doors of the Hotel Forum in Budapest. She was nervous of the coming meeting and, as always when she was nervous, she fretted more than usual over her appearance. For ten minutes she busied herself in front of the mirror in the Ladies', adjusting the tilt of her fur hat, the spread of her hair on the collar, small details that she usually allowed to happen of their own accord.

She wasn't sure she should have come. It could be a trick, some new device of Zoltan's to get round her. But she didn't have to listen, she told herself as she left the hotel and walked down the river front. If she didn't like what she was hearing she could always walk away.

The Vigardo Hall was designed by some architect who wondered what would happen if the gothic, the art nouveau and the faintly ridiculous were all to collide in the same building. Elaine Kasinczy-Landsberg was waiting under one of the arches.

'I'm so glad you've come,' she said.

The pale blue eyes swept her from head to foot with,

Terezia felt, a slight suggestion of relief that she was not going to be an embarrassment to her.

'You had something to tell me.'

'Yes—' Elaine was restless, wanting to get this over with as much as she did, Terezia realised. With a limp gesture of her hand she said, 'Why don't we go outside?'

They walked along the Danube together. Elaine glanced across at the river, at Buda Palace rising above the far shore, white and frosted like a cake at a child's party.

'You must think me very strange ringing you like that,' she began. 'I felt I must talk to you. I heard that you turned down the offer my husband made for the house.'

'I did.'

'You want to keep it yourself?'

'Is that so hard to understand?'

Elaine shook her head. She was playing with the pearls at her neck, twisting them round her fingers.

'No, don't get me wrong. You've got your reasons, I dare-say. But I don't think you realise, my husband is determined to have it.'

'His lawyer said I might be able to keep it.'

'No,' she said flatly. 'Never. Zoltan will never let you keep it. He will do everything in his power to get it. And believe me, he's got some power. I know you don't want to, but I really think you'd be clever to take the money.'

'If that's all you've got to say, I think we should end this now.'

'No, you don't understand—'

'I think I do.'

'You don't realise the limits he's prepared to go to; you don't realise what he's already done to get his hands on that wretched house. That Englishman from the university. I don't remember his name—'

'Dr Verity?'

'Zoltan told your friend he'd never met him but it's not true. He came round one evening.'

She paused, staring across the river as though shocked by what she was saying. Taking a handkerchief from her pocket she touched it to her nose.

'You should know this,' she said distantly. 'It's right . . .'

Terezia stood waiting, her hands in her pockets, with a nasty feeling that, right or not, she wasn't going to like what she heard.

'He came to see Zoltan,' Elaine went on. 'About eight in the evening . . . we were meant to be going out. They weren't together very long . . . fifteen minutes at most. Then Zoltan had him thrown out. I've never seen him so angry. After that . . .'

Her voice trailed off in the cold air. Terezia prompted her to go on.

'Are you saying that Zoltan had something to do with his death?'

'He died, that's all I know.'

'Straight after Zoltan saw him?'

She nodded unhappily. 'Two, three days later. You mustn't ask me to say this again. I'm only telling you now because I think you should understand what you're dealing with.'

'Do you know what they talked about?'

She shook her head and touched the handkerchief to her nose again, breathing in the scent as though it gave her strength. Then she looked round and Terezia saw her eyes were moist. It could have been the cold air or it could have been that she knew she was selling out her husband.

'Take the money,' she said.

Terezia shook her head.

'I really don't know who you are, or where you come

from, but you don't understand. My husband's obsessed with that house. He's lost all sense of reason over it. It's not worth fighting him so get wise. Let him have it beforc . . .'

'Before?'

'Before something terrible happens.'

The long black Cadillac drew into the kerbside where a man stood waiting. He was slight and pale and lean as a whippet, dressed in a denim jacket with a woollen cap on his head.

He opened the rear door and got in quickly. The curtains were drawn, making the inside gloomy. He sat on the small seat, his back to the driver, facing the other two passengers.

As the car cruised out into the traffic again, Vargas said, 'This is Gabor Erkell.'

'I'm pleased to meet you,' Zoltan told him.

The pale young man made no reply.

'You have been recommended to us,' Zoltan said. 'As a specialist.'

'I know my trade.'

'But what interests me is that you come with the most remarkable crcdentials.'

'I did what I had to do,' Erkell replied.

From the shadowed back seat, Zoltan looked him over. He was in his mid-thirties, a nondescript man, one who could easily be lost in a crowd. And yet there was a stillness to him, an intensity that gave him a strangely compelling presence in the car. Zoltan liked that; it was as he had expected, as he hoped.

Quietly he asked, 'And do you know who it is you are speaking to now?'

Erkell nodded.

'Does that bother you?'

'That depends what you want me for.'

'Nothing that you should find difficult.'

Zoltan had read the report on this man. He knew his past, knew the hatred that he had nurtured over the years. Almost casually he reached out to touch it.

'I hear you used to live in the village of Fetevis.'

'I did,' Erkell said flatly. 'Until the day she evicted me.'

'You must resent that.'

'She had no right to do it.'

'No,' Zoltan agreed. 'But she had her reasons, didn't she, Gabor? She had a very good reason to want to see you out of the village.'

'She had a reason; she didn't have a right.'

Zoltan saw the faint gleam that came into his eyes, the tightening of the skin. It was there. Oh yes, it was there all right, coiled up inside him like a snake. He could be useful, this one; useful but dangerous. He was going to have to be handled with care.

'You have a score to settle and that's good,' Zoltan said. 'You must hold that, Gabor, keep it. We can use it later. But first you must prove yourself.'

'In what way?'

'We have a problem that must be straightened out. It's very simple, very quick but it must be done right, Gabor. Do you follow me?'

'Tell me what it is.'

After she left Elaine, Terezia walked up into Varosomarty Square. Pigeons were standing huddled in the snow, steam rising through the gratings over the metro. By the wrapped statue she paused, undecided. The British Embassy wasn't far from here. Her car was parked in the opposite direction near the river. But now that she was so close it was tempting to go round and see Max. And she knew, to her slight annoyance, that once the possibility had raised itself she wasn't going to be able to resist it.

Her heart pounding like a young girl on her first date, she marched in through the bronze doors. But he should hear what Elaine had said, she told herself. It concerned him as much as her. And there was no loss of face. He'd made the first move by sending the flowers, hadn't he?

The officer on the desk was surprised.

'Anderson?'

'I'd like to speak to him please.' She'd play it cool, she promised herself. She'd match her mood to his. If he was distant she'd be distant back. She'd just deliver the information and leave. It was nothing more than politeness, like returning a phone call.

The officer said, 'But he doesn't work here.'

'Yes, he does. He's First Secretary.'

'No, I mean he's not with us any more. He's left.'

She felt a twist of apprehension. 'He can't have left; he was here just a few days ago.'

'No, he's . . . not here. Wait one moment please.'

He picked up a phone and summoned down a girl that Terezia recognised as Max's secretary. She was blonde and pretty in a solid way and greeted Terezia with flustered concern.

'Oh Lord,' she said. 'Max isn't here. Didn't you know?'

'But where's he gone?'

'We don't know. It's terrible. We've been doing everything to find him. But we don't have any idea where he is.'

Terezia was lost. 'But what happened?'

'He was meant to leave. Didn't he tell you that?'

'No, he didn't tell me anything.'

'He was asked to leave. Because of that horrid business

with the murder. But he didn't go. He's still here somewhere. The police are looking for him.'

'I didn't know.' Terezia's hands had flown up to her cheeks. 'He didn't say anything.'

'We must find him,' Janet whispered urgently. 'If the police find him here it'll be the end of his career.'

'But what's he doing?'

'I don't know. I think he must be trying to find some way of proving his innocence. But it won't do him any good. He doesn't understand.' She was looking at Terezia earnestly as though she were holding something back. 'You don't have any idea where he could be?'

'No. No, I don't know anything. I didn't realise this was happening.'

'If the police find him they'll arrest him.'

'But I don't know where he is.'

'If he gets in touch you must get him to come back.'

She promised she would and Janet went back to her office upstairs. Terezia didn't like to tell her that she doubted whether Max would ever get in touch with her again.

It was growing dark as she walked back towards her car, the street lights marking the line of the pavement with pools of orange phosphorescence. On the river bank she paused and stared down at the black water of the Danube, filled with a bleak, aching sense of loneliness.

Why hadn't he told her? Why hadn't he let her know he was in trouble? All this time she'd been smugly waiting for him to come back to her, with a note or flowers, some nice comfortable gesture that would break the ice. It was just a game, a little ritual that has to be acted out in every relationship before it can move forwards. She didn't realise that he had better things to be doing than flattering her ego. She'd pictured him sulking in his office, wondering how best to make up. In fact he probably hadn't even given her a thought.

'You silly cow,' she said under her breath.

It was her own fault. He hadn't told her he was being kicked out of the country because she hadn't given him the chance. Right from the start she'd been determined to ignore what had happened to him. She'd let him help her and done nothing in return. Nothing, that is, except shout at him.

Angrily she moved on down the river, hugging herself for warmth, when a voice behind her spoke softly.

'Countess?'

She spun around. A figure was following her, emerging out of the darkness towards her. She felt a start of apprehension and stepped back but at the same time she recognised him as one of the men from the security desk of the Embassy.

He paused as he reached her, glancing back in the direction he'd come.

'You were asking after Anderson,' he said quickly.

'Yes.' She felt a spark of hope. 'Do you know where he is?'

The man shook his head. He seemed in a hurry.

'Speak to Norton,' he said. 'Sergeant Norton. He might be able to help you.'

'Who is he?'

'He works in the Embassy. But don't try to speak to him there.'

'Where then?'

'He usually has lunch in a *sörözó* called the "Pilota".' He was moving on as he spoke. 'You'll find him there.'

Hope turned to panic. She didn't know enough and already he was going. She ran forward a couple of steps, trying to keep up with him.

'But how will I recognise him?'

'They know him there,' he said over his shoulder and before she could ask more he'd vanished into the night.

Half a mile away, in an area of Pest that had once had its charm but had long since given way to the dreariness of modern development, Max sat in the corner of a beer cellar. His cheeks were darkened by two days' growth of beard, the collar of his coat was turned up and he kept his head down as he read the daily paper, avoiding eye contact with the men at the bar. But still he felt exposed here, as though a spotlight was beamed down on to him.

Why can't you break the habit of a lifetime and be on time today, you stupid Irish layabout, he said to himself as he scanned the printed columns.

There was no mention of his name there which was good in its own way. It meant he didn't have to worry about some sneak back at his digs grassing him to the police. Not that he did worry about that too much. He was left pretty much to himself. The landlord, Gombos, spent most of the night mesmerised by the television set that lit up his basement flat like a fish tank and the rest of the time sleeping. He wasn't a very happy man, Max was told by the woman who lived opposite. His wife had left him and that had driven him to what she called 'the you-know-what'.

She had delivered the confidence by way of introduction and the next day asked him if he'd like a cup of cocoa. She had drooping hair and drooping breasts and smelled faintly of cabbage and disinfectant. Max had declined without, he hoped, being cool. It was a difficult balance. He didn't want to be too friendly or too unfriendly around the place, either of which drew attention to yourself. The only real answer was not to be seen at all.

He found that left to himself time dragged, particularly in the evenings. He had plenty to keep him occupied in the day but he'd never realised how much time there was at night until now, and in the past two days he'd spent hours prowling the streets or lying on his bed reading.

'Who's been a naughty boy then?'

He looked up from the paper as Michael Gallagher slipped into the chair opposite. He looked, as he usually did, amused and rather sleepy, as though he'd just woken up from a particularly funny dream.

He ordered a drink – 'Bushmills and don't go ruining it with any of that ice' – and then nodded towards the paper he was reading.

'You won't find your face in there,' he said vaguely. 'The police aren't releasing information about you. I don't know why not. I expect your lot have managed to get the story muzzled.' The sleepy eyes were drifting over him. 'Talking of faces, you look a fright.'

'I didn't mean to startle you.'

'No, it suits you. You should do this more often.'

'Did you find those dates?'

Gallagher nodded and leaned back in his chair as the waiter put the Irish whiskey in front of him.

'Any good?' Max asked.

'Smack on – to within a week.' He ran the glass under his nose, caught the peaty scent of home and took a sip. 'Can't think why it wasn't spotted at the time.'

Fishing a notebook out of his pocket he extracted a slip of paper and handed it to Max. 'Of course, you're keeping all this for your darling boy, aren't you?' Whenever he was serious he allowed a musical-hall Irish slang to creep into his words.

'Who else would I give it to?'

'Just checking, because I'd hate for to see you burn in hell in the next life for lying to a friend.'

'Could you do something for me?'

'I just have.'

'I need a car.'

'Don't we all? If only the good Lord had thought to make a tree that grew them wouldn't we all have one less reason to work on his day of rest?'

'The police will find mine some day and I can't rent another without showing my driving licence.'

'So you want me to perjure myself and get one for you.'

'I'll pay you later.'

'You're not forgetting who gets the story?'

'I'm not forgetting.'

Two bars of the electric heater were glowing in the corner of the room overlooking the Danube. It was chilly, the slut had complained when Strossmayer had brought her up here and he wouldn't want her getting cold later on, would he? He had taken her meaning. She was no fool this one; she knew what was coming; she knew what was for afters.

It was 11.30 at night and the remains of dinner were scattered across the plain wooden table. Nothing fancy, just bread and sausage washed down with red wine and a half-bottle of slivovitz. She'd drunk her share of that, he'd been pleased to see, taking it straight from the bottle, some of it trickling round the glass neck and down her chin. Now she stood leaning against the wall, black hair falling in a tangled mass, her face turned up to him. One knee was raised, a mute warning of the damage she could inflict if she didn't like what he gave her, but the slack lips were parted, the eyes dark and insolent.

She was asking for it, the saucy bitch.

Strossmayer took her breast in his hand, felt the weight of it in his palm. She looked down at the touch, as though she didn't know what was going on, but at the same time he felt her hips squirm up against his. Her head was back and she was laughing, her breath fetid with wine and lust. He reached down, pulled up her skirt and one bare leg snaked up around his with the grip of a gin-trap.

Roughly her hand searched up his inner thigh, testing the scale of his arousal, and then her fingers were fumbling at the zip. He wanted her, needed her. He pushed her hard against the wooden wall. His breathing was loud in his throat and he didn't hear the door open. It was only as the shadow of the intruder fell on him that his head jerked around.

Erkell stood in the doorway, his arms behind his back. Strossmayer's eyes bulged. He pushed the woman aside and straightened up.

'What the fuck—?' His voice was thick with wine.

'I have a message.'

Strossmayer swore at him, his face dark with anger. He told him to get the hell out of it before he broke his neck for him. The woman's face was sour as she pulled away to straighten her dress. The moment was gone, ruined by this little pale-faced bastard.

'I think you should listen,' Erkell said.

'Stuff your message.'

Strossmayer lurched over to the table and picked up a bottle. Who was this guy to poke his nose in here? He'd tear his bloody guts out.

Erkell didn't move. 'It's from Count Zoltan,' he said.

Strossmayer hesitated. What did this creep know about Count Zoltan? No one knew about that, apart from the lawyer, Vargas.

'What's he want?' he asked and with the question the woman realised she was taking third place in the room.

'Get him out of here,' she spat.

Strossmayer told her to shut it. He held the bottle in his hand, thrust out towards Erkell.

'Who are you from then? Vargas? Is that it? Has Vargas sent you here?'

'Count Zoltan sent me – with a message.'

'Say it and get out.'

'He's not pleased with you.'

'Well he can go fuck himself—'

'He gave you a job and you fouled up. The police have been round asking questions.'

Strossmayer splintered the bottle against the table. 'And that's the message, is it?' He took a step towards the creep, the broken bottle held out and moving slowly from side to side like a snake about to strike. He'd have this little sod and the woman afterwards.

But Erkell just stood there in the doorway, thin and pale as some poncing ballet dancer.

'No,' he said, raising his right arm from behind his back. 'This is the message.'

The silenced gun in his hand spat once.

'He says you're fired.'

The woman gave a moan as Strossmayer fell across the table. She stumbled backwards. Her eyes were rolling in her head and as Erkell turned to her she slumped to her knees.

'Please,' she whispered but Erkell shook his head.

'Wrong time, wrong place, lady.'

And the gun spat a second time.

20

There's nothing more sordid than the sight of last night's dinner first thing in the morning. And this was worse than most, Colonel Biszku thought sourly as he viewed the wreckage of the room. Black bread, a half-gnawed *kolbász* sausage and a bottle of red wine that could have doubled as battery acid, their appearance not improved by the fact that the whole greasy collection had been scattered across the floor when the man hit the table.

Some romantic evening.

'A professional job,' the Captain was saying. 'Both shots in the head.'

'How did he get in?'

'Cut a hole in the fence and knocked out the security camera with shaving foam.'

Terrific. As if they didn't have troubles enough, they now had an assassin who knew how to get round all the gadgets that technology tried putting in the path of crime.

He looked at the chalked outline of the two figures on the ground. 'Who was he then?'

'Jeno Strossmayer: fifteen years in the police, good record, made it to lieutenant then discharged in '90. A few odd jobs before he got a post here as security officer three years ago.'

Discharged when the new regime came in. How often had he heard that? A little too fond of the cosh, was that it? Biszku wondered. A little too fond of the back-hander, the kick-back? Found himself out in the cold when the world changed around his ears, and had to turn his hand to a bit of security work.

'He might have been taking on private contract jobs,' the Captain went on. 'Always had a lot of money in his pocket, bragged around the place that his work here was just a front.'

That old line. Probably went down a treat with the girls. Only in his case there was a margin of truth in it. But better if he'd kept his mouth shut about it; better if he hadn't wanted everyone to be impressed.

Biszku nodded towards the other silhouette. 'How about her?'

'Some girl he picked up in a bar earlier in the evening. He often brought them back here.' The Captain didn't rate her in the scheme of things. 'There was a gun in his jacket pocket. Ballistics are checking it with the bullet that killed Verity.'

And a fat lot of good it would be if it did match, Biszku told himself later as they drove back to Budapest. All it would prove was that they had found their man too late. With Strossmayer dead they were no further forward than they were when they started. And it was only 8.30 in the morning.

'Stop the car,' he said wearily.

The Captain glanced round at him in surprise. 'You want to go back?'

'No, I want to see if you can get a cup of coffee in this damned petrol station.'

*

'You left no trace?'

'None.'

'You're sure of that?'

'There is no way the police can trace me.'

'Good,' Zoltan said from the back seat of the Cadillac as it eased its way through the morning traffic in Kossuth Utca. 'You've done well.'

He studied the man opposite him, searching for traces of pride or elation in the aftermath of his grisly task. But there was none that he could detect. Erkell had none of the weaknesses of his trade. He just sat there, pale and silent, a weapon that carries out the wishes of its owner, taking neither credit nor responsibility for the deed.

'But can you be more subtle, Gabor? What you've done is good. Don't get me wrong. I'm pleased. You've done well but it's easy for a man with your background. It's part of your trade. What I want to know is whether you can be more . . . measured.'

'In what way measured?'

'I want you to go to Fetevis Palace.'

He saw it again: that gleam in his eyes, the look of the hunter, the predator sighting its prey.

'To do what?' Erkell asked.

'The Kovacs girl.' He disliked calling Terezia by any other name. 'I want you to put pressure on her. Nothing violent. I don't want you hurting her. But I want you to scare her, Gabor; I want you to scare the living daylights out of her. Can you do that?'

'How do you wish me to do it?'

'That's for you to decide.'

The Pilota was one of the new 'English-style' pubs in Pest, designed around the belief that all pubs in England are decorated with dimpled glass windows, models of square-riggers and solid wooden tables where the customers sit around drinking stale beer from pewter tankards as they wait to be press-ganged into the King's Navy. The modern world had intruded in the form of piped music, designer lagers and one-armed bandits that winked malevolently at Terezia as she came in.

It was just after midday and the place was only beginning to fill.

'I'm looking for someone called Nauchen,' she told the barman. 'Sergeant Nauchen.'

The name didn't register with him. He wore a white nylon shirt, sleeves rolled back from white arms, and an expression as blank as white paper as he shook his head. 'Can't say I know him, lady.'

Terezia couldn't be sure she had the name right. She'd only grasped it as the man passed. 'They said he comes in here at lunchtime.'

The barman turned to one of the others, who was filling a tankard from a copper pipe that protruded from a porcelain model of a beer keg. 'You know a Sergeant Nauchen?'

'What's he then – police sergeant?'

'No, he's English,' Terezia told him.

'Works in the Embassy?'

'That's right.'

The second barman scraped the froth off the glass and set it down on a cardboard mat on the counter. He punched the price into the cash till and said, 'Sure, I know the one.'

'Is he here now?'

'Can't say I've seen him today.'

This barman was much the same age as the first and wearing the same semi-transparent white shirt, but the way he came over to her now, taking over the conversation from the other, suggested he was the boss in the place.

'If I waited here would you tell me if he comes in?' Terezia asked.

His eyes roamed across her briefly. He was a busy man with better things to be doing, but he liked what he saw so he said, 'Sure. What are you drinking then, lady?'

'I don't want to drink anything, thank you.'

'This is a bar not a railway station.'

Terezia looked along the counter but she didn't recognise any of the names on the beer-pulls. 'Do you have wine?'

He hoist a bottle from beneath the bar and filled a glass. 'White,' he said. 'Right?'

'Yes, right.'

'Women always drink white at lunchtime.'

Terezia wished she'd said red with a dash of vodka in it, just to give him an idea of what it's like not to be right all the time.

'Take a pew. I'll tell you if he comes in.' A white hand that hadn't seen enough daylight in its time opened in front of her. 'That'll be two hundred forints.'

She took the glass over to a table and sipped at it tentatively, her eyes resting on the doorway that flipped open from time to time to let in the lunchtime crowd.

Since being given the name of this place she'd been charged with a sense of nervous anticipation. The stable hands had felt it in her that morning but put it down to excitement at the impending arrival of the brood mare.

She'd struck a price for the horse over the phone, haggled a bit out of habit and fixed the transfer of the money with the bank. Joszef was going to go over to the farm to pick it up when Rosza was out of hospital. They were going to stay a few days, look up some friends, make a holiday of it.

Buying the horse was the moment they'd been working for all these months but now that it had come she'd scarcely given it a second thought.

'You waiting for me?'

She glanced up to see a short, middle-aged man with thinning hair standing at her shoulder. There was a glass of beer in his hand and a look of gentle expectation in his face.

'Are you Sergeant Nauchen?'

'I could be,' he said. 'May I join you?'

She nodded and he slid himself into place across the table, his eyes roaming across her.

'I see you've got a drink already, pretty lady.'

'Yes,' she said.

'I'd have bought you one.'

She didn't particularly like the way he was looking at her, or the familiarity he seemed to have assumed before he'd even discovered who she was.

'That's kind of you,' she said.

'So what do you want?'

'I'm looking for Max.' It was strange, she thought, he didn't sound English. 'They said you may be able to help.'

The balding man's smile seemed to have set on his face. 'No,' he said patiently. 'I mean, what do you charge?'

'Charge?'

Terezia glanced across to the barman. He shook his head and nodded over to another table.

'For your time,' the man prompted.

'Oh pooh,' she said. The little toad thought she was a tart, sitting there with a glass of wine waiting to be picked up. She got to her feet. 'If that's what you want you'll have to look somewhere else.'

He took this as part of the bargaining. 'I'm prepared to pay over the odds.'

'You still couldn't afford me,' she told him, going over to the bar where the barman was smirking to himself as he cleaned a glass.

'Looks like you found a friend there, lady.'

Terezia wasn't interested in what he thought. He'd probably put the man up to it in the first place.

'Did you say Nauchen had come in?'

The barman repeated his nod across the room. 'English bloke from the Embassy? He's over there.'

He was sitting in a corner alcove, a quiet, neat-looking man in a mackintosh, doing the crossword puzzle on the back page of a folded newspaper.

'Sergeant Nauchen?'

He looked up from the paper, two steady Anglo-Saxon eyes frisking her briefly up and down. Then he clicked the ballpoint pen shut and put it in his upper pocket.

'Norton, Miss. Sergeant Norton. Same as the motorcycle.'

He said this in English so Terezia didn't understand anything more than that she had mispronounced his name.

'I'm Terezia Kasinczy-Landsberg.'

He nodded, the way forcigners do to show that they understand. Terezia slid herself on to the bench opposite him.

'I'm looking for Max Anderson,' she said. 'I was told you may be able to help me.'

There was a look of patient incomprehension on his face.

'Max,' she said.

He nodded and repeated the name.

'I was told you know where he is.'

He smiled and shook his head in apology and with a sinking feeling she realised he couldn't understand a word she was saying.

'I'm looking for Max.'

'You keep giving me all this Max talk,' he said in English, 'but I'm afraid it's not getting through.'

'I want to find Max.' She said the words very slowly but he shook his head again.

'It's no good, Miss. I just haven't got the hang of your language.'

Terezia looked around the bar, panic rising.

'May I be of assistance?'

A man who had been sitting at the table next to them came across. He was in his sixties, a dapper little figure in a grey suit and bow tie, smiling eyes, goatee beard and pince-nez spectacles giving him the look of a house-trained and well-dressed satyr. He bowed and flicked out a business card by way of introduction.

'I couldn't help overhearing your conversation. Perhaps I could be of assistance?'

'Could you?'

'My name's Hoffman and I'm a dentist,' he said as though this were credentials enough. 'I speak a little English.'

'That would be so kind.'

'I myself am German but I've lived in this country long enough to know that your language is a precious relic of the past but, like all relics, unfortunately dead.'

He delivered the observation with an immaculately trimmed accent and then turned and smiled benignly at Norton who stared back at him with the silent wonder of a man watching an impenetrable puppet show.

'Now what is it you were trying to ask?'

'I'm looking for Max Anderson,' she said. 'I think he might know where he is.'

They conferred together.

'He says,' the dentist told her, 'that Úr Anderson has gone back to England.'

'No.' She spoke directly to Norton. 'His secretary says he's still here.'

Norton shook his head as this was translated to him.

'He says he's left. He had no visa to remain.'

Terezia felt a clutch of panic. He must still be here; she'd pinned her hopes on him being here.

'Is that all he knows?' she asked the dentist.

She watched as the two men spoke together but there was no hope. She could see that. Norton was shaking his head.

'He is not in this country,' the dentist told her. He could see that this was not the answer she was wanting. He gave a little shrug and said, 'I'm sorry.'

'But he is here,' Terezia said.

'He says he can't be.'

Then why was the Embassy getting so stirred up about it all, she asked herself. His secretary had practically been in tears. She looked at Norton but he seemed to have lost all interest in the subject and had returned to his crossword.

She was suddenly furious that he could just dismiss the whole business so easily. Max had been his friend; he could at least show some interest.

'He must be here!'

'Perhaps,' the dentist ventured, 'if you were to contact his place of work they could give you his new address.'

'They're the ones who said he was here.'

The dentist smiled and bowed again as he withdrew. 'I'm sorry I cannot be of any further help.'

'No, I'm sorry.' It wasn't his fault. 'It was good of you to try.'

Putting his pen away, Norton stood up to leave, dropping the newspaper in front of her. He spoke briefly to the dentist as he passed.

'What did he say?' she asked.

'It was nothing,' the dentist replied quickly. He was embarrassed. 'He said perhaps you'd have more luck with the crossword than he has.'

What a stupid thing to say. Why should she want to do a bloody crossword at a moment like this? Anyway, how was she going to read it? It was in English, she couldn't understand a word. She shot Norton an angry glance as he left.

He was standing in the half-opened doorway. He met her eyes, looked down at the paper and up again.

In sudden understanding she glanced down at the printed page. Written amongst the words and doodles he'd made as he worked on the crossword was a phone number. Above it a name. Shackleton.

How stupid of her. She saw it now. He wasn't going to say anything with a third person present. No one was meant to know where Max had gone. She flashed a smile of gratitude at him across the crowded room.

Norton nodded and stepped out into the street.

Erkell eased open the high shutters. The hinges gave a groan at the unaccustomed movement but that didn't worry him. No one was going to see or hear him round here at the back of the Palace. The old man had gone down to the village some time ago, one of the stable hands was out exercising a horse, the other was working in the stable yard well out of earshot.

The window inside was locked. Erkell ran the blade of his knife between the frames, felt the catch give way easily. There was no security to this place. What would once have been guarded by dogs and servants was now open to anyone who wanted to break in.

He stepped over the sill, closed first the shutters and then the window after him. In the semi-darkness he walked through the derelict rooms of the huge house, feasting his eyes on the crumbling decorations, the cold fireplaces, the gaping holes in the ceilings where chandeliers had hung.

Until the girl had summoned him up here to evict him he'd never met any of the Kasinczy-Landsbergs before. His hatred for them had been focused on this great arrogant house standing above the trees and it gave him a rare glow of pleasure to see that it was now a wreck. This had been the nerve centre of their empire, their private world. Here they had lived their daily lives, here they had eaten and slept, fornicated and bred, spoiling themselves on the obscene wealth they had stolen from the labour of others. Erkell thought of the thousands of workers who had slaved all their lives in the mills and factories to build this house, living no better than animals so that the Kasinczy-Landsbergs could live like kings. And now it was a ruin, a hollow shell that had outlived its masters.

He stood in the remains of the ballroom. The skylights had caved in, fragments of the mirrors that had lined the walls were strewn across the floor. There would be no more music played here. The dancing and drinking and lechery were all over for them. What had been the showpiece of their wealth was now a grotesque reminder of their failure.

Silently he made his way up to the top floor of the house. These were the servants' rooms. He could tell. They were small and mean. There had been no need for the Kasinczy-Landsbergs to make them comfortable. They would never have come to this part of the house. They were probably hardly even aware it existed.

His grandmother would have known it. She'd worked in the house as a girl. This is where she would have slept at night, exhausted by a day that started at dawn and ended only when everyone else had gone to bed. That was until she'd become pregnant and been dismissed. Maids weren't allowed to have feelings and emotions, that was the privilege of the rich. She had been banished from the house without references or money to bring up her child in poverty.

Methodically, Erkell searched the rooms until he found one that suited him. The shutters were open, the window thick with dirt. But one pane was missing. Through it he could see down the length of the house to the lodge at the end where the girl lived with her foster parents. More importantly, it gave him a view in the other direction over the stable yard.

One of the stable hands was grooming a horse that stood tethered in the yard, sweeping the brush across the animal's flanks with long, practised strokes, whistling as he worked. The other was mucking out one of the stables, carting away the soiled hay round the back, bringing out fresh from a store in the yard. Erkell studied the position of this barn with interest. It was in the end wall, close to the entrance gate, high double doors leading into a dark interior.

The temperature in the room around him was touching freezing but he didn't feel it. Cold and hunger and fatigue were petty distractions that got in the way. He could banish them from his mind at will and concentrate on the task.

As night fell, he moved from his place by the window and threaded his way back down the house. He moved slowly, memorising the way in the dark. He needed to be able to get around easily and silently. In an empty house even the smallest noise is enough to give you away.

Climbing out of the window he'd come in through he made his way down through the trees to the village. He went into the bar and ordered a beer.

The barman recognised him. 'What brings you back in town then, Gabor?' he asked.

'A bit of business.'

'Oh yes?' He had the disinterested curiosity of all barmen as he slid the glass on to the counter. 'What sort of business is that then?'

Erkell took a pull at the beer and put the glass down again, wiping the back of his hand across his mouth.

'Just finishing off a few things I should have done earlier.'

'I'm looking for someone called Shackleton,' she told the man coming out of the door of the apartment block.

He checked the name in his mental register and shook his head.

'He's English,' she persisted.

'English? I don't know of any English. They say there's an American bloke on the second floor.'

Terezia wasn't sure. Max could have said he was American. The language was the same. She knew the accent was different but not that a Hungarian would notice.

'Been here about three days.' The man was on his way to work, his dinner in a box under his arm. 'Keeps himself to himself, they say.'

'That may be him.'

'Second floor, door at the end of the passage.'

He let her inside. There was no hallway, just a space filled by a rack of pigeonholes, gas meters and a flight of uncarpeted stairs. The air reeked. Terezia knew the fertile smells of farms and stables but this was different. It was the stale, urban smell of cigarette smoke, unclean bodies and yesterday's cooking.

As she came to the door she lost her nerve. There was no way of telling whether this apartment belonged to Max. No bell push with a nameplate, not even a number. It could be anyone inside. And if it was Max, would he speak to her? The last time she'd seen him he'd said she was a whingeing nuisance. He might kick her straight back down the stairs.

For one wild moment she toyed with the idea of going away, creeping back the way she'd come and leaving whoever this American was to himself. But she told herself she was being ridiculous. There was no point in running away after she'd got this far. Steeling her nerve she knocked on the door.

There was a movement inside. She stepped back out of range and the sound stopped. Perhaps she was mistaken and there was no one in. That would be better, much better now she came to think of it. She could go and wait outside and see if Max turned up.

The door opened a crack and a voice said, 'Hallo?'

'Max?' she faltered. 'It's me.'

'Terezia?'

The door opened fully and there he stood, gazing at her in astonishment. She felt suddenly shy and foolish and lost for words. Holding out her arms she made a little fanfare.

'Ta-da.'

All he said was, 'What the heck are you doing here?'

His voice was abrupt. This wasn't going to work, she realised. She shouldn't have come.

'I was looking for you,' she said.

He looked terrible, his hair tousled, eyes sunk and his cheeks dark with the beginnings of a beard. His eyes flicked away from her and down the passage.

'Did anyone see you come here?' he asked.

'No.' She didn't know, she didn't care. She just wanted him to say he was glad she was there. 'No,' she said, 'I don't think so.'

As she spoke there were footsteps on the stairs and they both looked round. A man in a vest and braces with a belly that sagged over his trousers heaved into sight. He stood at the end of the passage surveying the scene.

'There's no women in here, Shackleton,' he wheezed. 'Not after six.'

He seemed oblivious of Terezia's presence and addressed the remark to Max alone. The door beside them opened and a woman's eyes glared out at her for an instant through the crack.

'This won't take a moment,' Max said.

'That's the rules,' the fat man said.

'She's just delivering something.'

Max's eyes met hers as he spoke and with a little thrill of pleasure she knew it was all right between them.

'She'll be gone in a moment,' he added.

The fat man nodded. 'There's no women in here after six. I told you that at the start.'

'I'll get rid of her.'

The man ambled on down the passage and Max drew her into the room and closed the door.

'How in God's name did you find me here?'

'I talked to your friend Norton. He gave me a number to ring.'

They were both talking in whispers, like two children who've narrowly escaped being caught at a prank.

'No one said you'd rung.'

'I didn't give your name. I said I'd found a handbag with the number in it. They gave me the address.' She touched his arm. 'Tell me I've been clever.'

Max smiled at her and put his hand on her cheek. She nestled her face against it.

'Why didn't you tell me you had to leave?' she whispered.

'It didn't seem a brilliant conversation.'

'You are silly. I could have helped.'

'I didn't think it would come to that – having to leave, I mean. By the time it did we had other things to talk about.'

She took his meaning. 'I didn't mean to shout,' she said. 'It just took me by surprise. Seeing you get out of Zoltan's car like that; I thought you had some plot going.'

'You saw me in the car, did you?'

'I was coming round to see you when this great black car turned up.' She shook her head. 'But you should have said something. You didn't have to come here; you could have stayed at Fetevis.'

'That's the first place the police would have looked.'

'Better than this dump.'

'Don't you like it?'

Terezia glanced around the dingy room. It was completely unfurnished except for a bed with a sleeping bag on it.

'It's a dump.'

'I think the interior designer was making a statement,' he agreed. 'But it has it points. It's got a shunting yard out the back to give me an early call at five in the morning. Then there's the loo next door so I can keep a check in the night that everyone's regular. And it's got running water. Through the ceiling, admittedly, but if you put a bucket in the right place there's enough for coffee by the morning.'

Terezia was laughing as she ran her fingers through his hair. 'God, it's good to see you again, Max. I'm not so sure about this sandpaper on your chin.'

'Old trick I learned from the movies: if the "Wanted" posters have a shaved face, grow a beard.'

'Let's go round all the posters and draw a beard on them, then you'll have to cut it off.'

There was knocking at the door.

'Can I help you?' Max called out.

'I want her out of there,' the fat man called from the passage. 'It's after six, Shackleton; I told you.'

'Who *is* he?' Terezia hissed.

'The landlord. His name's Gombos which is short for pig.'

'There's no women allowed, Shackleton.'

'Let's get out of here, Max.'

'It's all right, Gombos,' he called. 'I've just checked and she's not a woman after all.'

'I want her out, Shackleton.'

'How do you think I feel?'

'There's no women allowed.'

'Let's *go*, Max.'

'I think you're right.' He raised his voice again. 'We're coming out with our hands up, Gombos, so don't fire.'

21

The bar in the next street had cut a few corners in its image-presentation programme but it suited their purposes well enough. It was dark and warm and there were only a dozen drinkers in the place, none of whom gave them more than a glance as they came in.

Max ordered a couple of glasses of red wine and took them over to the table in the corner where Terezia was sitting. She'd taken off her fur hat and her hair now fell gleaming around her shoulders, like beads of melted snow. She cupped her hands around her glass as though it would warm them.

'Why did you stay in the country, Max?' she asked as he took a seat opposite her.

'Several reasons.'

She ran her fingers over the back of his hand, brushing the hairs of his wrist. 'The Embassy's very worried about you. I was round there yesterday. They think you should go in.'

'I bet they do.'

'Your secretary said it would be bad if you stayed out here – for your career, I mean.'

'If I went back to the Embassy they'd ship me out of the country as quick as they could. Sort it out when you get back, old boy, and all that. I can't let it happen. I was kicked out of Moscow a couple of years ago.'

'I didn't know that.'

'I don't think *Collective-Farmer's Weekly* covered the story.'

Terezia smiled with narrowed eyes. 'You shouldn't be nasty about people who have to share a tractor.'

'It was a tit-for-tat job – I don't know what the Hungarian for that would be. We found the Russian Embassy in London was crawling with spies and had them fumigated. So they had to pretend our Embassy in Moscow was the same and before I could say *Glasnost* I was on the first Aeroflot flight out of town. If it happens once nothing sticks; everyone knows it's just a game. But twice and questions get asked.'

'But how did it help to stay here?'

'I needed to do some research on your family.'

'Research?' It was not the answer she was expecting. 'What sort of research?'

Max turned the glass of wine on the table, watching the concentric ripples spring out across its surface.

'Your family used to own a hunk of silver called the Hunyadi Venus,' he said. 'Do you know it?'

Terezia nodded. 'My father hid it in the hills at the end of the war.'

'Verity was looking for it.'

'In those boxes up in the library?'

'No,' he said thoughtfully. 'He knew it wouldn't be there. But he knew the game books would be.'

'Game books?'

'The records of all the hunting that used to go on at your place. There's dozens of them. I've looked through them.

Your father's gamekeeper used to write them up at the end of the day's sport – who was there, what they killed and where they killed it.'

Terezia understood. 'So Verity reckoned if he could find where they'd been hunting that day he could find the Venus.'

'It wasn't a bad idea – worth coming all the way from his nice warm rooms in Oxford to try out.'

'Did he find it?'

Max shook his head. 'He went and looked. It was up in a place called Castle Rock.'

'I know it,' she said excitedly.

'But he didn't find it.'

'Everyone says the Russians took it away years ago.'

'No,' Max said. 'The Russians never found it. Neither did Zoltan or Verity when they came looking, for the simple reason that it's not up there any more.'

The green-grey eyes studied him. 'Where has it gone?'

'Your father took it away.'

'My father?'

'He went back there and dug it up.'

Terezia looked at him seriously. 'Why should he want to do that?'

'To stop Zoltan getting his hands on it.'

As he spoke she felt a slight, uncomfortable fear in her stomach. The earth was shifting, she knew, on a secret that had been buried fifty years.

'How do you know this?'

Max glanced across to where a man was playing the pinball machine, the heavy unrhythmic thudding drowning the talk from the other tables.

'When was your father arrested?'

She calculated rapidly. 'Fourteen years ago.'

'And when did Zoltan turn up here in Hungary?'

"I don't know,' she said slowly. 'About the same time.'

'Not about the same time. At exactly the same time.' Max was leaning forward, his voice low. 'When Zoltan turned up in Hungary there was a big piece about him in the papers, about what he was going to do for the country and how clever the Government had been in getting him to move back and all the rest of it. The day after it came out your father was arrested at Fetevis.'

Terezia sat back in her chair, her hands cupped over her mouth.

'I checked with a journalist friend of mine,' Max said.

'You think he went back and moved the Venus when he heard Zoltan was back?'

'It looks like it.'

Terezia nodded into her hands. 'He wouldn't want him to have it,' she said. 'He hated Zoltan.'

'Why's that?'

'I don't know. I never knew Papa hate anyone. But he hated Zoltan.'

Max had guessed something of the sort. In the past few days he'd turned the image of those days over in his mind. He could see what happened, feel it, as though he'd been there himself.

'Do you know where he was when he was arrested?' he asked.

'At the house somewhere.'

'But where exactly?'

'I don't know.'

'Wherever he put it,' Max said, 'it's probably still there. He didn't have it with him when the police found him so he must have left it somewhere.'

'Do you think Verity found it?'

Max shook his head.

'He did go round and see Zoltan,' she said, eager to tell him her news. 'You were right. I talked to his wife. She said there was a terrible yelling match between them.'

'It can't have been over the Venus.'

'He might have just found it, by chance.'

Max shook his head. 'I tried that kind of line on your cousin Alexander and got a right chewing for it. And he had a point. If Verity had tried to sell the Venus to Zoltan he'd have bought it, and it would be sitting on his drawing room mantelpiece right now.'

Terezia paused. 'I don't understand. If Verity didn't find the Venus why did he die?'

'I don't know. There's something that Zoltan's hiding. Something he doesn't want anyone to know about.'

'But what can it be?'

'That,' Max said, 'is the sixty-four-million-dollar question.'

Terezia was silent for a moment, thinking. Then she smiled. 'God, Max, you've been doing some homework.'

'There's nothing like fleas in a bed for getting you up bright and early.'

'And I thought you were sitting in the Embassy, sulking because of what I'd said to you.'

'I was,' he said. 'But not in the Embassy.'

'Are there really fleas in your bed?'

'Battalions. Even the fleas get flea bites.'

Terezia cocked her wrist and looked at her watch. 'Oh Lord, I must go. There's a train at half past seven. I should try to get it.'

'Didn't you drive?'

'No. Joszef's got the car. That's the trouble. Gyorgy's there all by himself. I promised I'd be back.' She looked across the table at him, suddenly realising their time together was up.

'I'll drive you back if you like.'

She was pleased with the offer. 'Will you?'

'Sure.'

Her hand stole over his. 'I don't want to be a nuisance.'

'You're not,' he said, getting up. 'I rented a car. Just a Lada but it's the de luxe version with fitted engine and revolving wheels.

Her eyes were shining. 'That would be much better.'

On the top floor of the Palace, Gabor Erkell crouched perfectly still. Every hunter can tell you that it's movement that catches the eye; movement that gives away your position. Only when you are still are you invisible.

Through the cracked pane of glass he watched the stables below. One of the hands was in the office, the other sweeping the cobbled yard, washing it down with a hose and then brushing the water into the central gutter. Just after six he knocked off work and cycled down to the village, calling out loudly to his mate as he went out of the gateway. Off to his dinner, off to put away a few drinks in the bar and brag and flirt. A life without much care, without much pay; a life without importance to Erkell the moment he vanished into the night.

The other went round the stables checking the horses before going over to the house. He was the more senior of the two, the more responsible. Erkell watched him walk down the length of the driveway, hands in pockets, whistling tunelessly as he went inside. There was a stove in there, a table to put his feet up on, a radio to listen to.

He felt only contempt for these men. By working for the girl they betrayed their class and demeaned themselves. It was easy for them to justify their labour, easy to say they needed the money, easy to tell themselves they had wives and children to support. But they would know in their hearts that they had sold themselves to the enemy.

Like others of his elite section, Erkell had sat through daily sessions with political specialists. He'd listened to their words, noted what they said. But in the end there had been nothing there he hadn't already known. All he'd learned in those classes had been the language with which to put into words what he already knew.

Going downstairs, moving easily through the darkened house, he climbed out of the window. He felt no nerves, but the fire of anticipation burned in his belly. He liked that, welcomed the sensation. It sharpened his senses, gave him a strength. When the fire burned in him he was invincible.

Silently he worked his way round to the far side of the stable yard. The wall was high, like a fortress, but there was a loft door high up, a small aperture with a lifting hoist above. With quick, sure movements he climbed up to it, feeling his fingers into the cracks in the stonework, lifting himself up the wall with the strength and agility of a cat.

A wooden ladder in the loft led down into the stable yard. The only light was a single bulb over the office door. Keeping to the shadows he made his way round to the tack room. A horse neighed softly as he passed and he froze for an instant. He could sense the animals there in the darkness, silent witnesses to his intrusion.

Feeling his way round the heavy oiled tack he found a spirit lamp. He'd seen the girl using one the night before, going round the stables with it in her hand. Crossing the yard he took it into the hay barn. It was pitch black in there but he could smell the warm scent of the hay around him. He inched forward until he touched the stacked bales with one foot.

Unscrewing the cap of the lamp he splashed some of the paraffin on the ground and standing back he flicked open his lighter and touched the flame to the wick. A warm glow of light filled the barn.

In it, Erkell's expression was one of spiritual serenity.

'How's Rosza?'

'Still in hospital,' Terezia said. She was curled up in the seat of the car, watching Max as he drove. The windows were closed but even at the machine's maximum speed of fifty m.p.h. it was draughty and she hugged her coat round herself for warmth. 'But they'll let her out soon. They'll have to; they'll go mad if they don't. She sits there all day telling the nurses they don't know how to make a bed, or how to cook.'

'The perfect patient.'

'She was very pleased with your flowers. She's never had any from a diplomat before.'

'Ex-diplomat.'

'You'll get back, Max.'

'Maybe.'

'They can't blame you for something you didn't do.'

Max was beginning to wonder whether he really cared any more. He wanted to get back to civilisation, to be able to walk down a street without looking over his shoulder, to sleep without straining to hear the sounds in the passage outside. But whether he got back his desk in the Embassy was the least of his concerns at that moment.

Terezia held out her hands to the sickly heater in the dashboard. 'How did you know she'd gone into hospital?' she asked.

'I saw something about it in the papers.'

He drew to a halt in front of the gates and they got out

into the night. It was cold and raw, flecks of snow drifting restlessly in the wind.

'I don't think there's much to eat in the house,' Terezia said as she undid the padlock. 'There may be some eggs.'

'You've put a new light in the stables.'

'I don't think so.' She was fumbling with the key.

'It's all lit up.'

Terezia glanced up at the Palace. There was a glow of light over the west wing which housed the stable block. 'So it is.' She frowned. 'That must be . . .' The words died on her lips. She looked round at Max, her eyes wide with realisation. 'Oh my God, it's not . . .'

Max grabbed the padlock from her. 'Get back in the car!'

He wrenched the key around. The clasp opened, the chains parting with a clank. He tore them open and began dragging the gates wide.

Terezia was running back to the car. He jumped in beside her and hit the ignition.

The engine turned over but didn't fire.

'Come on, you bastard,' he hissed. He tried again.

Still nothing.

'Stop messing about!' Terezia shouted.

'I'm not messing about!'

On the fourth try the engine caught. He gunned the revs and slammed the gear lever into first. Dirt spurted from the front wheels and the machine slewed to the side as it sped forward through the entrance.

They could see sparks over the stables as they approached. They were like swarms of brilliant gold insects lifting gently up into the night sky.

'Come on, come on!' Terezia pleaded. She was banging her knees together with impatience.

The sight that greeted them as they skidded to a halt in the driveway was one from hell. Through the high arched gate, the stable yard was ablaze with light. The barn at the far end was engulfed in flame, the orange tongues licking out of the narrow windows, sucking in the cold night air for energy and reaching up into the darkness above.

Above the roaring of the fire they could hear the horses stamping and neighing, their heads silhouetted against the blaze as they tossed and reared in panic.

A figure ran towards them. It was Gyorgy, hair awry, dragging a hosepipe in his hand. His mouth was working but they couldn't hear a word he said above the din.

'The horses!' Terezia shouted at him. 'Get the horses out!'

He nodded and made for the nearest of the stables with her, tripping over the coils of the hose as he ran. Together they pulled the animal out into the yard. Max went to the next, slamming back the bolt and throwing open the doors.

There was no bridle on the horse inside, nothing to get hold of. It was standing quite still, its eyes rolling and bright orange with the reflection of the fire. He grabbed hold of its mane and began heaving it towards the yard. The horse gave a screaming whinny and pulled back, lifting him from his feet. He kept his grasp, fighting to draw it out. Then Terezia was there with him, talking to the creature, coaxing it to move. Between them they moved it forwards. Suddenly the horse sensed freedom and clattered out on to the cobbles, bolting away into the night.

The fire was spreading, the flames reaching out to embrace the office building, feeling its way into the door and windows.

They ran to the next stable and as they did so there was a

roar as part of the barn roof fell down into the yard, sparks hissing and spiralling upwards. One burning beam crashed across the stable door next to the office.

Without pausing, Terezia began running towards it. Max ran too, calling her to stop.

It was hopeless. In the light of the flames he could see the horse inside the stable, a dark form pawing and neighing. But there was no way of getting it out. Already the fire had taken to the frame of the doorway, running along the painted woodwork as quickly as a fuse to a barrel of powder. But Terezia kept running, the black silhouette of her coat flapping around her, like a moth drawn to the flames.

Max caught her when they were twenty feet away, pulling her to the ground. The heat was searing his face and hands as they rolled over on the hard cobbles.

Terezia fought him like a wildcat, struggling and writhing in his grasp.

'You can't go in there!' he shouted.

'Let me go!' She was beating at his face with her fists.

'It's too late!'

'I must!' She was crying. 'I must!'

With a kick of her legs she twisted herself free of his grip. Struggling to her feet she ran to the stable door and diving in under the burning beam she vanished from sight.

Afterwards Max couldn't have said whether he followed her to try to help her, or save her from herself, or whether he went after her because there was nothing else that he could do. But he ran. In through the doorway, ducking under the burning timber.

The stable was full of smoke and brilliant light, the heat burning in his throat as he fought for breath.

Terezia was holding the horse around its neck and over the

sound of the fire he could hear her talking to it. And to his amazement it seemed to respond to her. It grew calm, it's eyes still rolling horribly but standing stiff and still.

Max took it by the mane. He could feel the creature trembling and shivering beneath his hands and even in that heat its coat was wet with sweat. But there was no way out, he realised. They'd come in under the blazing beam, but they were never going to get the animal out past it. There wasn't the space.

One arm over his face, he cast around the stable. There was a bucket in the corner. Not much but at least it was metal. It would come between flesh and fire.

Holding it out at arm's length he lowered his head and ran at the beam. The two met with a shower of sparks but the heavy timber didn't move. He tried again, throwing his weight behind the blow. He could hear Terezia coughing now as she talked to the horse.

As he butted it for the third time the beam gave way and fell into the yard, breaking into pieces as it hit the ground.

The horse came forward. Max grabbed hold of it by the mane and the thick hairs of its coat and dragged it with him. As he did so, part of the roof collapsed behind them. A spray of sparks. The horse gave a buck and cantered forwards over the embers of the beam, the darkness swallowing it as it went.

Dimly Max was aware that the yard was full of other horses. Gyorgy had cleared the rest of the stables and the terrified animals were fighting their way out into the night.

He looked round but Terezia wasn't there.

Then he saw her.

She had fallen in a heap in the doorway of the stable, the timbers of the collapsed roof arched above her like a guard of honour over a bride emerging from the church.

She was very still.

Dropping to his knees he crawled back to where she lay huddled. He couldn't see or breathe, tears were streaming down his face from the acrid, choking fumes. Tearing open his shirt he held it to his face, gulping at the cleaner air that filtered through.

Terezia didn't move as he caught hold of her. He tried to lift her but she was a dead weight. Locking his arms under hers he dragged her forward across the cobbles.

Miraculously, as he hauled her along, he felt the weight lift from him.

It was Gyorgy, running in to help.

'I've got her,' he shouted in his ear.

Max made it to his feet and between them they pulled Terezia away from the fire to the other side of the yard. They lowered her to the ground and Max fell down beside her. The air was fresh and wonderfully cool on his face and hands and he drank it in gratefully as he examined her.

She lay face down without moving a muscle. Frantically he brushed aside the mane of golden hair and turned her head. Her eyes were closed, the skin as pale as snow.

There was no sight of breathing.

But she was alive, he told himself. She had to be alive.

'It was the smoke,' Gyorgy was whimpering. 'It was the smoke.'

Max raised himself on his knees, placed his hands on her back and punched down on her with his full weight. He'd read somewhere that the muscles of the lungs became paralysed. They must be made to move again.

'It's no good.' Gyorgy was crying. 'The smoke's done for her.'

He kept going. She had to be alive. She'd been there with him as they came out of the doorway. She'd been that close to getting out. He couldn't believe she'd gone when she was so close. He wouldn't believe it.

Another thought struck him. Rolling her over roughly on to her back he put his mouth to hers and breathed hard into her throat. He could taste the smoke. Laboriously he dragged the air in and out of her lungs until he had to stop, gasping for breath. As he did so he thought he saw her eyelids flicker.

It could have been chance, the breeze on her lashes. But then she arched her back and coughed. At first weakly and then deeply and painfully. And rolling over on her side she retched on the ground.

He'd never before been so glad to see someone throw up. When she was done he helped her up into a sitting position.

She looked up at him, disorientated.

'Great way to react to a kiss,' he said.

She went on staring at him, blankly, as though she'd never clapped eyes on him before, and then turned her head to look at the burning barn, the memory spreading back into her mind.

'Are they out?' she asked.

'The horses? Yes, they're out. They'll be in Romania by now, the rate they were going.'

She nodded thoughtfully, as though this were something that had to be taken into consideration. Then she asked, 'When did you kiss me?'

'Just now.'

'Why?'

'You have to take your chances when they come.'

She considered him gravely for a moment and then she began to laugh, long and helplessly. Somewhere in the middle it turned to tears and he held her close to him.

The yard had filled with flashing blue lights. Black-clad

figures were rolling hoses out across the ground. The officer in charge came over to them. He had short legs, short hair and wore a bright plastic helmet.

'Hay barn?' he asked irrelevantly.

Terezia had got shakily to her feet. She nodded.

The officer looked at the burning barn. 'Bitches, hay barns,' he said.

'Yes,' she agreed.

Three storeys above, under the eaves of the house, Gabor Erkell stood by the window. Even at that distance he could feel the warmth of the fire on his face and all around him the unearthly orange light danced and flickered on the walls.

Through the broken pane of glass he watched the firemen working on the blaze. They had it under control now. The hay had been the only really inflammable ingredient and now that it was burnt out the fire was beginning to die away. That didn't matter. It had done its work; served its purpose. Erkell had never intended to burn the stables to the ground. He just wanted the girl to realise that she was under threat; he just wanted her to know he was there.

Moving his head, he looked round to where she and the two men were rounding up the horses in the driveway. They'd got bridles on to them and tethered them to the trees where they stood docile and quiet now that the danger had passed.

Erkell had watched Terezia run into the burning stable to save the horse with a feeling of disgust. There was something obscene about the performance. She'd risked her neck for a horse. Would she ever have done that for a human? No chance. They were all like that, the Kasinczy-Landsbergs and their kind. More interested in horses than people. They'd paid incredible sums for them, kept them in beautiful stables, treated them with a care and concern they'd never shown to the wretched souls who slaved in their houses and factories.

Erkell's eyes followed Terezia as she moved between the patient creatures tethered in the dark. There wasn't one of her family who would have dreamed of turning an animal out into the night but they'd turned poor Elsie, his grandmother, out. They hadn't cared what became of her after she was gone. They hadn't cared what became of her daughter, his own mother, either. She'd worked in one of their mills from the age of twelve. Children weren't supposed to work in factories but it was wartime and they needed the money to make ends meet and so the foreman had turned a blind eye.

Fifteen hours a day she'd worked in that hell until the toxic fumes had destroyed her lungs. Erkell could remember the sound of her coughing in the bed beside him; he could remember the way the cancer had eaten into her day by day until she'd grown thin and wrinkled, an old crone by the time she'd died at the age of twenty-three.

He'd been taken away and put in an orphanage. Thin, cold and frightened. He'd had no family, no clothes, no money. He was a dispossessed child with nothing in his life except a name and the right to hate.

An hour later, Terezia hung up the phone and came back into the kitchen.

'He says he can bring some hay over in the morning.' She'd been talking to a farmer who lived further down the valley. 'He's going to charge for delivery but that's too bad. We've got to have it.'

'Where will we store it?' Gyorgy asked.

'There's room in one of the stables by the gate.'

She sat down at the table and rested her chin on her hands. She looked exhausted, skin pale, dark smudges round her eyes.

'Are you going to tell the owners?' It was Elek, the younger of the stable hands, who asked. He'd arrived, wide-eyed and shocked, while they were putting the horses back in the stables. He hadn't seen the fire but had been alerted by the wailing of the fire engine and pedalled up to the Palace.

Terezia looked at him dubiously. 'Maybe I should.'

'Tomorrow,' Max told her firmly. 'There's no need to do that now. None of the horses are harmed. You can tell them about it in the morning.'

He poured hot water from the kettle into four glasses of tea and put them on the table. Terezia took one, added a spoonful of sugar and stirred as she stared away into the distance.

'How did it start?'

'I can't think,' Gyorgy said.

'Could it have been one of the spirit lamps?'

'We didn't use one this evening. Anyway we never take them into the hay barn.'

'The fireman reckoned it would be a cigarette. But no one was smoking were they?' There was a strict rule against smoking in the stables.

'No one,' Elek said. 'I had a fag earlier. But I was out in the driveway. It couldn't have started a fire from there.'

Terezia nodded. The easy way he offered the information was enough to convince her it was true.

'Something must have started it,' she said.

'It could be anything,' Max put in. 'A rake falling over on a stone floor will make a spark.'

'Enough to start a fire?' Terezia asked.

'Could do.'

Elek was looking uncomfortable. 'It might have been something else,' he said slowly.

Terezia looked round at him. 'How's that?'

The boy shook his head, not sure of what he was saying, 'I mean, it may not have been an accident.'

There was silence in the room.

'You think someone started it?' Terezia asked.

'It was something I heard . . . in the village this evening. It may not be anything.'

Terezia leaned forward, coaxing him to speak. 'What did you hear, Elek?'

'When I was in the bar someone said that Gabor Erkell had been in earlier.'

The name didn't mean anything to Max. But he could see it meant something to the other two. At the mention of it, there was a tension in the room, as though the air had suddenly got cramp.

'Have I missed something here?' he asked but Terezia didn't answer him.

'Did he say what he wanted?' she fired at Elek.

'He said he'd come back to do something . . . some business.'

In the silence that greeted this remark, Max said, 'Who is this Gabor Erkell?'

Terezia turned to him, pushing her hair from her eyes. 'He's the bastard who reported my father to the police – years ago. I kicked him out of his house. He was living here rent-free in one of my houses. Can you believe that? I told him to get out.'

'Is that enough to make him do this?'

'Yes,' she said carefully. 'I think it might be.'

'He used to work for the AVO,' Gyorgy put in from the doorway.

Max remembered someone telling him that she'd evicted a man from his house. He'd said she'd done it for no reason.

'He's all screwed up,' Terezia said. 'Full of hate. But I didn't think he'd do a thing like this. He could have killed the horses.'

'He could have killed you,' Max said.

'I think that's probably what he was hoping,' she said bitterly.

'You say he worked for the AVO?'

'Yes. I didn't know it at the time.'

'Nice friends you make.' In their prime the AVO were more vicious, more calculating than their cousins in Russia, the KGB.

'Not that it would have made any difference if I had known,' she added defiantly. 'I'd still have had him out.'

'He must be mad,' Gyorgy said.

Terezia shook her head slowly. 'This isn't him,' she said. 'It's Zoltan.'

'Do you reckon so?' Max asked.

She nodded through the tangle of her hair. 'Rats like Erkell don't do anything off their own initiative. They take orders. And the only person who'd want this done is Zoltan.'

Max got to his feet and went over to the window. Was he out there now, he wondered. It's said that arsonists like to watch the fires they start; it's part of the kick. He could be out there now, watching, gloating.

'I don't think you should stay here tonight,' he told Terezia.

'I'll be all right.'

'I know somewhere you could go.'

'I'll be all right,' she insisted. 'I need to be here with the horses.'

'Gyorgy and Elek can stay with them.'

He looked across at the two boys for confirmation of this. Gyorgy gave a nod and said, 'Yes, sure.'

'Take the gun over there,' Max told him. 'And use it if you see anyone you don't like.'

'It will be a pleasure,' Gyorgy said. Picking up the gun from behind the door he broke open the breech and dropped in a couple of cartridges. They went out into the night together.

'What about you?' Terezia asked in a small voice when they had gone. 'Aren't you staying?'

'I can't. The police will be around sometime – maybe tonight. I'd rather not be here when they arrive.'

Going through to the passage he made a call. When he came back, Terezia was standing by the window looking out into the darkness. There was a stillness to her.

'I'm not going to let him do it,' she said.

'Who – Zoltan?'

'I'm not going to let him drive me out of the house. That's what he wants. He thinks that if he scares me enough I'll go. But I won't. This is mine!'

She turned to him as she spoke and her eyes were cold, the pupils lost in a sea of frozen emerald.

'I understand,' he said.

'It's horrible and broken-down and it's sad. But it's mine; I won't let anyone take it away from me!'

'It's all right,' Max said calmly. 'We're on your side.'

'Are you, Max?'

'Yes, I am. Of course I am.' He put his arm round her and she buried her face into his neck, holding him tightly.

'You think I'm out of my mind, don't you,' she whispered.

'No—'

'It's not what I was saying the other day.'

'It doesn't matter what you were saying the other day.'

'It takes time to realise these things.' She'd lifted her face away and was studying the lapel of his jacket as she spoke. 'It's hard to explain, but when I'm here I know who I am . . . I know where I came from. Without it I'm nobody. I don't even have a name. I'm just someone drifting about for no reason.'

'Then we must keep it.'

'It's silly, isn't it? I can't look after it or mend it; I can't do anything for it but I need it.'

'It belongs to you.'

She nodded. 'It's just the remains of a house but I can't let anyone take it away from me.'

'They won't.'

She looked at him intently then glanced away towards the passage. 'Who were you ringing just now?'

'I was fixing somewhere for you to stay tonight.'

'Stay? Who with?'

'With a friend of mine – you'll like her.'

'But it's very late. She won't want me turning up in the middle of the night.'

Max smiled. 'She won't mind,' he said. 'She's been waiting a long time to meet you.'

22

It was after eleven when they reached Eleanor's home. The shutters were closed, no light showing, but the daughter opened the door at the first ring. The indifference she'd shown when Max first turned up was gone, and she was smiling in welcome.

'I've made up the bed ready,' she said as she ushered them inside.

There's nothing like a crisis for bringing out the best in the Hungarians.

'Is your mother still up?' Max asked her.

She nodded. 'In the kitchen.'

There was only a single bulb burning above the scrubbed pine table. Eleanor was sitting by the stove, as she had been when he was there before, half lost in shadow. But she was awake and alert, a cigarette in one hand, its smoke writhing up around her face.

'So, Mr Anderson,' she said, a glint of humour in her eyes. 'The last time we met you told me you were leaving the country.'

'Something came up. I decided to stay.'

She gave her dry cackle. 'I thought so; I thought I'd be

seeing you again. You didn't look like a man who was leaving.' She lifted one hand and waved away the smoke that was troubling her and glanced beyond him. 'Have you brought her then?' she asked.

Max turned to where Terezia was standing by the door. 'She's here.'

Eleanor leaned forward, peering into the dark.

'Come closer, girl. I can't see a thing these days.'

Terezia came up beside Max. As the light fell on her, the expression on the old woman's face froze and she drew in her breath through her teeth.

'Ah yes,' she said quietly. 'I thought so. I'd have known you anywhere. Come closer.'

Terezia hesitated.

'Sit beside me,' the old woman said. 'I want to look at you.'

Terezia turned to Max. 'Who is this?'

'Eleanor Jankovics,' he said. 'You'd know her better as Eleanor Hargreaves.'

The old woman was watching Terezia keenly all the while, trying to judge her reaction to the name, and Max realised that for all her brusqueness she was nervous.

'Does that name mean anything to you?' she inquired.

Terezia smiled. 'Yes,' she said. 'Yes, of course,' and going over she kissed her lightly on the cheek.

It was a simple, almost childlike gesture but it affected the old woman strongly. Silver filaments of tears glittered in her eyes.

'I knew your father,' she said carefully.

Terezia sat down beside her, her coat falling open as she crossed her long jeans-clad legs.

'I know,' she said. 'He told me about you.'

It was what she wanted to hear and she smiled and shook

her head in pleasure. Then turning to her daughter who was standing, arms folded in the doorway she said, 'Don't just stand there – get some wine. We must have something to drink.'

'It's late,' the other woman chided. 'You should be in bed.'

'Bed? I'm not going to bed. We need to celebrate. It's not every day we have Karoly's daughter to stay.'

Maria shook her head but she wasn't going to argue. Hoisting out a bottle from the rack in the corner she gave it to Max, along with a corkscrew, and fetched glasses from the cupboard.

'Can I get you anything?' she asked Terezia.

Terezia shook her head then, seeing that the question was genuinely meant, she hesitated. 'Well, actually, if you had something to eat . . .'

'Are you hungry?'

'Starving—'

'When did you last eat today?' Eleanor put in sharply.

'I don't think I've eaten anything today.'

'Silly girl.' She was the governess again, in charge of the domestic agenda. 'No wonder you're looking so pale. You should eat regularly.'

'I've got some bacon,' Maria told her. 'And some eggs. Will that do?'

'Wonderful. I don't want to put you to any trouble.'

'It's no trouble.' The air was warming with the rich smell of butter. 'How about you, Úr Anderson?'

Max shook his head. He was sitting at the kitchen table, glass in hand.

Satisfied, Eleanor went back to the reason they were there. 'Max told me someone set fire to the stable block.'

Terezia nodded, eyes downcast at the memory.

'How bad is the damage?'

'Bad enough. The hay barn and the office are gone, so are two of the stables. But it could have been worse.'

'So you can keep going?'

Terezia nodded.

'Any of the horses hurt?'

'No, not hurt. We got them out in time. But I don't know if any of the owners will let them stay once they hear what's happened.'

'I shouldn't worry about the owners.' Eleanor wasn't concerned with minor details. 'Provided the animals aren't hurt they'll leave them where they are. And if they don't you can always find more. There's more horses than people in this country and from what I hear you've got quite a way with the brutes.'

Terezia smiled sadly. 'With the owners or the horses?'

'Both.'

Maria put a plate on to the table. It held soft fried eggs and bacon that was brown and corrugated from the pan. Terezia glanced at Eleanor who waved her hand impatiently.

'Eat girl, before it gets cold.'

She sat opposite Max and ate ravenously while Eleanor plied her with questions.

'Do you know who set fire to the place?'

'Yes, I think so. It was someone working for Zoltan.'

Eleanor touched the cigarette to her lips. 'You think he's behind it?'

Terezia nodded as she ate. 'Yes, I'm sure he is. He tried to buy me off the other day, promised a fortune if I'd leave the country. But I didn't go for it, so now he does this.'

'Can you prove it?'

'No – that's the trouble.'

They were interrupted by Maria bundling back into the room.

'There's a police car outside,' she said.

'Hell!' Max was on his feet.

Eleanor glanced up at him sharply. 'Are they looking for you?'

There wasn't time for explanations.

'Is there a way out at the back?' he asked.

Eleanor nodded towards the back of the house. 'Through there,' she said calmly. 'There's a door leading out into the garden. You can get into the road at the end.'

Terezia followed him through into the darkened room. 'When will I see you?'

'I'll ring you.' Max had the door opened, the cold night air gripping them. 'In the morning.'

He reached out, fingers touching her cheek, and was gone.

Terezia closed the door and went back into the kitchen. Her heart was thumping. Outside, a gloved fist was pounding on the front door. Maria went to open it. Eleanor lifted a bony hand and pointed to the table.

'Take your coat off and sit down,' she said quietly. 'Finish your dinner, girl, and don't let them see you're nervous.' Fifty years of police rule had taught her how to handle these situations.

The police didn't wait to be invited in. As the latch opened, they moved into the kitchen: two men, bulky in anoraks, their hands low on their belts close to the automatics that bulged from their hips.

The scene that greeted them was innocent enough, the two women looking up at them in surprise, one eating at the table, knife and fork in her hands, the other smoking by the range.

Their eyes probed the room.

'Where is he?'

'Who?' Eleanor asked.

'Anderson.' He fumbled the foreign name so it came out as *Undertern*. 'We heard he is here.'

'He's gone.'

'Where?'

'I couldn't say.

The policeman gave a grunt. He had a pale face and short blond hair under his peaked cap. He glanced around the room again, his attention settling on Terezia.

'What's your name?' he asked.

'She's a friend of the family,' Eleanor said testily.

'I asked what her name is.'

'Terezia,' she said. 'Terezia Kasinczy-Landsberg.'

It seemed to mean something to him. 'What are you doing here?'

'She's staying the night,' Eleanor said. 'She's had a fire at her home.'

'Is that so?' he asked Terezia.

She nodded.

'You'd know it yourself if you checked your files,' Eleanor told him.

The explanation took some of the wind out of his sails. 'Do you know where he's gone?'

Terezia shook her head. 'I couldn't say.'

'He just went off into the night, did he? No word of where he was going – nothing?'

Terezia looked over to the door they'd come in through and back again, eyes wide with innocence. 'Yes,' she said.

'How long ago?'

'I couldn't say, a few minutes ago—'

'You're late, Janos,' Eleanor cut in from the shadows. 'You were always late for school as a boy and now that you've grown up you're still late.'

'This is serious, Eleanor.'

'Go back to the station and tell them he's gone. It's someone else's problem now.'

'He's wanted by the police.'

'Then the police are fools. He's done nothing wrong, now take your hat off and have a drink.'

'We can't do that, Eleanor.'

'You might as well; you're not going to find him here.'

The policeman glanced at his mate, then with a jerk of the head he told him to check the house.

He was back within five minutes. A shake of his head told the other the place was clean.

'See,' Eleanor said in triumph.

'You realise it's a crime to harbour a wanted man.'

'We weren't harbouring him. He came by for a few minutes, now he's gone.'

The policeman nodded; if that was the way they wanted it.

Eleanor eyed him from her chair. 'Now clear off and leave us in peace, Janos. Come back again when you're not wearing a uniform.'

'I'm just doing my job.'

As they went back to the door, she asked, 'How did you know he was here?'

The policeman paused. He didn't have to tell her how he knew, he didn't have to tell her anything, but the answer came just the same. 'We had a tip-off,' he said.

Erkell swung the motorcycle round the curve of the bend, the dark shadows of the pine trees flashing past, his knee almost touching the tarmac, shifting up into top gear as the road straightened again.

He didn't get a kick out of the machines but he preferred

them to cars. They were more versatile. They could go off track and thread their way through traffic jams. They could lose themselves amongst other vehicles on a road, particularly at night when the single headlight was almost impossible to detect. And best of all, they could be hidden more easily than a car.

For the past two days he'd had the machine up in the trees near the Palace. When he saw Anderson and the girl leaving, he'd freewheeled it down the drive, let in the clutch as he came through the gates, the engine firing of its own accord, and caught them up before they were two miles out of the village.

He could see Anderson now, about half a mile up the road ahead. While his car had been parked in the road Erkell had taken the precaution of removing the cover from the offside rear light so that now one burned red, the other yellow. Even at this range he could trail it in the traffic as it made its way into Budapest.

'Don't fret, girl,' Eleanor said. 'He'll be back in the morning. Come and sit down.'

Terezia did as she was told, not sitting but kneeling down by the warmth of the range. She could feel Eleanor's eyes on her, as they had been since she first came in the room.

'So your father told you of me?' the old woman said.

Terezia nodded. 'But he never said anything about you being here. He thought you'd gone to America with the others.'

'England,' she said. 'I never went to America, I went back to England. And that was a mistake. England was a depressing dump after the war. They'd won the war and lost everything they'd ever had. The socialists had wormed their way into power and were busy making everyone feel bad about what had happened and who they were. They'd got guilt, good old-fashioned guilt, and that's more destructive than anything an enemy can do.'

'So you came back here.'

Eleanor nodded and stared back into the past. 'I got a job as the teacher in the village at Fetevis.'

'Was that any better than England?'

'Not really, but it's where I wanted to be.' She picked up the stub of the cigarette she'd been smoking and put it to her lips, fumbling with the disposable lighter. 'Will you light this for me, girl? My fingers are so stiff.'

Terezia flicked out the flame and lit the tip of the cigarette, sitting back on her heels. 'You must have loved him very much,' she said lightly.

'Who?'

'My father.'

'Why do you say that?' There was a wariness in her voice.

'To have come back the way you did.'

The old woman looked down at her through the smoke and then she gave a grunt. 'Is it that obvious?'

'Why else would you have done it?'

Eleanor shook her head. 'No one else has ever suggested it.'

'I saw the look on your face when I came in.'

'Yes,' she said with a sudden weariness. 'I came back to look for him. No one knew what had become of him, you see. There was no information. It was all banned. People just vanished after the war and we never heard of them again.' She blew out smoke and watched it curl away to the ceiling. 'I thought that if I stayed close to the Palace he'd come back one day.'

'He did.'

She nodded. 'Yes,' she agreed. 'He did. But by that time it was all too late.' She spoke of something she had understood and come to accept. 'No one ever told me he'd got married.'

'So had you.'

'I had,' she nodded. 'Life goes on. We can't live in our dreams for ever.'

'He thought you were in love with his brother.'

Eleanor smiled faintly. 'I know. And I let him think that. It was safer that way. You had to be discreet in those days. A girlish crush on your employer was one thing, but any suggestion that I was in love with Karoly would have been a disaster. It wasn't my place; it wouldn't have been allowed. He was unmarried, you see – eligible. I'd have lost my job on the spot.'

It seemed so complicated, Terezia thought. Complicated and rather absurd. But in some ways it wasn't so different from the world she'd been brought up in. Jobs had been fragile under the communists. A misconstrued remark, a connection with someone in disfavour, even an unfounded rumour, could get you the sack. They had just been the rules of the day that you'd learned to understand and accept and get round if you had the chance.

Eleanor touched the cigarette to her lips, staring away into the past with narrowed eyes as if seeing it differently for the first time.

'Tell me about your mother,' she said after a moment.

'There's not much to tell,' Terezia said quickly. 'I never really knew her.'

'But they were married? They were actually married?' The old woman rapped out the question.

'Yes, they were married.'

'But how did it happen?'

'I'm not really sure,' Terezia said. 'I can only tell you what I know.'

The foal had turned in the mare's womb and it took Karoly two hours to move it around until it was facing the right way.

It was a warm evening in July and the air was thick with the pungent scents of horse and sweat and straw. One of the yard hands held the mare's head, stroking the damp coat of her neck while Kalman Imre, the boss of the farm, stood watching with his hands in his pockets. Occasionally he'd grunt a question out through his shaggy moustache but otherwise he'd make no direct interference.

Erzsebet could feel the tension in the close, humid stall. It was at moments such as this that she knew the fortune of a stud farm hung in the balance. The mare had been sired by a thoroughbred racehorse from a stables two hundred miles further south. The match had been made almost a year before, the bloodstock examined, the deal made. As expensive and contrived an arrangement, she thought, as any royal wedding. But the foal, if it arrived in this world fit and strong, could be immensely valuable to them.

The men hadn't noticed her standing there in the corner of the stable. She'd come over to show Karoly the letter she had clutched in her apron pocket but finding them absorbed in their task she'd slipped inside without disturbing them.

She watched as Karoly felt under the mare's belly with the palms of his hands, sensing the position of the unborn creature beneath. His shirtsleeves were rolled to the shoulder, patches of damp in his armpits and down his back. The wing of fair hair fell in his eyes and he tossed it back with a quick, familiar gesture. In the shadows of the stable he appeared to her no different from the day she'd first met him, the aquiline features calm, his voice, when he spoke to the boss, quiet and polite as though he were making small talk in a drawing room.

Reaching down lower, he ran his arm under the horse. It was usual for a mare to be lying down as she delivered her foal but he had encouraged her on to her legs.

Pressing his shoulder into the taut, swollen belly, like a man finding the balance of a sack of grain, he lifted the burden of the foal inside and slowly began to knead it around in the womb.

She knew the operation couldn't be rushed. If the umbilical cord became tangled the oxygen to the foal's brain would be cut off. And if that happened, even for a split second, the animal would have to be put down at the moment of birth. There were ropes and forceps for this job but Karoly preferred not to use them. Nature could not be forced.

It was three years since they'd come to the farm. At first Karoly had been given odd jobs around the yard but within weeks his experience with horses had caught the attention of Kalman Imre. A horseman can spot the gift in others and he'd moved him on to more useful work.

To the other grooms and yard hands he was just plain Karoly. He didn't have another name. He worked with them, ate with them, joked with them but he remained anonymous. And they'd left it that way. Even Erzsebet knew nothing of his life before they'd met. He spoke to her occasionally of his days in jail and often of the jobs he'd had around the country after that. But of his childhood and upbringing he remained silent. It was as though that part of him didn't exist any longer.

The birth came as it was getting dark, the foal edging out into view, first its front hooves then its head appearing, like a dog jumping through a hoop in slow motion.

With powerful contractions of the body, the mare eased the foal out on to the hay where it lay, sleek and damp, an ungainly mound of limbs. At the sight of it, Erzsebet clapped her hands in delight. The men too grinned and shook their heads, the tension lifting, the moment of uncertainty past.

Karoly went outside and rolled a cigarette. He talked briefly with Kalman, the two men glancing at the newborn foal, assessing it, comparing their first impressions.

Released of the burden, the mare had become suddenly animated, nudging and licking the foal into life until in less than an hour it stumbled to its legs and staggered slowly round the stable like someone awakened from a deep sleep.

Leaving the yard hand to clean out, they moved the mare to the fresh straw of a neighbouring stall, the foal following drunkenly beneath its mother's legs.

Kalman Imre went back to the farmhouse telling Karoly that there was a drink up there for him if he wanted to drop by later. Karoly nodded his thanks and went over to the tack room. Erzsebet followed him.

'That was a close thing,' she whispered.

'Too close for my liking.' The birth of the foal had filled him with a physical sense of exhilaration. She could almost touch it in him.

He ran the taps in the sink, took off his shirt and began to wash his hands and arms.

'Were you worried, Karoly?' she asked.

'Worried?' It wasn't the word he had in mind. 'I was scared out of my wits. I didn't think the little fellow wanted to come out.'

He took a towel from the hook on the wall and began to rub himself down, drying his hair and combing it back in place with his fingers. Above him, the single bulb gleamed on the oily blackness of harness and polished brass. A weedy tune came from the radio in the corner.

After a moment Erzsebet said, 'I've had a letter from the lawyers.'

He paused. 'Oh yes?'

'It's my divorce.' She took the envelope from her apron and offered it to him.

Drying his hands, he took out the printed pages very carefully as if they were some precious relic and Erzsebet felt a flutter of nerves in her stomach. They'd talked of her chances of divorcing Gyula over and over again but now that the moment had come she wasn't sure how Karoly would respond.

'It's come through,' she said inadequately.

'The devil.' He spoke in a kind of wonder as he glanced across the print. 'I never thought he'd go through with it.'

'I'm free,' she said.

'How d'you feel about it?'

'Wonderful.' She shook her head, unable to find better words to describe the sensation that had grown within her since reading the letter. It was a pleasure that was sharp and hard in her. A feeling of deep cleanliness like standing under a mountain waterfall on a hot day.

Karoly dropped the papers on a feed bin. Taking her hand he touched it to his lips and she felt the green warmth of his smiling eyes on her face.

'Then we must celebrate,' he whispered.

Moving her hand outwards, he drew her in close to him with his other arm.

'What are you doing?' she asked breathlessly.

'Dancing.'

She was laughing now. 'But I can't dance, Karoly.'

'You're already doin' it.'

'But there's not room in here to dance.'

'Then imagine we're not here.' His voice was soft in her ear as they moved. The music bounced along, the smell of horse and leather filled their heads. 'Imagine we're a long way from here. Years away. The chandeliers are lit, the room's full of uniforms and long dresses. The orchestra's playin' one of the tunes my grandmama used to get that little fellow Lehar to knock up for her.'

Erzsebet was listening. She felt scared and happy at the same time but she was listening now with every fibre of her being.

'Where are we, Karoly?' she whispered.

'I've asked Ottokar to leave the windows open.' The music still carried them around. This was a new skill in Karoly. A skill that belonged to another part of him. 'So we can dance out on the terrace. Down there the trees are full of lanterns. The whole place is lit up.'

Erzsebet stopped, his face cupped in her hands. 'Where are we, Karoly?' she asked urgently.

His eyes were full of the dream. 'At home,' he said.

'Where's home?'

He hesitated and for a moment she thought she'd lost him. Then he smiled and said, 'Why, Fetevis, of course.'

At the word she felt a shock pass through her like a current of electricity. She knew it. She'd seen it. On a school outing some years ago they'd driven past the Palace of Fetevis. She remembered it spread out huge and gracious above the lake and the sight of it had drawn a gasp of amazement from the children in the coach. The teacher had been quick to pour cold water on their interest. The house, she had told them, had been built by enemies of the people. They had lived off the labour of others, sapped the strength of the country. Her classmates had all gazed at the house.

They heard the teacher's words. They knew what they were supposed to mean. But as they looked across the water at that vision they had all briefly touched a world that could never be theirs.

'Oh, Karoly,' she whispered. 'I'm so sorry.'

'Sorry?' he asked. 'Sorry for what?'

'For . . . what happened to you.'

He saw she didn't understand.

'Nothin' happened to me,' he told her.

'Your whole life—'

He drew her hands together and kissed them. 'I'm a lucky man,' he said. 'Most men have one life. I've had several.'

'Why did you never tell me before?'

'Tellin' people has never been a good idea.'

'But you can tell me!'

'Yes,' he said as if it were a thought that was new to him. 'I can tell you.'

And she put her arms around him, burying his head into her neck, holding his secret tight to her.

It was three days later that Karoly was called into Kalman's office. The farmer was sitting in a high-backed chair, his desk a healthy scrabble of paperwork. He appeared uneasy.

'I had a call from the police just now,' he began. 'They wanted to know whether you were working here on the farm. It seems they've had some sort of tip-off about you.'

He glanced up quickly at Karoly to see if he was going to give any hint of who might have done this.

But Karoly just said, 'Can I ask what you told them?'

'I said you had done some odd jobs around the place a few years ago and then moved on.' He looked down at his hands. 'They're coming round later today to check.'

'I see.'

'There was nothing else I could say, Karoly.'

'No—'

'I don't know what it is you're supposed to have done or why they want you but if they find you've been working here all this time we'll all be in the dung heap.'

'Yes, I understand that, sir.'

Kalman scratched the back of his neck, a man easier with actions than with words. 'I don't mind telling you,' he said roughly, 'I don't want to lose you. You're the best I've got. If there was some way I could get round it . . .' He shrugged, letting the thought trail away.

Karoly said, 'I'll collect my things, sir.'

'The men won't say a thing.'

'No,' he said, 'I'm sure they won't.'

'It may be worth your while going up to the Bukk Mountains.' Now that the worst of what he had to say was over, Kalman spoke with more confidence. 'I have a friend there who might take you on.'

'That's kind of you,' Karoly said.

'I've written to him recommending he tries you out. I've also told him about the fire.'

'Fire, sir?'

'That fire we had in the barn last year. I told him a lot of your things were burned in it. Particularly your work papers.'

The two men looked at each other in silence for a moment. Then Karoly smiled and said, 'I'd forgotten that, sir.'

'I've told him I'll be sending them on as soon as they've been replaced.' He searched Karoly's face. 'If you could give me your name I'll get it done.'

Karoly was momentarily at a loss for words. The farmer pressed him.

'You must have a name, Karoly.'

'No, sir . . . I'm not sure I have any more.'

Kalman's gaze didn't waver. 'If you were to have papers,' he said carefully, 'there'd be nothing to stop you from marrying Erzsebet. You know that?'

Karoly was looking out across the farmyard, his mind far away.

'She'd like that, you know, Karoly.'

He smiled at thoughts he'd never had before. 'Yes,' he said. 'I think she might like that.'

'You must give me the name.'

He paused, reaching deep within himself. Then he said, 'Kasinczy.'

'Kasinczy?'

'It's an everyday sort of name, wouldn't you say?'

Kalman looked at him, long and hard.

'Almost common, sir.'

For a long while Eleanor sat staring into the darkness. Then she stubbed out the cigarette and impatiently brushed away the smoke that rose from the ashtray.

'So that was the way of it,' she said brusquely. 'And everyone said he'd never do it.'

Maria came into the room to say that the bed was made up in the spare room. She looked hard at her mother as she spoke.

'It's all right. I'm coming, I'm coming.' Eleanor could take a hint. She waited until her daughter had left the room again. 'Fuss,' she said with a glint of amusement. 'That's all that girl does. Anyone would think I was an invalid.'

Terezia sat with one knee raised, hugging it in her arms. She could feel the tiredness rolling over her like a wave but there was something she wanted to know and the moment might not be right again.

'Could I ask you something?'

Eleanor paused as she was getting to her feet. 'What's that?'

'Why did my father hate Zoltan?'

'Zoltan?' She frowned. 'He never hated Zoltan.'

Terezia nodded.

'Not in my day,' Eleanor said. 'He was very fond of Zoltan, treated him like a son. He was the heir, you see, and that made a difference to Karoly. There was a sort of bond between them, an understanding.'

'Then he must have done something to have changed it.'

'No, I was there the last day they saw each other. Karoly didn't hate him. He could be stern if Zoltan did something he didn't approve of but that was his way. But he never hated him; he couldn't. Zoltan was his favourite.'

'He wouldn't even have his name mentioned in the house.'

'I can't believe it.'

Terezia nodded.

'Then something must have happened,' Eleanor said.

'But what?'

'I can't imagine.'

23

At nine the following morning, Gombos hammered on the door. 'There's a call for you, Shackleton.'

'Did they give a name?' Max asked.

He shook his head. 'It was a woman's voice.'

'Are they allowed to call at this time of the day?'

Gombos wasn't amused. 'Just answer the phone, Shackleton. There's others wanting to use it if you don't.

It was Eleanor, he discovered when he picked up the receiver that was dangling from its flex in the plywood booth on the ground floor.

She spoke in English. 'So you made it back in one piece.'

'They'll have to be a little quicker next time.'

'Why Shackleton?' she asked.

'One of my heroes.'

'Good choice,' she approved.

'Is Terezia still there?'

'No, she's gone back. Said she had to feed the horses. That's why I'm ringing.'

'You don't want me to help?'

'No, stupid, just listen and don't make smart remarks. There's something I meant to give her. I'm going soft in my old age; I'll forget my name next. I have something here that belongs to her. Had it for years. And now when I get the chance to give it to her I forget.'

What the heck could she have got that belonged to Terezia? She'd never met her before, didn't even know of her existence until the past few months.

'Can't it wait until she comes back?' he asked.

'She's not coming back. She thinks it's not a good idea to stay here now the police know about it. Maybe right. That's why I need you to come by and pick this up.'

'Nothing personal, Eleanor, but it's not a great idea for me to be hanging around your place either.'

'How can I get it to you then?'

Max thought. 'Could you get it over to your granddaughter?'

'Trudi?'

'At the schoolhouse in the village. I can pick it up from there.'

'I'll get Maria to drive over.'

A mile away, in a quiet street off Andrassy Utca, the long black Cadillac eased over into the kerb. Erkell opened the rear door and got in. He sat with his back to the driver as he had before, facing Count Zoltan and his lawyer. The curtains were drawn, their faces dark silhouettes against a dark ground.

'I hear the fire engines were out last night,' Zoltan said as the car pulled back into the traffic.

'The stables burned down.'

'Your handiwork?'

Erkell nodded.

'I trust you were discreet about it.'

'How discreet can a fire be?'

'But you didn't let them know you'd started it.'

'I made it perfectly clear I'd started it.'

The lawyer leaned forward and began to speak but Erkell cut him short.

'There's no connection he can make with you,' he said calmly. 'They'll think I did it to set the record straight, nothing more. But they needed to know that it was me. It'll make them wonder what's coming next. They'll know something is coming, but they won't know when. That's how it begins to hurt.'

'In their minds, you mean?' Zoltan said.

'All pain is in the mind.'

Vargas was uneasy about it. 'But what if they make the connection with the Count?'

'They can make the connection,' Erkell said. 'They can't prove it.'

'God, what started it?'

'A spirit lamp.'

'You're sure?'

'Gyorgy found it in the ashes this morning. It had been thrown in there.'

Joszef stared at the blackened shell of the barn in disgust. The morning light shone peacefully through the gutted windows. The water that the fire engine had used to douse the flames had frozen in the night into long icicles that hung from the sills and gutters, sharp and white as shark's teeth.

'You must go to the police, Tereyki,' he said.

'They were here this morning.'

'You told them?'

Terezia hefted the saddle on to the horse's back. 'Yes,' she said. 'I told them.'

'What did they say?'

'What do you think they said? They didn't believe it was anything more than an accident.'

Joszef was appalled. 'They can see what happened, for Christ's sake.'

'They thought one of the stable hands had left the lamp in there by mistake.'

'The lamps are never taken in the barn.'

'They don't know that.'

'But Erkell was here—'

'They said we have no evidence that he did anything else but stop by and have a drink in the café.'

'But you said he told someone he had unfinished business here. I mean, what else do you need?'

'The police reckon that if he'd meant he was coming up here he'd never have said that.'

Joszef swore to himself. Terezia could see the frustration, the sense of utter helplessness, that she'd felt herself mirrored in his face as he stumped away to look at the remains of the barn.

She swung the girth under the horse's belly and buckled it tight. She'd spent an hour that morning talking to the owners, telling them what had happened. Their reactions had been mixed. Some had taken the news philosophically – it could have been worse, accidents will happen, but at least no one was hurt. One had even been sympathetic, asked if he could help. But four had told her they were removing their animals immediately, another had said he was coming over that afternoon to see how bad the damage was.

But it didn't matter, she told herself. They had enough money in the kitty to buy more hay and straw and they could store it in the empty stables. And the mare they'd bought would be here in a few days. Joszef was going down to the country that afternoon with Rosza to pick it up. They didn't need to be a hotel for other people's horses any more. They could get on with doing what they had always intended to be doing. And Max was back. That was the important part. She wasn't going to let this get to her.

Putting her foot into the stirrup she swung herself up into the saddle. As she was walking the horse out through the gate, Gyorgy emerged from the house.

'There's a call for you.'

It was Vargas.

'I hear there was an accident last night,' he said as she picked up the phone.

'What has it got to do with you?'

'The police told us this morning.'

'Why should they tell you?'

'The Count is most concerned about his property.'

'If the Count is so concerned about his precious property he should call that bastard Erkell off!' Terezia shouted at him.

'Are you suggesting—'

'Yes, I am,' she said and slammed down the receiver. She didn't need to listen to him any longer; she could guess what he was going to say and she found herself shaking with anger as she went back outside.

Mounting the horse, she rode up into the hills behind the house. The ground was frozen and she couldn't take the animal at anything more than a walk so it took her half an hour to reach the point called Castle Rock.

It was a little plateau set beneath an outcrop of granite, high above the tree-line. In the distance, across the wooded landscape, hazy and purple in the winter light, she could see the curve of the Danube and beyond it, on the far hilltop, the silhouette of Visegrad Castle.

It was here the two brothers and the son they had thought

would one day inherit had buried the Venus. Here their lives together in Hungary had ended. But she felt nothing as she stood there on this desolate ridge. It was rather disappointing. She wanted to feel something, to touch their presence here. But the ghosts of the past had vanished.

Over by the rock face she noticed the ground had recently been dug up. That would be that little rat Verity. He must have come up here and tried his luck, hacking in the ground for buried treasure. She'd been mad to let him go through her possessions like that, mad to have let him roam around untended. Not that it had done him any good. He must have been furious when he didn't find what he was looking for. So close, so near, and still nothing. Zoltan too. He must have felt the same anger and frustration when he came up here in search of his inheritance.

Did Zoltan know where the Venus had gone, she wondered. He'd told Max that the Russians had taken it off at the end of the war. Did he believe that, or did he know in his heart that the truth was closer to home; that the uncle who'd once loved him as a son had taken it from him?

She stared down into the valley where the roofs of the Palace could just be seen above the trees. Her father had been in his seventies when he came back to Fetevis. She could visualise him in exact detail; the blond hair turned silver white, the lean, gaunt features of his face and that slight smile that seemed to hover around the edge of his lips and in his eyes, as if there were a joke to his life that he was just beginning to understand.

Eleanor said he didn't hate Zoltan. But he had left home, climbed his way up here and dug up the Venus to stop Zoltan from getting it. For that he'd forfeited his family and his freedom. And if that wasn't hate she didn't know what was.

Swinging herself back in the saddle she made her way downhill, letting the horse find its own way. Where had her father taken the Venus? It wasn't with him when he was arrested. Had he hidden it somewhere new, thinking he'd be able to find it later, or, seeing the police coming, had he just thrown it away? It could be lying under a bush, half covered in earth and leaves, or down at the bottom of the lake. Possessions hadn't meant much to him towards the end of his life. He'd learned to live without the comfort they promise.

'You've been off for a while,' Joszef remarked as she returned to the stable yard.

'I tried a new way, got a bit lost.'

He shot her a quick, keen look. 'Max rang earlier. He said he's got something for you.'

'Is he coming over?'

'He doesn't want to come here; thinks the police might be hanging around. He's gone to some place he knows near here. I've got the directions. He'll meet you there.'

The hunting lodge was pre-war and set in the woods. The floor was cut down into the earth so that the roof met the ground with no side walls to let in the cold. The snow had drifted over it so that all that was visible from outside was a white mound with a tunnel to come in by. It was a place to sit by the fire; a place to eat, drink and get as close to hibernation as the human body can achieve.

Max had spent a weekend there a year ago with a girl. He knew the owner and had persuaded him to give him a room in the upper floor: stripped pine and shutters set in the angle of the roof.

Terezia arrived, cheeks glowing, lips cold as they kissed.

'How did you find this place?' she asked.

'I've been here before.'

'I bet you brought a girl here.'

Max shrugged and she smiled with sweet female malice.

'Poor thing,' she sympathised. 'She can't have stood a chance.'

A waitress appeared with wine, bread and a tureen of soup. Terezia gave a purr of approval and taking off her coat she sat down at the table. She was wearing a blue jumper, belted at the waist, and a white turtle-neck sweater beneath.

She ladled out the soup and began eating.

'You're not hungry again?' Max asked.

'Starving.'

'There's never a time when you're not.'

'You should try being out in this weather all day.'

Reaching over, Max extracted a wad of envelopes from his jacket which was hanging on the back of the chair and dumped them down on the table.

'I got these from Eleanor this morning.'

Terezia paused, spoon raised in her hand. 'What are they?'

'Letters. Sent to your father from his brother in America after the war. He didn't know where your father was so he sent them to her in the hope she'd be able to pass them on. But she didn't know any better than he, so she's had them all these years.'

The envelopes were brittle and discoloured with age. Terezia put down her spoon and picked up the top one gingerly. It was addressed to Count Karoly Kasinczy-Landsberg, c/o Eleanor Hargreaves.

'She wants you to have them,' Max said.

'I don't think I want to read them.'

'I think you should.'

'Why, what's in them?'

'I don't know. But she thinks they might be important.'

Terezia studied the handwriting, undecided, and then picked up a knife and slit the envelope open. There were three sheets of paper inside, covered in a neat, dense script.

She flashed him a nervous smile. 'Rosza always says it's rude to read at table.'

'Read it.'

Her lashes went down and she started on the letter, at first skimming the page and then reading more slowly. After a while she put it down, her face serious.

'Are there any earlier ones there?' she asked. 'He keeps referring to other letters.'

Max sorted through them. The postmarks were almost lost but in her meticulous fashion Eleanor had noted the arrival date in the corner of each one. He passed over a couple.

Terezia read the first, quickly and urgently, her eyes flickering over the lines. Impatiently she put it down and opened the next. It was thicker than the others, and Max could see it contained some printed pages along with the handwritten.

After a moment Terezia put it down and sat back, her eyes closed.

'Oh, God,' she whispered. 'That's it.'

'That's what?'

'This is what Zoltan doesn't want me to know.'

Max looked at the pages scattered out beneath her hands. It wasn't his business what the two brothers had said to each other fifty years ago. But he wanted to know.

'What's it say?'

'Read it,' she whispered.

He picked up the letter and went through it. Much of the information was technical but he didn't need to bother with that. The gist of what was said was on the first page.

'Christ,' he said.

Terezia was leaning forward, watching him keenly as he read. 'Do you think it's still true?'

'I'm sure.'

'It might have changed.'

'The only person who could have changed this would have been your father and he knew nothing about it.'

'Who do you think does know about it?'

'I don't know. I guess just Zoltan and Zoltan. It's not something he's going to broadcast to anyone else, is it?'

'It says the papers are with their solicitors in London. Do you think they've still got them?'

Max got to his feet. 'I think we should find out.'

He went downstairs, extracted the number from international directory enquiries and put the call through. In less than ten minutes he was back.

'Yes,' he said. 'They've got them. Had them there for fifty years.'

Terezia was standing staring out through the tiny dormer window at the frozen landscape.

'Damn him!' she said, turning round to face him. 'This is what it is, isn't it? This is why Zoltan has been hounding me. It's not the house, not the Venus. It's this.'

'I suppose so.'

'No wonder he wanted to pay me off. No wonder the bastard was so hellfired up about getting rid of me. He didn't want me to find this.'

And she might not have, Max thought. Had she not kicked him out of the house that night and left him wandering about the village they might never have come across it.

'He's known,' she said. 'Ever since he met me he's known and he's never said a thing. Damn him!'

With sudden violence she flung her wine glass across the room. It exploded against the wall.

'*Zdorovie*,' Max said.

She glared at him for a moment and then the anger left her. She let her shoulders sag and shook her head.

'Oh Christ, Max, I don't think I want this.'

'It's not all bad, is it?'

'No? I can't think what's good about it.'

'It might give you a problem,' Max said evenly, 'but it cures a few as well, doesn't it?'

Terezia sat down again and, taking the letters, she scanned over the pages listlessly.

'I just don't think I can cope.'

'You don't have to, do you?'

Dropping the pages on the table she stared across the room to where the wine was trickling down the wooden walls. Max went and crouched down beside her, running his hand across her shoulders until his fingers stroked the soft hairs at the base of her neck.

She smiled distantly. 'Oh Christ, Max—'

'Don't fight it.'

'I bet the last girl you brought here didn't start smashing glasses, did she?'

'As far as I remember she didn't do anything.'

'Serves you right.' She searched his face intently for a moment. 'I can't believe he's done this,' she said quietly. 'To one of his own family.'

Zoltan didn't believe she was one of his family, that was the point. He couldn't believe it.

'At least now we know,' he said. 'That's all that matters. Now we know about it, there's nothing more he can do.'

In the book-lined office of the Landsberg Corporation, Zoltan put down the phone.

'She knows,' he said.

Vargas waited for him to explain himself. When he didn't he ventured, 'Knows?'

Zoltan was staring away into space, his face haggard.

'Go find that man of yours,' he said.

'Erkell?'

'Tell him to finish it.'

'Finish?'

The green-grey eyes flashed round to him, cold and hard. 'Yes, finish,' he shouted. 'Do I have to spell it out to you? I want her dead, out of the way for good. Is that too hard for you to understand?'

24

Nine-fifteen a.m. in Deak Ter: the Christmas trees still switched on, morning traffic impatient at the lights, their tyres cutting dark tracks in the overnight snow; the cold air misty with exhaust fumes and the tendrils of steam that lifted from the metro gratings.

The Lada drew off into a side street and parked. Anderson got out to push coins into the meter, the girl came round beside him, hugging herself for warmth. She was wearing her long grey overcoat and a fur hat; beneath it a scarf, not coiled round the neck like a college student but wrapped artfully round her face. Very classy, Erkell told himself, very eyecatching, like some toffee-nosed model in a glossy magazine. The peasant handkerchief round her hair seemed to have been shelved since she'd taken up with Anderson.

Erkell lit a cigarette as he followed them up the street. As a rule he didn't smoke but a cigarette gave a man a reason to be loitering, it let him blend in with the scenery.

They parted near the opera house, Anderson crossing the road, the girl walking on up Andrassy Utca. She was hot as a bitch on heat. He could tell from the way she'd pressed against him as they kissed goodbye, from the glow of anticipation in her face. The silly creature had probably told herself she was in love.

He'd put a stop to that quick enough.

Count Zoltan's lawyer had been nervous as hell when he passed on the instructions the night before. He'd tried to sound calm but his anxiety had come through loud and clear in his voice. He was in over his head. Probably good at bullying other suits in the boardroom but useless when it came to this kind of work.

Erkell had known all along it would end like this. He'd never have taken on the job if he had thought it would lead to anything else. And he guessed Count Zoltan knew it too. He was no fool. From the moment he had brought in a specialist like himself he must have known what the final solution would be.

And at the thought of it, the fire burned hot in his belly.

Turning off the main street, the girl went up the steps of a high building: one of those ornate, grandiose affairs you get around this part of town that looks as though it should be the private house of someone with more money than sense but turns out to be an office.

Going down to the bus stop on the corner he sat down and pulled the newspaper from his pocket. No one ever looks at a man reading a paper while he waits for his bus; he could sit here for as long as he liked.

Half a mile away in the New York Café, Michael Gallagher put the letter down reverently on the table.

'Ah, darling boy,' he murmured.

'Not bad, eh?'

'It's the most beautiful sight I've seen since I came to this land of sin.'

'I thought you'd like it.'

'This is the real thing, Max, my boy. I couldn't see it before, y'see. It didn't feel right. Old family houses, hunks of Renaissance silver are nice toys but you don't lose your head over them. Not when you're as rich as old man K-L. But this is different. This is the real McCoy. For this he'd tweak the devil's tail itself.'

'Can you run with it?'

'Oh, I can run with it all right. But we need evidence.'

'It's there in front of you.'

'And it'd make a lovely column in the business pages. But that's not what people want to know about. It's the lengths to which Zoltan's been going to keep this hidden that the reader wants to hear. This is a murder story – with a bit of GBH and arson to season it on the side. It's good old-fashioned stuff. But to get it on the page we need evidence. It's no good rushing into the editor's office bare-arsed and breathless if we can't back the story up with hard facts.'

'What do you need?'

'Can you prove he had the stables burned down?'

'A spirit lamp was chucked into the hay barn.'

'By some screwball who wants to see your Countess stamped out. What links him with Zoltan?'

'Just a hunch.'

Gallagher nodded. 'And that little gremlin Verity. How do you know it was Zoltan who gave the order to have him killed?'

'His wife overheard them yelling at each other.'

'But you can bet your back teeth she won't testify in court.'

'The police know who pulled the trigger.'

'You sure?'

'It was a man called Strossmayer. They've got pictures of him.'

'How do you know that?'

'I gave them to them.'

'Did you just.' He smiled sleepily, folded the photocopy of the letter and tucked it into his pocket. 'Then I think it's time I started asking a few questions.'

The girl was in the solicitor's office for more than forty minutes. When she emerged, she seemed more preoccupied than she had been before, walking down the steps, her hands buried in her overcoat pocket.

Casually rolling his paper, Erkell stuffed it away and sauntered after her – a man who has got tired of waiting for his bus and decided it's quicker to walk. He didn't have to keep close as she headed up towards Heroes Square. There was hardly anyone else in the street. He could keep his distance.

Crossing the road he looked in a shop window, taking a container from his pocket as he did so. It was not much larger than a packet of cigarettes. In it was a syringe that he'd modified for his purposes. The body and plunger he'd shortened so that it would lie snugly in the palm of his hand. The needle was the type used by vets, thicker and stronger than the usual so that it wouldn't snap when plunged into the flesh of some fretful animal. He'd reduced its length by almost half. On the tip of it was a cork to stop any of the colourless liquid in the syringe from leaking out. It was hydrocyanic acid, HCN, fast-acting, deadly and almost impossible to trace afterwards.

She'd almost reached the square now. Quickening his pace, he moved up nearer to her. He didn't like to make a hit up close like this. Direct physical contact is unpredictable. It puts you in the scene, implicates you in the act. It's the professional's way to work at a distance, with remote-controlled explosives, with sniping rifles that can be fired from a secure point from which the escape has been planned ahead.

But this was an exception. When he struck down this girl he wanted the satisfaction of being there beside her, the satisfaction of seeing the shock of realisation in her eyes, the satisfaction of seeing her collapse at his feet.

HCN works fast. There'd only be a few seconds between the time she felt the prick of the needle and the oblivion that followed. But in that brief instant she'd know. She'd turn and she'd see him and she'd know who'd killed her.

And Erkell wanted her to know that. Not just for himself; he wanted it for the thousands who had suffered under the tyranny of this cursed family. It was a judgement that had been a long time coming but it would be all the sweeter for that.

She was coming into Heroes Square, crossing the road, stepping over the slushy puddles in the kerb.

Erkell slipped the syringe into his hand, nestling it into place so that only the needle showed, sticking out between the closed fingers. Flicking off the cork cap he fell in behind her.

Terezia glanced at her watch. It was just after ten. Twenty minutes to kill before she met Max at Robinson's restaurant. It was on the edge of the lake; she could see it there on the other side of the square. But she didn't want to go straight to it. It was all right for Max. He was used to that kind of smart, expensive place, but she'd feel uneasy sitting there alone.

There was the museum. That at least was warm. But you had to pay to go in. Perhaps she could just look around the bookshop.

She went over to the zebra crossing. The lights had turned

green, the traffic lumbering forwards. She stood waiting, thinking back over the conversation she'd had with Victor Szelkely. He'd raised a problem, a bad problem that had to be solved and she urgently wanted to talk to Max about it.

A bus passed slowly. She saw herself reflected in the glass of the window. Then the image flicked away and there she was in the next window. Fur hat and overcoat, face framed by the swathe of the scarf. It was like looking at the stills of a film. Flick and she was there again; another and she was no longer alone. A man was beside her. Head down, black coat, collar turned up. Flick to the next and he was turned towards her. Flick and she saw his pale face, his eyes on her.

And she knew him.

Erkell.

She spun round. Fear gripped her, a dull ache in her stomach, unformed, unspecific. It took the strength from her legs. She felt them buckle, gave a small sobbing cry and staggered backwards as Erkell's arm struck out at her.

His gloved fist brushed her sleeve. She felt it snag for an instant as she stepped back into the road. There was a squeal of brakes. Someone was shouting at her but it was a long way away. She saw nothing but Erkell standing there in front of her.

He'd hesitated, just for an instant, those pale eyes of his on her, watching, waiting.

What was he waiting for?'

The instant passed. She saw the spark of anger awake in his face. A flick of his arm and he threw something away into the snow, reached in his pocket. And he was coming at her. There was something in his hand, held low and close to his body. Oh God; it was a blade, short and bright and thin.

Stumbling round the bonnet of the car that had come within an inch of hitting her, she ran out into the traffic.

Her fear was alive in her now, screaming in every nerve. She didn't think what she was doing or look where she was going. In her mind she saw only this man with his black coat and his pale eyes coming after her.

A sudden movement; the angry blare of a horn. She ducked to the left and a car swerved behind her. She heard the brakes locking, the tyres tearing at the road.

And then a heavy thump.

She snatched a look over her shoulder as she made the pavement on the far side.

The car had hit Erkell. He was down in the road. She felt a burst of hope and half turned, breaking the rhythm of her stride. Let him be dead, she prayed, let him be finished. But he'd rolled over in the road and was on his feet again, picking up the trail, running with his head low, his eyes fixed on her.

Heart hammering, she sprinted away up the pavement. Could she outstrip him? Men can usually run faster than women, but she was taller than most women and fit from hours in the saddle. At school she'd often beaten boys in races. But not now. Not now that it mattered. She could hear him behind her, feet pounding on the packed snow. He was catching her up, catching her up with that short, bright knife in his hand.

In front of her was the frozen lake. It was teeming with skaters. Without consciously thinking it, her instinct directed her towards them. Safety in numbers. Safety in amongst all those people, away from this cold desolate place.

Crossing the road, weaving between the cars, she hurtled down the flight of steps. There was a queue of people at the entrance. She pushed her way through them. Cries of protest, a hand grabbing at her arm. She tried to squeeze through the turnstile but the steel bar was locked. It hit her across the thighs, sending her sprawling.

A voice was shouting at her, telling her to get a ticket.

She tumbled over the turnstile on to the ground, glancing back up the stairs. Erkell was there, coming down. But more slowly now, wary in a crowd.

A shrill woman's voice said, 'Wait your turn,' but she wasn't listening. Scrambling to her feet, she ran out on to the lake side. The silver expanse of the ice stretched out before her, black figures swarming on its surface like bees.

Without breaking stride, she ran out amongst them. Within four paces a skater cannoned into her, and they fell sprawling on the ice. 'Christ, woman, what the hell are you playing at?'

She hadn't time to explain; hadn't time to apologise. Disentangling herself, she scrambled to her feet, glancing back. Erkell was standing on the shoreline. He wasn't coming after her, she realised. Not on the ice, not with everyone watching.

She felt a surge of hope and headed onwards, picking her way across the ice, figures flashing around her.

Halfway across, she caught sight of him again and her hopes were dashed. He was up on the bridge. He hadn't tried to follow her. He'd gone back to the road that ran over the lake. You stupid fool, she sobbed to herself. He'd reach the other side way before she could.

For a moment they stood, facing each other across the frozen whiteness. Then, turning round, she began heading away in the opposite direction, working her way through the skaters towards the castle.

She was getting used to the slippery surface now, able to move more quickly. As she reached the shore she was fifty yards ahead of him. Panting for breath she clambered up the snow-covered bank to the pathway.

She could see him coming through the trees, homing in

on her. She was never going to outrun him. Her heart was pounding, breath aching in her lungs.

Then, between the trees, she saw a bus. It was parked in the kerb, two women getting on.

She shouted for it to wait but the driver didn't hear. As she came out into the road she heard the hydraulic hiss of the door closing and it moved off, exhaust spiralling in the cold air.

It wasn't moving fast, just lumbering forwards, shifting up from first gear. She caught up with it, banging on the closed door. It had to stop for her. She could see the driver up above her. She shouted for him to stop but he shook his head.

The bus was picking up speed.

It mustn't go. It mustn't leave her. In desperation she pounded on the door again. Then reaching up she caught hold of the wing mirror, swinging herself off the ground.

A hiss of brakes and the machine shuddered to a halt.

'Are you mad?' the driver shouted as the door pulled open.

Terezia tumbled herself inside. 'Quick, go!' she panted.

'What's your problem then?'

'Go. Please go,' she implored him. 'There's someone after me.'

Slowly the driver looked back down the road. There were only a few people on the bus. They were all staring at this wild-eyed girl who'd forced her way on board.

Through the rear window she saw Erkell coming up the road towards them.

'Go, please!'

The driver gave a shrug and let in the clutch. The bus moved in a leisurely fashion up the road.

'Bloke in the coat?' he asked.

Terezia nodded. She was leaning against the driver's compartment, a sheen of sweat on her face, fighting for breath.

'Following you, was he?' he asked.

She nodded. It was a simpler explanation than the true one.

The driver wasn't unsympathetic. 'You get them all in the park these days,' he said. 'Drunks, acid-heads, weirdos.'

She looked back through the rear window. Erkell was standing in the road, watching the bus draw away.

'You know what I think,' the driver went on. 'I think the police should round them up, put them in the army. That'd sort them out, give them a bit of pride in themselves.'

Terezia nodded, not interested in how he was going to save the world. She glanced back through the window.

And the road was empty.

A mile further on the bus dropped her in a suburb of drab stucco and high-rise concrete.

She sat on a park bench and began to shake violently. It was a reaction, she knew that. The release from shock, the release from the primeval instincts of the hunted.

Her mind was clearer now, the confused images of her escape falling into place, linking together into a logical sequence. She went back over it, reliving each moment. It was painful but a healing process, the mind's way of coming to terms with the experience.

It was only then, as her hands steadied, strength returning, that she began to think ahead. What was she going to do, she wondered as she looked about herself. And where the heck was she anyway?

She walked down the road until she found a phone booth. Scratching in her bag, she found coins, pushed them into the slot. The operator found the number for Robinson's restaurant and put through the connection.

Mr Anderson? No, the waiter didn't know him. But he sounded polite and concerned and she explained he was an Englishman, early thirties, brown hair.

She stood waiting in the booth, with its graffiti and dirty floor and cards advertising girls who promised a good time, while the waiter went to look.

Please let him be there; please let him come to the phone.

But it was the waiter who came back on the line. He was sorry, Mr Anderson had left about twenty minutes ago. No, he didn't know where he'd gone.

She punched the button for a further call, held it down as she thought. Then she dialled Fetevis.

It was Gyorgy who answered.

'Has Max called?' she asked.

'Yes – about ten minutes ago. He was looking for you.'

Her heart leapt. 'Do you know where he is?'

'He didn't say. He's going to ring back again in about half an hour.'

'Tell him I'm going round to his place,' Terezia said. 'I'll wait for him there. Tell him to hurry.'

'Are you all right, Terezia?'

'No—'

'He sounded worried.'

She shook her head, the feeling of panic rising again. 'I think someone's trying to kill me.' Think? She didn't think it; she knew it. 'Oh, Gyorgy,' she cried. 'Tell him to come quickly.'

The President put down the phone in disgust. Pressing the buzzer on his desk, he summoned his aide through.

'Did you hear that?'

The aide nodded. He monitored all calls that came through on the security lines.

'Who is this bastard Gallagher?' the President asked.

The aide gave one of his faint smiles that the President found so infuriatingly superior. Thirty-two years old, polished at Harvard Business School, fluent in eight languages and the author of two books scanning the ether of central European politics, he had no trouble answering a simple question like this.

'A British journalist working here in Budapest. Writes for some of the heavyweight papers here but sends most of his stuff back for the home market.'

'How's he know so much?'

'He doesn't, Mr President. He's just digging.'

'Then we've got to stop him digging any deeper. If this gets into the papers it's not going to look good.'

'It's a long way from that.'

'Not long enough. Didn't you hear what they said in security? He's been asking some damned impertinent questions.'

'Then it might be as well to put a damage limitation exercise into operation.'

'What are the options?'

The aide smiled again; he'd already considered this and come up with answers.

'There are several.'

'Give me the best,' the President said. 'And make sure it's good.'

Taking the metro, avoiding the central area of Pest, Terezia made her way out to the suburb of the city where Max had been living for the past week.

The journey was agonising. Every time the doors slid

open at a station she pictured Erkell stepping on board, trapping her in the confined space of the compartment, and she sat huddled in the corner.

It was after midday when she reached the street. She wasn't going to try to get into the building, not with that pot-bellied landlord down in the basement. She'd hang around until Max turned up. It was unlikely he'd made it there before her. Even if he'd received the message straight away it would take him a good hour to get out here.

She went over to the café across the street. It was quiet and uncrowded. A string of fairy lights over the window, the hiss of a paraffin stove in the corner, music coming from a radio. A couple of workmen looked her up and down as she came in. The woman behind the counter directed her to a telephone in the passage.

She got through to Gyorgy.

'Did he call back?'

'About half an hour ago.' He sounded worried and confused, not sure what was going on. 'He's coming round now. Where are you calling from?'

'A café near the house. I'll wait here until he comes.'

'He said it'd be forty minutes.'

'That's okay, I'll wait. I can see him when he comes.'

'Are you all right, Terezia?'

'No, Gyorgy,' she said. 'I'm scared as hell.'

As she came back into the café, the woman behind the counter asked her what she wanted. Use of the telephone didn't come free.

She ordered coffee, took it over to the window. Through the lettering on the glass pane she could see Max's house. It looked dead, only one light gleaming in a window on the third floor.

It was a good place to wait. As soon as he came she could

run out and catch him before he went inside. They could be gone in a few seconds. She sipped her coffee. Now that she knew what was happening she felt calmer and began sketching hurried plans in her mind.

She needed to get away – right away – until this whole business was solved. Abroad would be best but she didn't have her passport with her. It would have to be somewhere in the country. Not a hotel; she didn't have the money for that. It would have to be with a friend, someone she could trust.

But she couldn't think who. She had friends, but none close enough to involve with this. It was a sad truth, she told herself. She was twenty-six years old and there was no one outside her adopted family she could turn to in a crisis. They'd never stayed in one place long enough to make roots.

A motorbike was coming down the road but she didn't pay it any attention.

Maybe Max would know someone. He always seemed to have connections everywhere he went. She glanced at her watch. It was forty-five minutes since he had run Fetevis. Where was he? He should be here by now.

The motorbike stopped outside the window. Terezia glanced up and froze.

It was Erkell.

He was sitting astride the motorbike, not ten paces from her. So close she could see the whiteness of his knuckles as he gripped the handlebar, the worn creases in his leather jacket, the stubble of hair on the back of his neck.

He hadn't seen her. He was close but he hadn't seen her. His head was turned away and he was staring up at the tenement block.

Slowly his foot came down, kicked the support down from the bike. He killed the engine and climbed off.

Terezia sat, paralysed with fear. One move, one sound from her and she knew he'd turn. Those pale eyes would see her.

Her heart was pumping, the blood hot and singing in her ears. She let her breath out slowly through her mouth.

It sounded so loud. He'd hear her, sense her sitting there so close to him.

But he didn't hear. Crossing the road he ran up the steps of the building and hit the buzzer with his thumb.

His head was still turned from her. He was rapping on the door, impatient, hostile. This was her chance to move; this was her chance to get away from that window.

Shakily she got to her feet and backed across the café.

The door of the apartment block had opened and the landlord was standing in the entrance, cigarette in hand, irritated by this disturbance. They stood talking together.

'Anything the matter?'

She looked round in surprise. It was the woman behind the counter who spoke. Slowly she realised they were looking at her. Everyone in the room. There was silence at the tables. They'd all stopped talking to stare at her.

Dumbly she shook her head.

Across the street, she saw Erkell go inside. The door closed.

It had to be now, she told herself. In a moment he'd be back. He'd cross the road and then he'd spot her. If she was going to get out of this place it had to be now.

She darted over to the door and pulled it open. The cold air hit her and she stopped, uncertain, her nerve failing her. If he came out now there'd be no escape. He'd see her, trap her.

But the street was empty and the craving for freedom on her. Without conscious thought she felt herself bolting out from the doorway and starting to run up the pavement.

So slowly. Her whole body was caught in glue. She heard her feet hammering along the snow-packed ground, felt her coat flying behind. But she seemed to be moving in slow motion.

He'd seen her. He must have seen her by now. He only had to open the door, to look out of a window and he'd see her crawling laboriously along the pavement.

The metro station was in front of her. She snatched a glance over her shoulder.

No sign of him. The street was still empty.

She clattered down the stairs, stumbling in her haste, clutching the railing for balance.

On to the platform. It was deserted. No sign of a train; she must have just missed one. She paced the platform, adrenaline burning in her veins, forcing her to move.

A figure stepped out from the pillars. She gave a little cry and jumped back. But it was a woman, head down, expression blank, trundling along with shopping.

Terezia craned forward, looking up the tunnel. Why wasn't a train coming, its lights searching through the darkness, air shovelling out ahead? She needed it to come now. She needed to be moving, to be getting away. Any moment now he'd come; he'd realise she wasn't in Max's house and he'd be coming for her.

She couldn't wait here.

Bounding up the stairs at the other end of the platform she reached the road. Fresh air, cold and sharp in her lungs. A glance round. Still no Erkell. She ran a few yards up the street then dived off into another. It didn't matter where she was going or why. It was enough just to be moving.

The car swung into the kerb, screeched to a halt and Max jumped out.

Gyorgy's message had been garbled and unspecific. All he'd managed to get out of him for certain was that Terezia was in some sort of trouble. But he didn't need to be told that; he'd guessed it when she didn't turn up at the restaurant.

There was no sign of her in the street. He unlocked the front door of the block, went into the sour-smelling hallway. Gombos's head appeared at the top of the basement stairs but when he saw who it was he ducked away out of sight.

So much the better; the less he had to make small talk to Gombos the sunnier the day appeared.

He went upstairs, half expecting to find Terezia skulking on the landing. She might easily have got inside the building; she'd done it before.

But still no sign of her.

He felt the ache of apprehension as he let himself inside. She was unlikely to have got into his room. He opened the door. No sign of her. And no note slipped underneath.

Where the hell had she got to?

He went back downstairs and rang Gyorgy from the pay-phone in the passage.

'She rang,' he told her hurriedly. 'She said she's in the café across the road.'

'I'll go and check.'

'I don't know why she didn't see you; she said she'd see you when you came.'

'Must have missed me.'

It was possible but it still didn't feel right. He put the receiver down, heard the coins clank down inside and went round to the hallway.

'That's the bastard.'

Gombos stood in the hallway, hands on hips, eyes sullen, barring the door with his bulk. Beside him were two uniformed policemen.

One of them said, 'Is your name Anderson?'

'What makes you think that?'

'Answer the question,' he said. One hand was on the butt of his pistol, the other reached out, palm punching into Max's chest, pushing him against the wall.

'Calls himself Shackleton,' Gombos said. 'But that's the one.'

The policeman was staring at him with that lazy intensity that comes to men at moments of conflict.

'You're coming with us,' he said.

'For what?'

'For having the wrong name. For having a face I don't like.' The stare never blinked, his outstretched palm prodding Max's chest. 'What's it to you?' he asked. 'You're on the wanted list and that means you come down the station with us.'

Max glanced over at the door but the other had it covered.

'Don't even think about it,' the first said. He took him by the wrist – grip like a wrench – twisted it up behind his back, a quick, practised movement, and thrust him forwards. Not the first time he'd bounced a man out into the street.

Gombos assumed a look of disgust as he passed.

'I knew you were wrong,' he said. 'From the moment I saw you I knew you were wrong.'

'You should let a few women in here,' Max told him. 'It would take your mind off those girlie magazines you keep down there.'

'Fuck you, Shackleton.'

'Who's he?'

25

In the woods below Fetevis, Erkell loosened the screw on the telephone cable, working quickly, deftly. He was angry at himself. He'd never failed in a hit before.

It had been pure chance that the girl had seen his reflection in the bus window. But that was no excuse. He should never have tried to take her in the open like that. A few grams of Semtex on the petrol can of the car would have blown her and her boyfriend into the past tense. Less satisfying, less dramatic but reliable.

Twisting the exposed end of the electrical flex around the thread of the screw, he tightened it again. The other end he dropped to the ground and jumped down after it, his boots crunching on the hard-packed earth. Above him, through the bare branches of the trees, loomed the roofs and towers of the Palace, set hard and dark against the evening sky.

Limping over to his rucksack, he sat down and massaged his bruised leg. The damned car had nearly broken it. He didn't know what had got into him. Running after her like that, he must have been out of his mind. Anyone could have seen him; anyone could have described him to the police.

Unstrapping the flap, he took out the tape recorder. It

was in a plastic sandwich box, sealed and watertight. He plugged the flex into its socket and buried it against the root of a tree, brushing leaves over it with his foot.

He stood back and viewed the effect. No one would see it unless they were looking for it. Now it was just a matter of waiting for her to call. She would call; he was sure of that. She'd be wanting help, wanting comfort. Sooner or later she'd ring.

And he would be waiting for her.

Terezia stood by the telephone booth. Inside a man in a blue workman's jacket leaned against the pay-box, taking his time. His eyes strayed over her as he talked, looking her up and down with lazy interest.

She turned away, holding her collar tight around her throat. It was four-thirty, getting dark and getting cold. She couldn't say where the past few hours had gone. It was a blur, already fading in her mind. Her only impression was of getting off one bus and on to another, letting them take her where they liked, an endless succession of short, directionless journeys that had ended up in this small town.

She looked down the street. A double row of identical, box-like houses, built to provide homes for workers for the factory she'd seen from the bus as they came in. Where exactly it was she didn't know. According to the road sign, Budapest was forty miles away but whether it was north, south, east or west of here she hadn't the faintest idea.

She felt cold and tired and very much alone. The only consolation was that if she didn't know where she was there was every chance Erkell didn't know either.

Keep ahead of the bastard, that's what mattered. Don't do anything predictable; don't do anything that could give him a clue to her whereabouts.

With a grunt of apology, the man came out of the telephone booth and she slipped in after him. It smelled of stale cigarette smoke but it was out of the wind, that was something. She dialled Fetevis, praying that by now it would be Max who answered.

But it was Gyorgy.

'Where are you?' He sounded frantic.

'I don't know, Gyorgy. Some town outside Budapest; it doesn't matter. Is Max there?'

'No. I thought he was with you.'

'No, he's not here.' She could feel panic in her stomach, sick and heavy. 'He hasn't rung you?'

'No, nothing. The last I heard he was coming round to you. Didn't you find him?'

'I had to go.' It was too hard to explain. 'Oh God, Gyorgy, he mustn't go back to his place. Erkell's there. He knows where he lives.'

Gyorgy swore softly.

'If he rings you must tell him to keep away,' she said. 'Tell him not to go near the place.'

'Yes, sure.'

'And find out where he is. I'll call back later.'

'Where are you?'

'It doesn't matter; I'll be gone in a minute. I'll call later.'

She put down the receiver and went outside. Street lamps cast feeble pools of light on the pavement. She walked down to the bus stop and sat on the bench, her coat huddled around her.

Where was Max? Why hadn't he called? She thought of Erkell waiting back there in the block of apartments, the small, bright knife in his hand, then pushed the image from her mind before it could take hold. That wasn't what had happened; it couldn't be what had happened. Max was all right; she knew it. She mustn't let wild, irrational ideas creep into her mind or she'd give in.

She stared across the road. What she needed was to get some place where she could be found; some place where Max would know how to find her. And as she thought it, the solution came to her.

Jumping to her feet she studied the timetable on the side of the bus stop. There was a bus due in twenty minutes. It was heading for Budapest. She might not have to go that far; it depended where she was. The bus driver would know.

She sat down again, feeling stronger. While she had a plan, something to be doing, she stood a chance.

Think positive.

She'd get there and ring back home. Max would have made contact by then. He'd come and pick her up and she'd be safe.

That was how it was going to be. She *knew* it was how it was going to be.

'I have to make a call.'

'No calls—'

'This is important, really important. If it's not stopped there's going—'

'No calls,' the police sergeant cut in.

'Then let me talk to a lawyer.'

'Later.'

He opened the door of the duty room, pushed Max in ahead and told him to sit down.

There were a couple of uniformed men inside, slouched in their chairs, jackets off, taking it easy.

The Sergeant snapped his fingers at one and he came over and sat down behind a typewriter that would be blowing out fifty candles on its next birthday. That was if it could blow. As it was, it didn't look as if it could type.

The Sergeant sat down between them, hunched forward, elbows on knees, his eyes fixed like a hunter on Max.

'Name?'

'Anderson.'

'In full—'

'Maxwell Anderson.'

'How do you spell that?' the typist wanted to know.

The Sergeant spelled it out letter by letter, each one followed by a clack on the typewriter. Then he turned back to Max.

'Occupation?'

'Diplomatic corps.'

'Previously employed in the diplomatic corps,' the Sergeant corrected for him.

The typist went back, deleted the text and replaced it with the new. He had short, plump fingers, hair on the backs of his hands but none on his pale forearms.

Max glanced round the room. It was institutional white and green, table tops lined with some wood-effect plastic. An aged television set glowed faintly with a black and white image of the outer hallway and behind him was a basin that would get an award for breeding bacteria. It was a dour, depressing place that almost exactly reflected his mood.

Three hours they had kept him in the cell at the end of the passage, in the company of a slop bucket and an iron bed, before they had found time in their heavy schedule to interview him.

'How long have you been living at the address where you were apprehended?' the Sergeant asked.

'About three days, maybe four.'

'Which?'

'Does it matter?'

'Answer the question!'

'Four.'

The plump fingers prodded out the letters.

The Sergeant turned to him again. 'And were you aware you were living in the country without a visa?'

'I suppose so.'

'What's that mean?' the typist asked.

'It means yes.' The Sergeant's eyes never left Max's face. 'Why were you using a false name?'

'To stop me from being brought in here to answer a pack of asinine questions.'

'Don't get funny, Anderson.'

'What do you want me to say?'

The Sergeant didn't reply; he had questions of his own. 'It was your intention to deceive the landlord?'

'Yes, of course it was my intention to deceive him. Now can I use the phone? There's someone I must speak to.'

He made to get up but the Sergeant's palm hit him in the chest, keeping him in place.

'No calls, Anderson.'

'Look, you don't understand what's happening out there—'

'Forget what's happening outside,' he said softly. 'What's happening out there is in the past. It doesn't concern you any more.'

The Hungarian public transport system has never won prizes for its speed or efficiency, and so it took Terezia over two hours to reach the hunting lodge in the woods.

The place was more crowded than it had been before. Through the swing door by the reception desk she could see a log fire burning in an open grate, hear the restless growl of conversation and over it the sound of dance music being hammered out on a piano.

The manageress arrived, stout and comfortable, dressed in an embroidered peasant dress and white blouse. Yes, she had a space for the night, she told her, taking a key off the hook.

The room she showed Terezia was up in the angle of the roof. It had a painted wardrobe, crisp white sheets and a duvet that looked so soft and warm that she could have crawled under it and been asleep on the spot.

The manageress bustled around, showing her bathroom, towels and light switches. As she left she said, 'I'll get one of the boys to bring your stuff in.'

'It's all right,' Terezia told her quickly. 'I don't have any.'

'No?' A note of caution crept into the woman's voice. She hovered in the doorway.

'There's some coming later . . . someone's bringing some things over.'

The manageress's glance shifted momentarily to the single bed. Terezia could see her thinking, assessing the situation.

'My car broke down,' Terezia improvised artlessly. 'I had to get here by bus.'

The manageress was taking in Terezia's pale face, tired eyes. 'You were here yesterday, weren't you?' she said.

Was it only yesterday? It seemed a lifetime ago.

'Yes,' she said.

The woman nodded, coming to a decision. 'Well, you make yourself at home,' she said closing the door.

Terezia pulled off her hat and scarf and stood in front of the mirror. God, she looked a wreck: eyes dark-rimmed and smudged, hair tangled. Delving in her handbag she found a comb and began repairing the damage. No reason really. She wasn't intending to be seen by anyone. But it was somehow comforting. Going into the bathroom she washed her face. She was tempted to strip off and take a shower. But she had nothing clean to change into and the thought of putting on the same dirty clothes she found repellent.

Sitting on the bed she checked through her finances. There were a couple of notes and a few coins in her bag. Small change, nothing like enough to pay for this place.

Going downstairs she found a pay-phone by the reception desk and dialled Fetevis.

Don't raise your hopes, she told herself as it connected, don't even think about it. Then there could be no disappointment. But surely there'd be some news. Max would have made contact; he must have made contact by now.

Gyorgy's voice sounded sleepy as he came on the line.

'Where are you?' he asked, suddenly alert.

'In a hotel, not far away.' She paused, not wanting to ask; not wanting to *have* to ask.

'Are you all right?' Gyorgy inquired.

'Yes—' Again she paused, giving him time. Then she asked. 'Have you heard from Max?'

'No.'

Her heart sank. Where *was* he?

'Oh, Gyorgy,' she whispered. 'What's happened?'

'I don't know.'

'Have you been out at all?'

'Not much, and never far. I'd have heard the phone.'

She dropped her head against the wall, the plastic of the booth cool on her forehead, and for a moment she thought she was going to burst into tears like a small child whose mother has forgotten to pick her up from a party.

'Terezia?'

'It's all right, I'm still here,' she said faintly.

'I'm sorry.'

'I know.' She gave a little sniffle, the back of her hand against her nose. 'I'd just hoped. Did you manage to get hold of Joszef?'

'I can't find out where he is. I'll try again in the morning.'

She nodded in understanding and said, 'Gyorgy, could you do something for me?'

'Yes, sure.'

'I now it's late but I haven't got any money.'

'Do you want me to bring some?'

'Could you? There's a tin on the shelf by the oven.'

'I know it—'

'There should be some in there. Could you bring it over to me?'

'Yes, sure, I'll get it. Is there anything else you want?'

What she really wanted was some clean clothes: a shirt and underwear. But she couldn't ask him to get those for her, could she? No, it was too personal. She'd known Gyorgy for four months, he was a kind, honest boy but he was still someone she employed. She couldn't ask him to go through her drawers.

'No,' she said. 'Just the money in the tin.'

'I'll go and get it. Tell me how to get to you.'

Erkell waited until the red light went off on the tape recorder, then ran it back and punched the 'Play' button.

And there she was, scared out of her wits, her voice babbling out the directions to her hideaway in the darkness.

He ran it over twice, memorising the directions, and then reset the machine and tucked it away out of sight. He glanced up at the Palace but there was no sign of a car as yet. The boy would be looking for the money to take over to her.

That gave him a few minutes' lead.

His motorbike was further down the hill. He hefted it

over the wall, kicked the engine into life and drove off into the night.

It took him under half an hour to reach the hunting lodge in the hills. Coasting the motorbike into the car park he cut the ignition and sat resting on the handlebars as he studied the squat building.

So this was where she'd gone to earth. A cosy little bunker if ever he saw one. She must think she was safe up here, miles from anywhere. And so she would have been if she'd kept her mouth shut. But of course she couldn't do that. The cow had to talk; she'd had to tell someone where she was.

And the moment she'd done that she'd signed her death warrant.

The door opened and a group came out. He had a glimpse of a brightly lit interior, the sound of voices and music before it closed again.

He couldn't go in there after her; he was going to have to get her outside in the dark.

Reaching under his jacket he took a gun from his trouser belt. It was a Beretta, small and neat in his hand but powerful enough to punch a bullet through sheet metal.

He screwed the silencer on to the muzzle. It was going to have to be quick. Two shots, one to the body to drop her, another to the head to make sure the job was done, and then get the hell out of here before anyone could raise the alarm.

A car was coming. Headlights searching up the road.

Erkell got off his bike as the Lada swung into the car park. He watched as it bumped its way across the matted snow, the boy at the wheel peering up at the name over the door, and drew to a halt opposite the door. Closer to the building, closer to the light than he would have liked. But no problem.

His right arm behind his back, he moved up beside the driver's door. The engine was still turning over, the boy leaning over to the other seat. He'd be picking up the money to take into his boss inside. She was going to be so glad to see him, so grateful. The boy would like that. He was under her spell, Erkell had sensed it from the way he talked to her. The boy was her slave. She must be quite a turn-on to a pimply youth like this. Oh yes, he could see it. With her long legs and her arrogant eyes and the blood of tyrants in her veins, she must be quite a turn-on. The devil's children are always the most beautiful.

He put his left hand on the door handle and pulled it open. The boy looked round, mouth open in surprise, but before he could speak Erkell's right hand had snaked out from behind his back and pressed the muzzle of the gun into the boy's chest.

'Move over,' he said softly.

The boy felt the gun in his ribs but he didn't look down at it. He was looking up into Erkell's eyes.

And he knew he was dead.

'Move,' Erkell said.

In silent terror the boy fumbled back over the gear lever. Keeping his arm outstretched, Erkell slipped into the driver's seat beside him. The boy began to whimper, finding his voice in the sound.

'Don't shoot!' His hands were above his head, eyes stretched wide. 'Please God, don't shoot!'

Erkell glanced over at the door of the lodge. It was silent, empty. He looked back at the boy. 'No?'

He squeezed the trigger as he spoke. Just a soft plop and a sudden jolt in the boy's chest as if he'd taken a massive electric shock. His legs kicked up and he was thrown against the far door. In the light of the doorway, Erkell saw a worm of blood appear at the corner of his mouth, saw his body give a twitch and then he was still.

Erkell smiled and asked, 'Why not?'

Reaching over, he pulled the boy's cap from his head and put it on. Then grasping him roughly by the collar he rolled him down beneath the seat, out of sight.

The whole operation lasted less than twenty seconds. He glanced up at the door again.

Still no one in sight.

Putting the car into gear he drove it over to the far side of the car park, cut the engine and got out. Then, pulling the boy's cap over his eyes, he sauntered over to the front door of the lodge.

In the opera house, the first act had just come to an end. The bar was filling with dark suits and evening dresses. There was the flutter of programmes, the glint of gold cufflinks, the occasional flash of diamonds, slightly tarnished from their years of exile in some foreign bank vault.

Bela Bessenyei pushed his way to the front of the queue. He'd found the performance cripplingly dull so far. A soprano thirty years too old to be a courtesan singing at full volume to a lover who would have a coronary if he tried making a pass at her wasn't his idea of an evening out. Nor was it helped by the fact that he was there with a delegation from Bulgaria who appeared to be under the impression that they were attending a funeral.

He'd left them in the box with a bottle of white wine and some stiffening smoked salmon sandwiches while he made a getaway. Catching the barman's eye he ordered champagne. He'd jumped several spaces up the queue but with his reputation for generous tipping he had an unfair advantage over the others.

As he was turning, glass in hand, his neighbour jogged his arm and he spilt the contents over the young woman beside him.

'Damn you,' she said angrily, jumping back.

'I'm so sorry.'

Head down, arms spread, she inspected the damage. 'Look what you've done!'

Flicking the handkerchief from his top pocket Bessenyei handed it to her. 'How very clumsy of me,' he said smoothly. 'You must let me pay to have it cleaned.'

Unplacated, she dabbed at the stain. 'Don't you ever look where you're going?'

There was no real reason to apologise further. It was an accident and he'd made the appropriate noises. He had every right to move on. But the girl had slim brown arms, wonderful legs in high heels and a figure that could make a man lose sleep, so he said, 'Perhaps I could buy you a glass of champagne?'

A toss of the shiny brown hair and she looked up at him, angry eyes assessing him in one quick glance. 'Champagne?'

'As a peace offering.'

'I'd rather not, if you don't mind,' she said and turning on her heel she marched off in the direction of the Ladies'.

'Terezia Kasinczy?'

Terezia glanced up at the waitress. She was standing at her elbow, carrying a tray with a plate of steaming goulash and a basket of bread wrapped in white linen.

'Yes,' she said cautiously. She hadn't given anyone her name.

'There's someone here to see you.'

She glanced around the room but there was no sign of Gyorgy amongst the crowd.

'He's out in the car park,' the girl told her. 'He said to tell you he's waiting for you there.'

Silly boy, there was no reason he couldn't come in. In fact she'd rather hoped he would. She needed a friendly face right now, someone to talk to. He could have stayed for a drink. She pushed back her chair and got to her feet.

'What shall I do with your supper?'

'Leave it there,' Terezia said over her shoulder. 'I'll be back in a moment.'

A party of Austrians was in the hallway preparing to leave, the women chatting together, cosy and dimpled, the men jovial with drink, shrugging on overcoats, calling out farewells as they left. One of them held the door open for her, bowing regally as she slipped outside.

The cold air hit her. She wrapped her coat around her and looked across the car park.

The van was over on the very far side, not parked in amongst the other cars but ready to go, the engine turning over.

She waved at Gyorgy but he didn't respond.

She hurried towards him, expecting him to get out to greet her. But he stayed where he was. It was strange. He was always so helpful, so deferential with her. It wasn't like him to be passive. Strange too that he had come into the hotel and gone out again. He must think she didn't want them to be seen together.

She paused a moment. It was Gyorgy all right. She could see him sitting there, silhouetted against the paleness of the snow, his cap pulled over his eyes.

From across the car park came a burst of laughter from the Austrians as they loaded themselves into their cars.

Terezia hurried on towards the van. The window was open. Gyorgy was leaning out.

'Is that you, Gyorgy?' she said breathlessly as she came close.

He nodded.

At that moment a car drew in from the road, its headlights sweeping round the car park. The beam flickered over trees and cars and for one brief instant it touched the face of the driver of the van.

A pale, gaunt face beneath the peak of the cap. Pale eyes fixed on her.

Not Gyorgy.

Erkell.

26

The headlights were on him for just a split second. No longer than the flash of a camera. But it was enough. Enough for the image to print itself in her mind as clearly and sharply as if it had been daylight.

She saw Erkell. In the frame of the van window. One elbow out, the dull gleam of a pistol cradled in the crook of his elbow.

In his eyes the cold blaze of triumph.

The terror of the past few hours ignited in her veins. She heard someone scream. Strength and thought left her. Her legs gave way and she half dived, half collapsed in a heap on the ground.

As she fell there as a sharp ripping sound and she felt the cold air punch at her cheek. Then she was down, spread-eagled on the hard-packed snow.

The car that had drawn in off the road lumbered between them, unwittingly shielding her from the man at the window of the van. She rolled over, getting to her feet. There was no conscious idea, no plan. Her mind was a void, panic and despair bursting like star-shells in the darkness. What drove her to her feet, propelling her forwards was beyond reason or control. It was the lore of the hunted, the instinct for survival that lies dormant in every creature.

Crouched low, she ran back towards the building, towards the light, towards cover. And as she ran the car was between her and Erkell.

Just chance.

She didn't know it; she didn't devise it. But it was there between them as she ran, obstructing his view, robbing him of the opportunity to get off a second shot.

In front of her was the group of Austrians, standing together, mouths open, expressions stupid with surprise. They'd heard her scream, saw her running.

The car had stopped; the driver was getting out.

There was nothing between her and Erkell now. He'd fire again. In her mind she could hear the soft, obscene detonation of the gun as she ran, feel the impact of the bullet tearing into her back.

Then she was in amongst the group, diving in amongst the protection of their bodies.

'Don't let him shoot me!'

Shoot her? Who was trying to shoot her? They were talking at once. What the hell was going on here?

Terezia was on her knees, grasping hold of one of the men, holding him between herself and Erkell.

'That man,' she sobbed. 'He tried to shoot me.'

Jesus Christ, was that true? They were looking across the car park at the van. Which man? You mean that guy in the car? They were calling out, telling him to stop.

But the window had slammed shut, the tyres were spinning on the snow.

'Hey! Hold it there a minute.'

The van swung round in a three-point turn, gears crashing into first, and it was gone, tearing off into the night.

Terezia let go of the man's coat, her hands dropping to the ground, fighting for breath. They were holding her now, helping her to her feet. The voices were loud, women shrill with alarm. 'Steady there. You're all right now. What happened then?' Their voices were around her, comforting, calming. 'Come back inside, you've had a fright. Who was he then?'

They were leading her towards the hotel but she pulled back, looking over her shoulder at the road.

'No,' she pleaded. 'I must go!'

'Come back inside for a minute. We'll call the police.'

'No—'

'We must get the police.'

'No please, not the police. I must go. He'll be back.'

They stood around her, awed, concerned, unable to follow what was going on.

'I must go,' Terezia whispered.

'Where to?' one asked.

'It doesn't matter. Anywhere.'

'I think we should call the police, get this sorted out.'

She shook her head, backing away from them. They meant well but they didn't understand.

'I need to get away from here,' she said.

One said, 'If that's what you want.'

She nodded.

He looked around at his friends. 'I could take you down to the town. Would that help?'

'Yes – please.'

Anywhere. It didn't matter where it was so long as it was away from this place.

The key turned in the lock and the Sergeant came into the cell. He jerked a thumb towards the passage and said, 'Out.'

Max stood up from the bed. He felt stiff and mentally numbed after sitting there with nothing more to occupy him that staring at the cracks in the ceiling. He'd tried moving around the confined space but he found it only increased his sense of impatience.

'You're going for a trip,' the Sergeant told him.

'Where?'

'That doesn't matter.'

'How about that lawyer you were going to get me?'

'Later.' The Sergeant was holding open the door with his foot, one hand resting on the butt of his pistol.

As he passed, Max said, 'You'll have to empty the bucket before you have anyone else to stay.'

'You've used it?' The Sergeant managed to make it sound as though he'd desecrated a work of art.

'I got overexcited waiting here.'

The Sergeant pushed him out into the passage. When they reached the hallway he told Max to wait. From his belt he unclipped a pair of handcuffs, businesslike implements that looked as though they'd been used before.

The door opened and a couple of drunks were propelled inside. They were shouting in the bleary way of men who've marinated their brains so long they can't remember which planet they're on.

'Keep the noise down!' the Sergeant ordered as he clipped one end of the handcuffs to his wrist.

A uniformed policeman came out from the duty room. One of the drunks swung a punch. It was slow and lazy and so obvious that anyone could have seen it coming. Anyone except a twenty-year-old rookie who'd spent the past hour playing poker in the warmth of the duty room.

It caught him on the jaw and sent him spinning into the Sergeant.

He gave a curse, pushed the policeman out of the way and launched his shoulder into the drunk. They went back against the wall with a crash, beery breath bursting from the man's lungs. The policeman who'd brought him in came in from behind, got his arm around the man's neck. It would have brought matters under control if the other drunk hadn't decided to pull the fire extinguisher off the wall and swing it into the Sergeant's ribs.

The Sergeant said a word that paraphrased his opinion of the drunk's ancestors' sexual behaviour and hit him in the gut. The drunk went down, pulling the Sergeant after him. The fire extinguisher clattered off across the floor.

And Max was standing alone.

He put his hand on the handle of the door beside him. It opened and he stepped through into an office beyond.

It couldn't last; they'd have seen him go.

But the noise from the hallway kept on going. He glanced around the office. A couple of desks strewn with paper, tin filing cabinet, posters on the wall. A window on the far side, barred with a wire grill.

A door to one side.

He slipped through it. It came out in a passage. A flight of stairs, ornate with fancy wrought-iron bannisters. The place must once have been a private house, he told himself pointlessly as he ran up them.

It was night-time; no one around.

On the landing he tried another door. Locked. He went on down, tried another. This time it opened.

Somewhere below he heard shouting. Not riot control any longer but orders being issued, sharp with exasperation.

There wasn't much time.

He was in a storeroom. Shelves and stacked cardboard boxes. And a window beyond.

He pulled it open, looked out. A sheer drop down into the darkness of a back yard. To his left there was a fire escape. He climbed out on to the window ledge, stepped over to the next, hands grasping for a hold on the rough brick wall.

Reaching over he caught hold of the iron railing and swung himself over on to the fire escape. The steps rang like gongs as he ran down them.

They'd hear; they *must* hear.

Adrenaline burning through his veins, he reached the ground. Cold air on his face and hands, sharp in his throat as he panted for breath.

An alley led out into the street.

A police car was parked in front of the station. He shrank back but there was no one in it.

He stepped out on to the pavement. A few people passing by. They weren't looking at him, weren't interested in his problems. He walked with them, keeping in close. Slow down, he told himself. Act natural. His legs were aching to run but he mustn't do it. Running gave the game away, running made you a fugitive.

There was a cinema up ahead. Bright lights, swing doors, a few people milling round outside. He didn't want to pass that. It was like walking on to a lit stage.

He turned down the passage to the side. It was dark and narrow and led out into another street. He walked on until he came to a main road. A bus was drawing into the kerb. It was going in exactly the direction he wanted.

Away.

27

Terezia awoke with the morning light shining through a crack in the wall straight into her eyes. She stared at it for a few moments without knowing where she was.

Then memory returned, heavy, dull and sickening.

She blinked and pushed herself up on one arm. Her neck was stiff, shoulder aching from sleeping on the hard-packed floor. She checked her watch. It was seven-forty. That late? She must have been exhausted to have managed to sleep on the ground so long.

Brushing her hair from her eyes, she looked round the shed. Logs were piled to the roof, a few tools hanging on the wall. Through the open door she could see an apple orchard and a house beyond, distant and grey in the dawn light.

Vaguely she remembered coming to this place in the dark. There hadn't been any conscious decision on her part. It had just been the first piece of shelter she'd come across as she reached the point when she was too tired to go on.

Yawning, she stretched her arms above her head. Her mouth was dry as if she'd been eating talcum powder and she felt dirty and crumpled. She ran her fingers through her hair and found it thick with wood chippings.

One by one she picked them out, combing out the knots and tangles as best she could with her fingers. There was a dull pain in her hip. Pushing down her jeans she found a livid bruise on the pale skin. It must have been from when she fell on the ice. She pulled the zip up again and, sitting straight, she spent a few minutes taking stock of her physical condition, feeling her legs and arms. It was a simple enough ritual but she found the sensation of her hands stroking down over her body curiously therapeutic. She was dirty and dishevelled but still alive. That was the point. There'd been two attempts on her life and she'd survived them both.

It gave her hope. She could come through this, she told herself. If she used her wits she could survive.

There was a movement outside. A woman had come out of the house and was feeding the chickens, tossing scraps from a bucket. Terezia held perfectly still in the shadow of the shed as she watched the woman give the base of the bucket a final slap with her hand and go back indoors.

Getting to her feet Terezia brushed the dirt from her jeans. She had to get going. In a minute someone would find her here.

Going over to the doorway she took a quick look around. The coast was clear. She slipped out, feeling a twist of nerves as she left the sanctuary of the dark shed. She was alone again; on the run. It was not a new sensation, she realised. Sharper, more immediate but familiar. She'd been on the run all her life. Because of her name, because of the family she was born into; all the elements of her existence over which she had no control.

Following the path between two allotments she found her way back to the road she'd come along the night before. It led into the village, a scattering of houses around a yellow-and-white church with an onion-domed steeple.

In a telephone booth in the road she searched for coins but there were none left. Just a hundred-forint note. She went to a shop further down and asked for change. Looking around the stacked shelves she realised how hungry she was and bought a bread roll, devouring it as she went back to the phone.

For a moment as she dialled she had a wild hope that it would be Gyorgy who answered.

But it was Elek, worried and uncertain, audibly relieved to hear her. 'Gyorgy?' he said. 'No, he's not here. He hasn't come in. I don't know where he is.'

Terezia felt the sickening weight return. 'I think something's happened to him,' she said quietly. 'Something . . . terrible.'

There was silence at the other end of the line.

'Can you look after things, Elek?' she asked.

'Yes.' He sounded shocked and lost. 'Yes, I guess so.'

'You must find Joszef. There's a number in the house where you should be able to contact him.'

'Aren't you coming then?'

'No,' she said. 'Not for a while. I can't. You'll have to do the best you can.'

'Okay then.'

'Can you do that, Elek?'

'What's happened to Gyorgy then?' The boy was scared out of his wits.

Terezia didn't want to say what she thought had happened. She didn't even want to think it.

'I don't know,' she whispered. 'Really I don't know.'

'Max called earlier.'

'Max?'

'He rang looking for you.'

She felt a sudden surge of hope and fought to control it. 'When was this?'

'Just now.'

'Where is he?'

'I don't know. He left a number.'

As soon as she had it she rang off, hitting the button for further calls, fumbling with haste as she dialled. She heard the line connect, the phone at the other end ringing. But no response.

She drummed her knuckles on the coin box. Come on; come on.

A click and the line came alive.

'Hallo?'

'Max?'

'Who do you want?' It was a man's voice at the other end speaking in Hungarian.

'I'm looking for . . .' Who was she looking for? He wouldn't use his real name. 'Is there an English person there?' she asked.

'English?'

'There should be someone English there,' she said in desperation. 'Please look, it's very important.'

The phone was put down. She heard the sound of voices speaking and suddenly he was there.

'Terezia?'

'Max?'

'Terezia, are you all right?'

'Oh Max, Max.' She heard herself babbling his name stupidly.

'Where are you?'

'I'm . . . I can't say. Oh, Max, where have you been?'

'Testing out your prison service. Where are you?'

'I can't say, Max.'

'You must. Tell me where you are and I'll come and fetch you.'

'No, I can't! I mustn't!' The strength she'd found earlier had vanished and she could hear the screech of hysteria rising in her voice. 'He knows,' she cried. 'He hears.'

'Who does?'

'Erkell. He hears everything I say.'

'He can't, Terezia.'

'I told Gyorgy where I was and Erkell came!'

'It's all right,' he said soothingly. 'It's all right.'

'He's killed him, Max. I know he's killed him.'

'Who, Gyorgy?'

'He came to bring me things. He said he'd come. But it wasn't Gyorgy; it was him.' She knew it didn't make sense but she couldn't get the words out right.

'It's all right.' Max spoke softly, calmly. 'Tell me where you are.'

'I can't,' she whispered.

'I can't help you unless I know where you are.'

'I'm so scared, Max.'

'You must tell me where you are.'

'I can't.' She was trembling with fear and relief. 'He's listening, Max. He hears everything.'

'I don't think he can. Honestly, I don't think he can be, Terezia.'

'He *hears*, Max.'

'Then we must meet somewhere else,' Max said. 'Somewhere he doesn't know.'

Terezia paused. Then in a steadier voice she said, 'How do you mean?'

'Can you describe somewhere you know without saying its name?'

She saw what he was getting at but her mind was a blank.

'No, Max . . . I don't know. I can't think of anywhere.'

'The photo album,' he said after a moment. 'You know that photo album I showed you?'

'What photo album?'

'At dinner that night.' He was speaking slowly and carefully, willing her to understand. 'I showed you some photos I'd found in the library.'

'I know—' She was with him now, her voice suddenly hopeful.

'Do you remember the picture of your father?'

'Which one?'

'They were on a sort of picnic. A whole lot of people – sitting on deckchairs. Your father was in the middle.'

'Yes,' she said excitedly. 'I know the one.'

'Do you remember where they were?'

'Yes, I—'

'Don't say anything.'

'No – I see.'

'Could you get there?'

'Yes,' she said. 'Yes, I could.'

'Good. I'll meet you there as soon as I can.'

Biszku slammed the phone down on the receiver.

'They had him!' he shouted. 'Three hours they had him without telling anyone. And then they lost him. What's the matter with these bastards? Are they all idiots?'

Captain Gruber refrained from giving his judgement on this point.

'I can't believe it,' Biszku said, sitting back in his chair and worrying his hair with his fingers. 'They picked him up in some apartment block and took him back to the station. But it didn't occur to them to tell anyone what they'd done.'

'Probably wanted to be heroes.'

'Then when they finally decided to bring him in they let him go. That was eleven last night. He could be anywhere by now.'

There was a knock on the door. A uniformed sergeant came in, the floppy paper of a fax in his hand.

'Report of a killing just come in,' he said. 'I thought you'd like to hear of it.'

Biszku gave a jerk of his head, telling him to go on.

'Boy found dead in a car; shot in the chest.'

'You know who he is?'

'Name of Georg Xantos.'

Biszku said, 'That meant to mean something to me?'

'Worked as a stable hand at Fetevis Palace.'

Biszku glanced round at Gruber, wide-eyed, and then stabbed his finger on the desk. 'Find Anderson!' he shouted. 'Put out a bulletin. Arrest him on sight. Get every goddamned policeman on the job but get Anderson!'

From a distance the pavilion on the water's edge appeared neat and spruce, a little white classical temple with a columned portico, half buried in trees. Up close it disintegrated into a ruin of lichen and crumbling stucco. The columns had rotted away in places, exposing a core of dark red brick.

The steps led straight down into the lake but the water was frozen along the shoreline and Max crunched his way over it and up into the porch. A mile away, on the far shore of the lake, the jagged roofline of Fetevis was printed against the winter sky.

The door of the pavilion stood ajar and he went through into a small round chamber lined with white marble pillars. In the centre was a pool, the surface of the water invisible beneath a haze of steam that lifted up into the domed roof. A single opening in the centre filled the place with a strange greenish light.

And it was warm, not just because it was out of the wind but warm as though the whole place were centrally heated.

Max put down the rucksack he'd brought and looked around in amazement. Whatever it was he was expecting, it wasn't this.

A sound from behind made him turn.

Terezia was standing between two of the columns. Her arms were wrapped around herself as though she were frozen cold, her green eyes fixed intently on him.

Without speaking he took her in his arms and she buried her head into his neck. Her hair was filled with the rich fertile smell of earth and wood and she was shivering like a frightened animal.

'Nice place you've got here,' he said.

Terezia didn't answer.

He sat on the white marble step, drawing her down beside him. 'Are you all right?'

She nodded and smiled, shaking her head. 'Christ, Max,' she said, 'where did you *get* to?'

'I was picked up by the police.'

'I was going round the bend trying to find you.'

'I went back to the flat like I said and there were a couple of them waiting for me. That slob Gombos must have called them.'

'And they let you go?'

'After a while. They had better things to be doing.'

Terezia's hands stroked his cheeks, the fingers just teasing his skin, while her eyes searched his face. She smiled again, gently this time and lazily. 'Why are you never around when I need you?' she asked.

'I'm here now.'

She nodded. 'You are,' she said and reaching forward she kissed him on the lips.

'How did Erkell find you?' he asked after a moment.

'I don't know.'

'What happened?'

'I don't want to talk about it,' she whispered. 'Not now.' Her fingers were in his hair and drawing him close she kissed him again, harder this time, her tongue pressing into his mouth. 'Later,' she promised and drawing back she shrugged off her coat. Then crossing her arms she stripped off her jumper.

One button of her shirt was open. Max slipped his hand inside, cupping her small, firm breast in its lacy bra.

'I feel so dirty,' she said.

'Sounds hopeful.'

'No, silly. Grubby. I haven't washed for over a day.'

'Then it looks as though we've come to the right place.'

'You don't mind?'

'I couldn't care less.'

She lay down on the damp stone floor beneath him, her hair spread out. Carefully, he parted her shirt, kissing her between her breasts and on her throat. Her hand strayed on to his inner thigh and moved stealthily upwards.

Softly she asked. 'Are you going to keep your clothes on then?'

He undressed, never an easy thing to do gracefully in these circumstances, while she lay watching him through lowered lashes.

'A strange place to be doing this,' he said as he leaned over her again.

'I think it's what it was built for. A bit wet.'

'I've got a rug,' he said and getting to his feet he went over to the rucksack he'd brought with him.

When he came back, Terezia had her back turned to him as she unfastened her bra. He touched her on the shoulder as he sat down beside her.

It seemed to take her unawares. She hadn't heard him return and she looked round, her eyes startled.

'I'm sorry,' he said, 'I didn't mean to give you a fright.'

'I didn't hear you.'

There was no perceptible change but her whole manner seemed to have stiffened. She knelt before him, her breasts bare and pale in the half light, her body suddenly tense.

'What's wrong?' he asked.

'It doesn't matter,' she said with a shake of her head. 'You surprised me, that's all.'

He thought she was referring to Erkell and said, 'It's all right; he can't find us here.'

'It's not that,' she said. 'Something else . . . It doesn't matter.'

'Tell me.'

'It's not important.'

She was in the grip of some phobia; he could see it.

'Tell me,' he said gently.

'It's nothing . . . Just something silly that happens occasionally. It doesn't matter.'

'Was it when I touched you?'

She paused. 'I get a fright sometimes when someone comes up behind me. It doesn't matter; it's gone now.'

But it hadn't gone. He could sense the tension still in her.

'Tell me about it.'

She shook her head, her eyes pleading with him. 'It's not important.'

'Was it something that happened to you?'

She sat very still, her gaze fixed on him, wanting to explain but unable to find the words.

'Don't be scared,' he said.

'It doesn't matter any more,' she said in a small, fierce voice. 'It *shouldn't* matter any more. It was years ago.'

'When you were a child?'

She nodded.

'It might help if you tell me about it,' he said quietly. 'Really, I think it might.'

She was still torn with indecision. But her eyes had lost the wild look and after a few moments she said, 'It was when I was at school. I was getting my coat and things.' The words came out slowly and falteringly. 'I was late. I'd stayed behind to talk to a teacher and I was late.'

Her voice broke off.

'Go on.'

'There were these boys . . . They knew who I was, you see. My father had been in court and they knew. They were always saying things. About my name, about my family. They said I should go to jail too. Because of who I was—'

'How many of them were there?'

'Four.' She looked down at her hands in her lap, the fingers twisting together. In the damp atmosphere, her body was wet, a bead of moisture running down between her breasts.

'They were there,' she said after a moment. 'Waiting for me. I didn't hear them. They came up behind me.' She shook her head, her hair falling about her face. 'It was horrible. I don't think anything happened, not anything . . . physical. But it was so horrible. I used to have nightmares about it.'

'How old were you?'

'I don't know. I can't remember exactly. About fourteen, I think.'

No longer a child, he thought. Already growing, her body

maturing. No longer a toothy girl but a woman, strange and different.

'Didn't anything happen to these boys,' Max asked, 'afterwards?'

She shook her head. 'Joszef didn't want to make a fuss. He thought it would only make things worse. So we moved. It was extraordinary. I'd only been living with them for about a year but they gave up everything: his job, their friends, everything. Just because of me.'

Max wondered what would have happened to her if they hadn't been there to help. She'd have wound up in some State orphanage presumably, an unwanted person in the system.

'It was a long time ago,' she said. 'I don't think about it much. I just get these sudden panics when someone comes up unexpectedly.'

He touched her cheek, running the back of his hand down the smooth damp skin.

'You think I'm mad, don't you?' she whispered.

'No,' he said. 'I think you've been through the mill.'

He stroked the back of her neck and even in that small contact he could feel the tension still alive in her. Her eyes were imploring him to go on but she wasn't ready. She needed time.

He lay back on the ground. He wasn't sure why or what he intended but he felt instinctively that at that moment any advance had to come from her.

In the silence he could hear the distant dripping of the moisture on the walls and the rattle of the branches on the roof outside.

Terezia made no movement. He lay perfectly still, wondering whether he hadn't made a mistake.

A full minute passed before he felt her hand steal on to his stomach. At first it was still. Then it moved, the fingers running over him lightly, shyly. Her hair brushed over him and he felt the softness of her lips as she bent to kiss him on the chest and shoulders.

Her hands were moving more quickly now, searching, exploring. She moved away and he heard the zip of her jeans come down. Then she slipped astride him, legs parted wide, naked now so that he felt the dampness of her sex on his stomach. Her lips were on his, hot and urgent, her hair enveloping them both.

And then almost roughly she rolled over on her back, her legs locked into his, and pulled him on top of her.

The tape ran back, the twin spools spinning, and clicked to a halt.

Crouched on the ground over it, Erkell pressed the button and listened to the recording over again. But there was nothing there to give him a clue to where the girl was or where she had gone. He noticed she was careful not to say where she was speaking from. She must have tumbled he had the phone tapped.

He heard the boy give her Anderson's number but there was no point in trying to trace it. He'd be gone from there by now.

They'd given him the slip.

But only for a while. He stared through the trees across the lake. She'd be back, he was sure of that. She was tied to the place emotionally and physically. She'd be back. It was just a matter of waiting.

And he could wait. He had all the patience in the world. Once he started a job he never rested until it was finished.

All he had to do was wait and she'd come to him.

*

Max rolled on his side and looked down at Terezia.

She was lying on her back, gazing up at the ceiling, a slight smile wrinkling the corners of her eyes.

'What are you grinning about?' he asked.

She turned and looked at him lazily. 'It's a secret.'

'Are you going to tell me?'

'It wouldn't be a secret then.'

'You can have secrets between people.'

'Oh, pooh,' she said. 'Don't try your clever lawyer talk on me.' Her eyes were laughing at him now. 'I'll tell you later.'

'Promise?'

She said she promised and, jumping to her feet, went over to the pool. Testing the water with one foot she waded out waist deep, the steam enveloping her, and dived under the surface. She was down almost a minute before bursting up for air. Then rolling over, lithe as a seal, she vanished under again.

Lying on his chest, Max felt the temperature of the water. Warm as a bath. There must be a natural hot spring below.

Terezia had come up and lay back in satisfaction, her hair fanned out around her head, letting the warm water soak away the dirt and stress of the past few days. From where he lay, he could see her throat and shoulders and the two soft snouts of her breasts above the surface but inexplicably nothing below. There seemed to be no translucence to the water.

He dipped his hand under the surface and it was almost invisible. He put it down further and it vanished completely.

'What are you doing?' she asked, wading over to the side, her wet hair sleek and shining.

'There's something in the water. It's dark.'

'Oh, that,' she said, pulling herself out beside him. 'It's

got some mineral in it – basalt or something. Didn't you know that?'

'I've never looked at it before.'

'That's how Fetevis got its name. It's short for *Fekete Vis*. I don't know how you'd say it in English.'

'Black Water.'

She tried the words out on her tongue, pulling a face at the alien sound. It was somehow fitting, he thought to himself, that the first piece of English he ever heard her say was the name of her house.

Inclining her head she took hold of the long shaft of her hair and ran her hands down it, ironing out the water. Her eyes were thoughtful.

'What are we going to do now?' she asked.

'We must get over to England.'

'Will they let you leave the country?'

'I don't know,' he said. 'I think so. If I go to the Embassy with my hands over my head I reckon they can have me shipped out of the country. It'll be a one-way ticket but that's all we need for now. Do you have a passport?'

She nodded. 'Back at the house.'

'Then we must try to get hold of it.'

'It won't work.'

'Your passport?'

She shook her head. 'Going to London.'

'We must get you to those solicitors of yours and show them who you are,' he said. 'After that you're safe. As soon as those papers are transferred into your name Zoltan won't be able to lay a finger on you.'

'But I can't get them,' she said. 'I talked to Victor Szelkely about it. He said they'll need proof of who I am before they can hand them over.'

'You mean they want to see your birth certificate?'

She nodded.

Hell and damnation, Max thought. Of course they would. Why else had Zoltan gone to such lengths to have it destroyed? He should have seen it from the start.

'Or something like it,' Terezia added. 'It doesn't have to be a birth certificate. He said that anything that proved who I was would do.'

'Such as?'

She shrugged. 'I don't know. Something that proves that I was born with the name I say I was.'

It was easy enough to say but he couldn't imagine what it was going to be. There would have to be a document, some piece of paper directly linking her with her father. Lawyers didn't understand anything unless it was in black and white.

After a moment Terezia asked, 'Do you think it would be worth going to the Municipal Hall where the certificate was meant to be?'

'Probably not. If it's gone it's gone.' He thought for a moment. 'Do you know where you were born?'

'Which hospital you mean?'

'They might keep records.' It didn't sound likely even to him. What hospital kept records back that far?

She shook her head. 'I don't know where it was.'

'Would Rosza know?'

'She might do. I never heard her say anything about it.' She stared across the steaming water, realising the impossibility of what was needed. 'What am I going to do?'

Max got to his feet and went over to where his clothes were scattered across the ground.

'There's someone I've come across who it might be worth talking to,' he said, taking his wallet out of his trouser pocket. From it he extracted a slip of paper and showed it to Terezia.

'What's that?' she asked.

'We found it in Verity's room. He'd jotted these numbers down on the back of a magazine. We thought maybe they were some sort of serial number, for a key or a hired car. Something like that. But it's not. It was only last night I realised what it is.'

'Last night?'

'In the police station. It's so obvious I could have kicked myself.'

'What is it?'

'When those goons picked me up they took me back and booked me. Then they put me up against the wall and took my photo, just like they do in the movies. I had to hold a number.'

'I see,' she said excitedly. 'And this is the same.'

'Kind of.' He took the slip of paper and tucked it back in his wallet. 'It's the identification number of a prisoner.'

'Can you find out whose?'

'I already have. I got on to Gallagher this morning and he checked it out. It belonged to someone called Kadar – Miklos Kadar.'

She gave a shake of her head; the name didn't mean anything to her. 'Who's he?'

'A journalist. He made the mistake of criticising the Government and did twenty years for political subversion.'

'How's that help us?'

'He shared a cell with your father.'

Terezia paused and stared at him in amazement.

Max said, 'Verity must have gone to see him.'

'You think we should do so too?'

'Have you got a better idea?'

'No, I haven't,' she said, bouncing to her feet and shaking the water from her hair. 'Where's he live?'

'Over towards Vac. It shouldn't take long from here.'

Terezia was pulling on her jeans. 'Would you mind if we stopped on the way?'

'Why's that?'

'For something to eat.'

'You're not hungry again, are you?'

'Starving.'

In a café between Szabadsag Ter and the spiky edifice of the Parliament building Bela Bessenyei sat reading a newspaper. He was due at Gundell's restaurant in half an hour's time for lunch with his wife's family – a pre-Christmas ritual that he could do without but, on balance, he found marginally better than having them there on the day itself. In the meantime he was preparing himself for the occasion with a couple of quiet drinks alone. Just to put him in the festive mood.

He took a sip at his glass. It was Chablis, chilled but not so cold that it drowned the taste. At official functions they were always obliged to produce Hungarian wine but as soon as he was out of sight of the press he allowed himself something cool and French.

A girl sat down at the table opposite. He glanced at her over the rim of the paper: olive skin and dark eyes, a dark fur coat that matched glossy brown hair. She had taken a pocket mirror from her bag and was quickly checking her appearance.

He put down the paper and said, 'Would you accept a glass of champagne this time?'

The girl looked round. 'I beg your pardon?'

'Last time I offered you had other things on your mind.'

She gave a slow smile, recognising him. 'If you promise not to throw it down me this time.'

Bessenyei got to his feet. 'May I join you?'

She glanced around the café. 'I was meeting a girlfriend. But she doesn't seem to have turned up yet.'

'Maybe until she arrives,' he said, sitting down opposite her.

A waiter appeared at his elbow. Bessenyei ordered a glass of wine and then held it.

'Why don't we make it a bottle?' he asked.

'If you're paying.'

Bessenyei asked for a bottle of Dom Perignon, giving instructions to have it put in ice, and rapidly calculating how he could extract himself from lunch with his in-laws.

'How many glasses?' he asked her.

The girl was reproachful. 'It should be three.'

His secretary could relay on the news that he had an unexpected meeting to attend to, he told himself. So sorry, pressures of State and all that. She'd done it for him before.

'Shall we say two and hope your friend takes a hint?'

The girl smiled again, with just a hint of interest in the dark eyes now, and said, 'I'm not sure I like the sound of this.'

28

Miklos Kadar lived with his son and his family in a residential block on the outskirts of town. It was a tall, soulless building, the type the Russians put up in the fifties and liked to call 'ideal' because they had water and electricity, a few square feet of space per person and a roof that only leaked when it rained.

It was the son who answered the door. He was in his forties, with the wide cheekbones and pale skin of the Slavs. He wore a checked shirt rolled up from well-muscled forearms.

'He's out,' he said, his eyes moving quickly between the two of them. 'Why do you want to see him?'

'I believe he was a friend of my father's,' Terezia said. She'd spent some time in the Ladies' while they stopped for lunch and her hair was brushed and glowing in the darkness of the passage.

The son accepted the explanation without comment, his manner neither hostile nor friendly but suspicious, as all Hungarians over the age of fifteen are conditioned to be.

'Kosice jail,' Max put in by way of explanation.

The son paused, 'Karoly?'

'That's right,' Terezia said. 'I'm his daughter.'

'My father has gone out for a walk,' he said. 'In the garden at the end of the road.' He turned and spoke rapidly to a woman inside and then came out into the passage. 'Come with me,' he said. 'I'll show you.'

They found Miklos sitting on a park bench, a walking stick between his knees, his hands folded above, staring into space with the tranquillity that only the very old and the very young can achieve.

He didn't see them approach. It was only when his son spoke that he looked round.

'Karoly's daughter?' he said.

Terezia sat down on the bench beside him. 'We were hoping you could help us,' she said gently.

'Ah yes,' the old man said. 'I can see it now.'

He was in his eighties, a scarf wrapped around his neck, a blue beret on his head, his eyes vacant and kindly in damp sockets.

Satisfied that there was some understanding between them, the son gave a nod and left them to it.

'I'm so glad to meet you, my dear,' Miklos said after he'd gone. 'I was looking for you. Some years ago.'

'Why was that?'

'He wanted me to find you. Your father did. I was let out before him, you see. He wanted me to find you to tell you he was well and that he thought about you.'

Terezia turned her head away quickly.

'But I didn't know where you were.' It seemed to cause the old man genuine regret. 'No one seemed to know anything about you in the village where you'd lived.'

'No,' she said. 'I'd changed my name and we'd moved away.'

'I thought maybe that was what had happened.' He paused,

not saying that there were other, less attractive, conclusions he could have drawn. 'Is your father still alive?'

She shook her head. 'No, he died a few years ago.'

'In Kosice?'

'Yes . . . they never let him out.'

'I'm sorry to hear it. He deserved better. Ten years I knew your father and in that time I never heard him say an angry word.'

Terezia gazed across the little park with its silver birches, thin and crisp in the weak winter's sun.

'You're so like him,' Miklos said. 'He often used to speak of you. It was difficult for him, not knowing what had become of you. It was very difficult for him.'

'Some friends of his took me in,' she said. 'I was all right.'

'He would have been glad to have known that . . . so very glad.'

Terezia pushed her hair from her eyes. 'When you were with him did he ever say anything about my birth?'

'Your birth?'

'I have a problem, you see.' She gave a shake of her head and glanced up at Max, unable to explain the situation in a few words. 'There's some complication about my birth certificate. We were wondering whether by any chance you know where I was born?'

'You were born at home,' he said as though he were surprised she should ask.

'Not in a hospital?'

'No, they couldn't get your mother into hospital. Did you not know that?'

Terezia shook her head.

'It was winter time.'

*

The snow was falling steadily, the flakes ghostly in the darkness, each one floating down slowly and silently as though trying to sneak past the window without her noticing.

Erzsebet watched them listlessly from the bed where she lay sprawled on her back. Her long hair was damp at the temples. One knee was raised, the other leg reaching down to the ground as she searched for relief from the burden of her swollen belly. It was so heavy and uncomfortable and unbalanced, a great boulder that made her back ache when she stood upright and kept her awake when she lay in bed at night.

Brushing her long hair from her eyes with the back of her arm she stared up at the ceiling. The contractions had started earlier that afternoon as she was ironing shirts in the kitchen. At first it had been just a twinge and she'd thought nothing of it. The baby wasn't due for at least two weeks. But then they had become more persistent, a hard, rhythmical movement of the muscles, that left her feeling faint and short of breath. She'd called for Karoly who was working in one of the barns outside. He'd helped her up to the bedroom and run down to ring the hospital.

What they could do she didn't know. It had been snowing now for over a day. The roads would all be cut off. Often at this time of year they could be isolated for two or three days before someone managed to cut a path down to the town.

Digging her elbows into the mattress, she arched her back, easing the ungainly bulk of her stomach. As she did so it came again. A deep, involuntary spasm that gripped her whole body, stopping the breath in her throat. This time, above the clutch of the muscles, she felt a new sensation. It wasn't much, just a slight ache following in the path of the other, remote and distant and yet all the more real for that, like the glimpse of a predatory creature far away.

'You two fightin' already?' Karoly asked as he came in and saw her lying pale and weak on the bed.

'Oh God, *draga*,' she said. 'It's like ten men trying to pull a boat up the beach in there.'

'Is that so?' He liked that image.

Undoing the buttons of her dress he ran his hands across the smooth, taut skin of her belly. She felt the fingers searching, probing, and remembered how they'd moved across the rough brown coat of poor Twilight as she lay in the street. Fifteen years ago that was. Half a lifetime away.

'How's the baby?' she asked.

'Strong.' His eyes smiled down at her. 'Strong as a horse.'

But for a moment his hands lingered, searching, as though there were a question there for which he still couldn't find an answer.

'Who were you talking to down there?' she asked.

'The hospital. They say they can't get an ambulance out until the roads have been cleared and that won't be until tomorrow. But there's a midwife about four miles from here. We may be able to get her over here.'

'We don't need a midwife, Karoly.'

'She could make you a bit more comfortable.'

'She'll never make it over in all this.'

'No, but we may be able to get a tractor over to her.'

'You can't bring the old girl here on a tractor.' She looked at him, horrified. 'Whatever will she think?'

Karoly wasn't too concerned what she might think. 'I reckon she'll have travelled worse in her time.' He did up the buttons of her dress again, smoothing out the wrinkles in the material. 'How y'feeling then?'

It was hard to describe the mixture of elation, nerves and exhaustion that were running through her. She shook her head. 'Weak.'

'Tea. That's what you need.'

'You couldn't put something in it, I suppose?'

'And have the little fellow come out with a hangover? Lord now, what sort of a woman are you, suggesting such a thing?'

She laughed and as she did so another spasm hit her and she clutched his hand until it had passed.

'Quick, go now,' she whispered.

While he was down in the kitchen the phone rang and she heard him talking, his voice low and urgent.

He brought up the tea in a jug.

'It's very hot,' he said as he put a mug of it in her hands.

And very sweet too, she discovered as she took a sip.

From the cupboard he took some pillows, stacking them under her head and shoulders so she could drink more easily.

'I'm just going out for a bit,' he said casually. 'You stay here and drink that and hang on until I get back.'

'Who were you talking to just now?'

'One of the lads tried taking a tractor out but it can't make it. The snow's drifted in the road.'

'Karoly.' She wanted an answer. 'You're not worried about delivering the baby, are you?'

'Can't say I've ever done it before.'

'It's no different from a foal, is it?'

'Bit smaller, I hope.'

His voice was easy, relaxed, but in the depths of his smiling eyes she could see a stillness.

After he was gone she sipped the tea and felt its sweetness give her strength. Through the open door of the cupboard she caught a glimpse of colour. It was the dress she'd worn on her wedding day. For someone already married and divorced, white had seemed inappropriate so instead she'd worn one of the local peasant costumes, a white shirt and tight bodice with an embroidered skirt below, puffed up with stiff petticoats that had rustled around her legs like dried leaves as she walked.

If he'd been married before the war, Karoly would have been in the fur-trimmed silks of the Hungarian aristocracy. As it was he wore his baggy flannel trousers and tweed jacket with patched elbows, and she'd have had it no other way. It was how she knew him and how she loved him.

The contractions came again and above it the wolf-bay of pain, closer now, more sure of itself. But she didn't fear it. She was calm and contented, the exhaustion she'd felt earlier turning to a drowsiness.

It was half an hour before he returned.

'Y'haven't started without me?' he asked cheerfully as he came in.

She smiled and shook her head.

He crouched down beside the bed and looked at her earnestly. 'There's no way of getting a tractor over to the old bat but we might just manage it on horseback.'

'I can't ride, Karoly!'

'You won't have to. I'll wrap you up snug in the blankets and we'll make it there together.'

She shook her head.

'Could you manage it, d'yer think?'

'No, Karoly.'

'It'll be easy as catching butterflies in a net.'

'I don't want to go there,' she whispered. 'I'll have the baby here.'

He went over to the window and looked out at the silent drifting of the snow. 'It wouldn't take more than half an hour,' he said, turning back to her.

Erzsebet gave a gasp as the contractions came again. It was beginning now, she could tell that. The movements were regular, insistent. Loosening her dress, Karoly held his palms to the muscles as they gripped and moved and again she felt his fingers delving and searching.

'Is there a problem?' she whispered.

'Problem?' The thought hadn't occurred to him. 'No, there's no problem.'

'Don't lie to me, *draga*.'

'I'm not lying.'

'You are so.' She smiled at him reproachfully. 'You always were a rotten liar. Tell me.'

He hesitated a moment and then said, 'It may not be easy.'

'It never is, is it?'

'No,' he said quietly. 'You don't understand—'

'Hush,' she chided. 'I understand.'

He looked down at her, his face grave. 'There might have to be . . . a decision.'

She nodded.

'You know it?'

'Of course,' she said dreamily. 'I've known it for years.'

He was a long time in speaking. 'If it has to be—'

'If it has to be,' she finished for him, 'you must look after the baby.'

'I . . . don't think I can do that.'

'You must.'

He looked up from his clasped hands and his eyes were suddenly silver with tears. 'I can't do that,' he whispered.

The contractions came, taking her breath from her. As they passed she drew him down to sit beside her on the bed. She touched his face with the tips of her fingers.

'I'm glad the midwife isn't here,' she said softly. 'We don't want anyone else with us.'

'Don't talk like this,' he said. 'It'll be all right—'

'I just want it to be you and me.'

'It'll be all right, *draga*!'

The pain was hard and persistent now, the start of a process that couldn't be halted but she was filled with a sleepy happiness that shone in her like sunlight. She held his hand.

'When the time comes,' she whispered, 'don't let her die.'

Terezia stared down at her hands folded tightly in her lap.

'I didn't know—'

'I don't think your father ever really forgave himself,' Miklos said carefully. 'I remember he moved away just after that. He didn't want to stay in the place where it had happened.'

'You remember it?' Max put in.

The old man looked round at him. 'Oh, it was talked about at the time.'

'You knew him back in those days, did you?'

'I didn't know him, but I lived in the same district. That's why we were put in a cell together, you see. And I heard about it; we all did.'

'But was no one else there at the time?' Max asked. 'No one who might have kept some sort of record of the baby being born?'

'No, I don't think there was anyone.'

It was hopeless even asking, Max realised. It had been an age of fear and suspicion when secrecy had been a way of life.

'How about the midwife?' he asked.

'She wasn't there, that was the trouble.'

'But she may remember it.' It was worth the try. 'Do you know her name?'

Miklos shook his head. 'I couldn't say. But you could ask Kalman Bartha, he was the doctor in the village at the time. He may remember.'

'Does he still live in the village?'

'I expect so.'

'I'll see if I can find out,' Max said. 'Is there a telephone around here?'

Miklos told him there was one on the corner of the next street and Max went off in search of it. When he had gone Terezia sat with the old man in the little park with its scraggy trees and overloaded litter bins.

'You must have talked a great deal with my father,' she said after a few moments.

'Talk, yes.' He smiled at the irony of it. 'There wasn't much else we were allowed to do.'

She found it difficult to be asking such personal questions of someone she'd never met before but his manner encouraged her to be bold.

'Perhaps, if you had the time, you could tell me about him.'

'I'm always here. About this time of the day. I like to smoke, you see, and my daughter-in-law won't have it in the house. So I come out here. I like to be outside.'

'What do you smoke?'

'Cigarettes. Any type if they're foreign. What I really like is those fancy little cigars but they're hard to get.'

Not for Max, she was sure of that. She smiled and said, 'I'll see what I can do.'

'It would be nice,' the old man said. 'I'd like to talk of Karoly, to remember him. He was someone I . . . liked.'

He had to search for the word that described his feeling and when he found the one he wanted it was plain and mundane but all the more potent for that.

'When you were together,' Terezia said, 'did he ever mention my cousin Zoltan?'

Miklos looked her over with his pale, kindly eyes. 'Oh yes,' he said. 'He told me a great deal about Zoltan.'

'One thing I've never understood is why he hated him so badly.'

'Have you not?' he inquired politely.

'My father didn't hate anyone.'

'No,' Miklos agreed. 'No, that's true. But then he had his reasons.' He sat and looked across the square, tucking the scarf around his neck.

'Are you cold?' Terezia asked.

'No. It is a little chilly. But no, I'm all right for now.'

'What reasons did he have for hating Zoltan?' Terezia prompted after a moment.

'He hurt one of his horses.'

'Zoltan did?'

'The day your family left Hungary your father went hunting with his brother. You probably know this.'

'Yes, but please go on.'

'Sometime in the afternoon they stopped and buried a piece of the family jewellery – I forget its name.'

'The Hunyadi Venus.'

'That's right,' Miklos agreed. He repeated the name to himself as though wanting to keep it in mind. 'Do you know who was there at the time?'

'My father,' she said, 'my Uncle Sandor and Zoltan.'

'Yes, them,' he agreed. 'But there was one more. A gamekeeper. Your father trusted him, you see. He didn't mind him being there. He knew he'd never tell a soul what he'd seen happen that afternoon. But Zoltan was not so trusting.'

Miklos paused as Max returned. Terezia glanced round at him. 'It's all right,' she said, 'I'd like Max to hear this.'

'On the way back down the hill,' Miklos went on, 'Zoltan nicked his horse with a knife so that it became lame. He asked the gamekeeper to take a look at it. The others didn't hear; they went on.'

'What did he do?' Terezia asked.

'When they got back to the house they loaded the cars and left. Your father stayed behind a few minutes. I think he wanted to take a last look around the stables. It was the part of the house he loved best. He found the horse, saw what Zoltan had done. Then the news came through that the gamekeeper was missing.'

'What had happened to him?' Terezia asked. She was listening to him speak with the intensity of a child having a frightening bedtime story read to her.

'They went back up the hill and found he'd been shot.'

'By Zoltan?'

'Your father believed so.'

'Is that why he didn't leave?' she asked carefully.

Miklos gave a little shrug. 'By then it was too late. The bridges over the river had been blown.'

Evening was drawing in, shadows darkening the gaunt silhouettes of the tower blocks. Terezia sat back on the park bench.

'I didn't realise,' she said.

'I don't think your father ever forgave him,' Miklos said. 'That's why he wasn't going to let Zoltan have the Venus. And now, if you don't mind, I'd like to get on back. It's turning rather chilly.'

They walked back with him to his block of flats. As they were standing waiting by the tin doors of the lift Max asked, 'Did he ever tell you what became of the Venus?'

'He dug it up,' Miklos said. 'Took it away with him.'

'Do you know where it is?'

'No, he never said.' He glanced at Terezia. 'He told me he'd left it to you in his will.'

'There's no mention of it,' Max said.

'Then I don't know where it is.' He was looking between

the two of them. 'But I explained all this to the man the other day.'

'Which man?' Terezia asked.

'From the university. He came asking about the Venus. He said he was working for you.'

'He was lying,' Terezia said quietly.

'I told him it was all in the will. Karoly said he'd left the Venus to you in his will.'

'Had Verity seen the will?' Max asked.

'No. He wanted to know where it was. I told him there was a copy in London. I know Karoly always sent these things to some firm of lawyers in London. He said it was safer there than Budapest.' He made a small gesture of apology. 'Did I do the wrong thing?'

'No,' Max said. 'Not at all. But it helps to explain something that we wanted to know.'

'The little rat,' Max said as they went back to the car. 'He must have hightailed it back to London reckoning he was going to get his hands on the Venus and, bingo, he found something much more valuable.'

He started the engine and headed out of town. Terezia fiddled with the heating controls, holding her hands over the grill in the dashboard for the first signs of warmth.

'If he'd had any sense,' Max said, 'he'd have kept quiet about what he found. But instead he decided to try blackmailing Zoltan. And that was goodbye, Dr Verity of Oxford University.'

Terezia was silent for a few miles. Then she asked, 'Did you find out about that doctor?'

'The telephone directory has someone called Bartha living in the village. I thought we'd give him a go.'

The address he'd found was for a small house about a mile

outside the main village. A woman in her fifties answered the door. She had greyish hair, greyish dress and the general air of being unhelpful.

'We're looking for a Dr Bartha,' Max said.

'He's not here.'

'Do you think we could wait until he comes back? It's very important.'

'What do you want him for?' She was holding the door half closed.

'We are trying to find a record of a child who was born here some time ago. We thought he might be able to remember it.'

'No,' she said.

'Could we ask him?'

'Dr Bartha died,' she told them. 'Three years ago.'

There was silence on the doorstep.

'I'm sorry,' Terezia said.

Now that she'd made her point the woman relented a degree. 'Who was this person's records you're looking for then?'

'They're mine,' Terezia said. 'I need to find someone who remembers my birth. It wasn't registered at the time.'

'I see. When was this?'

Terezia gave her birth date and the woman shook her head. 'He wouldn't have remembered. There are so many births around here; he wouldn't have remembered that far back.'

'This one was rather different,' Max explained. 'The roads were snowed up and the father delivered the baby himself. It was out on one of the stud farms.'

She considered. 'I could try asking the doctor who works here now. He might remember.'

'Could you?' Terezia said warmly.

'They were partners together for a while. But it's a long time ago. I'm not sure he'd even started work here then.'

Max took out a scrap of paper from his wallet and wrote down Michael Gallagher's number on it.

'If he remembers anything,' he said, giving it to her, 'anything at all, could you get him to ring this number?'

The woman took the piece of paper and the door closed on them.

'Hell,' Max said as they went back to the car. 'Helpful as a pin in a condom factory.'

'What do we do now?' Terezia asked.

She was looking despondent. Her hopes had been raised and dashed and the strain was showing in the way she stood, her head lowered, hands dug into her pockets. Max wondered how much more of this she could take.

'We should find somewhere to stay,' he said.

'Not here,' she said quickly. 'I don't want to stay here.'

Max unlocked the door. 'Well, maybe we should get back somewhere near Fetevis.'

She nodded.

'It's okay,' he said as she got in beside him. 'Something will turn up. It's just a matter of searching.'

She smiled but made no reply.

Bela Bessenyei reached out an arm for the glass of champagne on the bedside table and took a sip. It was flat, the bubbles only managing to raise a tingle on his palate. Hardly surprising, it was over two hours since he'd opened the bottle. Where the time had gone he couldn't say with any accuracy. It had all been lost in a whirlwind of desire and pleasure.

He lay back, balancing the glass on his bare chest, feeling satiated and drowsy. A quilt was spread over his legs but apart from that he was naked on the bed.

Through the bathroom door he could see the olive-skinned girl grooming herself in front of the mirror. She'd told him she was called Melinda. What her other name was he didn't know. He didn't particularly care either. Who needed names when you have a body that operates with the finesse and precision of a scientific instrument? He wondered where she had learned her tricks. None of the schools he'd come across in his brief stint in the Ministry of Education had the skills she'd developed on their curriculum.

Switching off the bathroom light, she came back into the room. She was wearing but a pair of long black gloves, and smiling at him.

Kneeling on the bed she drew back the quilt.

She couldn't want more. He was exhausted, spent like a fallen rocket. He took a sip of flat champagne and lay back with a groan. 'You're not thinking of starting again?'

'Last time was for you,' she purred, slipping off the bed and going over to the window. 'This one's for me.'

Unhooking the silk rope that tied back the curtains she sat astride his stomach and with quick, deft movements tied his wrists to the brass bedhead, her breasts brushing his face as she worked.

What did the crazy girl want now? Bessenyei wondered frantically. He had nothing more to give, nothing more he could do that he hadn't already done.

She was breathing heavily, her lips parted and thickened with expectation. Reaching over for the flimsy black bra she'd been wearing she put it between his teeth, knotting the straps behind his head. And then slowly and sensuously she started to stroke her hands down over his chest.

He couldn't do it again. Didn't the bitch realise that? He was finished, wrecked. But her fingernails were working over his ribs and down his body, teasing and gouging. And he could feel himself coming awake. There were darts of pleasure in his belly, hot and delicious.

And she was starting her tricks with him again. He groaned and arched his back, his arms held by the silk rope. It must stop; he couldn't take any more. But it was so good. Oh God, it was so good!

Crash!

The door burst open.

Bessenyei jerked his head up, eyes starting from his head.

There were figures in the doorway. And a voice said, 'Smile for the cameras, Minister!'

But he couldn't move. He was tied there to the bed.

The girl's face was between his legs, her teeth in his flesh. And all around him cameras were exploding.

He saw it all. In a flash he saw every step in the whole sordid, fucking set-up. But there was nothing he could do.

He was stuck there, trussed up like a bloody turkey.

The cameras stopped. The figures hustled out as quickly as they'd come. The girl jumped off him and ran after them, covering her nakedness with the quilt.

As she was leaving she paused and turned. And for one brief instant there was a look in her eyes that could have been an apology. Then she shook her head and the door closed.

Bessenyei fell back on the bed and said, 'Oh shit!'

But with the bra gagging his mouth he might as well have been saying 'Thank you'.

29

Max sat on the edge of the bed. Terezia was still asleep, her hair a storm of gold on the pillow.

He put the cup of coffee he'd brought up from the dining room on the bedside table and she stirred, opening her eyes. Turning on her back she smiled at him drowsily and then, seeing he was dressed she asked, 'What time is it?'

'About nine-thirty.'

She lifted herself up on her elbows in astonishment. 'I'd no idea it was so late,' she said. 'You should have woken me.'

'There's no rush.'

'I never sleep this long.'

'It's the best thing you could have done.' He didn't remind her that she'd been so tired when they arrived that she'd fallen asleep fully dressed on the bed and he'd had to help take off her clothes and crawl under the covers. He nodded at the table. 'I've brought some coffee up for you.'

'Have you had breakfast then?' she asked, sitting up and sipping at it.

'If you could call it that.'

They'd come across the hotel by chance the night before. It was about ten miles away from Fetevis, on the edge of a belt of woodland. It probably had its moment in the summer when the countryside was invaded by hikers and naturalists but right now it was almost deserted. Only one other table had been occupied when Max was in the dining room.

'There's no room service so I nicked this for you.' He took a bread roll from his pocket. It was wrapped in a paper serviette and filled with slices of ham and two thick chunks of cheese.

'What a hero you are.'

He watched as she ate, some of the crumbs spilling down her front to lodge on her bare breasts.

'I'm going into Budapest for a time,' he said.

She paused and swallowed. 'Why?'

'I need to talk to Gallagher, find out what's going on his end.'

'I'll get dressed.'

He shook his head. 'Best if you stay here.'

'Here?' She looked around the bare, functional room. 'But there's nothing going on here.'

'That's the point. I'll be back in a couple of hours.'

She looked rebellious. Wiping the back of her hand across her mouth she said, 'Couldn't you just talk to him on the phone?'

'No, I need to see him.' He swung his feet on to the ground and stood up. 'Apart from anything else he's got some cash for me.'

'But I'll go mad kicking around here.'

'I won't be long.'

Gallagher lived in the district below Buda Hill that they call The Watertown. His flat was on the fifth floor so Max was out of breath by the time he pressed the bell.

'Jesus Christ,' Gallagher said as he opened the door.

'Where the heck have you been? I've been trying to get in touch with you for the past two days.'

'Something came up.'

Gallagher took him through to a small sitting room and told him to take a seat. Which wasn't easy. The place looked as though it had been worked over by a burglar, with books, papers, magazines scattered everywhere.

'Where's the Countess?' Gallagher asked, going through to the kitchen. The gas stove lit with a whumph and he put the kettle on the flame.

'In a hotel out in the country.'

'Oh yeah?' That gave him something for his imagination to conjure with. 'Very nice too.'

'So why the excitement?'

'Because something weird's going on,' he said, coming through with a couple of mugs of coffee. Evicting a stack of books he perched himself on the arm of a chair. 'I've been asking a lot of questions around the place,' he said. 'Just putting in the ferrets to see whose head pops up the other end, you know the form. But I haven't been able to get much. The whole thing's sealed up tight as a nun's naughty. Then last night I get a call from some guy. Won't give his name but he says he's got something for me. Shifty as hell he is. I fixed to meet him first thing this morning. But he didn't show up. Then I get a call from him saying there's been a problem. I thought he meant the deal was off but he says he can get it to me by midday.'

'It?' Max queried. 'What is "it"?'

Gallagher shook his head. 'He won't say. But he says it's useful.'

'Where are you meeting him?'

'Buda Hill. I could do with you there.'

'Me?'

'Yea, you.'

'Won't it screw things up?'

'Not if you keep your head down. And I could do with a witness. I've got a feeling that this is going to be one of those moments when the more innocent bystanders around the better.'

'I'd better ring Terezia.'

He got through to the hotel. There were no phones in the rooms so he left a message to say he'd be back later in the afternoon. By the time he put down the receiver, Gallagher had put on a cap and an old leather bomber jacket and was waiting by the door.

'Okay,' he said. 'Let's go.'

On the other side of the street a man in jeans, trainers and anorak, a woollen skiing hat pulled over his ears, was reading the sports page of the paper as he leaned against the wall.

He glanced up briefly as Gallagher came out of the block of flats with the other man. Three days he'd been tailing the journalist around town, loitering in shops and cafés, sitting at bus stops, chatting to road workmen. And this was the pay-off, the moment he'd been waiting for.

Rolling the paper he sauntered over to his car and got in. Flicking open the channel on his mobile phone he spoke shortly, giving time, place and direction. And then he started the engine, drifted the car out into the traffic and followed on behind.

Bela Bessenyei stood at the window of the office on the second floor of Party Headquarters. Out of the side of his eye he watched the President's aide as he went through the sheaf of painfully clear black and white photos.

There was no sign of reaction, nothing by which he could

gauge what was going through the mind of this efficient, ambitious and somehow anonymous young man as he studied the explicit images. It was as though he were glancing through a budget report.

'This is the most unfortunate business,' he said after a moment, dropping the photos in a neat pile on the desk. 'Most unfortunate.'

'Isn't it just—'

'You say you met her by chance in a café?'

'She just sat down at a table near mine.'

'And you happened to strike up a conversation with her?'

'I'd met her before,' Bessenyei said testily. 'At the opera a couple of nights ago.' He didn't have to talk to this creep. He was a friend of the President. Any confessions would be to him and him alone.

'But you had no idea it was a set-up?' the aide inquired.

'Of course I didn't. And I'm not saying more until I have spoken to the President.'

'He's not in today, Minister.'

'Then I'd like a lawyer present.'

'If you wish.' The aide had no objections to that personally. 'But in the circumstances, the President thought you might prefer it if I were to talk to you in private before bringing in anyone from outside.'

'Oh yes? And what's he told you to say?'

'Naturally, his first concern is to keep this out of the papers. Pictures like this make an ugly sight on the breakfast table. But then you can't want to see them there yourself, can you Minister? You being a married man. Once those journalists get the whiff of scandal in their nostrils there's no knowing what else they may manage to unearth.' He paused. 'That gentlemen's club in Obuda, for example.' For the first time there was a glint of malice in his eyes. 'I'm sure you wouldn't want them checking down through the list of its members.'

Bessenyei wasn't going to play cat and mouse with the man. He came straight to the point. 'What do you want?'

The brutality of the question brought a thin smile to the aide's features. 'The President feels it might help if you were to give him a full explanation of your recent activities.'

'Activities?' He didn't know what the hell the bastard was on about.

'Your secret acquisition of Party funds from Count Zoltan Kasinczy-Landsberg.'

'Secret?' Bessenyei exploded. 'There's nothing secret about them. He's been paying donations to the Party for years. Everyone knows it.'

'On the contrary.' The aide's tone was glacial and Bessenyei realised that the conversation was being recorded. 'The President knew nothing of any such transactions taking place. And he'd never have allowed it had he done so. It is not our policy to accept private donations of that kind.'

'Don't give me that crap. He knows damned well about them.'

'You're wrong,' the aide said sharply. 'The President knew nothing of funds from Count Zoltan. Just as he knew nothing of how you arranged to have the birth certificate of one of the Count's relations destroyed.' The aide glanced down at the photos on the desk again. 'He has asked me to tell you that he would like a full account of how you came to do that.'

'He expects me to put that in writing?'

'Of course not.' The aide's expression never flickered. 'I've already done it for you. All you have to do is sign and the President will accept it.'

'Accept it? Accept it as what?'

'As your letter of resignation, Minister.'

Max's message made up Terezia's mind for her.

Ever since reading the short entry in the local paper she'd been torn with indecision. On one hand was Max's insistence that she stayed in the hotel. On the other was her sense of loyalty. She had to be there, she told herself. She would never forgive herself for not trying to attend.

Going to the pay-phone she made a call then checked the change in her bag. Max had given her some money. It should be enough to get her there and back. She went to the reception desk.

'Can I help you?' the girl asked.

'I need to call a taxi.'

'What's the time?'

'Twenty past twelve.'

'Where the heck's he got to?' Max asked.

'Give him time. This isn't a bus service.'

They were sitting in Gallagher's car, a beat-up Volvo that would never see its tenth birthday again. The engine was ticking over to keep the heater going and the window was misted with condensation. Max wiped a porthole and peered out up the street. The instructions Gallagher had been given were to go to Úri Utca and wait near the statue of the horseman.

They'd been there half an hour and there was no sign of life.

'This thing stinks,' Gallagher said after a while.

'The car?'

'No, this whole business.' He spoke with a quiet satisfaction. Nothing that didn't stink was of any use to him in his line of work. 'Some goon gives your friend Verity the bullet. You get some pictures of him and the next thing we know he's been put in the past tense himself. You'd think that was an interesting story, especially as it looks as though he was working for Old-Man KL at the time. But can I get anyone to stop and talk about it? Not a chance. No one has ever heard of it. I've tried them all: police, press, nurks in the civil service. Nothing. No one knows anything about it. It's as if it never happened. And you know what that means?'

'Someone's put the lid on it?'

'Put the lid on and nailed it down tight. And for that orders have to come from up high.' He aimed a finger at the patched sun roof of his car. 'Right up high.'

'Government?'

'Zoltan's been pumping money into their piggy bank for the past ten years. Serious money with more zeros on the end than you can count on your fingers. And for that he'll get a lot of people to look the other way when he wants it.'

He wiped the window with his forearm and looked out. Across the street was the bronze statue of Andras Hadik, a hussar commander riding a horse.

'Did you know,' Gallagher said after a while, 'that if you stroke that horse's bollocks you get a day's good luck?'

'Yeah, I heard.'

'It never worked for me.'

'It's probably just a rumour the horse liked to put around.'

They were interrupted by the sudden trilling of the mobile phone on the dashboard. Gallagher paused a moment and then picked it up.

'Gallagher speaking—'

'Who's that in the car with you?' The voice on the other end came out clear and nasal in the confined space.

'It's a friend of mine,' Gallagher said. Without moving his head he peered out through the misted window, trying to get a fix where the caller was watching them from.

'Police?' The voice asked.

'He's not the police.'

'What's he doing there?'

'Just making certain that what you've got for me didn't come from the pixies,' Gallagher said evenly. 'Where is it?'

There was a pause and then the voice said, 'You know the tomb of the Turkish Governor?'

'Yeah, I know it.' It was a couple of hundred yards away, a little monument on the fortress walls.

'You'll find it in the cannon beside the tomb,' the voice said. 'It's in the muzzle.'

'Okay, got you.'

'Alone, Úr Gallagher,' the voice warned. 'I want you there alone. Your friend stays back in the car.'

'Whatever you want,' Gallagher said and cut the line. He glanced over at Max. 'What do you reckon?'

'Sounds straight enough.'

'Could be a trap.'

'Why should they want to trap a second-rate hack who doesn't know his arse from his Olivetti?'

'You've a lovely way with words,' he said in wonder, opening the door of the car. 'Well there's only one way to find out, I guess. If I'm not back in fifteen minutes,' he added, ducking his head back in the car, 'cancel my subscription to the *Beano*.'

'You've got it.'

'And there's a gun in the glove pocket,' he said as he left. 'If anyone starts filling me with lead, feel free to start using it.'

'Get on with it,' Max said.

He watched Gallagher walk away up the street, tall and lean, his breath streaming out behind him. Was it a trap, Max wondered. He'd been asking a lot of questions in places where questions aren't allowed. It can't have made him any new friends.

He opened the glove compartment. A particularly unfriendly-looking weapon lay there. And let's hope it stays there, Max thought.

But he needn't have worried. Gallagher was back in just over five minutes, dumping himself down in the seat of the car empty-handed. 'Get anything?' Max asked.

Gallagher unzipped his jacket, pulled out a brown paper envelope and chucked it over on to Max's lap.

'Easy,' he said. 'Just sitting there in the postbox.' He spoke with the slight elation that sets in after danger.

'What's in it?'

'Hold on a second,' Gallagher said, starting the car. 'Don't open it here. We don't want any cameras watching us.'

Max waited until they were through the Vienna Gate and heading downhill before ripping open the envelope.

There was a single page inside, a photocopy of a letter.

'Holy shit,' he said.

'What have you got?'

'Bessenyei – he's resigned.'

'Now why should he want to go and do a thing like that?'

'He's been taking money from Zoltan on the side.' Max was rapidly skimming the letter. After a moment he said, 'Bloody hell. Look at this. He had the birth certificate taken.'

'It says that?'

'In black and white.'

'The name. Does it mention her name?'

'Name, title, the lot.'

'What's the date on it?'

'Today.'

Gallagher shook his head in wonder. 'Now how could our little chum have known about it yesterday then?'

Time was short. Already half the day had been wasted and Gallagher was burning to be getting on with his work.

'How long would it take you to fetch the Countess?' he asked as he brought the car to a skidding halt opposite his flat.

'About a couple of hours.'

He glanced at his watch. It was after one. 'Could you get her back here by three?'

'I guess so.'

'I'll meet you at the offices of *Magyar Hirlap* then. Do you know where they are?'

'I can find them.'

'I'll see you there, soon as you can.' He was measuring the time they had to the work that needed to be done. 'I'll get the editor and a couple of good lawyers. If we shift we can get this into tomorrow's papers.'

'Are you going to talk to Zoltan?'

'No, we'll just hit him with it. Blow the bastard out of the water before he can fire back. Will she talk?'

'Terezia?'

'Will she give us what we want?'

'I think so.'

'She's not renowned for co-operating with the press.'

'I think she'll do it.'

'We need facts, details, background from her. Is she looking presentable?'

'Enough to come into a newspaper office.'

'How about for some pictures?'

'She's been on the run for the past two days.'

'I'll bring along a hairdresser, get her to give her a workover. I want her looking like a film star.' He was thinking on his feet. 'It only has to be from the waist up. One of the girls in the office can probably lend her something to wear. There's a few of them who are presentable. Leave it with me. You go and get her.'

He crossed the road and disappeared into his flat. Max walked round to where his car was parked in the next street. There was a call box further up. It occurred to him that it wouldn't be a bad idea to give her a ring, tell her to be ready.

He pulled open the door and picked up the receiver. As he was searching in his pocket for change a hand clamped down on his wrist and he was thrown forcibly against the glass panel side.

'Nice and easy now,' a voice said in his ear.

He twisted his head round enough to see the blue and grey uniforms of a couple of policemen behind him, one with his shoulder into his back, the other groping for the handcuffs on his belt.

He kicked himself back, ducking down low, but there was no room to manoeuvre in the confined space and the policeman held him steady against the glass. He felt the steel jaws of the handcuffs snap shut around his wrist and he was pulled out into the street.

There was a police sergeant out there. He looked Max over quickly, keenly.

'Anderson?'

'What's it to you?'

'You're nicked,' he said dispassionately.

'For what?'

'For being someone the police want under arrest.'

'Look, you're wrong,' Max said desperately. 'I've done nothing wrong.'

'Then you'll have nothing to worry about, will you, sir,' the officer told him dryly. He had the calm, inoffensive manner of a man doing his job. He watched as the two policemen held Max up against the wall, frisking him over quickly and efficiently.

'There's someone I must go and get,' Max told him over his shoulder. 'It's important, really important. You must let me do it.'

He shook his head, scarcely listening.

'You can come with me. You can do anything you like but you must let me do it.'

'I don't think you understand, sir,' the officer said. 'It's not us that's coming with you. It's you who's coming with us.'

There was a police car at the kerb. They bundled him in the back, the policeman with the cuffs thrusting in on one side, the officer on the other. Max fought the panic that was rising in him.

'There's a journalist,' he said as the car moved off, swinging out into the traffic, its siren coming awake. 'In that street over there. Talk to him. He'll explain what's happening.'

'We're not talking to anyone, sir.'

'Then let me speak to your senior officer,' Max said.

The officer turned to him and there was a ghost of a smile on his face. 'Oh, you're going to,' he said softly. 'You're off to see the boss himself.'

30

The church was yellow and white, faded from weather and years of neglect. Beneath the onion dome, the clock had stopped, the hands stuck at two-fifteen, perpetually marking the time of the day when the mechanism had been removed, along with the church bells, to be melted down and put to more practical use in the new age of Soviet Enlightenment.

Gabor Erkell crouched in the shelter of the bushes at the far end of the graveyard and watched as the procession emerged from the side door. The coffin, heavy and cumbersome, was carried out first. A handful of figures followed in its wake, silent and grave-faced, uniform in their black clothing; a woman leaning on the arm of a grey-haired man, friends and family huddled around.

Grief and sympathy united.

Standing at the head of the grave, a dark mouth in the frozen earth, he could hear the priest intoning his words. For fifty years the Catholic Church had been persecuted in Hungary, its followers hounded, and yet here it was, alive, powerful and unchanged. The opium of the people had proved more addictive than Marx had ever guessed.

Erkell listened to the muttered lines of the prayers and it seemed to him appropriate that he should be here at this ritual of farewell for the stable boy. He hadn't known him in any conventional sense. Until a few days before he hadn't been aware of his existence at all, and yet in the brief seconds of his death he had known him more intimately than any of these others who stood lined up beside the grave.

It was as the coffin was being lowered down that he caught a movement out of the side of his eye. The church gate had opened and a tall, slim figure walked up the path. She had blonde hair and wore a long grey coat.

It was the girl.

Erkell felt a leap of excitement in his stomach. He'd known she'd come, he'd sensed it as the huntsman senses the behaviour patterns of his prey.

Silently she joined the others by the graveside, her head lowered, hands folded in front of her. She looked pale and tired, but then she would be consumed with guilt. This was her doing, her fault. It was astonishing that she dared to show herself at all on such an occasion. But Erkell understood she had to be there. She was tied to this place. However much she tried to run there would always be a reason she had to return.

It had been the same with her father. For thirty years he had kept away but in the end he had been compelled to come back. There was no force on this earth that could have stopped him.

He remembered seeing the Count. It had just been a rumour. Someone in the village had spotted a figure going up to the house. Was it him? Hard to be sure; it was so many years now.

Erkell had gone in search. He'd never seen Count Karoly before but he recognised him immediately. Not so much by his appearance as from his behaviour. He'd been standing by the lakeside, looking across the water at the house. It was the man's stillness that stuck in his mind, the trance-like stance, as though every sense of his body had closed down and he was absorbing the view through the pores of the skin.

He hadn't tried to confront him but for almost ten minutes he'd crouched in the woods and watched as the man drew in the sight of his lost estate. Then, after making his way back to the village, he'd made the call to the police.

They'd put the Count in the back of a van, hands cuffed, uniformed officers hustling him away.

As he climbed in, the Count had paused and gazed around the village, his eyes scanning the windows as though searching for the twitch of a curtain that would betray his informer. But Erkell had stood in the doorway of his house in full sight of the elderly man and he'd never even noticed him there.

He was too young to be the one. No one who had been born after the Count left Fetevis would have called the police. They had no reason to do so.

The brief service was over, the figures moving away from the graveside. Erkell saw the girl speak to the boy's mother, a few short, inadequate words. She touched the woman's hand and then left, walking slowly back to the gate.

Leaving his hiding place, Erkell stepped over the church wall and limped down to the road. His ankle had swollen in the night so that he found walking painful and running almost impossible.

A taxi was parked in the village. The driver emerged from the café as the girl came out of the church. She must have persuaded him to wait for her. She was good at getting men to do what she wanted. Leaving a taxi with its meter ticking over would cost a fortune but she'd probably flashed those green eyes at him and he'd found himself her slave, as the boy in the grave had been her slave.

There was no traffic on the road, so even dropping back half a mile at times he was able to follow the taxi without any trouble as it made its way back to the hotel in the woods.

Another bolthole, Erkell told himself as he studied it. He'd never have found it without her help.

Going down to the nearby village he found a phone booth and leafed through the directory for the number. Pushing a couple of coins into the slot he got through to the reception desk.

'This is Úr Anderson speaking,' he told the girl at the other end. 'I'd like to leave a message for a friend of mine who's staying there.' What name had she registered under, he wondered. Kovacs? Kasinczy? Or was she coyly in the book as Anderson?

As it was, it didn't matter. The receptionist knew who he was talking about.

'She's just come in,' she said brightly. 'Would you like me to get her?'

'That won't be necessary. Would you leave a message for her?'

'Of course.'

'Tell her I'm going to Fetevis. I'll meet her there.'

Colonel Biszku held up his hands, halting the flood of protest that poured from Max.

'I understand,' he said wearily. 'I understand.' He was sitting behind his desk, jacket slung over the chair, tie loose in the collar of his faded blue shirt.

'You have no right to hold me!'

'I have every right.'

'I've done nothing wrong.'

'You are living here without a visa. That gives me the right to arrest you. Now sit down.'

'Only because you had no reason to withdraw the damned thing. I never killed Verity.'

'I know,' Biszku said.

'You do?'

'Yes,' he said bluntly. We know.' He gave a shake of his shaggy head. 'We've known you didn't kill him for several days now.'

'So why the hell have you had your gorillas arrest me?'

'So that we can talk, Úr Anderson.' Biszku let the meaning of the words sink in. 'Now, for Christ's sake, sit down.'

Max dumped himself in the chair. The policeman gave a grunt of satisfaction and said, 'If you'd come to us earlier we might even have been able to help you.'

'If I'd come to you I'd be standing in the dole queue back in England and Terezia Kasinczy would be dead.'

'You reckon?'

'I know it.'

Rather to his surprise, Biszku accepted the criticism. 'I won't deny you were ahead of us on this one, Úr Anderson,' he said. 'That is why I need to speak with you now.'

'Later,' Max snapped. 'When I've got the time we'll have a cosy little chat and you can ask me anything you like. But right now I've got more important things to be doing.'

'No,' Biszku said mildly. 'We talk now.'

'About what?'

'About what you were doing on Buda Hill this morning for a start.'

'I was there picking up a confidential document that had leaked out on the pavement.'

'And what did it say?'

Max reckoned the policeman might as well know. He'd read it in the papers the next day anyway.

'It was a letter from Bessenyei to the President telling

him that he had Terezia Kasinczy's birth certificate removed in return for some hefty bribes from Count Zoltan.'

Bisku's eyes bored into him. 'You read this letter yourself?'

'Every word.'

'Where is it now?'

'Michael Gallagher has taken it over to the *Magyar Hirlap* offices. It'll be all over the morning papers.'

'And this is why you are in such a hurry?'

'They need Terezia. That's where I was going when you pulled me in.'

Biszku got to his feet and went next door. When he returned he'd come to a decision.

'Okay,' he said, putting on his jacket. 'Let's go and get her.'

'You reckoning on coming along?'

Biszku gave him an icy smile. 'You don't have a car,' he reminded him. 'Besides you'll find we get there a damned sight quicker with a siren going.'

Max refrained from telling him he'd have got there a damned sight quicker if he hadn't had to take the scenic route through police headquarters.

'Do you mind if I use your phone?' he asked. 'I'd better tell her what's going on. If she sees a police car turn up she'll be off like a shot.'

He dialled the hotel and got through to the desk.

'She's just gone out,' the receptionist told him.

'Out? Where?'

'I couldn't say. There was a message left in the pigeonhole for her. I gave it to her.'

'When was this?'

'About ten minutes ago.'

'Jesus.' He felt a twist of panic. 'You don't know what is said?'

'Afraid not.'

'But you must have taken the message.'

'That was the person before me.' The receptionist was beginning to sense this was an emergency. 'I've only just come on duty.'

'Can you find the other girl?'

'I'm not sure—'

'Please,' Max said. 'This is urgent. Find whoever it was, ask her what the message said. I'll ring back.'

He put the phone down.

'Problem?' Biszku was standing at his elbow.

'She's gone. Someone left a message for her and she's gone out.'

'You know who it could be?'

'No one,' Max said. 'No one knows she's there apart from me.'

'How about Gallagher?'

He shook his head. 'I never gave him the name of the place.'

'Then who?'

'I don't know.'

'In that case, my friend,' Biszku said quietly, 'I think we'd better get over there quick.'

A mile out of Fetevis, Terezia ran out of money.

'You'll have to drop me here,' she said. 'I haven't got enough to go any further.'

The driver drew into the kerb and asked her what she'd got. She showed him the notes in her bag. He counted through them, stuffed them in his pocket with a shrug. It wasn't his business to drive people around for free. But grudgingly he told her he'd take her as far as the village. He was going that way anyway.

The gates of the Palace were shut when she arrived. There was no sign of Max's car outside so she guessed she must have got there ahead of him. Clambering round the rusted ironwork she started to walk up the hill.

When she'd first read the note the receptionist gave her she couldn't see why Max should want to meet her here rather than pick her up directly from the hotel. But then she realised it was a good sign. He must have found something useful, something that proved her identity, and he wanted her to get over to Fetevis as quickly as possible to pick up her passport so that they could go to England.

She had no real image of what London would be like. Much the same as Budapest she supposed, only richer and smarter. Nor did she have any real idea of what direction her life would take once she got there. Only that it would be changed completely. Exactly how she hadn't had time to think about yet.

As she reached the house she went straight round to the stables. The horses greeted her with low whinnies and tossings of their heads. Quickly she went round them, stroking their firm necks, letting them nestle their velvet muzzles in her hands while anxiously she checked the condition of the stalls. For the past two days she'd been haunted by lurid thoughts of what was happening back here without her. But she needn't have worried. The place was in good order, better than she had dared to hope for. Elek had done well.

She'd talked to him briefly at the funeral and he'd told her he'd conscripted his elder brother to help out. And he'd managed to get a message through to Joszef down in the country. He was coming back immediately; he should be there by that evening so she could set her mind at rest.

Going through to the tack room she checked the level in

the feed bins and left by the side door. As she was closing it behind her she heard the horses suddenly stir, moving restlessly in their stalls, snorting and stamping.

Terezia froze.

It hadn't lasted more than two seconds, but she knew that sound in a horse. It was a signal of alarm. It came with the ears down flat on their heads, the eyes rolling back in their heads. The warning that an intruder was amongst them.

Icy fingers gripped her belly.

She glanced around herself. There was a belt of trees twenty yards away but there was no shelter in the bare winter trunks. Any movement in there would be spotted.

Ducking low, she ran along the crumbling stuccoed wall. An arched doorway further up led through to a small yard. It was where they'd once kept the hounds, a double row of kennels with a brick alley between. At the far end was a door, standing open, shadows beyond.

She slipped inside, crouching down.

Was she letting her imagination run away with her? It could be Max coming to find her. But she knew it wasn't. The horses would never have reacted like that to him. This had been someone they knew and feared.

And there was only one person that could be.

Erkell.

He had come into the stables three nights before and set fire to the hay barn. He was the one who would make the horses snort and stamp with fright.

Even as the thought flashed through her mind, she heard footsteps on the hard-packed ground outside. She shrank back into the shadows, her heart bumping painfully against her chest.

As she did so, Erkell limped past the doorway.

*

'Dammit!' Max said.

He prodded the button on the mobile phone, cutting the connection, and tossed it down on the seat between himself and Biszku.

'Still out?' the policeman asked.

'Still out.'

He'd put through a call to the hotel but the receptionist who'd taken the call for Terezia wasn't back yet.

'She'll probably be there by the time we arrive,' Biszku said.

'By the time we arrive is too late.'

He gave a grunt of agreement. They were doing ninety through the suburbs of Budapest, the police car flowing easily through the traffic, its siren clearing the other vehicles out of the way as if by magic.

Max stared out through the window at the untidy landscape of railway sidings and high-rise blocks. Across the plain the chimneys of a factory bristled up against the skyline, heavy coils of smoke lumbering away along the horizon.

A thought struck him, so bloody obvious he didn't know why he hadn't thought of it before.

'Get the driver to turn off,' he said to Biszku.

'Why's that?'

'There's no point in going to the hotel. She's not there.'

'Got a better idea?'

'The Landsberg Corporation,' he said.

Biszku turned, shooting him a quick, keen glance. 'You want to talk to Zoltan?'

'Yes, that's exactly who I want to talk to. If anyone knows where she is Zoltan does.'

Biszku was silent for a moment, undecided. 'Can you make this stick, Anderson?'

'I reckon so. It's worth a try.'

The policeman nodded. 'Okay,' he said. 'Let's do it.'

He leaned forwards, speaking shortly and quickly to the driver. The car pulled into the inner lane and drew off the main road.

'If we're going there,' Biszku said, 'I don't think it would do any harm to have a bit of muscle with us.'

He snapped his fingers towards the dashboard. Taking his hand off the gear lever, the driver passed him back the radio transmitter and Biszku put through an order for a couple of squad cars to go to the Landsberg Corporation offices.

'I hope you're right about this,' he said as he sat back.

'It's better than sitting here doing nothing.'

With the siren going they made it to the Corporation headquarters in under fifteen minutes. The barrier at the entrance was down but at the sight of Biszku's badge flashed out of the window it came up before the car had stopped.

There was one squad car there ahead of them, its two officers standing waiting. Biszku told them to follow him as he pushed his way through the revolving doors into the clean, sparse, brightly lit foyer of the Landsberg offices.

A secretary shimmered up but they ignored his questions and went straight to the lift.

'We're here to see Count Zoltan,' Max told the girl at the desk on the first floor.

In normal circumstances she would no doubt have told them that they needed an appointment and asked them to leave. But faced with two uniformed policemen and Biszku's badge, which flicked into view as his wallet snapped open like a snake's jaws, she decided to be more co-operative.

'He's not here today,' she said.

'Where is he?'

'I don't know.'

'Then who does?'

She looked between them, flustered. 'I don't know . . . perhaps you should talk to his son.'

'Is he here?' Max asked.

The girl had got to her feet, trying to assert some control. She went down the passage, knocked on a door.

A young man opened it. He looked them up and down rapidly. 'Can I help you?'

'We want a word with your boss.'

'He's busy at present.'

'Is this the office?' Max asked, going down to the polished double doors at the end of the passage.

'You can't go in there,' the secretary called out as he pushed them open.

Alexander Kasinczy-Landsberg was standing over by the high sash window, talking to another man, his jacket off, felt braces over a hand-made striped shirt, one hand in his pocket.

As Max burst in, Biszku on his heels, he broke off his conversation and turned towards them. He looked from one to the other and in a voice sharp with impatience said, 'What the bloody hell do you want?'

For a moment Erkell stood framed in the doorway of the kennels. His pale eyes swept slowly round the yard.

Then he moved on.

Terezia slumped down on her knees in the dark. She'd been certain he'd seen her; certain he'd known she was hiding in there. She'd wanted to jerk her head away from the window. But she'd known she mustn't. One movement and he'd have seen her.

Letting out her breath, she looked around the shed. In the gloom she could make out bare brick walls, a stash of wood up one end but no other door.

She had to get out. If he came back she'd be trapped in

here like a rat in a hole. But the thought of going out into the open again made her blood run cold in her veins. Frantically she looked around herself again. There must be a door, some way of getting into the house.

But there was nothing she could see.

She was going to have to go outside. But where to? There was no place to hide that was any safer than this.

Then she thought of the gun. It was standing behind the kitchen door. If she could get to that it would be something. It may not give her an edge over Erkell but it would give her a chance.

And that's what she needed.

With a purpose fixed in her mind she felt calmer, stronger. Crouching low she slipped out of the doorway and crept up the line of the kennels, her footsteps quiet on the mossy brick path.

Reaching the entrance she paused, hugging close to the wall. He could be out there waiting for her to make a move. Maybe he did see her and only pretended to walk on, knowing that if he left her she'd come out sooner or later.

Straight into a trap.

Ears straining she listened for the slightest sound that could betray the presence of a man on the other side of the wall. But there was silence, broken only by the distant cawing of the rooks in the trees.

With her back to the wall she turned her head round the frame of the door and looked out.

No one in sight.

She could see up the back of the house as far as the ruined shell of the orangery. But there was no movement, no sign of Erkell.

Now, she told herself. It had to be now. While he was round the other side of the house.

Stepping out into the open, she ran along the wall. It was the same direction as he'd taken but there was a covered passage further along that led through to the front of the house.

It was long and narrow, much narrower than she had ever noticed before. And the confined space amplified her footsteps so that they crashed and echoed around her as she ran.

Oh God, this was not a good idea, she told herself. He only had to pass by on either side and he'd see her in here. There was no shelter, nowhere to duck out of sight.

She felt naked, exposed.

But it was too late to change her mind now. Hugging close to the wall she reached the far end and flattened herself against the wall, heart hammering, breath coming in long unsteady gasps. There had been games like this when she was a child, games of hide and seek around the farm. But then the fear had been the whole point of playing, a delicious sensation they'd craved like junkies. Because it was safe, because it was all make-believe.

This was not make-believe.

Inching round the wall she crept up into the porch of the house, moving stealthily from column to column. Still no sign of Erkell. Where the hell was he?

She went down into the driveway, the Mercury fountain looming up above her.

Nearly there now.

Keeping to the shelter of the wall, she worked her way round to the little cottage at the rear of the house that had been their home for the past few months.

She tried the handle but the door was locked. Dragging round her bag that was slung over her back, she found the keys and fumbled one into the lock.

The kitchen was filled by the strange stillness that rooms

take on when they've been left deserted for some time. Familiar and yet unreal, as though they are only a replica of the real thing.

Reaching behind the door she grabbed hold of the gun. It felt solid and comforting in her hands. Snapping open the breech she dropped a couple of cartridges into the chambers and closed it again. As she did so she heard a sound that made her heart miss a beat.

It was the crunch of gravel outside.

Edging back the curtain with one hand she glanced out into the driveway. He was there, limping round the side of the house, heading straight towards her.

In a flash she realised what had given her away. The door. Dammit, she'd left the thing open. He'd seen it, realised where she was and was coming.

Stuffing a handful of cartridges in her pocket she ran through into Joszef and Rozsa's bedroom. Neat and plain. A white cover on the double bed, two framed photos on the side table. Dropping the gun to one side she wrenched at the window.

It wouldn't budge.

She tried again, frantic with haste.

Still nothing.

The catch. It was still on. She knocked it aside, and tore the window up.

Fresh air struck her in the face as she rolled over the sill, landing heavily on the ground. The gun clattered down beside her. Picking herself up she scuttled along the side of the house.

There was no cover here, nowhere to run to.

One of the shutters was dangling open. She stopped, breathless. The window inside was open. She glanced back. Erkell hadn't come out yet. Loading the gun through first, she scrambled in through the window, dropping to the hard wooden boards beyond.

For a few minutes she lay on her back in the dark listening, the gun held across her chest.

At first there was nothing. Maybe she was wrong. Maybe he hadn't noticed the door standing open.

Then she heard footsteps outside, strange, rhythmic footsteps as he limped down the side of the house.

She held her breath, clutching the gun to herself, as he came close. Was he going to see the open shutter and guess where she was? He was bound to. Where else would she have got to?

But the footsteps carried on past the window.

As they died into the distance she got to her feet and moved deeper into the house, walking slowly and carefully as every step was loud in the bare, empty building.

She'd never known Fetevis when it was a living house so she had no real concept of what purpose all these dark, hollow rooms had once served. But she could take a guess that where she had come in was once some sort of scullery. There were stone sinks to one side and long marble slabs on the other. A short passage led through the main kitchen, vast and stone-floored, and on into a series of smaller, dank chambers.

Double doors opened out into the gallery. Yellowish light from the dirty glass in the roof, dust and plaster crunching under her feet below. Softly she made her way through into the main hallway and looked up into the domed ceiling, feeling, rather than seeing, the space around her. And as she stood there she heard in the far distance a sound that made her skin crawl.

It was a door opening.

She turned around, every sense alert. It was impossible to pinpoint exactly where the sound had come from. The direction was lost in the echoing silence of the house. But it seemed to be off to her left somewhere.

Her first temptation was to run but she knew the sound would give her away. She had to go slowly.

Pulse racing, she tiptoed up the stairs to the first floor. On the landing she stopped and listened.

At first nothing but the silence of space and emptiness. Then she detected a slight movement down below. A soft tread. The sound of a man advancing slowly and warily. She inched back into the shadows, the gun up ready across her body, forefinger resting on the side of the trigger.

Then she heard his voice.

'Where are you, pretty lady?' It came from far away and seemed to float up the stairs towards her.

At the sound of it, she felt herself start trembling uncontrollably from head to foot. Crouching low, she crept on down the passage.

'There's no point in hiding, pretty lady.' The voice came again, soft and almost musical, gliding up out of the darkness to her. 'I can find you. I can always find you.'

In panic she ran, her feet clattering around her ears. And the voice followed her.

'So there you are, pretty lady. Upstairs, is it? Thought you could get away from me up there, did you?'

At the end of the passage she came to another flight of stairs, smaller and shorter. She fled up them, darted round the landing at the top and held still in the darkness.

Slow down, she sobbed to herself. Slow down!

'Did I scare you then?' the voice asked. It was coming from the top of the stairs now, moving in this direction.

Don't run, Terezia whispered to herself. Don't make a sound. She could feel the sweat on her face now, cold and clammy.

'Did I give you a fright there?' the voice asked. 'I'm so sorry. But you don't think you can escape, do you? You don't think you can get away from me?'

With infinite care she inched her way along the passage into a long bare room. Something dark and formless behind the door made her start but she saw it was only a grand piano. Too big to get out. Left to moulder away in silence.

'There's no need to run, pretty lady.' The voice followed her. 'I can always find you.'

Through the next door into a smaller room. But nowhere to hide. She must go up higher.

'I know you, you see,' the voice told her. 'I know how you think. I know what you will do before you know it yourself.'

Out into the passage and on down, past open doors until she found a way upstairs. When she'd first got the gun her intention had been to take it off somewhere to hide until Max turned up. He couldn't be far off. It was just a matter of waiting.

But now she understood that Max wasn't coming. The message hadn't been from him, it had been from Erkell. She should have realised it straight away. He'd used it to lure her away from the hotel.

And now she was here with him alone.

'Still hiding, pretty lady? Still think you can get away from me?' The voice floated up to her but with a flood of relief she realised it was further away.

The bastard had lost the trail.

Hope trickled into her veins. It might still be possible to hide from him here. The house was vast. If she could find some tiny niche to crawl into it might take him ages to find her.

She moved on down the passage. Unexpectedly, it took her out on to the gallery high above the main hallway. Above her the bell-like curve of the domed ceiling, below a sheer drop to the ground fifty feet below.

She looked across the dark well of space. On the far side of the gallery was a door. She'd no idea where it led. Maybe up into the dome. She might even be able to get out on to the roof.

Outside. It was a wonderful thought. She stepped forwards. But as soon as she put her weight on the gallery floor there was a groan and she felt the woodwork crack and sag beneath her. She jumped back, tripping on the step behind, tumbling down with a crash on the ground.

She heard the sound echo down through the deserted house, rolling on, giving away her hiding place.

And he'd heard.

Suddenly there were footsteps running towards her. Scrambling to her feet she sprinted back down the passage. It didn't matter where any more. All that mattered was to get away from the place where the sound of her fall had come from.

A flight of stairs took her down to the second floor. She ran on, dodging between doors until she came to a small dark room. Here she stopped, gasping for breath, and listened. There was silence.

Thank God, she'd lost him again.

Carefully she moved through to the next room and stopped dead in her tracks.

Erkell was standing in the centre of the floor.

He was just a dark silhouette, slight and still, but her eyes had accustomed themselves to the dark enough for her to see the smile on his pale face as he said, 'You didn't think you were going to get away from me, did you, pretty lady?'

She'd swung the gun round, holding it low, the barrel levelled at his chest but he shook his head.

'You're not intending to use that, are you?'

'If I have to,' she whispered.

He reached round his back and drew out his knife. It was small and thin, its blade a dull gleam in the dark.

Holding it out to one side he took a step towards her.

'Don't move!' she shouted.

'You're not going to use that thing.' He was almost reproachful as he told her the truth.

'I will,' she promised. 'If you come any closer I will.'

'In cold blood? No, pretty lady. You haven't got it in you.'

Terezia backed away from him. 'Why are you doing this to me?' she asked in a small voice.

Erkell paused, as though he were surprised she didn't know the answer already. 'Because you shouldn't be here, pretty lady. You're in the way; you're a nuisance.'

'I've done nothing wrong!'

'No one wants you alive,' he said quietly. 'So you must die. That's the way of it. Now put that gun down.'

His eyes held hers hypnotically. The knife lifted out to one side, he took another step towards her.

Terezia jerked up the gun. 'Don't move!'

'You won't shoot.'

'I will,' she sobbed. 'Take one more move and, so help me God, I will.'

'No, pretty lady.'

With the slow, stealthy grace of an acrobat on the high wire, he slid one foot forward and inched towards her.

'I'll shoot!'

'Then let's see you do it.'

Another step and a shaft of light from the shutters fell over his face. She saw the exaltation in his eyes.

He was enjoying it.

She fell back and felt the wall behind her. She could go no further.

Erkell's eyes were testing the distance between them. She saw him sway back like a cobra, his arms raised on either side. For an instant he paused. There was a smile on his face. He'd bettered her, defeated her. All he had to do was finish the job.

With a sudden lunge he struck.

And Terezia fired.

31

'Where's your father?'

'I really couldn't say,' Alexander Kasinczy-Landsberg told him lazily. 'Maybe back home, maybe at his club.'

'Call him.'

Alexander wasn't used to being spoken to in this way. He looked Max over with disdain and said, 'Why on earth should I?'

'Because we need to speak to him.'

'About what?'

'About what he's done with Terezia.'

Alexander made a small gesture of irritation. He was tired of this conversation.

'Really,' he said. 'I think we've been through all this before, Mr Anderson. My father has not *done* anything to the wretched girl. Now I'd be glad if you'd get the hell out of here.'

'Your father,' Max cut in, 'has a contract out on her life.'

'Oh, don't be so ridiculous!' He was angry now. 'Do you honestly think my father would put a contract on her because of a dispute over a piece of property? Use your common sense, man!'

'It's not over property.'

'What then?' he asked with heavy irony. 'Over a piece of silver that vanished years ago?'

'It's nothing to do with the house or a piece of silver,' Max told him. 'Your father is trying to kill her because she owns all this.'

'Owns all what?'

'Everything.' He waved an arm towards the window. 'Steel mills, armaments business, assets, the lot. The whole bloody Landsberg Corporation is hers.'

Alexander had gone very still. 'What are you talking about?' he asked quickly. 'She doesn't own the Corporation; she doesn't own anything.'

Max held up his hands. He hadn't time to explain in detail. That could come later. All that mattered was that Alexander understood the urgency of what was happening.

'When your family emigrated to America they restarted the family business. Right?'

Alexander nodded.

'Your grandfather set up the Landsberg Corporation. New name, new country but the same industry as before. He had to do it by himself as his brother was still over her in Hungary. No one knew what had become of him. They couldn't even get a letter through.'

'This is all ancient history, Anderson.'

'But the two brothers were very close, weren't they?'

'Twins.'

'And your grandfather was the younger of the two.'

Alexander nodded again.

'So he was not the heir,' Max said. 'That was Terezia's father. He was head of the family.'

'My grandfather may not have been the heir but he still founded the Landsberg Corporation.'

'In both their names.'

There was silence in the room.

'Both their names?' Alexander said. 'I've never heard anything of the Corporation being formed in both of them.'

'Your grandfather divided the shares between himself and his brother. Forty-nine per cent to himself and fifty-one per cent to his brother. Terezia's father may not have been there; he may not have even known about what was going on but your grandfather wanted him to have the main shareholding.'

'Because he was the head of the family?'

'That's the kind of man he was.'

Alexander stared at him long and hard. 'How the hell do you know all this?'

'We found letters.'

'They could be faked.'

'A solicitor's firm in London is holding the documents,' Max said. 'As soon as Terezia is able to claim them, fifty-one per cent of the Landsberg Corporation is hers.'

'So why hasn't she done it?'

'Because your father destroyed her birth certificate. And if we don't stop him now he'll destroy her too.'

It might have been that she lost aim as she jumped aside, or it might have been that she dropped the muzzle intentionally. She couldn't tell. But as Erkell lunged at her she fired down at his feet.

The gun lurched in her hands as it went off, the explosion huge and resonant in the empty room.

Erkell swore and jumped back, his face twisted with rage as the wooden boards splintered up with the impact of the shot.

He'd made a mistake, miscalculated her nerve. A few inches higher and she'd have had his legs off.

Dropping the gun, Terezia turned and ran. Out into the passage and down the wide curve of the stairs.

She could hear him coming behind her. As she reached the foot of the stairs she half turned to see where he was and missed the step. With a cry she tumbled down the last part, landing in an untidy heap of legs and arms.

The wind was knocked from her lungs, there was a pain in her shoulder. Rolling over, dizzy from the shock, she looked up to see Erkell coming down on her. He was moving slowly, impeded by his leg, one arm on the banister to steady himself.

She scrambled to her feet and ran across to the high front doors of the house. They were locked but the bolts top and bottom weren't drawn and as she pulled they bowed inwards, parting with a rattle.

Hair flying, she bounded down the steps of the porch and headed for the stables.

Alexander looked at him in silence for a moment. Then he turned to Biszku. 'Is this true?'

The policeman gave a shrug. 'I've not seen the letters myself,' he said evenly. 'But yes, I believe it is true.'

'So now that you know,' Max said, pointing his finger towards the phone on the desk, 'ring your father and tell him to call of his bloodhound.'

Alexander thought for a moment. Then picking up the receiver he dialled, spoke quickly and briefly, and put it down again.

'That was my mother,' he said. 'She says he went out a few minutes ago.'

'Did she know where?'

He shook his head. 'He was driving himself.'

Max picked up the phone and dialled the hotel. The receptionist was expecting him.

'I've spoken to the girl who took that message, Úr Anderson.'

'Does she remember what it was?'

'Oh yes.' She repeated the message she'd been given. 'But she says it was you who sent the message in the first place.'

'No,' Max said. 'Not me. Just someone who sounded like me.'

He put down the phone and looked across at the two men opposite.

'Where?' Alexander asked.

'Fetevis.'

It was instinct more than conscious thought that made her head for the stables. If she could reach one of the horses she could escape. It would have to be bareback. There'd be no chance of getting a saddle or bridle on. But that wasn't difficult. She'd often ridden like that. And once she reached the trees there'd be nothing Erkell could do. Even on motorbike he'd never catch her riding through trees.

She should have thought of it before. So easy, so obvious. If she could only get there ahead of him.

A glance behind as she reached the arch of the stable block. He was there, twenty or so yards back, running with that strange, limping gait, one arm swinging like a hunchback.

There was no time to make a decision. Reaching the first of the stalls she flung open the door. Inside was the big bay gelding she called Tempest Banker. The horse was facing inwards. Taking it by the head she stroked her hand down the curve of the neck, burying her fingers into the mane, urging it round.

The horse obeyed, turning obediently in the stall. But as

she tried to draw it out into the yard, its ears went back and it began tossing its head.

She looked round.

Erkell had come into the yard.

Snorting and rolling its eyes, the horse pulled back into the darkness of the stall. Terezia couldn't stop it. Without a bridle she had no way of holding it steady.

Erkell reached the stable door.

Letting go of the horse's mane she shrank back against the rear wall. She'd been so close, so near to breaking free.

But now she was trapped.

He stood staring at her. Then carefully he opened the stable door and came in, closing it again behind him. He was not letting her give him the slip this time.

Terezia moved round to the corner of the stable, keeping the bulk of the horse between them. It was standing quite still, trembling with fright, its coat soaked in sweat. She looked up at its head, saw the eyes rolling back. Dimly she realised this was the horse she'd dragged from the burning stable. It, of all of them, had reason to recognise him, to fear him.

Erkell moved to one side and she ducked round the other way. Another childish game. But this time in earnest. No smiles, no squeals of glee. A game played to the end.

Impatiently Erkell tried to push past the animal. It moved, suddenly throwing back its head and lashing out with its rear legs. The hooves crashed against the wooden wall of the stable.

Erkell leapt back.

'Jesus,' he cried out. 'Can't you control this brute?'

The horse turned. Erkell slapped his hand across its muzzle and it gave a high, crying neigh and reared up on its hind legs in the enclosed space.

'Call it off!' he yelled.

'I can't!'

Again the horse kicked out, rounding on him, its rump throwing him against the door.

'Get out!' she shouted. 'Get out of here!'

Rising up above him, the horse was pawing the air with its front hooves. One must have caught him because he gave a high, piercing scream. There was blood on his face.

Terezia shouted at him to get out but the horse gave him no chance. Kicking and rearing, it went for him. The air was full of the crash of hooves on wood and cobbles and the soft sickening sound as they struck flesh.

Dropping to her knees, she covered her head in her arms, partly to protect it from the wild, thrashing horse, partly to block her ears from the terrible screams of the man as he went down under the maddened creature.

Then there was silence.

Slowly she unwound her arms from her head and looked across the ground. The horse was standing still again, it's body flecked with sweat and foam.

Beneath it lay a huddled form, very still, the straw around it stained red.

Shakily she got to her feet and inched round the stable, keeping as far away from the hideous fallen figure as she could.

Pulling aside the bolt she went blindly out into the yard and closed the door behind her.

Max tapped the number of Fetevis into the mobile phone and hit the call button.

He was in the front seat by the driver, with Alexander and Biszku behind, trees flashing past the windscreen as they emerged from some woods, the silver serpent of the Danube appearing in the valley below.

The line connected, the phone at the other end started to ring. Max pictured her going over to pick it up, tossing back her hair as she put the receiver to her ear.

But it kept ringing.

He held on. She might be out in the driveway and only just have heard it. She could be running inside right at this moment. He concentrated on the image, willing her to answer. But a bright, recorded voice cut in and told him there was no response from the call and the line went dead.

He swore to himself.

'How much further?' Alexander asked from the back seat.

'About twenty-five kilometres,' the driver told him. He of all of them was untouched by what was happening, guiding the car with calm; almost clinical detachment. 'We'll be there in twenty minutes or so if we're not held up.'

'Which is the closest?' Biszku asked. 'Your father's home or the office?'

'The office, I guess,' Alexander said. 'Not much in it.'

'We may get there before him.'

To find what, Max wondered. He flashed up the number on the mobile again and mechanically prodded the call button.

Terezia went back indoors. She felt no sense of relief, just a lightheadedness as though she were floating on air. She stopped and leaned against the door frame. It could hardly have been more than fifteen minutes since she'd crept into the kitchen in search of the gun but already it seemed a long time ago, as if it had happened at another part of her life.

Going over to the sink she ran her hands under the tap and splashed cold water on to her face. It went some way towards focusing her mind and vaguely she began to wonder what she should do next. In the distance she could hear ringing. She dried her face and hands on a towel. The ringing continued but it was only gradually that the sound took on meaning and she realised it was the phone.

Out of habit she went over and picked it up. 'Hallo?'

'Terezia?' Max's voice as an explosion of surprise and relief.

'Max?'

'Are you all right?'

She closed her eyes and rested her forehead against the wall, feeling a mist of weariness sweeping over her.

'Terezia?' he called. 'Terezia – are you still there?'

She nodded although she realised he couldn't see and in a small voice she said, 'I think he's dead.'

'Who is?'

'He just came,' she whispered. 'The horses knew him . . . They made a sound, otherwise I wouldn't have realised . . . I thought it was you . . . He was talking . . .' Without shape or form the words spilled out of her. She knew they weren't making much sense but she couldn't stop them coming, a sudden warm release of the emotions cramped in her mind.

Max tried to break in on the flow. 'Terezia, listen,' he said.

But she couldn't stop the words and went on babbling incoherently. 'He was talking, Max . . . He kept talking . . . I was so scared . . .'

'Terezia, for God's sake listen!' he shouted.

Her voice petered off into silence.

'Now, listen,' he said more gently. 'You must get out of there, do you hear me?'

She nodded and said yes.

'Go out into the woods, go down to the village, anywhere. But get the hell out of there now.'

She nodded again.

'We're on the way,' he told her. 'We'll be there in about fifteen minutes. Get out of the place and don't come out until we show up. Okay?'

He didn't say why she should do it and she didn't ask. She didn't need to. The urgency of his voice told her to do as he said and ask questions later.

Running across to the sink she picked up her handbag. There was a draught. She could feel it on her face and she realised the bedroom window was still open. She hurried through and pulled it down, slipping across the latch.

As she returned a voice said, 'There's no rush.'

She spun around.

It was Zoltan.

He was standing in the doorway, filling the space, a dark silhouette against the brightness of the daylight. One hand was held in his pocket.

For a moment she stood and stared at him stupidly. Where had he come from? There had been no sound of his arrival, nothing to warn her.

'What are you doing here?' she asked.

He appeared to find some humour in the question. A bleak smile flicked across the patrician features of his face. 'Strange,' he said. 'I was going to ask you the same thing.'

This was what Max had been talking about, she realised. He'd known Zoltan was coming, tried to get her out of the house before it was too late.

Zoltan's eyes scoured the room, quickly, keenly. 'Where is he?' he asked.

She understood he meant Erkell. He wanted to know what had happened to him. She pictured the bloodstained straw, heard the screams and the crashing of the horse's hooves but she couldn't find the words to explain, and numbly she shook her head.

For a moment Zoltan's eyes bored into her, reading the situation for himself. 'Did you kill him?'

Again she shook her head. 'No,' she said simply. 'It was the horse.'

'Jesus Christ.' He said the words under his breath.

'It kicked him.'

Zoltan glanced over towards the stable block and back at her.

'I'll give you one thing,' he said lightly. 'You have a remarkably developed sense of survival.' He nodded towards the phone. 'Who were you talking to back there?'

She wanted to defy him, fight back against his questions but all the spirit had drained out of her. 'Max,' she said miserably.

He gave a grunt as though that was to be expected. 'Where is he?'

'Budapest.'

She didn't give the lie with any particular aim in mind but simply because she didn't want to help him. It must have fitted with what he'd heard because he gave a nod.

'Then we'd better go.'

'Go?' she asked slowly. 'Go where?'

'I want you to go and get in the car.'

His hand had come out of his pocket and she saw it held a gun, thick and short-barrelled, an obscene black object in his hand. She'd known it was there, sensed its presence in his pocket but at the sight of it she felt a sickness in her stomach.

He was going to use it. She could see that in his eyes. He was going to take her somewhere and finish her with that ugly little weapon.

As though reading the thoughts in her mind, Zoltan said softly, 'You should have taken the money.'

'I didn't want your money.'

'It was a good offer.'

'You call losing everything you own a good offer?' she said bitterly.

He gave a shrug as though he couldn't be blamed for the consequences if she refused and said, 'That was for you to decide.'

Terezia looked at the gun in his hand and somewhere in the back of her mind it occurred to her that Zoltan hadn't been expecting to find her here. He'd been expecting to find Erkell. And with a dry, empty sense of sickness she realised that's why he had come. Not to kill her but to kill Erkell. Just to tidy up the whole sordid business. He was not a man who would leave a trail behind him.

Zoltan saw her looking at the gun and he gave the barrel a twitch. 'Outside,' he said.

She pushed herself away from the wall, too tired and sick of mind to fight him.

As she passed him he said, 'I want you to get in the car. Don't try to do anything heroic or I'll be forced to shoot you in the back and believe me that's not a pleasant way to die.'

She turned and looked at him. It was the closest she'd ever been to this man who'd blighted her life for the past months, who'd plotted to destroy her, and in a flash of feminine spite she said, 'If you do anything to me you'll never know where the Venus is hidden.'

Zoltan wasn't going to be sidetracked by any tricks from her. Her shook his head. 'The Venus ain't here.'

'It is.'

'It was taken away by the Russians years ago. I've looked, everyone's looked. Even that creepy little guy the other day had a look for it and it ain't there.'

'That's because you were looking in the wrong place.'

Zoltan smiled and shook his head. 'You're forgetting I was there, lady. I know where it was buried and it ain't there any more.'

'My father moved it.'

Just for a moment she saw a cloud of doubt pass over Zoltan's face. She pressed home her advantage.

'He came back here and dug it up.'

'Oh yeah, why would he want to go and do a thing like that?'

'Because of what you did to that poor man on the day you left here.' She spat the words at him with malicious pleasure. 'My father didn't want you to get it. He came back and he moved it.'

Zoltan stared at her, his eyes hard as diamonds, then he shook his head and said, 'Is that a fact?'

'It is.'

'I always wondered whether that's what the crazy bastard did.'

'He wasn't crazy,' she said furiously.

'They locked him up for it.'

'Maybe that gives you some idea of how much he hated you.'

Zoltan nodded slowly. 'Yeah, maybe it does.' He wasn't going to let it get to him. He gave a jerk of his head. 'But you know where he put it. Right?'

'Yes,' she said. 'I know.'

'So how come it's still there?' he asked. 'If you know where it is why haven't you dug it up and flogged it? It would pay off some of the debts you've run up on your nags.'

'I didn't know where it was until just now.'

'Just now?'

'I saw it,' she said.

His eyes narrowed. 'Where?'

'I'm not going to tell you. If I tell you where it is you'll shoot me where I stand.'

'If it's somewhere around here I'll find it anyway.'

She shook her head. 'You'll never find it. If you searched all your life you'd never find it.'

She hadn't the slightest idea what she was talking about. All she knew was that she must play for time. Max would be here in a few minutes. She must hold on until then.

'So where is it?' Zoltan's voice was suddenly harsh.

'I'll show you.'

'Tell me!'

He was a fearsome man to defy, a man who'd held power and authority all his life and knew how to handle it, but she shook her head, feeling the tears welling up in her eyes.

'No,' she said in a small voice. 'I'll show you and then you must let me go.'

'No deals,' he said flatly.

'You must promise!'

Zoltan stared at her for a moment. 'You show me where it is first. We'll worry about what happens later.'

It wasn't much but it was the best she was going to get from him. She nodded over to the porch. 'It's in the house.'

'Okay,' he said. 'Let's go find it. No tricks, no clever behaviour. You got it?'

She nodded dumbly and they walked across the driveway, Zoltan a pace behind her, the gun held a few inches from the base of her spine. He wasn't bluffing, she was sure of that. If she tried to make a break for it he'd shoot her where she stood and she felt the skin on her back tingling with the anticipation of the shock.

As they reached the porch she glanced down the hill. Where had Max got to? He'd said he'd be there in fifteen minutes. But that must be up by now. Where was he?

'Get the bloody thing out of the way!' Biszku shouted.

The tractor stood blocking the way. One wheel of the trailer it was pulling had sunk into the kerb as it drew out of the gate and it had toppled sideways, spilling its load of sugar beet across the road.

Biszku had the window down and was cutting the air with his arm. 'Move the thing!'

The farmer spread his hands. There was nothing he could do about it. The wheel was bedded down in the ditch. He needed to get the whole machine unloaded, take the weight off the axle before he could pull it out.

'Can you get round it?' Biszku asked his driver.

He shook his head.

Biszku leaned out of the window again. 'Uncouple the tractor and get it out of the way.'

The farmer nodded and ambled over to the back of the machine.

'And get a bloody move on!'

Max glanced at his watch. It was twenty minutes since he'd rung Terezia and they were still five miles from Fetevis. Had she got out of the place before Zoltan arrived?

The coupling came free. The farmer climbed on board and with a spurt of exhaust, the tractor moved forwards. As soon as a gap appeared in the road the driver let in the clutch, bumping the car up the kerb round the trailer, and accelerated into the open road.

In the vastness of the hallway Terezia paused, looking around herself for inspiration. She didn't know what to do, where to go next. Zoltan was close by her shoulder. She could hear him breathing, feel his impatience.

'Where is it?' he demanded.

'I don't know—'

'Don't piss me about!'

She didn't know what to say. She had no scheme in mind. All she knew was that she must prevaricate, think of something to keep herself from being led down and bundled into his car. If she was taken away from here she was lost.

She looked up into the domed ceiling far above.

'Where?' Zoltan barked.

'Upstairs—'

He pushed her towards the staircase. As they climbed she sensed a change in Zoltan. He kept close to her and the hand with the gun held to her back never wavered but his attention had shifted. He was looking around himself in wonder and she realised that this was probably the first time he'd seen the inside of the house for over fifty years.

At the head of the stairs she paused again. Zoltan was staring round at the boarded-up windows, the walls crumbling like cake icing. He seemed transfixed by the sight. Was he seeing it as it used to be, she wondered: polished floors magnificent with Persian carpets, gilded furniture glowing in the sunlight?'

'Where now?' he asked jerking his attention back to her.

'This way, I think . . .'

'You think?'

'I'm not sure,' she cried fearfully. 'I don't remember the way.'

'You said you knew!'

'I do. I just don't remember the way to get there.' She could feel the tears welling up again. 'I don't know the way round like you do!'

'Where is it?'

'Further up,' she said desperately. Play for time. Keep him guessing. That was the only hope.

He pushed her forwards roughly.

Oh God, where was Max, she asked herself as they moved down the passageway. Why hadn't he come like he said he would?

One of the chandeliers had fallen from its bracket and lay spreadeagled across the floor, and they had to pick their way through the remains, their feet crunching on the shattered crystal. A door stood open. She turned aside into it but he stopped her.

'That doesn't lead anywhere.'

'Yes,' she said. 'It's through here.'

They came into a room of faded white and gold. It led through to another, smaller room. But there was no door. It was a dead end.

'This doesn't lead upstairs,' Zoltan said angrily. 'These are the morning rooms, they don't go anywhere.'

Morning rooms. Another world, another life.

'I thought it was the way,' she said.

He took her by the arm and threw her back the way they'd come.

'Tell me,' he shouted. 'Tell me where it is. I know the way.'

'I won't tell you!'

'I know this place; I know every inch of it. This is my house.'

'It's not your house!'

For a moment she thought he was going to hit her and she jumped back. But reaching out he grabbed her by the hair, drawing her face close to his.

'You're hurting me,' she cried.

'I'll hurt you more if you don't tell me where it is.'

'It's up,' she gasped. 'Further up.'

He let her go, pushing her out into the passage.

'There's a staircase round the corner,' he told her. 'It goes up to the gallery. Is that the right way?'

'Yes,' she said breathlessly. 'Yes, I think that's right.'

It was the one she'd been up earlier, dark and narrow, leading to the upper floor. Zoltan propelled her down the passage, his hand pressed close to the nape of her neck. She could feel the cold steel of the gun against her skin, hard and solid.

They were at the top of the house now. There was nowhere further they could go. She had to think of something, find a way of keeping on going. If he once thought she was fooling him it would be the end.

They came out into the brightness of the circular gallery above the hallway, the huge space opening suddenly beneath them.

Terezia stopped. She'd been here earlier. This was where she'd tripped and given away her hiding place to Erkell. She looked across the empty expanse to the doorway opposite.

And she knew what she had to do.

Zoltan was close beside her. 'Where?' he asked.

'It's up here.'

He cast his gaze up into the bell of the dome above them, the tattered gilding of its plasterwork glowing dully in the afternoon light.

'Where is it?' His voice was harsh.

'Across the other side,' she whispered.

'Show me.'

She shook her head. 'No, I'll stay here.'

'Show me!'

'Go to the other side,' she cried. 'I'll tell you where it is when you get there.'

'You'll come with me,' he said and taking her by the arm he started to drag her round the wooden gallery.

She held on to the railing, struggling against his grip.

'You said you'd let me go. If I told you where it is you said you'd let me go. You promised!'

'I made no promises.'

'I'll tell you where it is when you get there. But you must let me go!'

And then in the far distance she heard the sound she'd been waiting for.

It was the wail of a siren.

Zoltan held perfectly still, listening. Then he turned to her and the look in his eyes was terrible. 'What's that?' he asked softly.

'I don't know . . .'

A car was coming up the driveway. She heard it come to a halt outside, its tyres tearing at the gravel.

'I thought you said he was in Budapest.' Zoltan shouted the words at her in fury.

'He was . . . He was there. I don't know who that is.' She didn't know what she was saying, only that help was close.

Zoltan raised the gun to her head. He was going to shoot. Oh God, he was going to shoot.

There were voices outside. She heard her name called and ran to the balustrade but before she could shout out Zoltan swung his arm. The gun caught her on the side of the head and she fell sprawling across the wooden boards.

Slowly and sickeningly the world turned over before her eyes and she clutched at the banisters for support. Pulling herself to her knees she gave a yelp of alarm but before the sound had reached her lips Zoltan had clamped his hand across her mouth.

He pulled her to her feet, the gun pressed into her neck.

'You bitch!' he whispered. 'You knew, didn't you? You knew they were coming.'

Terezia struggled to free herself but he held her in a vice-like grip, drawing her back against the wall.

They were outside. She could hear them talking together somewhere close to the porch.

They mustn't go. They mustn't leave her here.

Throwing herself back against him, held firm in his grip, she lifted her feet off the ground and lashed out at the banisters.

There was a crash of breaking timber and a small piece broke off, spinning down into the hallway where it landed with a dry clatter.

Zoltan flung her round to the side, her head hitting the wall. Bright sparks of light exploded before her eyes.

'Keep still, you bitch,' he hissed into her ear.

His hand was on her face, the fingers digging into her cheeks, crushing her nose. She could feel his breath on her neck, feel the gun clamped beneath her ear.

They must have heard. The sound of the breaking wood hadn't been loud but surely it was enough to alert them.

But there was silence outside. The voices were no longer there.

The tiny ray of hope she'd felt turned to panic. Where were they? Where had they gone?

In desperation she began to struggle. They mustn't go. They mustn't get into the car again and leave her here with him.

Zoltan jerked her back. 'Keep still!'

She twisted her head in his grasp, trying to break free. Her mouth came open and she felt one of his fingers press into it, cutting off her breath. With all her strength she sank her teeth into it and tasted blood, warm and salty.

Zoltan gave a snarl of rage and his grip loosened. She

flung herself downwards, twisting round. As she did so there was an explosion that threw her head to the side and she felt the searing heat of the gun as it went off.

Ears ringing, she hit the ground and looked up at Zoltan.

He stood over her, his bleeding hand clamped to his mouth, the other holding the gun.

It was aimed at her face.

There were voices down below, shouting up at them but she didn't hear what they were saying. She was gazing into Zoltan's eyes.

And in them she saw no mercy.

Dimly she made out someone telling him to drop the gun. Zoltan glanced around and for a moment he seemed puzzled. She followed his gaze and saw that far down there was a group of men. Max was there but it was not him talking. It was Alexander. He was standing in the centre of the hallway, his head craned back, speaking to his father slowly and deliberately.

Zoltan stood quite still. Then he turned back to her and she saw the fury had gone out of him.

'Where is it?' he asked.

She didn't understand him. 'Where is what?'

'The Venus.' He spoke in a hoarse whisper.

Terezia drew herself up on one arm. Zoltan had dropped the gun to his side and his eyes were almost pleading with her.

'Where is it?' he asked.

In a small voice she said, 'I don't know.'

'Where is it?'

'I don't know!'

Zoltan looked across at the doorway on the far side of the circular gallery and then slowly his gaze went up into the dome above.

'It's there, isn't it?'

'No—'

'In the dome at the top. There's a room. I know it. It's there, isn't it?'

'No, it's not there,' she said. 'It's not anywhere.'

But she could see he didn't believe her. He was staring up above his head in wonder.

In the distance she could hear running feet, loud on the bare wooden boards. Zoltan glanced round at the gallery.

'Don't!' Terezia shouted. 'It's not safe!'

But he wasn't listening.

'There's nothing there!' Terezia told him.

He turned and looked at her for a moment and then, as though he had forgotten she existed, he stepped forward.

'Don't!' she shouted.

It happened quite slowly. As he walked round the gallery, still looking upwards, there was a cracking of the wood. Zoltan stopped for a moment and reached out for the balustrade. As he did so the gallery sagged. He stumbled and fell to his knees, letting go of the gun that tumbled down into the hallway below.

Terezia watched in cold fascination as he knelt there. He was staring at her, his expression one of bewilderment, as he realised what was happening. And then with a splintering of wood the whole thing gave way beneath him. As he slipped down he reached out and grasped hold of the banisters which stood out like spears facing an invisible enemy and hung there dangling in space.

Terezia covered her face with her hands, watching through splayed fingers.

'Help me,' he gasped.

She shook her head. She was huddled up against the wall, the hallway a gaping hole beneath her.

'Help me!'

She couldn't. If she went anywhere near him she'd slip down with him. But his eyes were on her, pleading for her help and she couldn't stop herself.

Crawling forward across the sloping floor she locked her arm round one of the supports that hadn't given way and reached out to him.

Her hand was almost a yard away from his. She lay down flat on the ground, legs spread, and slithered herself closer.

As her hand reached out to his he let go of the bannister he was holding and grabbed her by the wrist.

She gave a cry of fright, almost letting go as the sudden extra weight tore at the muscles of her back. She could feel herself slipping downwards. Her arm, locked around the wooden beam, was giving way. She couldn't hold on for long.

Zoltan was staring into her eyes, willing her to hold him. She pulled one leg around on the sagging floor, trying to find something to brace herself against. But there was nothing.

Then she felt Zoltan's grip give way. His hand slipped down from her wrist to her hand.

'I can't hold you!' she cried.

Zoltan's strength was weakening. It was now she who was holding him and he must have realised that she couldn't do so for much longer because he lifted back his head and said, 'Do you know?'

'Know what?'

'The Venus.' He was talking in a whisper. 'Do you know where the Venus is?'

She nodded.

'You know?' There was desperation in his voice.

'Yes,' she whispered. 'I know.'

For a moment Zoltan stared up at her with his furious green-grey eyes.

And then he let go.

32

It was ten days later that Terezia opened the high French windows of the Gritti Palace Hotel and stepped out on to the balcony. She was wearing only a long white bathrobe, the marble cold on her bare feet. Resting her coffee cup on the balustrade she watched the jostle of traffic making its way up the Grand Canal.

It had been Max's idea to bring her to Venice. He said she needed a complete change of scene, somewhere where she could rest and recover and start to plan for the future. And that, he told her, could only mean this strange, crooked city.

He knew the place like the back of his hand and when they had a few moments to themselves he'd taken her through the warren of streets, showing her windows from which distraught lovers had thrown themselves into the canal, columns where corpses had been strung up and bridges where rival gangs had fought pitched battles.

But there were times also when he left her to herself. With the particular sensitivity he had for these things, he understood she needed time alone; time to think and assess and come to terms with the responsibilities she faced. He had a room on the same floor as her suite and in the early hours of the morning he would slip out of her bed and go back there, leaving her to wake and start the day in her own time.

Often she spent these solitary moments walking around the churches. She'd had no real experience of religion. What faith her father might have once held he'd lost by the time she was born and Joszef had always treated ritual of any sort with grave suspicion, so she'd rarely attended a church service in her life but she was transfixed by the huge paintings over the altars. There was a serenity to the colours and patterns that intrigued her and she'd spent hours studying them.

She'd been in touch with Ottlik, the curator of the Museum of Fine Arts in Budapest, and made arrangements to buy back all the family pictures that they were holding in the basement. In time she intended to trace the other possessions that were buried away in museums and get them back. It was going to be no easy task but one she was looking forward to with some pleasure.

The rebuilding of Fetevis was the first and urgent priority in her mind. Max had made inquiries back in Budapest and already three architects had made the journey out to Venice to offer their services. There was one she'd liked in particular. He'd worked on the palaces in St Petersburg and later in Prague and he seemed in sympathy with what she wanted and what was needed. She'd commissioned him to put a team of engineers into the house to evaluate the damage and give her an assessment of what structural renovation had to be done.

Another visitor to the hotel had been the Director of Finances from the Landsberg Corporation. For two long afternoons he'd sat with her in the graceful drawing room of her suite, patiently defining the boundaries of the huge empire, describing its aims, its assets and investments. The figures he quoted had made her head spin. She'd never had to deal with finance of this complexity before and made no pretence of understanding everything he said. But by the end of the exhausting sessions she had some grasp of the scale and extent of what she was taking on.

Oh God, she thought, was she really taking it on?

She glanced at her watch. It was nine-fifteen. Max would be around in a few minutes. It was earlier than usual but this was no ordinary day. In under an hour she had to face the entire force of the Landsberg Corporation and announce the decisions she'd come up with, decisions that would affect not only their lives but the lives of thousands who worked beneath them.

At the thought of it she felt a flutter of nerves in her stomach. She knew exactly what she wanted to say; she'd rehearsed the lines with Max over and over again. But what if she dried up? What if she lost her nerve and started to muddle her words? She'd be a laughing stock before she'd even started.

Then you mustn't do it, she told herself firmly. You've got to be strong; you've got to cope. It was like taking a dangerous fence at horse trials. You could fuss and change your mind beforehand but once you were committed there must be no doubts, no second thoughts. You had to give it everything you'd got.

Going back inside she inspected the contents of her wardrobe. It had filled in the most satisfying way since she'd first arrived with nothing more than the contents of one small suitcase. She'd wasted no time in visiting the emporiums of Italian *haute couture* – Versace, Armani – sacred names that she'd only previously read of in magazines.

After a couple of false starts, she settled for a navy blue two-piece. It was plain and simple but beautifully cut, the type that Max called a power suit. But that was fine with her, she told herself. Power was what she needed right now.

As she zipped up the skirt she turned and inspected her outline in the mirror, running her hand down over her stomach. She was concerned that she was going to put on weight without horses to exercise. The stables back at Fetevis were going to be restored to their original glory. She would have the stalls filled; she might even do some breeding as she'd intended. But only for her own pleasure. There was no necessity to try to make a profit out of them. Quite the opposite, in fact. It seemed a little sad after all the effort and anxiety she'd put into them but she had no true regrets. The work wasn't wasted. With the wisdom of those brought up close to nature she understood it had been part of a process. The stables were the practical reason she'd found for taking on the house and if it hadn't been for that she wouldn't be standing here now in the most expensive suite of one of the greatest hotels in the world admiring her reflection in the mirror.

Nothing could be seen in isolation. It was part of a cycle that kept turning.

When Max arrived ten minutes later he found her ready and pacing.

'How do I look?' she asked, spinning round to face him.

Her voice was steady but he could tell from the way she held out her hands, fingers fluttering as though she were trying to dry nail varnish, that she was crackling with nerves.

'You look perfect,' he said.

'Are my heels too high?'

'Very sexy.'

She turned around, checking her appearance over her shoulder in the mirror. 'Do you mean tarty?'

'I'm never entirely sure where one starts and the other ends.'

'I could change them.'

'No,' he said calmly. There was no need for change. Change bred uncertainty and apprehension. 'You look exactly right.'

And so different, he thought to himself, from the pale, exhausted girl who had sat in the editor's office of *Magyar Hirlap* ten days ago, stammering out her story to the assembled audience of newspapermen, lawyers and police. These few days away had put the fire back in her, as he'd hoped it would. The rest would come. He knew there were still nightmares and moments of panic. He'd been there and felt them. What had happened to her would be with her for the rest of her life. But she was a resilient girl and he was sure that in time the wound would heal.

Gallagher's story, coupled with the death of Zoltan, had made the front pages of papers across the world. It had been a work of art, hard-hitting and to the point. The only one not impressed by it was Gallagher himself. Max had talked to him on the day they left for Italy. Gallagher had told him the story was all right as far as it went. The trouble was it didn't go far enough.

'What more do you want?' he'd asked.

'Bessenyei resigned,' Gallagher said in his distant, dreamy voice.

'He didn't have much option, did he?'

'The word is that he was forced to do it.'

Max had said it was hardly surprising in the circumstances and Gallagher had smiled sadly.

'You know something,' he'd said. 'In the bad old days in Russia, if your sledge was attacked by wolves what they used to do was to pick on the smallest and weakest person in it and pitch him out of the back. That way the wolves were so busy chewing him to shreds they let the others get away.'

'You think that's what happened?'

'If it weren't for having to get your story out before some other *eejit* gets hold of it, I think we could have had the whole sledgeful of the bastards.'

He was an artist in many ways, always wanting more than he'd achieved.

The story had reached Venice ahead of them. The hotel manager had greeted Terezia personally as the boat arrived from the airport and had taken pride in showing her the signatures of previous members of her family in the hotel registers. The paparazzi were next. A picture of the *Contessa* standing in the stern of her motor launch, tall and grave, had appeared in one of the local rags. Terezia didn't appear to show much interest in it, although Max noted she did cut it out and keep it. But she was still having nothing to do with the magazines who asked to interview her. In many ways she was a very private person.

'Are they all here?' she asked.

He nodded.

'Then we'd better get going.'

'They can wait,' he said. 'They're fuelling them up with coffee at present.'

'Oh no, Max. Let's go. I want to get this over with.'

The hotel had opened one of its state rooms for the occasion. Twenty or more grey-suited men were assembled beneath the chandeliers in the long salon, the air filled with a polite murmur of anticipation that stopped dead as Terezia came into the room.

Victor Szelkely came forward and, touching her hand to his lips, he made the introductions.

There were only a few faces she recognised but the others she'd been briefed on beforehand and she knew them to be the heads of various legal and executive departments of the Corporation. One by one she went between them, smiling and shaking hands.

When she came to her cousin Alexander she kissed him on both cheeks. Max had noticed that despite what had happened, or perhaps because of it, there was a growing bond between the two of them. He was staying at the Cipriani Hotel and she'd had lunch with him the day before, taking the opportunity to brief him on what she was about to say so that there would be no surprises in that quarter.

Formalities over, she took her place at the head of the table and began by thanking them all for coming all this way to be there. What she had to say after that took her less than fifteen minutes.

As the majority shareholder she told them that she intended to take her place as the head of the Landsberg Corporation but since she didn't have the necessary skills or experience to handle the day-to-day running of the business she was appointing Alexander as Managing Director.

There was a ripple of interest around the table at the announcement.

Terezia went on to say that she would in future attend all board meetings but would concern herself only with the moral and ethical implications of the business. Nothing, particularly in the field of armaments, would be allowed to go ahead that she didn't fully approve of and she'd reserve the right of veto for this.

Of the income owed to her over the past fifty years she would make no claim other than to ask for the complete rebuilding of Fetevis to be financed by the Corporation rather than by her personally. In return she would allow parts of the Palace to be used for formal events.

When she was finished she thanked them again for their time and attention and, getting to her feet, she strode out of the room.

Max followed her down the passage. As soon as she was out of sight of the doorway she slumped back against the wall and let out her breath with a rush.

'Christ, how did I do?'

'Brilliant.'

'I was shaking like a leaf.'

'It didn't show. They were eating out of your hand.'

'I thought I was going to faint.'

'What you need's a drink.'

She glanced round. 'Not here. I don't want to bump into them all again at the bar.'

'No, not here. I thought we should go out to Torcello.'

'Torcello?'

'It's an island across the lagoon. There's a restaurant there that knocks out the best lunch in the business and there are some Byzantine mosaics in the cathedral next door which you can swot up on afterwards.'

She thought for a moment and then her nose crinkled into a grin. 'You always have the right answer for things, don't you?'

'You should put me in charge of the Corporation catering.'

'No.' Her eyes were suddenly serious. 'No, Max. I don't want you doing that. I want you on the Board.'

'Of Landsberg's?'

'I need you there.'

'I don't know anything about business.'

'You know when people are talking out of their backsides

and that's what I need. You can give yourself a name. I don't know what – maybe Legal Adviser.'

'With my hat on.'

'I need you there,' she said. 'You're the only one I can be sure is on my side.'

From comments and evasions she'd made in the past few days, Max had been half expecting something of this sort but he wasn't sure it was a good idea.

'I don't know,' he said carefully. 'The Embassy has asked me to stay on.'

'That's good.' She was openly and genuinely pleased for him. 'Oh, Max, that really is good.'

'There might be some sort of promotion in it.' He smiled in his self-deprecating way.

'Couldn't you do both?'

'Maybe.'

She shook her head. 'But maybe what?'

He hated himself for what he was going to say but events were moving so fast they mustn't be allowed to get out of control. There had to be a balance. 'You're a rich woman now, the head of a billion-pound business.'

Terezia was very still. 'Does that threaten you?' she asked in a small voice.

'No,' he said carefully. 'I don't think threaten is the right word. But it makes a difference.'

'Oh, Max.' Her hand was on his. 'When I first met you I was just a stable girl.'

'That's the point.'

'But what's changed?'

'Nothing really.' The crow's feet round his eyes wrinkled into a slight smile. 'It's just that there are going to be a lot of guys trying to get their hands on your money. I don't want to be the first in line.'

'It's not you who's asking; it's me.'

'I know that—'

'I need you,' she whispered fiercely. 'I can't do this by myself.'

He nodded in understanding. 'Will you let me think on it?'

The concern melted from her eyes. She smiled luxuriously at him and said, 'You can think as long as you like. So long as you come up with the right answer.'

There was a sound in the passage. She was suddenly alert.

'Quick,' she said, drawing him away. 'They're coming out; they'll catch us here.'

They went down into the hallway where the morning light from the canal danced on the marble floor.

'Max?'

He paused as they came outside.

'What does Byzantine mean?'

'I don't know,' he said. 'But it sounds very grand and art-historical, doesn't it?'

A fortnight later Terezia returned to Hungary with Max and a mountain of luggage to find Fetevis already encased in scaffolding.

Her first instructions were to have the little cottage-like wing where she'd been living knocked down. The memories it held were not all happy ones and that, to her superstitious mind, meant it had go to. Instead she bought a house a couple of miles down the valley and installed herself in it with Rosza and Joszef. From there she drove over each morning to supervise the reconstruction work.

The renovation of Fetevis was not just a building job, it was a military campaign. A whole village of portable cabins had been set up in the driveway and gradually they filled with drawings, designs and samples. The entire building had been translated into a computer simulation that, to her delight, could be revolved and explored. In time stonemasons, sculptors and plasterers would be commissioned to translate the sterile white gridlines on the screen into a living reality.

The architect reckoned it would take five years to complete the construction work but, as Terezia told Max one evening, if it took all her life it would be time well spent.

She'd asked Eleanor over on numerous occasions, walking through the empty rooms with her, gathering every memory she held of how they had been used and decorated, and together they pored over the photographs Eleanor brought with her of the house as it had been before the war.

Regularly she drove herself in her dark blue Mercedes convertible over to the housing estate outside Vac. And there, in the scraggy park, she sat and talked with Miklos Kadar. On each occasion she brought a box of Romeo & Juliet panatellas, that she had sent to her from Dunhill in London, which the old man smoked with quiet pleasure as he recalled his days with her father.

When Max came over one Saturday in late February, he found her in the driveway sitting astride a horse in her familiar loose, Cossack stance. She was dressed in jeans and baggy sweater, as she had in the past, the silk scarf draped around her neck the only indication of the change of fortune in her life. There was a saddlebag across the pummel of the saddle.

'You off somewhere?' he asked.

She nodded down towards the lake. 'I thought we should go for a picnic.'

'Great,' he said. 'You show the way and I'll trot along behind.'

'No, stupid.' There was a lazy expectancy in her smile. 'You can hop up here with me.'

'On that thing?'

'There's plenty of room.'

'Won't it snap in half or something with the two of us on it?'

'Not if we go slowly. He won't even notice the difference.'

She cocked out her foot for him to step on and reaching down she hauled him up behind her.

They made their way down into the valley, Max sitting with his legs dangling, arms around her waist. He could feel the roll of her hips as she rode, smell the scent in her hair.

She turned towards him. 'Have you thought about what I asked you, back in Venice?'

'Yes.'

She waited for him to go on. When he didn't she asked, 'Yes, you've thought about it or yes you'll do it?'

'Yes, I'll do it. But on one condition.'

She twisted round until she could see him fully. 'What's that?'

'That if things don't work out with us for some reason,' he put the words carefully, 'we can break the agreement off. No dramas, no recriminations.'

She chuckled. 'Such a cautious man.'

'One step at a time.'

'If that's how you want it.'

'Is that a deal?'

She leaned back, the curve of her throat exposed, and kissed him. 'It's a deal.'

'You always knew I'd say yes.'

'I still wanted to hear you say it.'

A thaw had set in and the trees dripped on their heads as

the horse came out on the water's edge by the Winter Pavilion.

'You remember this place?' she asked.

'How could I forget? I cut a notch on one of the pillars.'

Kicking one leg over the horse's neck, she vaulted down to the ground. Throwing the reins over a branch she hefted down the saddlebag and slung it over her shoulder.

Max followed her into the greenish chamber where the steam floated above the pool. Sitting cross-legged on the ground Terezia took out a couple of glasses wrapped in a white napkin and a bottle of champagne which she passed across to him.

'I saw Biszku today,' he said as he peeled off the gold foil. 'He says they've traced Vargas.'

Terezia looked up.

'He's in Vienna and claims he had nothing to do with anyone's death. That was all Zoltan, according to him.'

'Just carrying out orders from above.'

'That sort of thing. Biszku reckons they'll never be able to prove otherwise.'

'You mean he won't get prosecuted?'

'Not unless they can find something solid to prove otherwise.'

Terezia thought for a moment. 'Well, I hope he crawls under a stone and stays there. If he comes back to Hungary I'll have him flayed alive.'

Max pulled off the cork and poured the champagne.

Terezia took a sip and smiled dreamily. 'If I could only have one drink ever again it would have to be champagne. It always tastes right.'

'Even at breakfast?'

'Especially at breakfast.'

'You've got a natural feel for decadence.'

'I'm not decadent,' she said with an aloof smile. 'I just have impeccable good taste.'

She studied the bubbles rising in the glass for a moment. 'You remember last time we were here—'

'You said you had a secret.'

She looked up, surprised he had followed her train of thought.

'There's something I want to show you.'

Leaning back she held out one leg.

'Your foot?' he asked.

'No, silly. I want you to pull my boot off.'

He tugged them both off. Wriggling out of her jeans, she slipped her jersey and T-shirt over her head and waded out into the pool. Steam writhed up around her bare waist. Ducking under the water she gave a kick of her legs and vanished from sight.

Her head appeared for a moment, grinning in satisfaction. Then she went down again and when she resurfaced he could see she was carrying something. There was a flash of light as though there was a shoal of fish down there and slowly she stood up.

In her arms was a silver figure of a girl, its face nuzzled against her naked breast.

To Max the twilit room seemed suddenly filled with brilliant light as she brought it over to him.

'You knew it was there?' He was staring at the gleaming figure.

She nodded, pleased with herself. 'No one was going to see it down there.'

'But how did you know?'

She looked down at the figure as though it were a child in her arms. 'It was in the will,' she said. 'My father said he'd left me everything he owned under the sun.'

'Is there a sun in here?'

'Look up.'

Max followed her gaze up into the dome of the ceiling. It was a mosaic, green-blue stones glittering darkly, except in the centre, around the circular aperture of the light, where flaming tongues spread out from a golden image of the sun.

'I never noticed,' he said in wonder.

'That's because you were looking the wrong way.'

'It's extraordinary—'

'It is, isn't it,' she said. 'Almost Byzantine.'

FINAL JEOPARDY

Linda Fairstein

The days of Assistant D.A. Alexandra Cooper often start off badly, but she's never faced the morning by reading her own obituary before.

It doesn't take long to sort out why it was printed: a woman's body with her face blown away, left in a car rented in Coop's name in the driveway of her weekend home. But it isn't so easy to work out why her lodger – an acclaimed Hollywood star – was murdered, or to be sure that the killer had found the right victim.

As Coop's job is to send rapists to jail there are plenty of suspects who might be seeking revenge, and whoever it is needs to be found before her obituary gets reprinted.

'Raw, real and mean. Linda Fairstein is wonderful'
Patricia Cornwell

POSTMORTEM

Patricia Cornwell

A serial killer is on the loose in Richmond, Virginia. Three women have died, brutalised and strangled in their own bedrooms. There is no pattern: the killer appears to strike at random – but always on Saturday mornings.

So when Dr Kay Scarpetta, chief medical examiner, is awakened at 2.33am, she knows the news is bad: there is a fourth victim. And she fears now for those that will follow unless she can dig up new forensic evidence to aid the police.

But not everyone is pleased to see a woman in this powerful job. Someone may even want to ruin her career and reputation . . .

'Terrific first novel, full of suspense, in which even the scientific bits grip'
The Times

CRUEL AND UNUSUAL

Patricia Cornwell

At 11.05 one December evening in Richmond, Virginia, convicted murderer Ronnie Joe Waddell is pronounced dead in the electric chair.

At the morgue Dr Kay Scarpetta waits for Waddell's body. Preparing to perform a postmortem before the subject is dead is a strange feeling, but Scarpetta has been here before. And Waddell's death is not the only newsworthy event on this freezing night: the grotesquely wounded body of a young boy is found propped against a rubbish skip. To Scarpetta the two cases seem unrelated, until she recalls that the body of Waddell's victim had been arranged in a strikingly similar position.

Then a third murder is discovered, the most puzzling of all. The crime scene yields very few clues: old blood stains, fragments of feather, and – most baffling – a bloody fingerprint that points to the one suspect who could not possibly have committed this murder.

'Chillingly detailed forensic thriller confirming Cornwell as the top gun in this field'
Daily Telegraph